*To Natalie
with love,
Pook & Nick
Xmas '08*

Double Murder
on Martha's Vineyard

Double Murder on Martha's Vineyard

by Cynthia Riggs

Including:

Deadly Nightshade
The Cranefly Orchid Murders

PUBLISHED BY VINEYARD STORIES
EDGARTOWN, MA 02539

PUBLISHED BY VINEYARD STORIES, 2007

Deadly Nightshade and *The Cranefly Orchid Murders* were originally published by St. Martin's Press, New York.

Cover and book design by Tony De Feria

Author photograph by Daniel Waters

Illustrations by Sydney Noyes Riggs. Page 1, Oak Bluffs, from the old steam-ship wharf; page 219, Stepping stones.

Printed in Canada

ISBN 978-0-9771384-4-9

For Dionis Coffin Riggs, Poet
1898-1997

AUTHOR'S NOTE

I try to work from ten o'clock in the morning until I run out of steam. When I'm immersed in writing, the sun rises over the kitchen roof, blazes through the windows, and disappears in the west, and I'm not even aware of it. I forget to eat, forget everything.

Every one of my Victoria Trumbull books – there are seven so far, since I started this series in 2001 – touches, subtly I hope, on a social issue – mixed race courtship, gambling, child molestation, spousal abuse, pastoral infidelity (normal infidelity is too normal), development versus conservation, drug use, gay rights, problems of aging (Victoria loses her driver's license), and overall represents an attempt to break aging stereotypes. Victoria, throughout the course of the books, has never aged a day beyond 92, and won't.

Because I have no idea where my stories are going when I write, I sometimes end up with what seems to be an insoluble problem. At one point the compost heap exploded. Why? How? And where does the story go from there? A skunk detonated pressure-sensitive explosives hidden in a zucchini that had been left on Victoria's doorstep but was put in the compost when it was gone-by. I haven't used this plot twist yet.

— Cynthia Riggs
West Tisbury, Maasachusetts
April, 2007

Deadly Nightshade

by Cynthia Riggs

CHAPTER ONE

The Man in the Water

WHEN she heard the scream, Victoria Trumbull had been waiting for her granddaughter Elizabeth to return from the outer harbor, where she and the harbor master had gone to check boats. The scream sent prickles along the back of her neck. She had never heard anything like it before.

She had waited almost an hour after a friend dropped her off at the harbor. She didn't mind waiting. As long as she had paper and a pen, she could always work on her poetry.

She watched sunset colors dance in the tidal ripples of the channel leading into the harbor basin, bold splashes of orange and red and purple. The incoming tide created a stained-glass mosaic of fractured color that washed against the boats tied up in the harbor.

The incoming tide rocked sailboats on their moorings, and set shrouds to slapping against aluminum masts with a mournful bell-like clang, a sound that repeated itself from boat to boat, until the whole was a cacophony of bells tolling.

Across the narrow channel, an osprey returned to its untidy nest of sticks on top of a telephone pole. Victoria watched it circle, wings spread wide. She could see its markings, gray and black and white. Colors flickered off the scales of a large fish that the bird held, struggling, in its talons. The osprey's chicks set up a greedy clamor, and Victoria could see their heads over the rim of the nest, beaks open wide. The osprey landed on the edge of the nest, feet extended, wings out to the sides. The fish flipped violently, its tail flicking sunset sparks, and the chicks' shrill peeping stopped abruptly.

Victoria rummaged in her old leather pocketbook for something to write on. An envelope would be fine, the ComElectric bill she had forgotten to give Elizabeth to mail last week. She turned it over to its blank back. She found a purple-and-green pen with stars, gold glitter, and the words *Victoria Trumbull has just won $25,000!!!*, and started to write in her loopy backhand scrawl.

The osprey lifted up from its nest, its wings spread wide. The darkening sky, now drained of fluorescent orange, silhouetted the bird. It cried, a mournful peeping cry, too feeble-sounding for the strong wings, talons, and beak.

The wind was picking up, a brisk breeze from the northwest. She was vaguely aware of the sound of men's voices across the harbor on the East Chop side, could almost make out words.

The scream jolted her out of her reverie. It echoed across the harbor and reverberated against the moored yachts, ricocheting off the shingled side of the harbor master's shack. Suddenly, it cut off. She stood up; the pen fell out of her lap, rolled toward the edge of the deck, and plopped into the water six feet below. She heard grunts, a scuffle, a splash, then nothing. The commotion came from across the harbor, near the yacht club's dock, where she thought she had heard men's voices earlier. But the light was fading quickly, and Victoria couldn't be sure. An engine whirred, coughed, caught. Was it a boat or a car? She thought she saw a plume of exhaust in the darkness on the other side of the dock. Tires skidded on sand, bit into a hard surface, and squealed as a vehicle turned. A sound came off the water. Was it an echo? Had the vehicle turned left or right? She couldn't tell.

Stillness settled again. It were as if no scream had ever spoiled the peace of the evening, no splash.

No one moved on the boats. No curious heads poked out of cuddies; no one stood up in cockpits. None of the strollers along the bulkhead paused to point and shout. Was she the only one who had heard the scream and splash, the sound of a motor, the squeal of tires?

Victoria looked at her watch. Not quite 7:30. What the devil could she do?

She hadn't the foggiest notion of how to use the radio in the shack to call the harbor master and Elizabeth, to tell them about the commotion, the scream, the splash.

She picked up the envelope on which she'd written the first line of her poem and put it back in her pocketbook. She paced the deck in front of the shack, no more than eight feet. She paced down the side of the shack, no more than twelve feet. She turned and paced back again.

Night was settling on the harbor. The bright sunset colors had faded and now dark purple wind clouds scudded across the darkening sky.

Finally, she heard, dimly, an outboard motor heading into the channel. The entry lights had come on, triggered by darkness, a flashing red on the right of the harbor entrance, green on the left. Victoria eased herself down the ramp that led to the floating dock where Elizabeth would tie up the harbor master's launch. She held the railing tightly with both hands. She was not going to act like an old lady, slipping and falling and breaking something. She had to tell the harbor master what she had heard, what she might or might not have seen, and she had to tell him immediately.

The launch turned into the channel and slowed, its bow settled down, leveled, and its wake dropped behind it in a long, curling V that broke in small combers against the rock sides of the channel. Elizabeth, lanky as a boy in the fading light, was in the stern, holding the tiller. Domingo sat in the bow seat, facing her, his arms folded over his broad chest, his dark baseball cap squared over his brow. Victoria knew that cap, the navy blue one that said NYPD in faded gold letters.

"Hey, Gram!" Elizabeth idled the engine and let the boat drift into the floating dock. "What's up?" Victoria could see her granddaughter's bright eyes in the dusk, her short gold-streaked hair tousled in damp curls.

Domingo turned, careful not to upset the boat's balance, and doffed his cap. "Sweetheart," he said to Victoria. "Be careful. Watch yourself." He remained seated.

"Grab the line, Grammy." Elizabeth reached for a cleat with slender fingers, held the boat against the floating dock, and passed the stern line to Victoria. Domingo still remained seated. Victoria, who'd been reared around boats, flung the line around a cleat and secured it. Elizabeth got out carefully and stood up straight, a tall young woman (thirty was young to Victoria) in tan shorts and white uniform shirt. The bow of the boat dipped lower in the water with the weight of the harbor master. Domingo uncrossed his arms long enough to hand her the bow line.

"Don't put the boat away yet." Victoria stood up and backed toward the railing on the ramp so she could hold on to something.

"What's up, sweetheart?" Domingo pulled his cap down over his close-cropped hair and adjusted it over his heavy black brows. The boat bumped gently against the fender of the floating dock.

"I heard something on the other side of the harbor." Victoria pointed toward the East Chop dock with her gnarled hand. "A scream. Then a splash." She held the railing and braced herself against the slight movement of the dock. "I thought I saw someone before I heard the scream, but I'm not sure."

"Get in," Domingo ordered.

Elizabeth held out her hand for her grandmother, and Victoria took it and settled herself onto the middle seat, her back to Elizabeth, who sat down again in the stern seat and started the motor. Domingo undid the lines and gave the dock a small shove with his hand. He leaned toward Victoria. "Show us where, sweetheart."

Elizabeth steered away from the floating dock, as much at home on the water as Victoria had been at her age. She piloted the launch among the sailboats moored in the center of the harbor, slowly, so the wake would not upset dishes or cocktail-hour glasses. Victoria heard music coming from the cockpits and cabins, music that varied from boat to boat. Rock, reggae, Bach, mostly contained within the boats. She could see the soft light of kerosene lamps, the glow of battery-operated lanterns.

"The scream was loud enough to wake the dead," Victoria said to Domingo. Elizabeth shifted slightly in the stern seat.

Domingo unfolded his arms long enough to gesture toward the music wafting from the boats. The whites of his eyes, contrasted with his dark face, made it look still darker. He shrugged, hands out, pale palms up, opened his eyes wide. His expression seemed to say, What do you expect? Victoria hadn't realized how loud the music must be inside the boats. Domingo peered out from under the peak of his cap, watching her. Victoria, who had gotten to know him well during the two months Elizabeth had worked for him, saw an expression of pleasure she had never seen before. Retired New York cop back in action, she thought.

Behind her, Elizabeth was quiet as she steered the launch slowly among the boats.

"Where did the sound come from?" Domingo asked. Victoria pointed toward the far shore. He lifted his chin at Elizabeth. "You," he said. "Slow down. You're making too much wake."

Elizabeth grunted and slowed the boat. The wake trailed off gently, met and broke against the whitecaps that wind and tide had stirred up in the harbor. The bow of the launch slapped small breaking waves, sending sprays of water over the harbor master's uniformed back, occasionally over Victoria. Her face glistened with salt spray, her beak-like nose dripped water, and diamonds of moisture sparkled in her white hair in the light from shore.

Above them, the sky had become black velvet, punctuated with stars so bright the lights from shore couldn't drown them out.

"The tide's changed," Domingo said. "The current will be full flood in another ten or fifteen minutes."

The launch's red and green running lights reflected off the darkening surface of the harbor; the stern light trailed a path of white glitter behind them.

Victoria lifted her right hand from the gunwale, gingerly, so as not to upset the balance, and pointed toward the dock, now dark. "More that way."

Elizabeth changed direction slightly, and the bow slapped the choppy water.

"Slow down," Domingo ordered Elizabeth. "There's no rush." Elizabeth cut the speed to bare headway. "Sweetheart, let me have the searchlight under your seat." Victoria felt around until she found the plastic-encased light and handed it to him. "You." He gestured to Elizabeth. "Back and forth, starting here."

Elizabeth gave the boat more power.

"What's your hurry? Slow down." He turned back to Victoria. "Sit still, sweetheart. Tell me if you see anything." He swept the searchlight across the dark surface of the water. The light reflected on foamy white wave tops.

Elizabeth turned the boat and steered slowly toward the light on the Harbor House. When she was even with the last of the moored boats, she turned again and steered toward the barely discernible osprey pole, a line against the pinkish gray evening sky. They were broadside to the waves now, and the launch rolled, shipping water with an occasional slurp, until an inch or so sloshed around in the bottom of the boat.

"The bailer is under the seat, Gram."

Victoria fumbled until she found the Clorox bottle scoop tied to a thwart with a length of fishing line. She spread her knees and leaned over to scoop up the water at her feet. She heaved it over the side, careful to toss it away from the wind.

"Your grandmother's a better sailor than you are." Domingo nodded at Victoria. Elizabeth snorted, a sound Victoria interpreted as a muffled laugh.

Domingo swept the light back and forth as they moved closer to shore. Victoria bailed. The Clorox scoop scraped against sand in the bottom of the boat. As they neared shore, the harbor surface, sheltered now by land, calmed. It reflected the stars, lights from the hotel. The boat steadied.

"Whoa!" Domingo said. "I see something."

Elizabeth idled the motor. Domingo held the light on a floating dark mass a couple of boat lengths from them. They drifted past, and Elizabeth steered the launch toward it, letting the boat's momentum carry them.

Victoria rose slightly in her seat.

"Watch it!" Domingo said, balancing the boat. "Looks like we found the source of your scream." He held the light high and aimed down at the dark mass.

"My God!" Elizabeth gasped.

"Careful!" Domingo ordered.

Victoria sat back. "How awful." She stared at the object. "He's not dead, is he?"

"Doesn't look too good, sweetheart."

"I heard him scream." Victoria stopped, then continued. "He screamed for help. And I did nothing."

"There was nothing you could do, sweetheart. Don't start thinking that way." Domingo turned to Elizabeth. "You!" he said. "Get the boat hook."

Victoria moved slightly so Elizabeth could slide the boat hook out from under the seat. She stared at the mass bobbing in the light from shore.

"Are you okay?" Domingo asked. "You're not cold, are you?"

"No," Victoria replied. "I was thinking about that man."

Domingo nodded and looked beyond Victoria to Elizabeth. "Pull it in. Get it next to the boat. That's it," he added as Elizabeth leaned out and hooked the neck of the dark sweatshirt, navy blue or black. "Go easy. That's it."

"For Christ's sake, Domingo," Elizabeth said, exasperation in her voice. "You don't need to tell me every single thing."

The body was that of a heavyset man. He was floating face down, arms spread over his head. His jeans were pulled down, so his plump bottom was exposed, two pale, gelatinous globes. His legs had sunk into the water, out of sight. It was difficult to tell much about him in the dim light. His wet hair seemed to be gray, held back in a short ponytail with an elastic band.

"Don't rock the boat." Victoria had leaned over to get a better look. "You," Domingo said to Elizabeth, "get a line out of the box and secure him. That is," he added, "if I'm not telling you too much." The sound Elizabeth made was the same noise Victoria had heard her make as a little girl when her mother told her to clean her room.

"Get the line under one of his arms," Domingo ordered. The boat shifted as Elizabeth unlatched the box, took out a length of line and reached out toward the body bumping against the right side of the boat. Victoria leaned slightly to her left for counterbalance.

Domingo unclipped the handheld radio from his belt and switched it on, twisting the dial until the static stopped, and speaking into the mike.

"Oak Bluffs harbor master on Channel Sixteen to Coast Guard."

"Coast Guard on Sixteen, sir," a woman's voice answered. "Switch to Channel Twenty-Two."

8

Domingo entered the numbers, two small beeps of sound. "We have a floating body in the harbor near the yacht club."

"Yes, sir." The Coast Guard woman repeated what Domingo had said.

"We're taking it to the dock."

"You're taking it to the dock, sir."

"I'm calling the state police and the Oak Bluffs police on Channel Four Oh Four."

"Yes, sir." The voice repeated that information.

"Switching back to Sixteen, and standing by," Domingo said.

"Standing by Channel Sixteen, sir."

"I've got his arm tied," Elizabeth said in a thick voice. "The other end of the line's around the thwart."

"Start her up and take the boat to the dock. We can secure him to the pilings until the police get there."

He radioed Communications on Channel 404. "Send the hearse." He refastened his radio to his belt. "Not that I expect much from them." He adjusted his cap and sat back in the bow seat, folded his arms over his chest again. "Hope you don't have to go anywhere, sweetheart. This might take awhile."

Elizabeth geared up and headed toward shore, where the dock was barely visible.

"Not so fast. Slow down." He looked down at Victoria. "Recognize him, sweetheart?"

Victoria looked at the body tied alongside, dragging through the water with a sloshing sound, and shook her head. Water washed over the head, lifted the ponytail, rippled down the back, dividing into three streams when it reached the pale, round buttocks.

"Who is it?" Elizabeth said from behind her grandmother.

Domingo didn't answer immediately, and Victoria looked up at him. "Bernie Marble," he said finally.

"Oh no!" Elizabeth gasped. "Are you sure?"

"Yes," Domingo said.

"How can you tell?" Victoria, one hand on each side of the boat, kept gazing at the body.

"Ponytail and fat ass," Domingo said.

Sirens whooped in the distance. Vehicles with blinking emergency lights sped toward the dock, then stopped on the road leading to it, red and blue lights still flashing.

Domingo turned around in his seat, his hands on the gunwales. "Ambulance and police cruisers." He turned back to Victoria. "I told them we needed a hearse. Watch Chief Medeiros's reaction when he sees whose body it is."

Domingo's face was hidden in darkness. Behind him, the strobing red and blue emergency lights backlit his chunky torso, framed his capped head.

"I mean it," he said to Victoria. "Watch the chief's face carefully. See what he does when he recognizes his crony."

Elizabeth throttled down the outboard engine, and the launch drifted toward shore. As they got closer, the dock loomed over them. Five or six figures — Victoria couldn't tell exactly how many — stood on the end of the dock, silhouetted by the strobe lights that swung round and round on the vehicles.

A voice came down from the dock, five feet above them. "That you, Mingo?"

"Yo!" Domingo said.

"What the hell have you done now?"

"Come and see." Domingo turned to Victoria. "You okay, sweetheart? Can you get up that ladder?" He paused. "You'll have to go to the police station to give a statement."

"There's nothing I can tell anyone." Victoria's eyes avoided the floating corpse a foot from her.

"I don't trust that chief," Domingo said under his breath. "But there's a procedure we have to follow."

"I can get up on the dock." Victoria looked up over her head. "Where's the ladder?"

"Yo, Chief!" Domingo shouted up to the man on the dock above them.

"Yo, yourself," Chief Medeiros said.

"How about giving Mrs. Trumbull a hand up, like a gentleman?"

"What the hell's she doing here?"

"She's a witness." Domingo turned to Elizabeth, who was attempting to secure the left side of the launch to the piling while the harbor master and police chief talked. The body was outboard. Victoria looked up at the dock far over her head. Of course she could climb up there. She simply had to make sure she had a firm hand hold and moved slowly.

Elizabeth looped a line around the barnacle-encrusted piling.

"You," Domingo said to her. "What are you doing?"

Elizabeth looked up at him. Victoria had turned slightly so she could see her granddaughter.

"Tying the boat up, of course."

"Those barnacles are razor-sharp." Elizabeth retrieved the line quickly. "You come back and the boat would be in the middle of the harbor, with crabs feeding on the corpse."

"Ugh!" Elizabeth said.

"Nice fat crabs," Domingo said. "Tasty."

A voice came from above them. "I'll take the line." Elizabeth, balancing herself cautiously, passed lines up to an extended hand. Someone tied the lines around dock cleats. A young man, his hair blond in the lights from the vehicles, scrambled down the ladder and got in the boat next to Victoria, then helped her to her feet. When she had straightened her legs, she reached for the uprights of the vertical wooden ladder. She looked up and saw faces peering down at her from the dock. *Thank goodness I don't wear those old-lady shoes,* she thought. Her hiking shoes with the hole cut in the top of one to ease the pressure on her toe had lugged soles. She put her right foot on the ladder, slick with seaweed, and held tightly to the sides. The blond boy was behind her. Left foot on the same rung. Right foot on the next rung. Left foot. She looked up and could see the top of the dock, hands reaching out to her.

At the top, two more people, another young man and a stocky woman Victoria recognized as an emergency medical technician at the hospital, helped her onto the dock.

Chief Medeiros stood off to one side, waiting for Domingo to climb the ladder.

"You," Domingo ordered Elizabeth, "stay there until I tell you to move."

"Asshole," Elizabeth muttered under her breath.

Chief Medeiros looked down at her and grinned. "You got that right, girlie."

Domingo's cap appeared at the top of the ladder, the faded gold NYPD showing clearly in the light from the vehicles.

Victoria realized how short the harbor master was when she saw him next to the police chief on the dock. He was even shorter than the woman, whose name she couldn't recall. Domingo was probably five foot seven, a squat man with broad shoulders. His chest widened to an ample stomach that hung over his belt buckle, then narrowed to slim hips.

"What've you got for us, Mingo?" Chief Medeiros said when Domingo walked to him.

"The body's tied up to the launch. Want to see it from down there?" Domingo hooked his thumbs into his uniform pockets, stood with his feet slightly apart, toes out. "We brought him in the way he was, floating face down. Didn't turn him over."

"Any idea who it is?" The chief placed his hand on Domingo's shoulder, damp from the ride across the choppy harbor.

"You tell me."

The chief turned to go down the steep ladder and disappeared from view.

"Want me to go back down to watch his reaction?" Victoria asked, looking anxiously at Domingo, who shook his head.

"I think we'll find out what we need to know," he said, so softly that only Victoria could hear. "You can sit on the bench, if you want, sweetheart. It's going to be awhile."

"Shit!" The police chief's voice exploded up from the launch. "Jesus Christ!" Domingo looked at Victoria and raised his eyebrows, moved his lips in a faint smile. The chief appeared on the ladder again.

"Bernie," he said to Domingo. "You knew it was Bernie, didn't you?"

"Who, me?" Domingo opened his eyes innocently. He spread his right hand across his chest, fingers splayed out. "How can I identify a corpse in the dark, a body floating face down?"

"Shit," the chief said again. "Excuse me, ma'am." He turned to Victoria, then back to Domingo. "What's her role in this?" He jerked his thumb at Victoria. "Witness, you said? We need to get back to the station as soon as we get him into the ambulance."

"You need the hearse, Medeiros, not the ambulance."

The chief ignored Domingo and turned to one of the patrolmen. "Call Toby, will you? You know, the undertaker," he said when the patrolman looked perplexed. Then, impatiently, he added, "He's dead, fool. He doesn't ride in the ambulance. Toby knows what to do." The patrolman walked quickly back to the police vehicle, and Victoria heard a burst of static as he got on the radio.

"Can you get the launch up to the beach?" the chief asked. Domingo nodded, his thumbs back in his pockets, feet apart. "Be easier to get him out there than to lift him up to the dock," the chief said. "Jesus Christ. What timing."

Domingo raised his eyebrows at Victoria.

Elizabeth started the motor, and a patrolman and medic passed lines down to her. She eased the boat toward shore, then lifted the outboard motor into the boat as the water shoaled. The corpse grounded in the shallow water, and water sloshed over his head, ponytail, back. His bare buttocks shook.

Victoria looked down from her perch on the dock. She counted six people altogether, not including the harbor master, her granddaughter, and herself. Lights circled around and around on top of the three vehicles. Victoria thought of strobe lights in the disco she had once gone to with Elizabeth and her granddaughter's now ex-husband. People seemed to flick in and out of visibility, red, blue, red, blue. Someone moved a vehicle to light up the scene with headlights, illuminating the launch and Elizabeth, the body, and its exposed bottom.

Victoria watched Elizabeth untie the body from the thwart. The medics and police waded into the water to turn it over, so they could load it onto the stretcher they had wheeled next to the shoreline, Victoria supposed. She couldn't see what they were doing because their backs shielded the body from her sight. She heard a splash. They must have turned it over, she realized. At the same instant, she heard mingled shouts, curses, grunts. She saw Elizabeth stand up in the boat, then sit down again quickly. Elizabeth leaned over the side of the launch, the side away from the corpse, put both hands on the port gunwale, and vomited into the harbor, over and over. She continued to heave even after nothing more came out.

Victoria stood up and walked stiffly down the dock, stepped down onto the boardwalk that crossed the sand, stepped off into the sand, and headed toward the group. Domingo blocked her way.

"No. You don't want to see this," he said. "You don't want to see what they did to him. No, sweetheart. Sit on the boardwalk until they load him into Toby's hearse. Then you'd better take care of my assistant back there. She needs you." He jerked his head toward the launch. "We've got a long evening ahead of us."

~ ~ ~

CHAPTER TWO

The Harbor Master's Shack

"I'VE put a password into the computer program." Howland Atherton peered down his nose at Elizabeth, who was sitting next to him in the harbor master's shack. Sunlight reflections danced off the water, glistened on Howland's high cheekbones, and flickered on the computer screen.

It was two days after Victoria, Domingo, and Elizabeth had found Bernie Marble's disemboweled, emasculated corpse floating in the harbor. Elizabeth was back at work, although nothing seemed normal to her anymore.

She could tell by Howland's expression – his turned-down mouth and the way he sneered at the computer – that he was irritated, probably with himself.

"Domingo pretends he's Denny the Dunce." Howland leaned back in his chair and ran his fingers through his hair, silvery on the sides, dark on top. "Then when you agree to help the poor guy, he springs the trap – snap – and you're caught up in whatever scheme he's got going." He keyed in a few numbers with his two forefingers. "And I fell for it. I did exactly what he wanted. He wanted to computerize the harbor."

Elizabeth shook her short hair off her forehead. She was dealing out a handful of receipts like a deck of cards.

"I'm sorry I got you involved in this job," Howland continued. "He can't be much fun to work for."

Elizabeth looked up from the receipts in surprise. "I love working here. It's what I needed after getting rid of my creepy husband." She returned to the receipts. "Domingo's hard to take sometimes, but I like him, sort of."

Howland's smile made his mouth turn down, not up. "Two mature people, you in your thirties, me in my fifties, groveling before a Latino tyrant."

Elizabeth laughed. "You didn't know my ex."

The harbor master's shack, set high on pilings driven into the harbor floor, moved gently in the tidal current. Water swashed past clumps of seaweed on the shack's footings.

The two worked quietly. After several minutes, Howland said, "If it weren't such a challenge to design this program, I'd be tempted to walk away." He moved the monitor slightly to cut glare from the harbor. "It's more complicated than I thought it would be, and Domingo doesn't make things easier."

A powerboat came through the channel into the harbor. Elizabeth went out on the deck, cupped her hands around her mouth, and yelled, "Slow down! No wake!"

The sunburned man at the wheel, his nose blistered and peeling, waved at her and slowed. The boat's wake trailed off.

"I hope the password you're putting in will keep the dock attendants from messing it up." Elizabeth came back in and sat down again. "Those kids think they know everything there is to know about computers."

The shack trembled, and Elizabeth looked up to see a couple in their sixties coming up the catwalk to the window.

"Customers." She got up again to greet them, slid the window open, exchanged pleasantries, and handed the woman a clipboard with a form to be filled out. The man signed the credit-card receipt and put his part in his wallet. The woman gave Elizabeth the completed form, and they left.

"The dock attendants know only enough about computers to screw up my program," Howland said after they'd gone. He typed in a series of words. "Maybe the password will keep them out, but who knows."

"What's the password?" Elizabeth picked up a receipt and placed it on one of the piles. The wind blew through the open south window, which looked out over boats in slips around the edge of the harbor, fluttering the papers on Elizabeth's desk. She brushed away tendrils of hair that blew into her eyes.

"The password is the harbor master's wife's nickname in Spanish." Howland keyed another set of words into the computer, then moved the monitor again to shade it from flickering reflections.

"That should be easy to remember," Elizabeth said wryly. She looked up from the receipts. "I have no idea what Mrs. D.'s nickname is in English, let alone Spanish."

" 'Woman.' " Howland glanced at Elizabeth with his turned-down smile.

" 'Woman'?" Elizabeth slapped the receipts down on the counter. "That's what Domingo calls his wife? 'Woman'?"

"Yes." Howland returned to the keyboard, held his hand over the monitor. "Still too much reflection."

"That pig!" Elizabeth leaned back in the rickety chair. "I don't see how Noreen puts up with him. 'Woman'! He's not in Colombia now."

"He never was." Howland pushed his chair away from the counter with both hands. The chair scraped on the sandy floor, and he stood up, gradually unfolding his tall frame. "He comes from Brooklyn; his father came from Colombia. The password is *'mujer.'* Write it down somewhere safe."

"Believe me, I'll remember that." Elizabeth picked up the receipts from the countertop and started to sort them again. After a few seconds, she threw them down. "I can't think straight. I can't concentrate on anything. I keep seeing that obscene corpse."

A sailboat came into the channel under power, and when Elizabeth saw the skipper, she waved.

"They're here for a week, all the way up from the Virgin Islands, and this is their first stop." The sailboat turned and backed toward a slip. "They've got a glorious day, and tomorrow is supposed to be just as beautiful."

"They clear U.S. Customs before they get here, don't they?" Howland asked.

"Technically, they're supposed to, in Miami or Washington or New York or Boston. But most don't. That boat can carry enough fuel and provisions to cross the Atlantic easily." She stood up and looked out the sliding window toward the boats and the Harbor House beyond them. "Where the devil are the dock attendants? They need to help with lines."

"How is your grandmother taking the murder?"

"You know the way Victoria is." Elizabeth turned to him. "She's more like a ten-year-old than a ninety-two-year-old. She loves action of any kind."

Howland moved the chair back under the counter, and it scraped again, fingernails on slate. Elizabeth winced.

"I might as well sweep the sand out of this dump." She got up. "The dock attendants are supposed to keep this place clean, but look at it." She gestured around the small office.

The shack had windows on all four sides. The window on the south, now open, could be pushed to one side, so the staff could take in money or give information to boaters. From that window, Elizabeth could look over the harbor with its moored and docked yachts, could see the activity of guests at the Harbor House. Through the window to her right, she could see the narrow channel leading into the harbor, and, across the channel, the osprey nest high on its pole. On weekday evenings, when the harbor was quiet, she liked to watch the ospreys. She had seen the male arrive early in the spring, even before she had taken the job in the harbor, and had watched the pair fix up the nest, watched them sit on their eggs, had seen the hatchlings when they emerged.

To the north, beyond the channel, she could see ferries coming and going on

Nantucket Sound, from Woods Hole on the mainland to the Oak Bluffs wharf. The computer and printer were on a counter that ran under that window.

The fourth window faced the parking lot to the east. Across the lot, pastel-colored Victorian houses, festooned with wooden gingerbread, faced the harbor. A desk under the window looked out at the catwalk that led from the shack across a hundred-foot stretch of water to the parking lot.

A grimy T-shirt hung limply out of an open desk drawer, and a torn chips wrapper and a crushed soda can lay on the floor.

The windows made the shack feel larger than it actually was. Elizabeth had measured it, and it was smaller than Victoria's upstairs bathroom, which was only eight feet by twelve.

"Those hotshot kids can't even hit the wastebasket." Elizabeth gestured at the rubbish on the floor, and Howland ducked to avoid her arm.

"Try to keep them away from the computer at least." Howland leaned over the monitor and, still standing, entered a couple of numbers. "I have more work to do on the program before it's safe from them."

"The program will never be safe from them. They've been playing with computers since kindergarten." Elizabeth moved the aluminum lawn chair that served as office furniture to one side and reached behind the door for the broom. She pulled the T-shirt out of the open desk drawer and tossed it, the soda can, and the chips bag into the trash container.

Footsteps pounded on the catwalk, shaking the small building. Elizabeth looked up to see two teenage boys tossing punches, hopping from one foot to the other, dancing toward the shack.

"Cut it out, you guys," Elizabeth shouted at them. "Go back and get the sailboat's lines. Go on!"

"He don't need help," the kid with green hair said.

"Go!" Elizabeth said.

"We need to get a pad of receipts," the taller kid said.

"I already checked out a receipt pad to Louie." Elizabeth nodded her head at the green-haired boy. Both were wearing khaki shorts and blue knit collared shirts with "Dock Attendant" across the back. Except for the hair and the difference in height, they looked identical.

"I don't know where it's at." Louie avoided Elizabeth's eyes.

"Help the sailboat; then keep looking until you find the receipts. They're numbered. If you've lost them, you're fired."

17

"Shiiit," said Louie. "C'mon, Dewey. Creepy old lady."

"Watch your mouth, or you're fired."

"You can't fire me. You ain't my boss. My father is on the Harbor Advisory Committee."

Elizabeth grabbed the broom and wrenched the door open, fire in her eyes.

"He didn't mean nothin'," Dewey said, backing away from Elizabeth, who was brandishing the broom. Both kids put their arms over their heads.

"Let's get outta here," Louie said, and they turned and sauntered down the catwalk. When they got to the bulkhead, they looked back at Elizabeth, and the green-haired kid jerked his head toward her in an insolent way.

"Dewey and Louie, hey?" Howland said.

"There's a third one we call Huey," Elizabeth said. "I've forgotten their real names."

Elizabeth leaned the broom against the door and dusted off her hands. "That's that."

"I doubt it." Howland watched the kids move as slowly as they could toward the sailboat. A crew member on the stern of the boat held a line, prepared to jump ashore and tie it off as the boat backed into the slip.

"Lazy bastards," Howland said of the kids, who were still too far away from the sailboat to help. "They need Domingo to get after them. New York cop meets Island bumpkins."

"Even Domingo can't handle the kids. 'You can't touch me; my father is ...' " Elizabeth mimicked the teenager, high voice and a wiggle of slim hips. "I almost feel sorry for Domingo." She straightened papers on the desk. "My grandmother thinks Domingo is wonderful, courtly, considerate, charming."

"He is, to her."

"Victoria flirts with him as if she were a girl." Elizabeth smiled. "She admits he might be difficult to work for. That's not exactly how I'd put it. 'Impossible' is more like it, much as I love the job and respect him." Elizabeth set the two chairs outside on the deck, then swept the sand into a heap mixed with paper scraps, dust balls, and twisted paper clips. "At times, I get fed up with the way he wants me to document every teensy-weensy thing. I go to the bathroom. 'Document it,' he says."

"Really?"

"Almost. And those dock attendants! If I had anything to say about it, I'd fire every single one of them. All they do all day long is show off for one another, boys flexing muscles, girls tossing their snaky hair."

She opened a lower desk drawer, took out a piece of cardboard, and swept the dirt pile onto it. "Every one of them is related to someone – a selectman's niece, a Harbor Advisory Committee member's girlfriend's son's girlfriend. Honestly, you can't say anything around here. It's as if we're surrounded by a pack of kid spies." She slid the pile of dirt off the cardboard and into the trash, then stepped out the door and slapped the cardboard on the railing, shaking off the remaining dust. A breeze eddied around the shack, flicking a cat's-paw of disturbed water across the harbor, rocking sailboats on their moorings.

For a few minutes, Elizabeth remained on the deck. She leaned her elbows on the railing and watched the wind on the water. Then she went back into the shack and swept vigorously.

Howland sneezed, then sneezed again. He reached into his pocket for his handkerchief.

"And to think" — he gestured around the small shack — "instead of all this, you could be gardening and taking care of Victoria."

"Victoria does not need taking care of," Elizabeth said. "She thinks she's taking care of me, and she's right." She changed the subject abruptly. "How did Domingo ever talk you into designing a harbor-management program?" She nodded at the computer.

"He's trying to convince me I can sell the program for a million dollars." Howland put his handkerchief back into his pocket. "He's wrong, of course, and he knows it. It's a game he plays. I'm simply using off-the-shelf software and adapting it to the harbor." Howland leaned back against the desk and crossed his right leg over his left, half-sitting. He was wearing worn boat shoes with no socks, and Elizabeth could see the big toe of his right foot through the broken stitching at the seam.

"He tells me it's a challenge, which it is, a challenge to design a simple, foolproof program that deals with a lot of variables."

"He's not thinking about you, though, is he." Elizabeth made it a statement, not a question. "He thinks there are leaks in the money-handling system, and he wants you to seal them off."

"Exactly," Howland said. "He's convinced that someone has been skimming money from the harbor receipts, a hundred thousand dollars or more a season."

"From mid-June to Labor Day?"

Howland nodded. "Two-and-a-half months."

Elizabeth whistled. "Not bad! Forty thousand a month."

"From what I see so far, he's probably right. The harbor seems to be taking in about that much extra this year." Howland opened one of the desk drawers and started to put his foot on it. He looked in and shut the drawer quickly. "Good heavens! You know what's in there?"

"No. Let me see." Elizabeth leaned forward to look. Howland opened the drawer a crack, and she saw a loose pile of twenty-dollar bills.

"Yeah. We have to take that to the bank tonight. Would you put it in one of the green bank bags? Second drawer down on the left side."

"No," Howland said. "I don't work here, remember? I don't want my fingerprints on anything." He shut the drawer again. "What were you saying?"

"I was going to say, before he took over the harbor master job, the town had a sloppy way of keeping records."

Howland raised his eyebrows. "Oh?" He opened the drawer.

"No, really. That money is all accounted for with receipts and paperwork. When your program is up and running, we can turn it over to the town accountant, but Domingo wants all the data entered into the computer before we do."

"In the meantime, we have how much in that drawer?"

"I think it's about fourteen thousand dollars."

"What!" Howland choked. "Fourteen thousand, you think? In a drawer? Loose?"

"No one's going to take it."

"They're eviscerating people right and left, and yet the money is safe in that drawer?"

"Don't remind me of that." Elizabeth turned to her work.

"We've got to enter that into the computer right away, even though the program isn't foolproof yet," Howland said. "Domingo suspected something funny was going on here at the harbor even before Bernie was killed."

"You think Bernie's death is related?"

Howland nodded.

"How?" she asked.

"Domingo seems to think the hundred thousand is, or was, a payoff for someone to keep quiet. He thinks he's a threat to somebody, and he's not sure who." Howland turned to look out the window. "How were they handling the money before?"

"The dock attendants would bundle up loose cash and loose checks and take the whole mess, uncounted, over to Town Hall."

"So between the time boaters paid their money and the treasurer counted it, no one had any control over it?"

"That's right. And a lot of the money was cash." Elizabeth straightened papers on the counter.

"The computer program will seal up most of the loopholes," Howland said. "Once we have all the boat names and owners' addresses entered, it will be easy to track the money. I'm not sure this is going to help Domingo, though. It's as though some town officials hope he fails, as though they're setting him up." He looked out the window again toward the parking lot. "Here he comes now with Victoria."

Elizabeth put the broom back behind the door and glanced out the window. Domingo was parking his white convertible in the harbor master's slot. Victoria sat on the left side of the front seat, her face shaded by a large floppy straw hat.

"Look at that car of his!" Elizabeth said. "If that isn't conspicuous consumption!"

"Rolls-Royce Corniche," Howland said. "Right-hand drive. He claims it fell off a truck when he was a New York cop."

"He's driving it for my grandmother's benefit. He usually drives Ernesto's pickup."

Domingo got out of the right-hand side and slammed the door shut with an expensive thunk. He reached into the back seat and retrieved a manila folder and a basket covered with a Black Dog napkin, walked around the back of the car, looked at the rear tires, walked down the left side, and opened the passenger door.

"Look at that, will you?" Elizabeth put both hands on the desk and leaned forward for a better look. "He's pretending he's a gentleman. Watch this!"

Domingo had taken off his navy blue cap. He bent slightly at the waist in a courtly bow and offered his right arm to Victoria, who took it and smiled up at him. Howland laughed.

Still holding the folder and the basket, Domingo put his cap back on, and with Victoria on his arm walked toward the catwalk leading to the shack. She swept her straw hat off with a girlish gesture, her smile revealing a complicated set of wrinkles upon wrinkles. She was wearing a lavender-colored pant suit, the pants riding high on her still-shapely long legs. The ends of the yellow ribbon she'd wound around the hat brim fluttered in the breeze. Victoria had tucked a bunch of black-eyed Susans into the ribbon, and the flowers were beginning to droop. She looked up at Domingo with her hooded eyes and gave him a smile.

"Trapped," Howland said. "I'd hoped to get away before he got here. Are you finished sweeping?" Elizabeth nodded, and he moved the two chairs back into the shack from the deck.

"You'd think she'd act her age." Elizabeth watched her grandmother and Domingo.

"If you're her age and still have it, you can act any way you want," Howland said.

Outside the shack, Domingo escorted Victoria to the bench where she'd sat two nights before, then set the basket beside her.

Water lapped gently around the pilings. A seagull flew overhead, soaring on the air currents rising from the harbor's surface. The osprey circled; a plane droned overhead. Domingo shaded his eyes with his hand.

"Won't be long before the president arrives," he said to Victoria. "Then we'll have planes and boats everywhere. Secret Service, the press. It's going to be a mess." He looked at Victoria, who was searching for something in her pocketbook. "Your lunch won't spoil, will it?"

"I didn't pack anything that would," Victoria said.

She took an envelope out of her pocketbook, then continued to search for something. Elizabeth, who had been watching her from inside the shack, reached into the cup of pens and pencils on the counter and found a thick pen inscribed with the words *This number qualifies Victoria Trumbull for the final round of the Million-Dollar Sweepstakes!* She walked outside and gave it to her grandmother.

Victoria pushed her straw hat back on her head, reached up for the ribbons floating in the breeze, and tied them under her chin. "Thank you," she said, taking the pen.

As soon as Elizabeth stepped back into the shack, Domingo followed her. He pointed his index finger at her. "You," he said. "Did you get all those receipts entered into the computer?"

"Not 'You.' I have a name," Elizabeth said. "No, I didn't enter them. I haven't even sorted them yet."

"Is something holding you up?"

"I am," Howland said. "I'm installing your million-dollar computer program."

"We're working against time." Domingo thrust his hands into his trousers pockets and set his feet apart. "The selectmen are getting impatient."

"To hell with the selectmen. I can only go so fast."

"That's very well for you to say." Domingo looked up at Howland with dark eyes. "They're not paying you."

"No kidding." Howland's mouth turned down. He put his head back and looked down at the harbor master through half-closed eyes. Reflections from the water flickered across his high cheekbones, gave his hazel eyes a leonine appearance.

"You don't understand," Domingo said. "They're setting me up, I tell you. Especially now, after what happened to Marble." He patted his shirt pocket, where he kept his pack of Camels.

"Surely they don't think you had anything to do with Bernie's death?" Elizabeth said.

"They're looking for a reason to fire me. Not turning over the receipts to the treasurer is reason enough, to their way of thinking." Domingo stood in the doorway and looked out at the Harbor House. "I'm not handing that loose cash over to the treasurer without getting a receipt. They won't give me a receipt unless we have the money accounted for on one of their forms. And we can't generate a form until Atherton gets the bugs out of his program."

"Debugging a new system takes time," Elizabeth said.

"They're not giving me that time."

"What can they fire you for?"

"They'll call it mismanagement, mark my words."

"But they hired you. Why would they want to fire you?"

"They hired him because they thought he was a dumb black cop who would do what they wanted him to do," Howland said.

"Yas," Domingo replied.

"They'd be crazy to fire you." Elizabeth looked steadily at the harbor master. "You've tightened up the money-handling system, closed loopholes, installed high-tech mooring systems. Why would they fire you?"

"Because they don't want the money-handling system tightened up," Domingo said. "Money is leaking out of the system into somebody's pockets; I've suspected that for months." He turned and looked directly at Elizabeth. "Get those receipts entered into the computer if you have to stay here all night." He patted the cigarette pack in his shirt pocket.

Elizabeth shrugged and turned to Howland. "What about it?"

"Go ahead. The database is ready. I'll enter some of the data for you, give you a break. Domingo's right. We have to get everything into the system before we can turn the money over, and we have to do it as soon as possible."

"Don't put your initials on it," Domingo said to Howland. "You don't work here, you know."

"Thank God."

Outside, Victoria was scribbling on the back of an envelope. Occasionally, she looked up as a boat came into the harbor, rocking the shack, or at the osprey nest, the birds bringing an endless supply of food to their chicks. The ospreys' plaintive cries echoed across the harbor.

Domingo looked out the window at Victoria. He pulled the pack of Camels out of his shirt pocket, shook one out, and started to light it with a battered Zippo.

"Not in here," Elizabeth said sharply. "No smoking. Don't you dare smoke in here."

Domingo put the cigarette back into the pack. He turned to Howland. "They're all alike."

"Yeah, yeah."

"Ms. Elizabeth" – Domingo stretched out the "Ms." – "I need to tell you something, and I don't want your grandmother to hear."

Elizabeth looked up, concerned at the harbor master's tone.

"No one knows what she saw two nights ago. She says she saw something – four people, maybe. She isn't sure." He put his hands in his pockets and continued to look over the harbor. "No one knows whether she can identify the vehicle she heard leave the scene. She doesn't think she can. She forgot to tell the police she thought she heard a boat. She's not sure. But as long as someone out there thinks she might have seen someone, recognized a voice, recognized a vehicle, she is in danger." He stopped.

Elizabeth stared at him, her face paling under her tan. Howland, who was leaning against the desk, put his hand up to his chin, stroked it. Elizabeth heard the slight scratch of afternoon whiskers.

"What can we do?" she said.

"I, for one, am going to talk to your West Tisbury police chief, have her or one of her patrolmen watch your house." He turned and looked at her, then at Howland. "I'll go by your place as often as I can." He thrust his hands deeper into his pockets. "I still have a valid gun permit."

"Gun?" Elizabeth turned back from the counter.

"Your car is not exactly inconspicuous," Howland said. "A white Rolls-Royce convertible?"

"The more conspicuous the better." Domingo patted his pocket. "I don't trust the Oak Bluffs cops. I don't trust the selectmen. I don't trust anyone on the Harbor Advisory Committee. The recently deceased Bernie Marble had ties to all of them. Owned a bar on Pequot Avenue, in partnership with two of the selectmen."

"The Good Times?" Elizabeth said. The radio in the shack crackled with static, and the three listened until it cut off.

"That's another of his properties. Meatloaf Staples is part owner of that. The two selectmen were partners with Bernie in the Sand Bar, two doors down from the Good Times."

"Meatloaf," Howland said thoughtfully. "He was always with Bernie, almost like a bodyguard."

"That is correct," Domingo said. "He knows how to spot power and cozy up to it."

"The advantages of not being in power." Howland moved away from the desk, headed toward the door. "I need to get home to feed my dogs."

"You better keep them hungry." Domingo moved out of Howland's way. "You never know when someone may find his way into the duchy. You want them hungry, ready to attack."

"Tigger and Rover, attack dogs?" Elizabeth said. "I don't think so."

"Damnation!" Howland halted at the door, his hand still on the knob, and looked toward the parking lot. A van had pulled into a slot. The door opened and an obese man slid out of the driver's seat. His two small feet touched the macadam. He faced the van and slammed the door, pushed his glasses back up his small nose, tugged his baseball cap down on his forehead, pulled his tan jacket over his gut, pulled his pant legs away from his crotch, and looked over at the harbor master's shack.

"Meatloaf," Howland said. "What's he doing here?"

"Get going with those entries, Ms. Elizabeth." Domingo turned to her. "We're running out of time."

~ ~ ~

CHAPTER THREE

Sleuths

MEATLOAF Staples stepped onto the catwalk, holding the railings on either side with small hands that seemed out of proportion to his body.

As he approached Victoria, who was sitting on the bench outside the shack, Elizabeth, still sitting at the computer, watched her grandmother's reflection in the computer screen.

Victoria looked up from her writing and shaded her eyes. "Good afternoon," she said.

Meatloaf turned his head toward her without answering. He pushed his sunglasses back onto his nose. Drops of sweat ran off his forehead in rivulets, traveled down the side of his face, and dripped onto the wooden catwalk, where they made fat dots that spread out on the boards. Sweat blotched the armpits of his tan shirt.

"How rude," Victoria said softly, although clearly enough that Meatloaf must have heard. Inside the shack, Elizabeth laughed.

"Watch yourselves." Domingo glanced out the window.

Meatloaf stepped over the doorsill and into the shack. "How can I help you?" Domingo said civilly.

Elizabeth turned back to the computer and began to enter receipts she hadn't yet sorted.

Howland leaned back against the desk and folded his arms across the chest of his thrift-shop shirt.

Meatloaf removed his sunglasses, took a crumpled handkerchief out of his pocket, and wiped his glasses. He lifted his baseball cap with "Araujo Septic Systems" on it and mopped his forehead. He put his sunglasses on, stuffed the handkerchief back into his pocket, and straightened his baseball cap. Elizabeth watched his reflection in the screen, heard his heavy breathing.

"I'm here about a complaint," Meatloaf said finally.

"Won't you sit down?" Domingo indicated the empty aluminum lawn chair. Meatloaf pulled the chair to the end of the shack, scraping it along the floor. He turned around, his back to the chair, put his hands on the armrests, and eased himself into it. Aluminum rubbed against aluminum; the synthetic webbing squeaked. He faced the three of them, Domingo standing beside the door,

Howland leaning against the desk at the end of the shack, and Elizabeth at the computer on the side.

"What's she doing out there?" Meatloaf looked at Domingo and jerked his head toward Victoria. He clasped his hands together on top of his belly.

"Writing poetry," Howland said.

"I asked you, Mingo, not him." Meatloaf turned his head toward Domingo, his eyes hidden by his sunglasses.

"It's public property. She can sit there if she wants." Domingo folded his arms over his chest like Howland. Elizabeth made soft clicking noises on the keyboard as she watched the reflections of Meatloaf and Domingo on the screen.

"What's the complaint?" Domingo said.

Overhead, a seagull cried, a long, mewling call ending in a series of short squawks.

"Seems you have one of the selectman's nieces working for you as dock attendant. Is that right?"

"That's correct." Domingo remained next to the door, his arms still folded. Water splashed gently against the pilings. A small motorboat went out of the harbor.

Domingo narrowed his eyes at Meatloaf. "Allison Phipps."

Elizabeth paused briefly, then continued typing. The osprey cried. Wind lifted papers on the counter next to her, and she put a rounded beach stone on top of them to hold them down. The telephone rang. She got up from the desk and answered it.

After a long wait, Meatloaf continued. "Her aunt lodged a complaint against you."

"What for?"

"You pretend you don't know?" Meatloaf laced his hands high on his belly. Water reflections, stirred up by the passing boat, danced on the ceiling of the shack.

The radio crackled, and a man's voice came over it. "Oak Bluffs Harbor, this is … yacht …" Static garbled the message. Elizabeth pushed her chair back, got up, and lifted the radio mike off its hook on the wall next to Domingo.

"Vessel calling the Oak Bluffs harbor master," Elizabeth said in her low voice. Domingo, Meatloaf, and Howland held their poses as if for a time exposure. "This is the Oak Bluffs harbor master on Channel Nine. Your radio message is breaking up. Please repeat. Over."

"She's not the harbor master." Meatloaf's voice was high-pitched, almost a soprano. He moved his head slightly to look at Elizabeth as she spoke into the radio mike. "You got her taking over your job?"

Domingo said nothing.

The voice came through more clearly. "This is the sailing yacht *Sea Slide*. I reserved a slip for five nights."

Elizabeth directed the boat into the harbor and told the skipper how to pay. She hung up the mike and sat again, where she could watch Meatloaf's reflection.

"*Sea Slide*, eh?" Meatloaf moved in the chair. "Where's she coming from?"

"I can tell you in just a sec." Elizabeth keyed something into the computer.

"The program can track boats from the time they first contact us until they leave here." Howland moved toward the screen, which was showing a list of boat names. "*Sea Slide* called us several weeks ago to request a slip."

Elizabeth scrolled down to the boat's name while Howland stood over her, one hand on top of the computer monitor, the other in his pocket.

"It's all in here," Elizabeth said. "*Sea Slide* left the Turks and Caicos four weeks ago, stopped at Saint Croix, and then sailed directly here to the Vineyard."

After a long silence, Meatloaf spoke, as if the information Elizabeth had given him meant nothing. He glanced toward Howland, then back at Domingo. "Looks like you need some better operating procedures." He wiggled his laced fingers.

"What was the selectman's complaint?" Domingo asked.

Meatloaf turned his sunglass gaze to Domingo. "Harassment."

Howland coughed, then sneezed. He took his handkerchief out of his pocket and blew his nose.

Elizabeth turned from the computer, her lips parted. "Harassment?" Domingo scowled.

Meatloaf shifted in his chair, and the aluminum frame creaked. "I'm only reporting what Liz Tate said. She's the one who filed the complaint against you, not me."

"How am I supposed to have harassed her?" Domingo leaned against the wall next to the radio. Looking at the computer screen, Elizabeth could see his jaw clench, could see Howland sit against the desk again, holding his chin in his right hand.

The telephone rang. Elizabeth answered, "Oak Bluffs harbor master." She listened. "Let me get your boat's name, its length and beam." She listened. "And the date you'll be arriving?" Howland, Domingo, and Meatloaf didn't move. Elizabeth clamped the telephone receiver next to her ear with her shoulder, filling out a form as she spoke. "Call on Channel Nine when you get here." She hung up the phone and returned to the keyboard.

Howland crossed one foot over the other.

"How am I supposed to have harassed the young woman?" Domingo repeated. He took his cigarette pack out of his pocket, shook one out, stuck it in his mouth, and put the pack back in his pocket. He reached into his pocket for his Zippo, flicked it a couple of times without lighting up, put it back in his pocket, took the cigarette out of his mouth, and held it, unlighted, between his index and third fingers.

"According to Liz Tate, her niece left work last Friday night in tears. She claims you abused her. Verbally."

Howland grunted, and when Elizabeth looked up at him and saw his expression, she suspected he was holding back some inappropriate witty comment that had occurred to him.

"Verbal abuse is not harassment," Domingo said.

"Harassment, abuse, same thing." Meatloaf unclasped his hands and pushed his sunglasses back with his forefinger.

"Tell Liz Tate to make her complaint to me in writing." Domingo put the unlighted cigarette in his mouth and let it dangle from his lower lip. "She set up the procedure."

"She's going to love this." Meatloaf hoisted himself out of the chair, stretched his arms, and yawned hugely. "She's no lady when you get her upset. Don't say I didn't warn you."

"Thanks." Domingo's cigarette danced on his lower lip.

The radio static crackled. The telephone rang. Howland leaned down and scratched his bare right ankle. A suntanned couple wearing identical madras shirts and khaki shorts came to the window. The woman held a credit card.

Elizabeth got up from her chair. "I'll be right with you," she told the couple at the window. She picked up the phone and said, "Please hold; I'll be with you in a moment." She lifted the radio mike. "Vessel calling Oak Bluffs harbor master, this is the Oak Bluffs harbor master."

Meatloaf shook his head. "I feel sorry for you, Mingo. Wouldn't want to be in your shoes." He lumbered out the door and squeezed past the couple in madras shirts. "Pardon me," he said, then walked down the catwalk to the parking lot.

Howland turned to Domingo, while Elizabeth finished giving directions on the radio. She filled out a charge form for the couple at the window, and took the telephone message.

"Allison Phipps is that skinny blond girl, isn't she?"

Domingo nodded.

"She's sneaky. I wouldn't trust her," Elizabeth said.

A boat whistled. Elizabeth looked up and saw the small passenger ferry *Cut-tyhunk* heading into the channel. People in bright summer clothes leaned on the rail. In the parking lot, three tour buses lined up, doors open. The drivers stood together in a small cluster, talking.

Howland pulled a chair out from the desk and sat facing the others. He crossed his right leg over his left.

Domingo unclenched his hands and thrust them into his pockets. He watched Meatloaf, his large dark eyes half-closed.

"Do you have a special reason for not trusting her?" he said to Elizabeth finally.

"A couple of times, I've come into the shack and she's been sitting at the desk, as if she'd been looking through stuff."

"Did you actually see her looking through something?"

The ferry's engines went into reverse, and the water in the channel foamed and bubbled. The ferry pulled alongside the bulkhead. A crew member on deck tossed a line to a darkly tanned man on shore, who dropped the end loop over a bollard. A young woman with red hair turned an iron crank that ratcheted the gangplank from ferry to shore. Then the tanned man secured the gangplank with lines.

"No, I didn't actually see her; it was just a feeling."

"A feeling," Domingo said. "A feeling. Can you document a feeling?"

"To hell with you." Elizabeth felt her face flush. "I don't trust her. That's all."

"Keep an eye on her, then," Domingo said. "If you see her doing anything she shouldn't be doing, doc — "

"Document it," Elizabeth replied, interrupting him.

On the shore, passengers from the ferry called to one another as they loaded into the tour buses. Meatloaf opened the door of his van and hoisted himself up onto the driver's seat with a small jump. His feet dangled above the pavement, the toes of his shoes pointed at each other. He wrote something in a notebook held high on his stomach. Elizabeth looked from Domingo to Howland to Meatloaf and then back at Domingo.

The unsmoked cigarette flipped up and down on Domingo's lower lip as he spoke. "That's the start of it."

The last passenger had walked down the gangplank and onto a tour bus. Blue smoke puffed out of exhaust pipes as bus engines started up. The buses backed out of their parking spaces and left. The parking lot was quiet again.

"What do you want us to do?" Howland watched Meatloaf through the window as he spoke to Domingo.

"Document everything." Domingo took the cigarette out of his mouth. "Dates, times, names, everything that transpires. Everything. Document going to the bathroom."

"Told you so," Elizabeth said to Howland.

A sailboat entered the channel under power. A crew member stood on the cabin roof, tying the loose mainsail onto the boom with long white ribbons. Elizabeth reached for the radio mike and directed the boat to a slip. A slim cigarette boat followed the sailboat, powerful engines so loud Elizabeth could barely hear the radio. The phone rang and she answered it. She saw the masts of two sailboats heading for the harbor entrance. A man walked up the catwalk toward the shack, a couple following him, and, behind them, a woman with two small boys. Elizabeth went out onto the deck, leaned over, and shouted above the engine noise, indicating a slip number for the cigarette boat and pointing to the slip.

Back in the shack, she told the man how to find the laundromat, told the couple where they could shower, and directed the woman with children to the carousel.

Domingo stepped out onto the deck, where Victoria was still sitting, and leaned his back against the rail, facing her. He took a deep breath and let it out again. He put the limp cigarette back in his mouth. "How're you doing, sweetheart?"

"What a rude man." Victoria looked down the catwalk to the parking lot and Meatloaf's van. A breeze flicked the ends of her yellow hat ribbon. "I hope you're not going to tell me I'm supposed to know who he is."

Domingo laughed and took out his Zippo. "You mind? Your granddaughter won't let me smoke."

Victoria shook her head. "Go ahead."

"How's the writing?" He lit the cigarette and inhaled deeply, held the smoke in.

She nodded.

"Finding that body was heavy stuff. Sorry you had to go through that, sweetheart." He let the smoke out slowly and leaned back, both elbows on the railing.

Victoria again looked toward the parking lot, where Meatloaf's van was pulling out of its space. "Who is he? I've never seen him before."

"Meatloaf Staples. He's fairly new to the Island. He's on the Harbor Advisory Committee."

He took another drag on his cigarette and threw it into the water, where it went out with a hiss.

"I couldn't help overhearing. Why is he accusing you of harassment?"

Domingo paused before he answered. He leaned back again, resting his elbows against the railing, and looked over at the osprey nest across the channel. The osprey returned with a fish in its talons. The chicks set up a shrill peeping. "I'm not sure yet. Something's going on that involves town officials — the selectmen, the Harbor Advisory Committee, the Oak Bluffs police. I haven't sorted it out."

"I know you think someone has been skimming money off the harbor receipts." Victoria watched him quietly, her eyes shaded by the straw hat.

"Money they were skimming off the harbor receipts is small potatoes compared to something bigger that's going on," he said.

"A hundred thousand dollars, small potatoes?" Victoria reached into the pocket of her lavender jacket, brought out a used paper napkin printed with fluorescent frogs, and dabbed at her nose.

"Yes, small potatoes," Domingo repeated. "You don't understand the scope of what we're dealing with." He turned, facing the Harbor House at the head of the harbor, his back to Victoria, elbows on the railing, hands clasped. "Someone is not pleased with Howland's computer program." He turned to face Victoria again, one elbow still on the railing. "The more loopholes I close up, the more frantic someone is getting."

"Who?"

Domingo shrugged.

On the shore, another set of tour buses pulled up to the *Cuttyhunk's* dock; these passengers got off the buses and boarded the ferry.

"But you're doing such a good job." Victoria tugged the brim of her hat to shade her eyes as she looked up at him.

"You don't understand, sweetheart. They don't want me to do a good job. They want me to go along with them. If I don't go along with them, who knows what they'll do?" He looked intently at Victoria, who was watching him, her hand on her hat brim.

Inside the shack, the phone rang. Elizabeth answered. A small sailboat came in the channel under sail. Domingo waved.

"How you doing, Cap'n?" he said to the small girl who was at the tiller. She grinned, big front teeth bright in the sunlight.

He looked at his watch. "Your granddaughter will be off in fifteen minutes. Tell her to be careful, will you? She's on duty again this evening, eight to midnight."

~ ~ ~

"Domingo's car has leather seats," Victoria said as she settled onto the frayed pink towel that covered the exposed foam of the passenger seat in Elizabeth's VW convertible. The car had been parked in the sun in front of the gingerbread houses, and the black surfaces of the dashboard and armrests radiated heat.

"His car is a Rolls-Royce," Elizabeth said, as if that explained it. She straightened the pink towel on the driver's side, sat, and swiveled her legs into the car. "At least my seat covers match."

The ferry's engines revved up and the whistle sounded. The crew ratcheted the gangplank back. A crew member lifted the hawser off the bollard and tossed it aboard, and the ferry moved out of the channel.

"They'll probably try to blame last year's missing money on Domingo." Elizabeth turned the key, and the engine caught with a metallic rattle. "Probably say he bought his car with the harbor money." The engine coughed and the convertible shook.

"Domingo's car is much quieter," Victoria said.

Elizabeth snorted. She looked behind her and backed out of the parking spot.

Victoria braced her hand on the dashboard. "I'm sure he's exaggerating the problem. He has a sense of the theatrical."

"He didn't exaggerate Bernie Marble's murder." Elizabeth drove slowly through the crowded street that ran next to the harbor, avoiding mopeds, bicycles, and tourists. "I wonder, by the way, who'll run the Harbor House now. He and Chief Medeiros were partners, but Bernie managed it."

"He let that wonderful hotel get run-down," Victoria said after a few minutes. "I remember when my grandparents used to take me there for Sunday dinner, all of us dressed up. It was so elegant. Now look at it." She indicated the weathered gray shingles and peeling paint. "And do you remember the time we went to the selectmen's meeting, and some woman said the five dollars he was charging boaters to take a shower at his hotel was too much?"

"I remember," Elizabeth said grimly. "It is too much. He hassled that woman, made her look foolish. Embarrassed her."

Elizabeth turned right onto the main road, which went past the harbor. Power yachts fringed the harbor on the right, their sterns facing the bulkhead. Tourists strolled past, viewing the boats; they stopped to talk with boaters sitting on deck chairs in cockpits, drinks in hand, bare feet propped up on transoms.

"Some of the boats that stay here have come a long way." Elizabeth stopped to let a couple wheeling a baby stroller cross the road. "Bermuda, the Caribbean. They come from all over. They go up to the Harbor House with their toilet-article kits and towels, wanting a hot freshwater shower, and have to pay a fee, on top of what they pay to keep their boat here." She started up again slowly, watched out for a boy and a girl wobbling next to the road on purple-and-pink bikes. "It's a rip-off."

On the left side of the road, a row of gingerbread houses faced the harbor, their window boxes full of flowers that matched the pastel trim. Guests sat in rockers on the big front porches, drinks in hand, watching tourists walking along the bulkhead past the boats, watching boaters with their drinks in hand watching them on their porches. Teenagers sat on porch railings, sandy bare feet swinging, sunburned faces, arms, and legs bright against sleeveless T-shirts and faded cutoff jeans. Guests rocked and talked. The women wore floral-print sundresses; the men sported slacks embroidered with whales.

Beyond the row of gingerbread houses, the Harbor House stood by itself, a sprawling Victorian building with cupolas, archways, carpenter's lace, balconies, and wraparound porches. Banks of bright blue hydrangea, yellow marigolds, and red salvia lined the front walk.

As they passed the hotel, Victoria said, "Remember how he spoke to that woman? Said he was sick of the females in Oak Bluffs telling him how to run his business."

"I remember." Elizabeth slowed the car to let a truck pull out of the parking lot next to the Harbor House.

"And he pointed at all the women there, each and every one of us, including me, and I hadn't said a thing."

"As I recall, you were carrying a sign that read 'Jail, Not Bail,' " her granddaughter said.

Victoria ignored her and went on. "Chief Medeiros was standing next to him, grinning like a baboon."

After they passed the Harbor House, they came to the far side of the harbor, next to the liquor store.

"Want to go the long way, around East Chop?" Elizabeth asked, her foot on the brake. "We can eat our sandwiches at the lighthouse."

"Maybe we can stop by the yacht club's dock, where all the action was."

"I thought so." Elizabeth looked over at her grandmother, saw the eager look in her eye. Victoria's nose lifted, as if she would find the perpetrators by sniffing them out.

"It's hard to believe it was only two nights ago," Victoria said. "It seems longer. There was nothing in the *Enquirer*."

"You wrote it up for your column, didn't you?"

"Yes, but Skelly called, said it was an Oak Bluffs item, not a West Tisbury one, and edited it out."

"They don't want to print anything that might mar the luster of this paradise, the president's vacation isle." Elizabeth turned onto East Chop Drive. The harbor was on their right. "Seems to me that's pretty important West Tisbury news, that the West Tisbury columnist for the *Enquirer* witnesses a murder."

"I don't know that I witnessed anything." Victoria looked straight ahead, her face shaded by her hat, the black-eyed Susans drooping. "I heard a scream, then a car or truck start up." Victoria looked over at Elizabeth. "I told them that at the police station when they took my statement."

They turned right onto the sandy road that led to the dock. "You'd think this would be roped off with yellow tape as a crime scene, the way they do in movies." Victoria sat up straight in her seat. "I forgot to tell the police I thought I heard an outboard motor right about the same time."

"You told Domingo, didn't you?"

"Yes."

"They've finished doing whatever they think they needed to do here." Elizabeth parked the car by the side of the rutted road, next to a hedge of wild roses. "Domingo said they took down the crime-scene tape the day after it happened."

"So we don't need to worry about destroying evidence," Victoria said. "Tire tracks or whatever."

"I don't think so." Elizabeth got out of the car. "We can walk from here."

When Victoria opened her door, it pushed aside a branch of wild roses, dropping pink petals onto the ground.

"There've been all kinds of vehicles in here." Elizabeth pointed at the ground. "That night, there were two police cruisers, the ambulance, and Toby's hearse." She reached into the back seat and lifted out the lilac branch she had carved into a walking stick for Victoria.

"We may find something that wouldn't mean anything to anyone else," Victoria said. "Sometimes it's just as well if you don't know what you're looking for."

Victoria walked around the front of the car, bracing herself on the hood, brushing between the rose hedge and the convertible. Elizabeth handed her the stick.

They walked up the beach toward the yacht club. With her stick, Victoria flicked over pebbles and bits of seaweed, shells, driftwood, a piece of glass, a plastic bottle. Elizabeth walked next to her, watching the objects her grandmother uncovered.

They'd gone a couple of hundred feet toward the yacht club when Victoria stopped.

"A boat pulled in here," she said. "It's not a fresh mark, and it's not where you landed with the body the other night. That was closer to the dock." She examined the long, straight mark in the sand. "It's well above the high-tide line."

Elizabeth saw the distinctive trace of a keel, footprints that were mere indentations in the sand, leading from the keel mark into the tall grass and wild roses on a slight bluff above the beach.

"No one ever uses this beach," Elizabeth said. "The yacht club people swim on the Sound side, where the water is deeper."

"I suppose we should look through the shrubbery and see if we find anything. You go." Victoria sat on a driftwood log and handed her stick to Elizabeth. "You can use this to go through the brambles."

"Thanks. You're as bad as Domingo." Elizabeth took her grandmother's stick and stepped up onto the two-foot-high bluff. Pebbles and sand slid down the face. Black roots showed at the top, holding clumps of dark soil onto the top of the sandy bank. "There's a sort of beaten-down way here," she called down to Victoria. "As if someone has been through here recently."

"Do you see anything on either side?" Victoria called back.

"No. The rosebushes and grass are thick. It's hard to see through them. I'll look down low, under the tops."

"I suppose they might have thrown something off to one side," Victoria said.

"If there's anything here. What am I supposed to find, a knife or something?"

Victoria heard her brush through the growth of wild rose, stiff bayberry, huckleberry, muttering an occasional "Ouch!" as the branches slapped her bare legs.

"Something like that." Victoria could see Elizabeth moving brush aside with the lilac stick.

"Why wouldn't they have tossed it overboard, instead of dropping it here?" Elizabeth was making slow progress. Branches snapped; dry leaves rustled.

"It's too shallow," Victoria called back to her. "At the end of the dock, it's only four feet deep, and the water is quite clear."

"Found something." Victoria heard her scrabbling through the rosebushes. "Never mind. It's a broken bottle."

"Bring it out," Victoria said. "Do you have a paper in your pocket you can handle it with?"

"A paper towel. I'll lay it in the path and keep looking."

"What does it look like?" Victoria said.

"The bottom is broken off," Elizabeth said. "It's wicked-looking. Jagged."

"A whiskey bottle?"

"Rum. Strange brand. Coulibri?"

"Never heard of it," Victoria called back.

"Me, neither. The top's still got the seal on it. Want me to keep looking?"

"Go to the end of the path, just in case there's something else. But I think we found what we came for."

Elizabeth carefully carried the broken bottle back to the car, laid it on the back seat, protected it with the pink towel from the driver's seat. Victoria walked slowly along the beach, turning seaweed over with her stick.

"This is interesting." She bent over to pick something up. "What is?" Elizabeth went over to her, her face alert.

"A plastic cover of some sort." Victoria stood the lilac stick in the sand. "The cover for a checkbook," she said. "No checks in it, but there's something under the flap."

Elizabeth had come abreast of her grandmother.

"It must have been in the water, drifted ashore with this clump of eelgrass." Victoria opened the flap carefully. Inside was a soggy deposit slip with a water-blurred name and account number, and a yellow deposit receipt, also water-blurred.

"I can't make out the name or numbers." Elizabeth peered over Victoria's shoulder.

"I can't, either. I think we need to show it to Domingo, see what he has to say." She reached into her pocket for the frog-printed napkin and wrapped the plastic cover in it. "It may be just a piece of flotsam, but who knows."

"I'll put it in the car with the other evidence." Elizabeth held out her hand.

"Handle it carefully," Victoria said. "Maybe when it's dry, we can read the lettering."

Elizabeth put it on the back seat of the car, next to the broken bottle, and laid the frayed pink towel over both.

"While we're here, we might as well go out to the end of the dock." Victoria started toward it.

They walked along the boards laid across the sand and onto the weathered dock.

"You were right." Elizabeth looked down into the water. "You can see right to the bottom. The water is crystal clear."

Below them a school of tiny fish swam in unison, abruptly changing direction with a flash of silver, as if the hundreds of fish were a single organism.

"Look how clearly you can see the harbor master's shack from here." Victoria put her hand up to shade her eyes from the glare. "I can even see Domingo leaning over the railing."

Elizabeth followed her grandmother's gaze. "My God," she said. "No wonder he's worried."

"What?" Victoria lowered her left hand and looked at Elizabeth.

"I didn't realize you could see across the harbor so easily, that's all."

~ ~ ~

CHAPTER FOUR

Dojan

AFTER supper Victoria had returned to the shack to help her granddaughter sort receipts. At sunset, she went out on deck for a few minutes to watch the osprey chicks, fledglings now, poised on the edge of their nest, their strengthening wings spread wide for tentative flight. The parents hovered above the nest, flying in circles, plaintive cries echoing around the harbor.

Darkness closed in around the shack. Victoria and Elizabeth worked quietly, commenting occasionally on a boat name, or asking each other to interpret handwriting.

Victoria heard the click of the wall clock above the east window and looked up. "Eleven-thirty. Only a half hour to go."

"This evening's gone fast." Elizabeth entered a few more receipts into the computer. "I should be finished in another fifteen minutes, Gram. Thanks a million for helping."

"Is it always this quiet?" Victoria, at the desk at the end of the shack, turned to face her granddaughter.

"Pretty much so. Most of the boats get in before dark. Not much happens after dark, usually."

The window that faced the parking lot and the gingerbread houses was a black mirror, reflecting the shack's brightly lit interior. Victoria peered into the dark surface and saw herself, her white hair softly disarrayed, Elizabeth sitting in front of the computer, half-turned toward her, hair wisping around her forehead. Elizabeth was as lean as Victoria had been at her age, and taller. Her uniform was still sharply creased after a full day.

"There's a nice feeling of privacy at night." Victoria smoothed her hair in the window mirror and looked at her granddaughter's reflection.

"It's deceptive." Elizabeth picked up a receipt and studied it. "I can't read the writing on this." She put the paper to one side. "Everybody in the world can see us, but we can't see them."

At that moment, there was a knock at the sliding window. "Who's there?" Elizabeth asked; then to Victoria, she said, "I didn't hear anybody coming."

Victoria glanced up at the clock. Eleven-forty-five. She had not heard or felt anything, either.

Elizabeth stood up, and her chair fell over with a metallic clatter. Victoria turned toward the sliding glass window. On the other side of the reflections, she could dimly see someone. "Who could it be at this time of night?" Elizabeth moved toward the window and slid it open a few inches. A tall man, half-hidden in the darkness, loomed on the other side.

"Frightened you, didn't I?" The man moved closer to the window. His shoulders filled the frame. Elizabeth stepped back.

"Can I help you?" Her voice was higher than usual. Victoria got to her feet.

"Two large vessels are coming in," the man said in a deep voice. "They need berths."

"Who are you?" Elizabeth slid the window open a few more inches. Victoria could see the man had a huge head of fluffy black hair stuck with osprey feathers, and a huge black beard that covered the lower half of his face. He was wearing a black mesh muscle shirt that exposed dark, hairy upper arms tattooed with intricate designs. Around his neck, he wore a black scarf printed with what looked like white skulls.

"Who am I?" He grinned at Elizabeth, teeth white against the blackness of his beard and the night. Victoria could see that his upper-right-front tooth was missing. "I am the Wind and the Rain. I am the messenger for the sheik of Qatar. It is the sheik's vessels that are arriving."

Victoria moved closer to the open window. Elizabeth glanced at the door. Victoria assumed it was to make sure it was locked. Elizabeth looked behind her. Victoria could tell she was wondering how to handle this situation.

"The vessels will be here in an hour," the apparition at the window said. "Two vessels, each one hundred and twenty-five feet in length."

Elizabeth's mouth opened slightly. Her hands were on the windowsill.

"They're coming from the Persian Gulf." He sounded impatient. "The sheik needs two berths for the night."

"Berths!" Elizabeth said. "We can't take boats that size; the channel isn't deep enough. We don't have slips large enough."

"The sheik expects you to find something." The Wind and the Rain scowled, and his dark hair, dark eyebrows, and dark beard almost met. His eyes showed a ring of white around dark irises. Victoria saw the tattoos on his upper arms writhe as he crossed his arms over his chest.

Victoria moved to the window. Elizabeth stepped forward to stop her, but Victoria slid the window open as wide as it would go. "You look familiar." She looked intently into the man's hairy face. "You're a Gay Head Indian, aren't you?"

"I am a Wampanoag." He flexed and unflexed his arm muscles and scowled, uncrossed his arms and put large grimy hands on the windowsill. "I am a Native American from Aquinnah." His raggedly bitten nails were rimmed with black. Elizabeth moved back, as if she thought he was going to vault through the window.

"I know you," Victoria said in a conversational voice, the voice she used at garden club meetings. "Aren't you one of the Minnowfish children?"

The man stared at Victoria. His dark irises floated in the glistening whites of his eyes. His pink mouth opened in a pale O. He leaned forward into the window. Elizabeth stepped backward again and fetched up against the computer keyboard. Victoria heard a humming noise and looked over to see a string of X's march across the screen. Victoria put her knobby hands on the sill between the Wampanoag's heavy calloused hands. The man continued to stare. Victoria heard Elizabeth's breathing. She heard the X's continue to march.

Victoria turned to Elizabeth. "Hadn't you better do something about that?" She indicated the screen. Elizabeth stepped away from the computer and the X's stopped.

Suddenly, the Wind and the Rain sagged. His muscles relaxed and his eyes closed partway.

"Yes, ma'am, I'm Bessie's boy. The youngest Minnowfish."

"I thought so." Victoria stood up straight, her hands on the sill, her arms extended. The man moved back from the window a half step, fingers with bitten nails still holding on.

"Your great-grandmother was Charity Minnowfish."

"Yes, ma'am." He opened his eyes, and the irises floated.

"Charity must have been your father's father's mother."

"Yes, ma'am." He let go of the windowsill.

"I went to school with Charity." Victoria leaned forward. "She was one of my pals. We looked for birds' nests together."

"Yes, ma'am." He shook his head, and Victoria heard the string of bones around his neck rattle. "That was a hundred years ago," he whispered. The osprey feathers in his hair quivered. His black skull-printed scarf moved in the night breeze coming off the harbor.

"Not quite." Victoria leaned out the window toward the man, who had backed up as far as he could to the railing. She put her elbows on the sill so she could see him better. "You must be Dojan, aren't you?"

"Yes, ma'am," he whispered.

"Well, Dojan," Victoria said in her Sunday school teacher's voice, "tell the sheik to come back tomorrow. We don't have room for him tonight." She leaned farther out the window, and Dojan moved to one side. "Give the sheik my respects."

"Yes, ma'am." Dojan moved along the railing, sideways like a crab, eyes fixed on Victoria. "A hundred years," he whispered.

"I remember when you were a little boy." Victoria pointed at him. "You haven't changed a bit. Do you still lobster?"

"Yes, ma'am," Dojan said. "I fish some, too."

"Wonderful!" Victoria said brightly.

"You like lobster?" he asked suddenly in a loud voice. A startled night bird flew up from the water, beating its wings, squawking.

"Of course." Victoria saw the breeze lift the ends of Dojan's skull scarf.

"Will you be here tomorrow?"

Victoria turned to Elizabeth, who was staring from her grandmother to the apparition beyond the window and back to her grandmother again.

"Will we?" Victoria said to Elizabeth.

Elizabeth nodded.

"I'll bring you a lobster." He moved his hands apart to indicate to Victoria the size of the lobster he would bring to her. "I'll bring you two lobsters tomorrow."

"How's Bessie?" Victoria still leaned part way out the window into the darkness.

"She's well, ma'am. Touch of arthritis."

"I know all about that." Victoria lifted her knobby hands. "Tell her hello from me, Victoria Trumbull."

"Yes, ma'am." Dojan raised his hand in a movie Indian's salute and sidled away from the window. His black hair, black shirt, black jeans, and bare feet faded down the catwalk.

Elizabeth let out her breath in a long sigh.

Victoria spread her hands in front of her and looked at them. "I'm glad you don't bite your fingernails, Elizabeth."

Elizabeth slid the window shut, locked it. Locked the window over the desk. Shut the two windows that looked out over Nantucket Sound. Deleted the strings of X's on the computer screen and turned it off.

"Dojan comes from a good family. He's quite bright. He can be a bit strange, but he's harmless. He's like his father, who was strange, too." Victoria gathered up her papers and dropped them into her pocketbook. "Did you finish what you were doing?"

"No way I can do it now," Elizabeth said. "I'll finish it tomorrow." She opened the desk drawer and rummaged around for the bank bag, stuffed it full of bills from another drawer.

"Wouldn't it be nice if he actually does bring us lobsters?" Victoria looked at her reflection in the window and patted her hair, turned her head to one side to examine her great nose.

"I don't see how you do it." Elizabeth looked in the bank bag and zipped it shut, locked it. She took a flashlight out of the top desk drawer, waited for Victoria to step out of the shack, then turned out the lights and pulled the door shut.

They drove the short two blocks to the bank, past the Steamship Authority dock, at night only a suggestion of a structure that faded into the distant deep water to their left. Waves lapped softly on the deserted beach below the bluff. Some creature swam beneath the surface of the water, trailing a stream of phosphorescence. A line of white foam lingered where waves broke onto the dark shore. A lone night bird cried. The breeze blew in from the sea.

Elizabeth parked in front of the closed bank, and Victoria watched as she unlocked the night deposit box, put in the bank bag, relocked the drawer, and got back into the car.

"That was harbor revenue we haven't turned over to the town treasurer yet." Elizabeth looked behind her and pulled out into the deserted street. "Domingo is determined to have every penny accounted for on the new computer forms, and he wants a receipt from the treasurer to prove he did."

The Flying Horses had closed for the night. They could hear laughter and shouts on Circuit Avenue, music coming out of the open doors of the Sand Bar on Pequot Avenue. The rest of the town was quiet.

Elizabeth drove along the route they had followed earlier in the day, past the gingerbread houses, past the boats. No one sat on the porches now or walked along the bulkhead. No one sat in boat cockpits with feet up on transoms. They passed the Harbor House and the road to East Chop.

Victoria looked in the side mirror. "There's a car behind us. It came out of the road next to the Harbor House."

"Can you make out what kind of car it is?" Elizabeth moved her head to one side. "The headlights are blinding me."

"It looks high, like a truck or a van."

"Wish they'd switch to low beam." Elizabeth moved the mirror to cut the glare. "I hope they turn off before we get to the curve near the hospital."

The vehicle stayed close behind them. Elizabeth slowed at a wide place in the road, where it could pass them easily, and the vehicle dropped back.

"I'm going to turn left onto the road that goes to the lobster hatchery, Gram." Elizabeth switched on her left-turn signal. "See if I can shake him."

"He's turned on his left-turn signal, too," Victoria said, looking in the side mirror.

"Damn." Elizabeth stepped harder on the accelerator.

"Why don't we stop at Domingo's?" Victoria said. "We can pull into his drive and wait there, let him pass."

"Good idea." Elizabeth moved her head so the lights behind them were not reflected into her eyes from the side mirror. She signaled a right turn onto Barnes Road, and the other driver did, too.

"I suppose it's possible that he happens to be going the same way we are." Elizabeth adjusted the mirror again.

"Unlikely this time of night." Victoria leaned forward to look into her side mirror again. "It's after midnight."

They halted at the stop sign by the fire station and the vehicle behind them stopped, too. No other cars were in sight.

"We're almost at Domingo's," Elizabeth said. "When I turn into his drive, see what kind of car it is, if you can." She passed the boxy privet hedge in front of the de los Fuerzos's and made an abrupt turn, without signaling or braking until she'd turned into the drive. Brakes squealed on the vehicle behind them before it accelerated and sped into the night.

"A Ford van," Victoria said. "Light color, gray or tan, not white. The license plate was muddy, but it started with 'FU.' "

"Nice going, Gram!" Elizabeth said with admiration. "Mr. D's lights are on. I suppose midnight isn't too late to call on someone."

"I think it's a good idea, under the circumstances." Elizabeth opened the car door.

"Besides, we need to tell Domingo about finding the bottle and checkbook cover."

Noreen and Domingo were sitting in wicker armchairs at the glass-topped table in the living room, watching a late-night rerun of the selectmen's meeting on Channel Nine. The room was dense with cigarette smoke. Elizabeth knocked on the sliding door and pushed it to one side.

Noreen stubbed out her cigarette and stood up. She was small and blond, almost a foot shorter than Elizabeth, who was six feet tall. She was wearing white sweatpants and white socks and a magenta T-shirt printed with exotic blue-and-gold flowers.

"Yo," Domingo said to Elizabeth, and remained seated. As soon as Victoria came through the door, he stood up and took off his baseball cap.

"Is everything okay?" Noreen turned down the volume on the TV with the remote and moved a chair over for Victoria.

"We were being followed and decided to stop here," Victoria said. "Besides, we found something."

"Did you identify who was following you?" Domingo put his cap back on and sat down again.

"Light-colored Ford van, license starting with 'FU,' " Victoria said.

" 'FU.' " Domingo laughed. "That's not Meatloaf. I don't know who it is, but I'll find out." He waved the smoke away from Victoria. It drifted toward Elizabeth, who cried, "Hey!" and fanned at it.

"They didn't try anything smart, did they?" Noreen asked.

"No," Elizabeth said. "They came out of the road next to the Harbor House and followed us here."

"Was the harbor busy tonight?" Noreen asked Elizabeth, who was sitting on the couch under Domingo's display of antique harpoons.

"Did you get all the receipts entered?" Domingo asked.

"Will you let me talk without you butting in?" Noreen turned to him, hands on her hips.

"Okay, honey, okay." Domingo took his cap off and placed it over his heart, then looked up at the ceiling with liquid brown eyes.

"No." Elizabeth yawned, then covered her mouth with her hand. "It was quiet until almost midnight. Then this weird, creepy man came by, saying a couple of huge boats were arriving."

"Oh?" Domingo looked at her.

"It was only Dojan Minnowfish," Victoria said. "I went to school with his great-grandmother."

"He frightened the hell out of me." Elizabeth stretched her arms over her head. "Black hair, black beard, black eyes, black clothes, rags and feathers and bones rattling and blowing in the wind." She looked up at Domingo's harpoons. "I hope those things are wired in place. Some weaponry."

"Dojan lives here in Oak Bluffs, doesn't he, Domingo?" Noreen asked.

Behind them, the TV showed two of the selectmen gesticulating at the third, Liz Tate, whose back was to the camera.

"I think he lives in the Camp Meeting Ground, behind Harbor House." Domingo paid no attention to the selectmen. "His family owns one of the wooden tents off Pawtucket Avenue."

Noreen turned to Victoria. "You went to school with his great-grandmother? She must have died twenty years ago."

"Yes," Victoria said. "In fact, I wrote a poem about her. I must find it and give a copy to Dojan." She watched the selectmen on TV. "It's better without the sound. Looks as if they're saying things I'd rather not hear."

"That is correct, sweetheart," Domingo said. "You know where the name Dojan comes from?" he asked suddenly, leaning forward in the wicker chair, hands clasped between his knees.

"No. Where?" Victoria said, interested. "Is it Wampanoag?"

"It's ancient Norse. It means 'dead.' " He looked first at Victoria, then cut his eyes at Noreen and then at Elizabeth.

"Christ!" Noreen sat up straight in her chair. "You're making that up."

Domingo shook his head. "His name means 'dead.' "

"Where do you get this stuff?" Elizabeth said.

"He's full of it." Noreen turned to Elizabeth. "What did Dojan want?"

"He told us a sheik was going to bring two huge boats into the harbor tonight." Elizabeth kicked off her shoes and put her feet up on the couch.

"He does that a couple of times a season," Domingo said.

"It's the first time I've seen him." Elizabeth yawned again.

"Why didn't you warn her, Domingo?" Noreen said. "He'd frighten anyone, sneaking up to the window at midnight."

"I assumed they had him locked up somewhere," Domingo said. "That nice jail in Edgartown. Country club."

"Cut out that shit, Domingo," Noreen said. "You're not funny." She turned to Victoria. "I'm sorry, Mrs. Trumbull."

"A couple of months ago, before you came on board, he got into an altercation with a drunk," Domingo continued.

Elizabeth waved her hand to direct his cigarette smoke away from her face.

Domingo opened the window.

"When I arrived at the scene, this drunk was lying on the ground. Dojan was hitting him over the head with what appeared to be a leg."

Noreen got up. "I've heard this before. Want some coffee?"

"Yes." Elizabeth covered another yawn.

"Then what happened?" Victoria said.

"There was blood all over the place," Domingo continued. "I thought Dojan had torn the guy's leg off." He looked at Victoria, who was watching, enthralled. "He had."

Victoria sat forward in her chair.

"It was an artificial leg," Domingo added, and sat back with a smirk.

"That's sick," Elizabeth said.

"It's the truth," Domingo said.

"Domingo, you're full of it," Noreen said.

"Come to think of it, Dojan drives a light Ford van."

"Talk about nightmares!" Elizabeth said. "Would you rather be tailed by Meatloaf or by some crazed Wampanoag named Dead?"

"You said you found something." Domingo turned to Victoria. "What did you find?" He leaned forward again, bright eyes fixed on her.

"We stopped by the East Chop dock on the way to have lunch at the lighthouse."

"You went to the crime scene. You couldn't help yourself. Go on."

"Let her tell her story her own way, Domingo," Noreen said.

Domingo reached for his pack of cigarettes and lit one.

"Why don't you just light it from the old butt?" Elizabeth said. "Save lighter fluid." She waved the smoke away.

"We walked along the beach toward the spit that goes out to the osprey pole," Victoria said.

"Go on." Domingo watched Victoria.

"Someone had pulled a boat above the high-tide mark."

"A lot of people do that." Domingo watched Victoria's face.

"Let her talk, Domingo," Noreen said.

Elizabeth held the mug in both hands, sipped her coffee, and looked at her grandmother over the rim.

"Not many people," Victoria said. "It's a kind of backwater. Flotsam washes up on the beach there, plastic oil containers, sunblock bottles, eelgrass. I would think boats would prefer to land on the beach near the dock, where it's cleaner. No one would want to swim there."

Domingo's expression never changed. "Do I understand you to say, sweetheart, you think that a boat landing several hundred feet north of the dock has something to do with the killing?"

"For God's sake, Domingo," Noreen said. "Shut up."

"Footprints led from the keel mark to a sort of path..."

"A path?" Domingo said.

"Not exactly a path, a trodden-down place at the top of the bank, where the rosebushes and bayberry were disturbed, and the grass was crushed down."

"Go on." Domingo took another drag on his cigarette.

"I sent Elizabeth along the path — the stepped-on place — to look for anything she could find that might seem unusual."

"Go on," he said. "She found something."

"Yes. A broken rum bottle."

Domingo slapped his hand on the glass tabletop. The vase of flowers clattered.

Noreen stood up. "You can't let anyone else say a word, can you? Don't pay any attention to him, Mrs. Trumbull."

"No, no, honey," Domingo said. "Do you understand what my girlfriend is saying? Three-quarters of the men on the New York force — men and women, that is — wouldn't have thought to do what she did. You realize that?" He looked at Noreen, then back at Victoria. "Go on, sweetheart. Where was the bottle?"

"Off to the right side, under the rosebushes. Elizabeth picked it up with a paper and put it in the back of the car."

Domingo stared at her, his expression wavering between admiration and horror. "You've got to remember, I'm an ex-cop. You don't mess casually with evidence."

"We had no reason to think it might be evidence."

Domingo shook his head.

"That's not all," Elizabeth said. "Tell him the rest, Gram."

"What else?"

"We were walking back to the car; I was turning things over with my stick, looking for interesting stones or shells ..."

"Go on," Domingo said.

"She's telling you just as fast as she can, asshole," Noreen said. "Give her a chance to talk." She turned to Victoria. "Sorry, Mrs. Trumbull."

"I turned over a clump of eelgrass and found a plastic checkbook cover. No checkbook inside, but there were a couple of deposit slips that had not been filled out and a deposit receipt."

"What makes you think that had anything to do with the events of two nights ago?"

"The plastic was still pretty fresh-looking," Victoria said, "and the paper deposit slips and receipt were soaking wet, but not turned to mush by being in the water. I would guess it was in the water less than two days, maybe washed up yesterday." Victoria looked at Domingo. "It probably has nothing to do with the murder. But who knows?"

Domingo stubbed his cigarette out in the full ashtray and looked intently at Victoria. Noreen took the ashtray from him and went into the kitchen, then brought it back clean.

"Where are they now?" Domingo said.

"In the back seat of the car," Elizabeth said.

"The proper procedure is to turn evidence over to the police," Domingo said.

"But we have no reason to believe this is evidence," Victoria said again.

Domingo nodded. "Yas," he said. "That is correct." Noreen sighed.

Elizabeth got to her feet and stretched. "I need fresh air. I'll bring the stuff in."

Victoria watched her lanky granddaughter slide the door open and head toward the car.

The papers in the plastic cover were still soggy. Domingo carefully peeled the plastic flap away from them.

"Get me a knife, honey." He reached out his hand without looking at Noreen, and she went back into the kitchen. She returned with a thin-bladed knife, making a gesture for Victoria's benefit, as if she were going to impale her husband with it before she put it in his outstretched hand.

"Thank you," he said, eyes bright.

Noreen went back into the kitchen and returned with a clear plastic cutting board and a handful of paper towels. Domingo looked up at her. Their eyes met. There was a faint smile on his face. Victoria felt a touch of electricity in the air. Noreen gave him a soft slap on his cheek and sat down again.

As carefully as a surgeon, Domingo slid the knife under the corner of the top paper and carefully separated it from the one beneath. He laid paper towels on the cutting board and gently set the two deposit slips and the yellow receipt on top.

"Can you make out any printing?" Victoria got up and leaned over Domingo's shoulder.

"Still too wet, sweetheart."

Noreen left the room again and came back with a clear piece of glass, a small windowpane. Domingo made a kissing sound in her direction, and Noreen punched him on the shoulder. He sandwiched the wet papers between paper towels and the glass and set a dictionary on top.

"It's probably nothing," Victoria said.

"Kept us entertained for a half hour," Domingo said. "By tomorrow morning, we may be able to see something."

Elizabeth yawned.

"I've got to get my granddaughter home." Victoria looked at her watch. "Good heavens, it's one-thirty."

"You want to spend the night?" Noreen said. "We have plenty of room."

"No thanks," Victoria said. "We'll be fine. I'm just curious to know what's on the papers we found today, that's all."

"They need to dry slowly," Domingo said. "The glass will keep them from curling as they dry. Air can get in around the edges, so it won't mildew."

"I guess we'll know tomorrow," Victoria said.

~ ~ ~

On the way home, Victoria looked in the side mirror. "There's a car following us. A different one. The lights are lower and closer together."

"It must be Domingo." Elizabeth frowned, and Victoria could see her face in the reflected light from the car behind, high cheekbones and wide mouth. "Funny, he didn't say anything about seeing us home."

The car followed them along Barnes Road, turned right when they did onto the Edgartown Road, followed them past the airport. When they turned into the driveway, it continued on past them, turning right on Old County Road, and Victoria could see its taillights disappear into the night.

~ ~ ~

CHAPTER FIVE

Victoria's Visitors

"I HAVEN'T seen much of Victoria since the murder," Chief Casey O'Neill said to her sergeant, who was sitting at the desk across from hers, which he shared with the two patrolmen. Casey leaned back in her chair and lifted coppery hair away from her uniform collar. "She knows who's related to whom, so I don't make insulting jokes about someone's third cousin twice removed." Junior grinned, eyes turned down, mouth turned up. His pale mustache seemed to have been pasted on to make him look grown-up.

"That was my father's sister-in-law's second cousin," he said. "It's okay to insult 'connections.' "

"I'm learning. After I've been here a few more years, maybe I'll understand the politics of this town."

Junior was filling out monthly reports. He erased something vigorously, then brushed eraser crumbs off his desk with the side of his hand. "Since Victoria heard that scream, she feels personally responsible for the investigation."

"She would," Casey said.

Junior scooped a handful of blunt pencils from his desk and took them over to the pencil sharpener screwed to the frame of the window that overlooked the pond. "She also feels she needs to protect her granddaughter after the divorce. I guess it was pretty messy."

"Tell me about it." Casey leaned back in her swivel chair. "How's your dad these days?"

"He's got a one-man show of his landscapes this fall."

"All right!" Casey said.

When Ben Norton, Junior's father, retired as chief of police, Junior assumed he would succeed his dad. Instead, the selectmen hired Mary Kathleen O'Neill, from off-Island.

After the first buzz of astonishment, the village settled down and waited. Casey was not one of them; she was trained in big-city crime. Wait and see, the village said, see how her graduate degrees equip her to handle wandering grandfathers, missing bicycles, farmer's market parking, and emergencies down unmarked dirt roads.

Junior had been ready to quit and move off-Island. But he, too, waited. The new chief was making an effort to understand her new town and its people. After six weeks, Junior stayed on.

He lined the pencils up on the windowsill and inserted them one at a time into the hand-cranked sharpener. In the pond, the pair of swans and their three half-grown cygnets were feeding, their long necks immersed in the shallow water, their tail feathers in the air. The cygnets' white adult feathers showed raggedly through gray baby down. On the other side of the pond, tall stalks of joe-pye weed had opened mauve blossoms.

"I suppose we won't see much of Victoria until she solves the murder?" Junior turned from the window to the chief.

"There's not enough action in West Tisbury for her at the moment." Casey keyed numbers into the computer. "These were supposed to save paperwork, not make more," she muttered.

"How's she getting to Oak Bluffs, now she's lost her license?" Junior blew shavings off a newly sharpened pencil.

Casey looked over her shoulder. "She hitchhikes. I picked her up on Old County Road the other day. Thumbing."

Junior laughed. "It's those long legs of hers," he said. "The first car that passes picks her up. Every time."

The phone rang. Junior put the pencils down and picked up the receiver. "West Tisbury Police Department, Sergeant Norton speaking."

The chief, who had turned back to her computer, could hear a man's voice and make out an occasional word. She heard the name Victoria a couple of times.

"That was Domingo," Junior said when he hung up the phone.

Casey sighed and stood. She wiped the dust off her polished boots on the back of her trousers, left foot, right foot.

"Sounds as if we've put a stop to her hitchhiking," Junior said. "Domingo asked us to keep a watch on her."

Casey paced the small area in front of the two desks. "We don't exactly have a lot of manpower to spare."

"We don't need police watching her," Junior said. "She's got friends. What about the guy who lives behind her?"

"Winthrop Lodge." Casey picked up a yellow pad and pen.

"He's like one of her grandkids." Junior brushed the top of his tidy desk. "How about the artist who lives in her attic?"

Casey felt her face redden. "Angelo Santellini." She turned her back to Junior, pushed her chair under her desk, tucked her uniform shirt firmly into her trousers. "You know, don't you, that Victoria was trying to play matchmaker?"

"You and Angelo?" Junior grinned.

Casey nodded.

Junior laughed. "In a way, her matchmaking worked. Angelo and Winthrop."

"I wasn't looking anyway." Casey leaned over, turned off her computer, and sat again. She straightened papers on her desk, put them in manila folders, opened her bottom desk drawer, and set the folders in it. "Let me see the schedule." Junior handed her a yellow sheet. "Josh or Adam can cruise past her place on a regular basis. I'll drive by when I can."

"My father has a thing for Elizabeth. I'm sure he'd like to help. Get back in action," Junior said.

"Your father?" Casey said, surprised. "Elizabeth is your age, isn't she?"

"Younger." Junior grinned. "He's only thirty-five years older. Lotta life in the old man yet."

Casey shrugged. "Well, sign him up." She made some notes on her yellow pad. "Among us, we should be able to cover her for a couple of weeks."

Junior scribbled with his newly sharpened pencil, occasionally moistening the lead with his tongue.

"Elizabeth is with her at night. If we include Domingo, that makes nine."

"I'll talk to Elizabeth," Casey said. "Victoria doesn't lock her doors, of course. I doubt if they have keys." She sighed. "No one in this town locks doors. The selectmen acted as if I was out of my mind when I demanded a lock for the station door."

"You're not in Brockton now."

"That's for sure," said Casey.

~ ~ ~

"It's a relief to have a morning off." Elizabeth was on her hands and knees next to Victoria, both of them pulling weeds in the iris border. "Domingo gets on my nerves after a while."

Victoria knelt on a padded kneeler with handles that Elizabeth's mother had given her.

"I'd like to stop by his house sometime today to see if we can read those bank slips," Victoria said.

The weeds rustled under the peonies, and McCavity stalked through the tall growth of red clover and sorrel. He settled on a patch of weeds directly in front of

Victoria, ones she was about to pull, and began to wash himself, reaching around with his long pink tongue to clean his shoulders. Victoria laughed, roughed his head with her grimy hand, levered herself up with the handles on the kneeler, and shifted to a new spot. The cat cleaned his head where she'd patted him, then moved again.

"Here's some catnip for him." Elizabeth pulled up a fuzzy-leafed plant and tossed it to McCavity, who scooped it up, rolled over onto his back, and pawed the catnip with his back feet.

"The ground is nice and soft. Last night's rain was just what we needed," Victoria said. They pulled weeds companionably, a gentle cropping sound, like animals munching. "I'll pull up this poison ivy. It doesn't seem to affect me."

"Do you want it on the burn pile?" Elizabeth got to her feet. Her jeans had a long rip in the right knee, worn through from kneeling in the garden.

"No." Victoria tossed the shiny-leafed plant to one side. "The oils get carried in the smoke, and if you breathe it in, you may have a problem."

"In your lungs, ugh." Elizabeth tossed grass clumps and lamb's-quarter and purslane and red clover, feverfew and mint and digitalis seedlings into a pile at the side for the compost heap. "What's this purple flower?"

"Which one?" Victoria asked.

"It's star-shaped, with yellow centers." Elizabeth moved peony leaves aside so Victoria could see. "Is it something you're trying to grow on purpose?"

"Nightshade," Victoria said. "Pull it out."

"It's poisonous, isn't it?" Elizabeth tugged the plant out by its roots. "Deadly nightshade."

"Same family as tomatoes and eggplant," Victoria said, shaking the dirt off the roots of a bunch of grass. "Better wash your hands right away. People have gotten sick from touching it."

"I'll put it on the burn pile. Guess we don't need it to seed itself any more than it has already." As she passed McCavity, who was lying on his back like a limp toy, the catnip resting on his soft belly fur, he suddenly reached out and swiped at her jean-clad leg.

"Whoa, McCavity! You crazy cat." She stepped over the iris spikes onto the grass. "There are enough weird weeds in this border alone to give everyone on the Island itchy rashes, or make them sick, or drive them crazy."

"Or worse," Victoria said.

~ ~ ~

"I can watch Victoria an hour or so a day." Noreen and Domingo were sitting at the glass-topped wicker table and she was making a list on a pad of legal paper. They were watching Court TV in a desultory way. A woman lawyer with heavy horn-rimmed glasses and a red dress gestured at something on an easel. Occasionally, Domingo would look over at the television.

"All right!" he would say. Or "Yas!" Or he would shake his head and say, "Don't do that!" Sometimes, he would laugh.

"Would you pay attention?" Noreen said. "This is serious."

"I am paying attention, honey. Who do you think called Chief O'Neill?"

"Ernesto can drive by on his way to and from work," Noreen said. "He could stop in for coffee. Victoria likes him."

"Glad somebody does." Domingo leaned back in his chair. "Keep him out of my way for another half hour."

"Don't talk that way about your son-in-law." Noreen wrote Ernesto's name. "He's married to your daughter, remember?"

"Yes, honey." Domingo took off his cap and blinked his eyes.

"You are full of it." Noreen shook a cigarette out of the package on the table near her, lighted it with a disposable green lighter, and inhaled.

"What about your friend on the board of selectmen?" She looked at Domingo through a screen of bluish smoke.

"Liz Tate is no friend of mine." He got to his feet and went up the step into the kitchen, poured himself a cup of coffee. "She accused me of harassing her niece."

"You're shittin' me!" Noreen's blue eyes opened wide. "Allison, the scrawny blond kid? Liz Tate claims you harassed the kid? You?" Noreen started to laugh. "What did you do?"

"I told her to pick up a candy wrapper on the dock. I can't even tell a female employee to pick up a candy wrapper?"

"You told her?" Noreen put her pen down. "How did you tell her, Domingo? With a pat on her fanny?"

"No, no," Domingo said. "I was very polite. Maybe my voice was a little forceful."

"Yeah, sure. 'Forceful.' You yelled at her, right? She probably went home in tears and told her auntie."

"Liz Tate is a scheming broad." Domingo looked at his wife with his wide-set dark eyes. "Excuse me, honey. Liz Tate is a scheming person. Meatloaf delivered the complaint."

"What does Meatloaf have to do with all this?"

"He was her messenger," Domingo said. "I told him — politely, of course — to have Liz Tate put the complaint in writing. I did call him a 'lackey.' "

"Cross her off the list." Noreen swiped her pen across the name she'd written. "We know a bunch of people who would be happy to watch Victoria."

"We can't trust half of them."

"What about your deputy harbor master? He's out of jail now, isn't he?" Noreen said. "What's his name again?"

"Aggie. Victoria knows him. Add his name to the list."

"That's what I just said," replied Noreen, clearly irritated. "How about listening to me occasionally?"

"Yes, honey," Domingo said.

~ ~ ~

Victoria opened the cabinet above the stove. "We're running low on coffee. Also, we've run out of coffee cake and cookies." She closed the cabinet and went from the kitchen into the cookroom, a small room that had served as a summer kitchen when Victoria was a girl.

The afternoon sun poured into the room, touched the bouquet of black-eyed Susans that blazed like orange flame against the checked tablecloth. Sunlight touched the pine woodwork and the wide floorboards. Victoria's baskets hung from the hand-hewn beams. Pots of spider plant and Swedish ivy and philodendron curtained the windows. Victoria stepped down carefully into the cookroom, her hands braced on the doorjamb, and sat in her caned bentwood armchair. She fished an envelope out of the trash, then took a pen out of the marmalade jar on the windowsill.

She was starting to write when McCavity stalked in, sprang into Victoria's lap, turned around, and settled himself, paws curled under him. Victoria patted him absently, and he purred, head up, eyes closed.

From her seat, Victoria could look through the west windows across the field, across New Lane, across Doane's pasture. She could see the West Tisbury town center a half mile away, the church spire with the sun glinting on the weather vane on top, the roof of the new library above the trees.

"I've never known a time when we had so many callers," she said to Elizabeth. "While you were at work, Ernesto stopped by. He had a cup of coffee with me and one of your rum raisin muffins. Two, actually. And Howland stopped by. He had two cups of coffee and a muffin. Ben Norton dropped in."

"Two cups of coffee, two muffins." Elizabeth pulled another caned chair up to the table, eased the ripped part of her jeans over her knee, and sat.

"I think he's set his cap for you," Victoria said. McCavity opened his yellow eyes and stared at Elizabeth. "I've started a grocery list. We'll need to go to Cronig's before it closes."

"For heaven's sake, Gram, he's older than my dad. Pair him up with Mom, not me." She ran slender fingers through her hair. "Besides, it's women who set their caps, not men."

"He's awfully nice," Victoria said.

"He is. His paintings are glorious, and it's fascinating to watch him at work. But no thanks."

"You could do worse." Victoria stroked McCavity. "Do we need more Bisquick?"

"Yes, large size. Why not set him up with Casey? They're closer in age, only twenty years' difference. Then Casey would be her sergeant's stepmother." Elizabeth laughed.

Victoria got to her feet and checked the soil in the philodendron in the west window.

"I'll water it." Elizabeth filled the teapot and watered the plants until they dripped onto the floor.

"Would you please move my pocketbook?" Victoria said.

"Sorry." Elizabeth took a paper towel out of her pocket and wiped the water spots off Victoria's leather pocketbook and put it on the table.

"Then Winthrop stopped by after work, had a cup of coffee and a muffin. Angelo joined us. Then Junior Norton."

"How weird." Elizabeth took the teapot back into the kitchen and put it on the counter next to the stove. "Do you have everything we need on the list? Bananas. We always need them."

When Victoria finished the list, they went out through the entry to the car. A long shelf in the entryway was covered with treasures generations of children had brought back from the beach. Victoria took her wide-brimmed straw hat from a nail next to the windows. The black-eyed Susans she had stuck in the ribbon hatband the day before had dried to brown crisps. She tossed them into the garden at the top of the steps, where the well used to be.

"Maybe they'll seed themselves. They'd be pretty against the shingles."

The convertible's top was down, and a brown leaf had drifted from the Norway maple onto the seat. Elizabeth shook out the towel seat covers, and then Victoria got in and slammed her door shut.

Elizabeth backed the car out of the spot under the tree and headed out the driveway, past the iris and peony border they had not finished weeding. Brown pointed tips of the iris leaves marked the close of the dry summer. Canada geese flew overhead. They passed the west meadow with its ancient lilacs, so old and so large, they were more trees than shrubs.

They drove under the ailanthus tree Victoria's grandfather had brought back from China in a pot 150 years ago. "Tree of Heaven," he'd called it. Every year, the tree produced hundreds of offspring, and when Elizabeth and her sister were children, her grandfather would pay them a penny for each seedling they uprooted.

"With the president about to visit, traffic will be awful in Vineyard Haven." Elizabeth checked the road to the left. A van with a dish antenna on its roof was coming toward them.

"They're going much too fast." Victoria watched the van as it disappeared down the small hill to their right. "Ever since they widened the road, it's been like a speedway."

"CBS News," Elizabeth said. The van left a stream of dust swirling in its wake.

"When is he due?" Victoria tied her hat ribbons under her chin as the brim of her hat flopped in the breeze from the van.

"Next week, I think." Elizabeth pulled into the road and turned left. "The Oak Bluffs Harbor is in a dither." They passed the police station, the small shingled building that had once been a one-room school. Victoria waved at Junior, who grinned back. They passed the old mill on the left, now the home of the garden club, the mill pond across the road from it.

"The Coast Guard came into the harbor to check out places to keep their cutters," Elizabeth said.

"Cutters! Imagine that," Victoria said.

"They're bringing in two cutters. A state police boat came in yesterday. The marine conservation officer will be in the harbor the whole time he's here. The Secret Service are all over the place, dressed the way they think Vineyarders ought to look, thinking they'll blend in, only they've forgotten to take off the price tags.

They all have microphones in their lapels."

"Why do they need all that security in the harbor? He's not staying in Oak Bluffs, is he?" Victoria put her hand on top of her hat as Elizabeth turned right past the mill pond and the breeze eddied from another direction.

"He's staying in Edgartown. But I guess they need to be ready for anything, from a plane crash to a fishing trip."

"That poor man. What a life, having someone watching you all the time."

"Hmm," Elizabeth said. "Yeah."

~ ~ ~

CHAPTER SIX

The ArtCliff Diner

THE SIREN whooped once as the ambulance backed up to the hospital entrance, its beeper warning anyone behind it. The EMT in the passenger seat opened her door, dashed around to the back of the vehicle, and yanked open the doors.

"Is he still with us?" she said to the technician inside, who was sitting next to a stretcher with a figure laid out on it like a corpse, hands folded over a large belly.

"He's still breathing." He unstrapped the stretcher from the ambulance floor. "Can you hear me, sir?" There was a moan from the stretcher.

"It's okay, sir. We're at the hospital."

A hospital tech flung the emergency room doors open as the EMTs wheeled the stretcher with the limp figure out of the ambulance and hurried him inside.

A small gray-haired man in a pink-and-blue-plaid shirt and open white coat came from behind the admitting desk, where he'd been filling out paperwork. He took a pair of glasses from his pocket, put them on, and inspected the man on the stretcher.

"Damned if it's not you, Meatloaf," he said. "I told you this was going to happen if you didn't stop stuffing yourself." Meatloaf moaned, eyes slits in his puffy face.

The doctor took his glasses off and put them back in the pocket of his lab coat. "Bring him in here. Might be his heart."

"Yes, sir, Dr. Erickson," the tech said.

Dr. Erickson gestured to another tech. "Get the portable cardio machine, stat." While the techs rushed off, Dr. Erickson unveiled Meatloaf, peeling off the light blanket the EMTs had placed over him, unzipping his windbreaker, unbuttoning his shirt, lifting up his undershirt to expose an expanse of pink belly with a smattering of hairy curls.

"If it didn't get you this time, it will the next," Dr. Erickson said unsympathetically. He slapped the side of Meatloaf's belly, and Meatloaf moaned.

A tech wheeled in the portable cardiograph machine and two techs, a nurse, and Dr. Erickson attached the wires to Meatloaf, first rubbing on splotches of jelly at each point where the wires were to be attached. Meatloaf shifted slightly, and the stretcher creaked.

"Don't move," Dr. Erickson ordered.

Meatloaf made bubbling noises through his pursed lips. His skin was a grayish green. His face sagged like a day-old balloon.

"Start 'er up." Dr. Erickson motioned like a conductor, and the techs switched on the machine.

"Odd." Dr. Erickson, his glasses on the end of his nose, held up one end of the paper, which showed regular, even peaks and valleys. "Curiouser than hell."

~ ~ ~

"Indigestion?" Noreen said. "Indigestion?" She had pulled her rusted red Volvo up to the emergency entrance of the hospital, where Victoria was waiting, her string bag of poetry books in one hand, her broad-brimmed straw hat in the other.

"That's what I heard as I was going through the emergency room." Victoria set her books on the floor of Noreen's car and swiveled herself in.

Noreen waited until Victoria was settled. "I heard on the scanner they were stopping at Meatloaf's place. I figured Domingo had jinxed him."

As Noreen pulled away from the grass strip in the emergency entrance's parking lot, Victoria indicated a lemon yellow pickup truck. "That's the new surgeon's car, a 1956 Jeep."

Noreen looked over at it. "That's the year he was born."

"He's younger than most of my grandchildren." Victoria shook her head. "It's amazing what children can do these days."

Noreen pulled out of the parking lot and waited for a string of cars to pass before she turned onto the main road. On their right, they could glimpse salt marsh, before trees closed in and the road veered away from the water. On their left, stone walls and fences had been moved back from the road to make way for the new bicycle path, and the gray lichen-covered sides of the stones no longer lined up the way they had for a century or more.

"I suppose the road by your house was dirt when you were a girl." Noreen braked at the stop sign by the fire department.

"It was sandy, with wagon ruts on either side of a high center." Victoria looked in the side mirror, where the road spun out behind them. "One night, a boy from Edgartown who was courting one of my sisters and my cousin Leonard from West Tisbury, who was courting an Edgartown girl, both fell asleep on the way home. When their horses met at Deep Bottom, they stopped, nose-to-nose. The boys slept on."

Noreen laughed. "Imagine that happening today." She waited for cars coming from her left, then turned right. "It must have taken a couple of hours to go the eight miles or so from Edgartown to West Tisbury."

"Now we get in a car and think nothing of driving from one end of the Island to the other. We used to go to Oak Bluffs two or three times a year, a great occasion. Now, Elizabeth commutes, drives there every day."

"Domingo told me Liz Tate accused him of harassing her niece, one of the dock attendants."

"Domingo's too refined," Victoria said.

"Domingo, my husband?" Noreen turned to Victoria in astonishment. She swerved and a car horn honked. She moved back to her side of the road. "You gotta be kidding me."

"He has such courtly manners," Victoria said.

Noreen raised her eyebrows. "Are we talking about the same person?" She sneaked a quick look at Victoria.

"And he knows so much about poetry." Victoria looked straight ahead, her nose lifted. "He appreciates it. Not many people do these days." She moved slightly in her seat.

"I'll give you that." Noreen turned into her drive. "Domingo likes Elizabethan poetry because the guys who wrote it were sneaky, plotting, and conniving, and wrote in code."

Noreen stepped outside the car and leaned in through the driver's side to talk to Victoria. "He identifies with that shit. Excuse me, Mrs. Trumbull." She opened the back door to take out the groceries. "Come in and have a cup of coffee."

Victoria carried one of Noreen's bags into the house and dropped it onto the couch. She sat in the wicker armchair in front of the glass-topped table while Noreen brought in the rest. Sunlight filled the large, sprawling room. At one end, opposite the table, a wall of mirrors reflected green plants and sunlight, and the couch with Domingo's harpoons above it. Afternoon light poured through two skylights on either side of a brick chimney behind a large black wood-burning stove.

Noreen stepped up into the kitchen, returned with two mugs of coffee, and sat across from Victoria. Sunlight filtering through the plant-filled window lit up Victoria's face, made her wrinkles stand out in strong relief, hummocks and gullies of time. Her eagle's beak of a nose cast a long shadow on her cheek. Her eyelids drooped over her bright brown eyes. She put a knobby hand up to her face to brush back a loose strand of hair that waved naturally around her face in a white halo.

"You and Domingo have a thing going with that poetry." Noreen stirred her coffee. "If I didn't know my husband pretty well, I'd worry about you two."

Victoria looked down modestly. "The best thing about getting old," she said, "is that you can flirt with the men and their wives don't mind."

Noreen sipped her coffee and watched Victoria's face. "I'm not so sure about that, Mrs. Trumbull."

A car pulled into the drive. Noreen pushed the plants aside and looked out.

"Elizabeth. She's early. Domingo must have gone softheaded." The white Rolls-Royce pulled in next to Elizabeth's car. "And here he is. Wonder who they left in charge?"

Elizabeth pushed the sliding door aside, came in, and dropped onto the couch.

"What a day!"

"Domingo giving you a hard time?" Noreen poured a cup of coffee and handed it to her as Domingo came into the room.

"Thanks." Elizabeth took the cup and sniffed the fragrance. "No, it's not so much Domingo, for a wonder." Domingo rolled his eyes. "It's the dock attendants, the treasurer, the selectmen, the Harbor Advisory Committee. The harbor is busy, but that's okay. It's just the whole atmosphere."

"Did you enter the harbor receipts you were worried about into the computer?" Victoria asked Domingo.

"All done, sweetheart."

"Except for a bunch we can't read," Elizabeth said. "We've got enough entered so Domingo can fill out the paperwork and get that cash to the treasurer."

"You mean, *I* can fill out the paperwork." Noreen stepped down from the kitchen. "I'm the one he's going to get to do it."

"You heard what Howland's code word is, didn't you?" Elizabeth looked up at Noreen.

"I'm not sure I want to know."

"It's your nickname in Spanish."

"He calls me 'woman' when he thinks he's being cute. What is it, *'mujer'?*" She tugged on a strand of Domingo's hair.

"Ouch!" he said. "You know I love you, honey."

"You're full of shit." Noreen gave him a swat with the back of her hand.

"At least one good thing happened today," Elizabeth said. "Meatloaf Staples didn't show up." She kicked off her shoes and wriggled her toes in the soft carpet.

"You heard he was taken to the emergency room?" Noreen said. "Suspected heart attack."

"No!" Elizabeth sat up.

"It was indigestion," Victoria said.

"Shucks." Elizabeth leaned back against the couch cushions again. "Since Allison's aunt filed the complaint against Domingo, the dock attendants are acting surlier than usual. Domingo walks by and they put on this big act of being terrified."

"They ought to be terrified of him," Noreen said.

Elizabeth said, "I don't see why Domingo can't fire all of them. We're trying to institute controls on money transactions, and the kids lost one of the receipt books, fifty numbers' worth. That could easily translate to five thousand dollars."

"How can you lose a receipt book? They're not exactly small." Noreen picked a yellowed leaf off a plant in the window.

"We designed them so you couldn't slip the book in your pocket and take it home by mistake," Elizabeth said. "I don't think you do lose them."

~ ~ ~

"Here he comes, Mr. America!" one of the lunchtime regulars at the corner table in the ArtCliff Diner sang out as Meatloaf lumbered through the door. The diner was on Beach Road, across from the Mobil Mart and down the road from the shipyard.

"Whaddaya say, Cap'n?"

"Hey, Dorothy!" a bald guy with a fringe of sandy red hair and bushy coppery eyebrows shouted to the woman in the kitchen. "Bring Meatloaf a double order of sausage and gravy."

"With fried potatoes and onions," said a cadaverous-looking man with prominent cheekbones, who was wearing a greasy red baseball cap with "George's Auto Body" printed on it.

"Add a couple of rashers of bacon to the order, Dotty," said Red, the guy with the bushy red eyebrows. "Put it on my tab."

Meatloaf shambled over to the round corner table. Lunch patrons in the diner looked up and moved aside to let him pass. The diner had five small tables in addition to the big corner table, and a counter with five stools that ran partway across one side. Meatloaf squeezed past the counter, pushed his baseball cap up on his forehead, and took off his sunglasses.

"You guys cut that out," Dorothy, a sturdily built woman in her forties, called out from the kitchen. "You wanna kill him?"

"Yeah," said one. "Why not?" said another. "Who'll know the difference?" asked the third.

Meatloaf pulled out one of the captain's chairs around the big table and sat down with a grunt.

"So, you're dieting, I hear," said Red. "Have a carrot stick, Meatloaf."

"It wasn't funny." The three men at the table laughed. The one sitting to Meatloaf's right slapped him on the back.

"How many EMTs did it take to carry you in?" asked the first man, a gray-beard wearing the ubiquitous baseball cap, this one emblazoned with "Martha's Vineyard Shipyard."

"One to screw in the lightbulb and four to turn the stretcher," Red said.

Shipyard brayed with laughter.

"Wrong joke," said Meatloaf, his mouth turned down. More raucous laughter.

"Whatsa matter, baby?" Beanie, the cadaverous man, sitting on Meatloaf's left, asked solicitously, putting his arm partway around Meatloaf's broad back. "Can't take a joke any more? Diet getting to you?"

"Lay off me." Meatloaf's face was getting red.

"Temper, temper!" sang out Shipyard.

"Yeah, lay off him." Dorothy set in front of Meatloaf a plate with a hamburger patty, a tomato slice, and a dab of cottage cheese.

"Oooh, girls!" Shipyard looked at Meatloaf's plate.

"I mean it," Dorothy said. "Lay off. The guy almost died."

"Almost died, my aunt Fanny," Beanie said.

"Almost killed the EMTs who had to carry him in is more like it," Red said.

"You about finished with your witticisms?" Meatloaf stabbed the hamburger with his fork held tines down and carried a chunk of it to his mouth. "Real funny guys, you are." He chewed the blood-red meat. "Real funny."

"What's the news at the harbor with that nigger spick?" Beanie leaned forward, bony elbows on the table.

Dorothy scooted out from behind the counter, grabbed Beanie's collar. "You watch your goddamned mouth around here." She shook him. "Hear me? Nobody talks like that in my place."

"Awright, awright." Beanie shrugged her off and straightened his collar.

"I mean it." Dorothy scrubbed the table in front of Beanie with her wet dishcloth, then flicked it at him.

"You trying to put me back in the hospital?" Meatloaf said, mouth full of hamburger. "That guy is screwing things up."

"Cutting back the wife's shopping money, is he?" Shipyard said. "Everybody knows you was on to a good deal."

"The black guy is smarter than you give him credit for," Beanie said. "Smarter than all of youse put together."

"Anything new with the murder investigation?" Red asked.

Meatloaf choked suddenly, coughed, his face turning red. Beanie slapped him on the back. Meatloaf coughed a few more times and wiped his watering eyes.

Shipyard brayed. "Almost got you that time."

"What about the old lady who saw it all?" Red said. "Mrs. Trumbull, wasn't it? West Tisbury?"

"She has no idea what she saw or heard. She's in her nineties, for God's sake." Meatloaf coughed a couple of times. "She doesn't know diddly-squat. Medeiros, the cop, not the plumber, talked to her." He chewed. "Whaddaya expect from an old bag?"

"She's a pretty damn smart old bag," Shipyard said. "Not much gets past her, from what I hear. She rides around with West Tisbury's police chief."

"So?" Meatloaf said.

"Writes the West Tisbury column for the paper, don't she?" Beanie said.

"Don't give me any more shit about Mingo or the old lady. Let me eat my lunch in peace, will you?" Meatloaf jabbed another hunk of hamburger with the fork and carried it to his mouth.

"Getting some pretty big boats in the harbor this year, ain't you?" Shipyard said. "I see that professor's boat is next to the fuel dock."

Dorothy brought a fistful of heavy white mugs of steaming coffee from the kitchen and chunked them down on the red-checked vinyl tablecloth in front of each of the men.

"Which one's his boat?" Red put his hands around his mug and turned to Shipyard. "That big motor sailer?"

"Yeah." Shipyard stirred a heaping spoonful of sugar into his coffee. "His boat's the sixty-five-footer with the black hull, teak deck."

"Dawn Chorus," Meatloaf said through his hamburger.

Shipyard pulled a paper napkin out of the black dispenser in the middle of the table and wiped his own face vigorously. "Hey, Meatloaf! Can't you keep your food in your own mouth?"

"Professors make enough money to keep a boat like that?" Beanie asked.

"He's got plenty of money. You know which house he bought, don't you?" Shipyard looked at Beanie over his mug.

"That big house on the Sound, backing on Lake Tashmoo." Beanie dumped two spoonfuls of sugar into his mug.

"Yeah, five million dollars' worth," Red said. "Let me have the sugar when you're through, if you left any."

"That what he bought it for?" asked Beanie. "God A'mighty! Real estate prices are outta sight."

"Definitely not a professor's salary." Red looked toward the kitchen. "Hey, Dotty, how about some cream?"

Dorothy returned with a small stainless-steel pitcher and plunked it in front of Red. "Sorry, boys, forgot all about it."

"Where does he get his money?" asked Beanie.

Red shrugged. "Someone said he developed some astrophysics software program."

"You mean there's enough call for astrophysics computer programs to make someone a millionaire?" Beanie said, looking at Red in astonishment.

"Astrophysics ain't what you think," replied Shipyard. "No one looks through telescopes anymore. It's stuff like *Star Wars.*"

"That's old hat now." Beanie sipped from his mug.

"Yeah, well, it's other shit like that. Greenhouse effect. Ozone layer. Somebody told me he was working in Puerto Rico on a big radio telescope." Shipyard looked at Meatloaf, who sat there chewing. "Guess we finally shut him up."

"Where's he teach, Harvard?" Beanie stirred his coffee.

"MIT, I think," Red said.

"He used to," Shipyard said. "I heard he got fired."

"Professors don't get fired."

"Something about the guy ain't right," Shipyard said. "He's too good to be true."

"You're jealous," said Red.

Meatloaf wiped his mouth on a paper napkin, then reached for a second napkin and wiped his forehead. "Can't you guys think of anything else to talk about?" He balled up the napkins, dropped them on his plate, and pushed his plate away from him.

Dorothy bustled over to the table. "You done, Meatloaf? You left your cottage cheese."

"Yeah. I lost my appetite. Don't need a special diet when I'm around them." Meatloaf jerked his head at the others.

"Poor dear." Shipyard brayed his short laugh. Dorothy took Meatloaf's plate with its balled-up napkins, pool of blood, and dab of cottage cheese, then wiped the vinyl cloth in front of him. Meatloaf leaned his elbows on the table, small hands dangling in front of his gut.

"So what are you doing about the harbor master?" Red said.

"You can't hardly fire the guy. He's doing a pretty good job, from everything I hear." Beanie moved his coffee mug in circles on the vinyl cloth.

"Don't you worry your sweet asses. We'll get rid of him," Meatloaf said, reaching for the cream pitcher. "And the old lady, too."

Shipyard leaned back on two legs of his chair to talk to Dorothy. "Better bring two more pitchers of cream for Meatloaf. Another bowl of sugar, too."

"And two jelly doughnuts," Beanie said loudly.

"And a double slice of your banana cream pie," Red said.

"With two scoops of vanilla ice cream," Shipyard added.

"Holy smokes," Meatloaf said. "There are ways to get rid of you guys, too."

~ ~ ~

CHAPTER SEVEN

Howland's Program

LOUIE, the green-haired dock attendant, sat back in the aluminum lawn chair in the harbor master's shack. "That computer guy musta put in some kind of code word," he mumbled to Allison, who was sitting on the desk, kicking her feet, her boating shoes dangling off the ends of her toes. "I can't get into the program."

Allison snapped her chewing gum. "So? Who cares?" She was sketching something in a stenography notebook.

"I want to see what Mr. D is trying to hide. What's he got in there? Why does he need to keep anyone out of the program?"

"To keep you guys from, like, messing it up?" Allison swung her feet.

"While you're sitting there doing nothing, check the desk drawers, will you? See if they left any loose money in there, or any receipt books."

"They lock them up. Only Mr. D and Elizabeth have keys." She swung her feet, hands on the edge of the desk, and snapped her gum.

"Try the drawers. I want to see what's there." Louie typed a word into the computer and hit the enter key. The computer beeped.

"I'm not touching a thing. I don't want Mr. D on my case again, you know?"

"What could he have used for a code word?" Louie said, half to himself, trying another combination. "You got nothing to worry about, Allie." He paused to look at her. "Your aunt is about to sue him, isn't she? Because he hassled you? He wouldn't dare touch you." He hit the enter key again. The computer beeped.

"I got plenty to worry about. He didn't harass me. He hollered at me is all." She swung her feet, and one of her boat shoes fell off. "I don't really blame him, you know? My father woulda smacked me if I gave him the lip I give Mr. D." She slipped off the desk, put her shoe back on, and lifted herself onto the desk again. "Mr. D isn't so bad, you know?"

Louie tried another word, and when the computer beeped yet again, he said, "Shit. I'll never figure it out this way." He turned to Allison. "Your aunt was hoping for something to nail him with. Damn that guy. There's no way to figure out what code word he used. I tried all the obvious things."

"Maybe he wrote it down somewhere."

"I doubt it." Louie looked up from the computer. "What're you drawing?"

"None of your, like, business," Allison said.

Louie looked toward the parking lot. "Here comes Howland now, with Mr. D."

Allison glanced over her shoulder and got off the desk in a hurry, gathered up her receipt book and a pencil, and scuttled out the door.

Domingo was ambling from the parking lot along the catwalk that led to the shack over the water, feet splayed out. Allison moved to one side to let him pass. He stopped.

"Did you clean up the mess in the shack?" His thumbs were hooked in his trouser pockets. He looked at her intently.

"No." She peered down at the wooden decking at her feet.

" 'No' what?"

"No, *sir.*" She emphasized the last word.

"And why not?" Domingo looked at her.

"It's, like, already perfectly clean," she said. "Sir."

"Come back to the shack and we'll take a look."

Allison shrugged, tossed her long hair back from her face, turned, and retraced her steps to the shack.

Louie was standing as far from the computer as he could get, paging through his receipt book, apparently counting. Domingo looked at him, and Louie avoided his eyes. "Still haven't figured out the code word, eh?"

"Who gives a shit about some code word?"

"Watch your language." Domingo stared at him. "Get out of the shack and patrol the harbor. Pick up the trash, empty the barrels into the Dumpster, and check boat lines."

Louie slapped his receipt book against his hand and avoided Domingo's eyes. "This isn't a job; it's slavery."

Domingo's eyes got brighter. "You don't know what slavery is, kid. Get out of here before I kick you someplace the bruises won't show, give your father something to complain about."

Louie hitched up his shorts and mouthed something.

"You say, 'Yes, sir,' understand?"

"Yeah."

Domingo grasped Louie's upper arm and looked at him. Domingo grinned, teeth white against his dark face.

"Yes, sir," Louie said hurriedly. Domingo released him, and the dock attendant scurried out of the shack and joined Allison on the catwalk. The two flew past Howland, who was giving directions to a tourist, pointing toward something on Circuit Avenue. Howland glanced at them as they passed.

"You abusing those poor children again, Domingo?"

Domingo stood in the middle of the floor, thumbs in his pockets, feet apart, toes facing out, looking at the computer, at the desk, at the window locks.

"So it would appear." Domingo reached into his shirt pocket for his cigarettes. "You sure the program is safe from them?"

Howland stood in front of the computer and entered a series of words. "They're not likely to hit on the code word. I'm more concerned that they'll accidentally erase something or hang up the hard drive. I don't suppose we can ban them from the shack?"

Domingo didn't reply immediately. He shook out a cigarette, then put it back in the pack. "My assistant's got me afraid to smoke in my own office." He put his hands in his pockets and paced the small shack. "We can't lock them out, if that's what you're saying. They have to come in here with receipts, fill out time sheets, check the schedule. We can't keep them out."

"A pity." Howland sat in front of the computer and entered a string of words. "When did that motor sailer come in?"

"*Dawn Chorus.* This morning, early. Owned by T. R. Folger, old-time summer family. A couple years ago, he bought that big house on Tashmoo."

"That's an expensive boat," Howland said as he continued typing.

"He's got a live-aboard captain, too." Domingo paced the shack. "That's not cheap." He stepped outside and stood at the railing, looking out at the Harbor House.

"A yacht and a five-million-dollar house on a professor's salary?" Howland lifted his eyebrows.

"The money comes from something else." Domingo turned his back to the railing and put his elbows on it. "If I'm not mistaken," he said with a slight smile, his bright eyes on Howland, *"he* made his money developing a computer program."

Howland looked up at the harbor master, and his mouth turned down. "Why didn't you ask him to develop the harbor-management program instead of me?"

"He's too busy."

"I suppose I'm not?"

Deadly Nightshade

Domingo continued to talk as if to himself. "In the couple of years he's lived here, he's become a pillar of the community. Volunteers at the hospital. Teaches in the literacy program." He glanced from the Harbor House to Howland. "You could be doing good works, if you'd only get going with that harbor program."

"Yeah, yeah." Howland went back to the keyboard.

The door of the shack was swinging slightly. Domingo leaned down and propped it open with a rounded beach rock. He turned and looked at Howland. "How are you coming with those receipts?"

"Between Elizabeth and me, everything's entered except the ones in this pile." Howland picked up an inch-thick stack of receipts. "These, we couldn't read. Those kids can't write." He pointed to the top one. "Can you read this?"

Domingo fished in his pocket for his glasses and looked at the name written in the space designated "Boat owner." He shook his head and handed the stack of receipts back to Howland.

"Or this one." Howland handed the next receipt on the stack to Domingo. "What's that boat name?"

Domingo looked at it and shook his head again. "Looks like *Otter Creek.*"

"Or is it *Sweet Life,* or *Other Wife?*" Howland slapped the pile of receipts. "Figuring out this program is difficult enough without having to deal with illiterate kids."

Domingo grinned. "Their aunts or fathers will probably cite me for abuse if I tell them to print clearly."

"In addition to the dock attendants' lousy writing," Howland continued, "boat owners give boats the most ridiculous names, spelled in improbable ways. We registered four boats named *Why Not,* spelled four different ways. Puns, professions, pet names, naughty names. We registered three boats named *Wet Dream.*"

Howland glanced up from his computer to look out at the parking lot. "Who's that?" He indicated a tall, extremely slender man with curly dark hair, white on the sides, and a large black mustache who was walking from the parking lot toward the catwalk. He was wearing tan chino slacks and a light blue knit collared shirt.

"That's the professor."

"*Dawn Chorus,* a five-million-dollar house on the beach." Howland looked closely at the man coming down the catwalk. "Inventor of a multimillion-dollar software program."

"Right."

The tall man approached the shack and grinned, perfect white teeth dazzling in his tanned face, as Domingo went outside to greet him. He thrust out his hand, Domingo thrust out his, and they shook.

"How're you doing, Professor?"

"Not bad. You having a good season?" Standing next to Domingo, he leaned his elbow on the railing, crossed his left foot over his right, and peered genially down at the small harbor master. The boat shoes on his sockless feet were new and polished.

"You heard about Bernie Marble's murder?" Domingo, leaning with his back against the railing, looked up at the professor.

"Not something you expect on the Island. Do they know who did it?" He raised his thick eyebrows in an upside-down V.

Domingo shook his head. "If they do, no one's saying."

"Probably don't want to make too much fuss with the president coming in a week or so. Wouldn't look good."

Howland, who had been listening from inside the shack, got up from his seat in front of the computer and joined Domingo and the professor on the deck. The professor was at least three inches taller and much slimmer than Howland.

The professor straightened up and extended his hand. "Name's Rocky," he said.

"Howland Atherton." Howland lifted his head so he could look down his nose at the taller man.

"Understand you're developing the computer program with my drinking buddy here."

Domingo turned to face the harbor, elbows on the railing, looking at the Harbor House.

"I believe you're the one who ought to be developing this program." Howland glanced at Domingo's back. "My experience is with the three-eight-six."

"That's what you need for this job. You don't want a high-tech program. Mind if I take a look at it?" the professor asked. "I don't want to intrude, of course. Believe me, I know what it's like to work out the bugs in one of these programs."

"Not at all." Howland bowed slightly and held his hand out for the professor to lead the way. The professor ducked through the door, Howland following. He pulled the second aluminum lawn chair up to the computer and both sat.

Domingo lifted a hand. "I've got to check the dock attendants." He went down the catwalk and disappeared behind the tent with the butterfly display next to the snack bar.

"Good man," the professor said after Domingo had left.

"The selectmen don't seem to think so." Howland pressed a key and the screen demanded a code word. The professor averted his eyes politely while Howland typed in *"mujer."* Howland hit the enter key and the harbor-management program popped up on the screen.

"Nice. Straightforward, simple." The professor leaned forward in the lawn chair. "You must have had the deuce of a time setting that up. The simpler the application, in my experience, the more difficult the programming."

"It did take some thought."

"I can imagine. More than some. Would you mind showing me how you did that?" The professor sat back. "If you don't mind."

"No, no. I'm certainly delighted to show you."

The phone rang.

"Do you need to answer?"

"No," Howland said. "The machine will pick up on it. I don't work here."

The phone stopped after a few rings, and they could hear the answering machine whir.

"I'm interested in how you handled problems such as differing boat lengths and beams, varying slip sizes, where boats came from, and the length of stay."

Howland put a stack of clean paper into the printer. "I'll give you copies of forms we use for reservations. As I said, it's not original; I'm basing my work on existing software."

"All the more impressive. Domingo mentioned earlier that you've developed forms for the turnover reports. I take it those are the reports that accompany checks and cash you turn over to the town?" The professor moved his chair closer to the computer.

"Yes, that's right."

"Ingenious. Knowing Domingo, he probably doesn't appreciate what you've done."

"True, to some extent."

"He's not free with his compliments." The professor leaned back in the chair while Howland printed out copies of the forms he had designed. "He's pretty shrewd, Domingo is," the professor continued. "I wouldn't like to be on his wrong side."

The radio crackled on the wall behind them. A voice came on, saying, "Oak Bluffs harbor master, Oak Bluffs harbor master." The professor raised his eyebrows at Howland.

"Domingo has a handheld radio. He'll take care of it."

"You were saying about the program?"

"I think this management program will protect him to some extent." Howland turned to look at the other man. "We'll have all the information he needs to run the harbor — registration numbers, addresses, that sort of thing."

"Domingo seems to believe money is slipping through loopholes in the system," the professor said.

Howland paused before he answered. "Yes."

The professor showed concern. "You'd think the selectmen would support him more than they seem to be doing."

"Yeah," said Howland. "You would think so."

The shack swayed slightly on its pilings, and the professor looked up.

"Domingo's assistant, Elizabeth Trumbull," Howland said.

"Oh?" The professor raised his eyebrows.

"She's Victoria Trumbull's granddaughter, lives with her."

"Good place to be," the professor said.

Elizabeth reached the door and hesitated when she saw someone with Howland at the computer. She brushed her hair away from her face with the back of her hand. The freckles on her nose stood out against her tan.

"Come on in," Howland said. "Meet the owner of *Dawn Chorus*, Professor Folger. Elizabeth Trumbull." The professor got to his feet and extended his hand to Elizabeth, who shook it firmly.

"I don't often have to look up to anyone." Elizabeth tipped her head back.

The professor bowed slightly. "I understand there aren't many people you need to look up to," he said graciously. "So you're Victoria Trumbull's granddaughter?"

Elizabeth smiled and nodded.

"I'm a great admirer of her poetry. I believe I have all of her books. She must be along in years."

"She's ninety-two."

"And still writing, from what I read in the *Enquirer.*"

"Please, sit down." Elizabeth stepped into the shack. "I'll sit on the desk and watch you work."

"It was your grandmother who witnessed Bernie Marble's murder, wasn't it?" the professor asked.

"I don't believe she actually witnessed it," Elizabeth said cautiously. "She heard a scream."

Howland said, "Victoria, Domingo, and Elizabeth found the body"

"That must have been a horrible experience."

Elizabeth nodded.

"The professor developed an astrophysics program," Howland said to Elizabeth. "I'm showing him our harbor application."

"Call me Rocky. My students do."

"Where do you teach?" Elizabeth sat on the edge of the desk.

"I was teaching at MIT," Rocky said. "However, I'm now an independent consultant."

Elizabeth looked out the window. *"Dawn Chorus* is beautiful."

"She's about thirty years old."

Elizabeth whistled. "She looks brand-new. What a lot of work to keep up that teak and all the brightwork."

"Would you care to come aboard?"

"I'm on duty today." Elizabeth looked at the sleek boat at the fuel dock. "How much longer will you be here in the harbor?"

"I'll be here for a while. It would be my pleasure to have you aboard for drinks. And you, Mr. Atherton?"

"Call me Howland."

The professor got to his feet. "Elizabeth, I'll send you an invitation, you and your grandmother, for drinks aboard." He went through the door, ducking his head.

Elizabeth sat on the edge of the desk and watched the professor stride along the bulkhead toward his boat. "Maybe my grandmother could practice her matchmaking on him." She turned back to Howland. "She's trying to pair me up with Ben Norton, who's at least thirty years older than me. This professor seems to have money, brains, and he's tall."

Howland gazed at her. "Too good to be true, right?"

"He's probably married." Elizabeth sighed. "Where did he get his money, from his computer program?"

Howland shrugged and turned back to the screen.

Elizabeth continued talking. "If you were to market your harbor program the way Domingo thinks you should, maybe you'd make your fortune, too."

"A million-dollar yacht with live-aboard captain?" Howland shook his head. "With the proceeds of a computer program?"

"You're just jealous." Elizabeth slid off the desk and sat next to him. "I guess we'd better try matching this pile of receipts with whatever we can that's in the computer."

"Who's guarding Victoria right now?" Howland paused in his data entry and glanced at Elizabeth.

"Chief O'Neill assigned the two West Tisbury patrolmen to watch her, and Ben Norton was going to stop by later. I don't believe there's anyone with her right now."

Howland finished the entry he was working on, stood up abruptly, picked up his green canvas briefcase, and put a sheaf of papers into it.

"I've got to go. Will you be okay, Elizabeth?"

"Of course. Why the sudden concern? I've been working here alone for more than two months now."

"Sorry. I don't mean to sound protective. See you later."

~~~

Victoria was opening a small can of cat food when Howland knocked. McCavity was on his hind legs, front paws up high, mewing. "Come in; the door's open." Victoria dished cat food into McCavity's bowl and set it on the floor. As the cat dodged under the table, his tail bumped the table leaf, which banged. By the time Howland entered, McCavity's head was in the bowl.

"Haven't seen you since this morning." Victoria looked up at Howland with a twinkle in her eyes. "Nice to be so popular."

"Can't stay away from you. Do you have any coffee left from this morning?" He lifted the pot off the burner.

"I've never seen anything like it. Everybody in town has dropped in for coffee. I've gone through three pots so far today. I haven't had a moment alone to write."

"Anyone you don't know?" Howland reached the cobalt blue mug down from the cupboard over the sink and poured himself a cup.

"Yes. The nicest man came by, left only a few minutes ago. He had copies of all of my books, and he asked me to autograph them." Victoria went into the cookroom and sat at the table.

"Oh? Who was it?" Howland poured milk into his coffee and sat across from Victoria at the table.

"T. R. something. I wrote it down to make sure I spelled it right in his books." She sorted through some papers on the telephone table. "It's here somewhere."

"T. R. Folger."

"Yes. That's right. Do you know him?"

"I met him today. About an hour ago, at the harbor."

"He must have come right here. Imagine that." She picked out a couple of wilted zinnias from the bowl of flowers in the center of the table and laid them next to her.

"What did he have to say?" Howland sipped his coffee.

"He's a great admirer of mine. He introduced himself, then asked if I would autograph my books he'd bought over the years. Oh, yes, something else." She got up stiffly from her chair.

"Can I get something for you?"

"No, I have to get it." Victoria opened the cabinet over the refrigerator. "It's where I keep my stash of sweets." She looked over her shoulder at Howland. "I don't want anyone to see how much I've hidden away here."

She returned with a small box of Chilmark Chocolates. "Rocky brought me this. Have a piece. Or two."

"Thank you." Howland watched her slip the golden elastic band off the box and put it on her wrist. She lifted the lid of the white box. "Have you eaten any yet?"

"Not yet." Victoria looked over the selection laid out in the box. "Such a treat. I don't often have them given to me." She poised her hand above one, then changed her mind. "Rocky must have known how much I like chocolate."

"You can hardly miss with those." Howland picked out a fat cream, turned it over, and looked at the bottom. He put it back in the box and picked out a second candy, turned it over, looked at the bottom. He did the same with a third piece.

"I wouldn't ever allow my children to do that, Howland," Victoria said tartly. " 'Look as long as you want,' I'd tell them, 'but once you put your fingers on a piece, it's yours.' "

"I'm sorry. That was rude of me. Let me take the box and I'll bring you a new one."

"That's not necessary." Victoria put the lid back on the box, slipped the golden elastic back around it, and pushed the box toward him. "It's yours if you want it. Take it."

"Thank you." Howland picked up the box, zipped open his briefcase, dropped the chocolates into it, got up from the table, and left.

~ ~ ~

"Did you notice the stars when you came in?" Victoria said to Elizabeth, who'd returned from her day at the harbor. The night was cool and clear, with a touch of fall in the air. "Orion is so brilliant, you can imagine the hunter striding across the sky with his starry belt and sword."

Elizabeth fetched the rum bottle and cranberry juice jug from the cupboard under the kitchen counter and mixed two drinks. She followed Victoria into the parlor, set the drinks on the coffee table, and knelt by the fireplace, where a fire was laid, ready to light. She put a match to the paper underneath and waited for the paper and kindling to catch before she got up.

"I'll bring in more wood," she said.

She had lifted the canvas log carrier out of the wood basket and was at the dining room door when Victoria said suddenly, "Howland came by."

Elizabeth turned at the tone of her grandmother's voice. Victoria was sitting in the mouse-colored wing chair next to the sofa. "He did the strangest thing this afternoon."

"He can be pretty weird. What did he do this time?"

"He came over for a cup of coffee, and when I offered him a piece of chocolate from a box that nice man Rocky Folger brought me, he mauled several pieces, and when I told him sarcastically to take the whole box, he did." She held up her glass and looked thoughtfully at the firelight flickering through the ruby red cranberry juice. "That's not like Howland at all. He usually has such impeccable manners."

"I didn't realize the professor had come by." Elizabeth set the log carrier down on a chair.

"Yes. Shortly before Howland showed up."

"Mr. Folger was at the harbor today. He asked Howland to show him the harbor computer program."

"Yes, he told me," Victoria said. "He also told me about his own program, not that I understood what he was talking about."

"He seems like a nice man." Elizabeth looked through half-closed eyes at her grandmother. "He's closer to my age than Ben Norton is."

Victoria's face crinkled in amusement. "I can't start matchmaking until I know him better."

Elizabeth sighed. "I'm not interested anyway, Gram. I need to get my head back together before I look at another guy." She left the room with the log carrier and returned in a few minutes with a load of wood, which she stacked in the basket next to the hearth. Flames flared up briefly; a log shifted. She prodded the fire with tongs until it burned evenly, then sat on the couch next to her grandmother's chair.

"Rocky has invited us aboard his yacht," she said.

Victoria looked thoughtfully at her granddaughter. "I hardly know what to tell him about Howland and the chocolates."

"You don't need to say anything."

"I suppose not. I'll tell him, again, how pleased I was." They sat quietly, looking into the flames for long minutes.

Victoria glanced up suddenly. "Is someone at the door?"

Elizabeth put her drink on the coffee table and went to the kitchen. Howland stood in the dark entry with a white pasteboard box in his hand.

"Come on in," Elizabeth said. "I hear you've suddenly acquired a sweet tooth."

"Sorry about that." Howland strode into the parlor and presented Victoria with the box he was holding, a box of Chilmark Chocolates, twice the size of the one Rocky had given her.

Victoria looked up, puzzled. "What is this all about?"

"It's my apology for being so rude this afternoon." Howland moved in front of the fireplace, put his elbow on the mantel, and looked down at the hearth.

"Will you join us for drinks?" Victoria asked him as she put the candy box on the end table next to her.

Howland shook his head. "No, thanks. I've got to go."

The fire sizzled and hummed. A log snapped and broke with a shower of sparks.

"I'll see you tomorrow," he said to Elizabeth. "You're on duty at the harbor, three to midnight, aren't you?"

"Yes."

Victoria lifted her glass to him. "Good night."

Howland nodded, then disappeared into the starry night.

"What is wrong with him? He's certainly acting odd." Victoria looked into the flickering fire. "I suppose it will sort itself out eventually."

~ ~ ~

CHAPTER EIGHT

The Medi-Van to Boston

VICTORIA ALMOST canceled her trip to Boston when she saw Meatloaf Staples driving the medi-van. This was the first time she'd used the free van, and it hadn't occurred to her to question who the driver might be. However, Dr. Erickson had made an appointment with the foot specialist, Elizabeth had dropped her off at the ferry terminal, and she could hardly back out now. She hoped Meatloaf would not remember her from that brief encounter at the harbor master's shack. Really, she had nothing against him, except his rudeness that time.

Victoria, who was sitting in the backseat, watched as a frail woman with a walker smiled up at Meatloaf, who helped her into the van. "You're so thoughtful, Mr. Staples." Meatloaf had set out a milk crate as a step, folded the woman's walker, and stowed it behind the front seat.

The woman patted his arm, and he pushed his sunglasses back on his nose. She settled into the middle seat, next to a man wearing a red plaid jacket and a yellow-and-green Hawaiian shirt.

The medi-van was the first vehicle in the ferry line. Mist drifted up from the harbor's glassy surface, which reflected sailboats moored between the breakwater and the ferry lane. Gulls circled and mewed; one dived and hooked a silvery fish in its bill, then soared into the air on strong wings. The harbor's mirror surface shattered into myriad sunrise colors where the bird had touched it.

Behind the rose-colored clouds over the shipyard to the east, the sun shot out bright rays. The masts of the topsail schooner *Shenandoah* etched black lines against the dawn sky,

The woman introduced herself to the man in the Hawaiian shirt, and they exchanged pleasantries about the sunrise. She shifted in her seat and peered at the people sitting behind her.

"George dear, what's taking you to Boston?" George was next to a black-haired woman, who was wedged between him and Victoria.

"Meatloaf's van." George gave a horse-toothed laugh. The frail woman tittered. "Actually, my stomach's acting up again." He adjusted himself between the women on either side of him. "I'm going for tests."

"It's terrible getting old, isn't it?" She turned with her arm across the back of the seat. "And Victoria! This is the first time I've ever seen you use the van."

"Dr. Erickson wants someone to look at my toe."

The woman next to Victoria smiled at her. Victoria scowled back. The woman had plastered her face with makeup, as if she were an actress. It made her look spooky, clown-like. "One needs to take care of one's feet," the woman said brightly. Victoria's usually good-natured face wrinkled into a sour expression.

Meatloaf aimed his sunglasses through the open side door. "Everybody here?" He counted the passengers, pointing a thick forefinger at each one. When he came to Victoria, he paused. She saw him purse his soft lips. He remembers me, she thought.

"Let's see, five," Meatloaf continued. "One more's supposed to come." He looked at his watch. "They'd better hurry."

The sun broke above the clouds and the harbor brightened. Sunlight glinted off white hulls and sparkled on the quiet water. Tendrils of mist writhed up from the harbor's surface and vanished. The day was going to be warm.

A short elderly man, his face flushed, darted toward them. "Medi-van?" he gasped, mopping his head with a handkerchief.

"None other." Meatloaf nodded. "Take your time, mister. You ride in front with me. I got laundry in back."

"Landry?" The man put his hand behind his ear, puzzled.

"Lawn-dree," Meatloaf said loudly. "When I do this medical run, I cart dirty lawn-dree from the Harbor House to the commercial laundry in Boston."

Victoria looked behind her and saw two folding metal carts with canvas sacks bulging with towels and sheets slung from them.

"Ah." The man regained his breath. "Killing two birds."

"You could say that." Meatloaf helped him into the front seat and slammed the door shut. An attendant beckoned the van toward the ferry. The line of cars and trucks followed up the gangplank, where they stopped to give the deckhand a ticket.

"Whaddaya say, Meatloaf?"

"Nothin' much, Beanie."

"See you at the diner this evening." Beanie tore off a portion of the ticket and handed the rest back to Meatloaf, who put the ticket under the visor and drove onto the vessel. The metal deck plates clanged under his wheels. He nodded to the deck hand, who directed him into the left center lane, and stopped behind the chain strung across the bow.

Once he'd pulled on the parking brake and shut off the engine, Meatloaf reached into his shirt pocket and brought out a folded slip of paper. Victoria saw him take a pen out of his pocket and scribble what looked like numbers.

The vessel's diesel engines rumbled. The vehicle deck vibrated as a second line of trucks and cars formed in the right center lane, headed by two eighteen-wheelers. The ferry rocked as each truck drove on board.

"Anyone want to get out, go up to the snack bar?" Meatloaf turned to his passengers. "This van's not going anyplace else for forty-five minutes."

The woman in the middle seat and the woman next to Victoria raised their hands. Meatloaf set down the milk carton step and helped them out of the van. Victoria got out with them, taking Meatloaf's cold, moist hand reluctantly. "Watch your step, girls; the deck's slick." He peered into the van. "Anyone else?"

As she climbed the iron stairway that led to the upper deck, Victoria felt someone watching her. Halfway up the stairs, she looked down and saw Meatloaf turn away quickly. He got back in the driver's seat, folded his hands over his stomach, and tilted his head back against the seat. His sunglasses covered his eyes.

At the top of the stairs, Victoria opened the watertight door that led into the lunchroom, then seated herself with the two other van passengers in a booth across from the lunch counter.

"How you doing, Mrs. Trumbull? Off to America?" Victoria looked up to see Eddie Schultz, the electrician.

"Doctor's appointment. What about you?"

"I'm off to get some pipe sections myself. Christ, you'd think they was gold-plated." He tipped his dirty red baseball cap to the three women. "Have a good day. See you around."

He moved to the urn in front of the lunch counter and poured himself a large cup of coffee. "Keep the change," he said to the blonde behind the counter.

"Whaddaya say, Eddie?" A bulky, bearded man slapped him on the back. "Catch any blues lately?"

"They ain't running too good up to Menemsha. How about you?"

"Running pretty good around Wasque, I hear. Give me one of them crullers." The man pointed to a sugary doughnut and the blonde lifted the plastic cover, picked one up with a piece of waxed paper, and handed it to him.

"Rough out there?" Eddie asked her.

She shrugged. "Slick calm."

The ferry whistled and pulled away from the slip. Victoria could see boats on moorings in the harbor, all pointing east. She nodded to a neighbor, who had come up the stairs into the lunchroom. Noting the clunky high heels of a young woman with two small children, Victoria marveled at how she managed to look so stylish with children hanging on her. She looked around at the other four booths, all of which were occupied, and recognized a woman from church, who smiled at her. She turned back to the two women sitting across from her, and they talked about the children's posters displayed on the bulkhead above the table. The black-haired woman brought three cups of coffee to the table. They discussed summer crowds and how autumn was almost upon them. They continued chatting until the ferry turned into the channel between the barren-looking Elizabeth Islands and Woods Hole.

When the purser announced the vessel was docking, they returned to the van. The ferry's big doors opened, engines roared into reverse, and the vessel slid into the slip with a bump that rocked the vehicles on the car deck.

Meatloaf started up the van and led the procession of cars and trucks and motorcycles off the ferry.

As they left Woods Hole behind them, conversation died down, and the van's passengers dozed or read until they reached the outskirts of Boston.

"Medical Center, first stop." Meatloaf inclined his head toward the back of the van. "Tufts next, Beth Israel." He checked the side mirror and changed lanes, cutting in front of a bus.

"I've got to drop off the laundry. I may be late, so keep your shirts on, girls." Victoria scowled.

~~~

When her appointment was over, Victoria strolled through the Commons until it was time for the van to arrive, then returned to the clinic entrance and sat on a bench under a tree. The shade felt good after the walk in the hot sun.

She took her pen and a pad of paper out of her pocketbook, intending to write. Before she put down the first word, she looked up and saw a stout man wearing sunglasses cross the street in front of her. At first, she thought it was Meatloaf, and for an instant she had a pang of fright. However, the man was no one she knew. Her heart was thumping. What was she afraid of?

Her poem vanished like the morning's mist. She thought about Meatloaf. He shouldn't be transporting a load of dirty hotel laundry in the same vehicle with elderly, possibly ailing, passengers. Surely the health department would not approve. If he were engaged to drive the medi-van, it seemed unscrupulous to wring extra money out of the deal by combining it with a laundry run. Come to think of it, why drive the laundry off-Island, anyway? The commercial laundry had a regular Island route. She'd seen the truck in Vineyard Haven. She shook her head.

While she was musing, the van pulled to the curb next to her and Meatloaf opened the door. Victoria's was the last pickup. The three already in the back seat moved so she could take the same seat by the window that she'd had on the trip into town. Before she settled herself, she leaned over the back seat. The laundry carts now were loaded with cardboard boxes, taped shut. Clean laundry, she assumed. When she looked up, Meatloaf's sunglasses were reflected in the rearview mirror, lenses shining at her.

It must be the way the light reflects off his glasses, Victoria told herself.

During the trip to Woods Hole, she avoided looking toward the rearview mirror and Meatloaf's glassy stare. She wasn't one for chatter, especially about ailments, and after a few attempts, she gave up and looked out the window at the late-summer foliage. Whenever she glanced up, Meatloaf's bug-eyed sunglasses seemed to be aimed at her.

At the top of the hill approaching Woods Hole, where she could see the harbor and the islands beyond, she always felt a surge of pleasure. This time, she felt relief, as well.

The van continued down the hill, across the bridge, into the staging area for the ferry, and onto the waiting boat.

When they docked at Vineyard Haven, Victoria's head ached from tension, and she was glad to be out of the van.

She went inside the terminal building to wait for Elizabeth. While she waited, she had an eerie, prickly sensation that someone was staring at her. She looked around, expecting to see Meatloaf standing behind a column, but no one was there.

"Sorry I'm late."

Victoria started. She had been so preoccupied she had not noticed her granddaughter come into the waiting room. When she looked up, she saw concern on Elizabeth's lean, freckled face.

"Are you okay, Gram? I didn't mean to frighten you." She put her hand on her grandmother's back. "How was the appointment?"

"A lot of nonsense over a toe. It doesn't hurt and I have no trouble walking, now that you cut that hole in my shoe."

"How did the day go otherwise?"

"I spent too much of it with Meatloaf."

At Elizabeth's frown, Victoria told her about the trip.

As they walked to the parked car, Elizabeth said, "Domingo wants us to stop by. He's acting mysterious, as usual."

"Maybe he's identified those slips in the checkbook we found washed up on the beach."

~ ~ ~

When they entered the living room, Domingo stood.

"Did you find out whose checkbook it was?" Victoria asked immediately, going over to him.

"I know whose deposit slip it was. And how much money was deposited on a certain date. Sit down." Domingo gestured to a chair, and when Victoria sat, he did, too. "Honey!" he shouted into the room off the kitchen. "Bring me the papers."

Noreen bustled into the kitchen and down the single step to the living room, placed both fists on her hips, and leaned toward Domingo, her face six inches from his. "You can't even say 'please,' can you?"

"Please, honey. Thank you. I'm sorry." His eyes opened innocently. "Please, if you would bring me those papers?"

"Asshole." She flounced out of the room and returned a few minutes later with the bank receipt and the deposit slip still enclosed in two pieces of glass. She set the glass on the tabletop with a clink.

Victoria, in the chair, and Elizabeth, still standing, leaned over it.

"The numbers on the account are clear." Domingo wiped the top piece of glass with a paper napkin. "The name is more difficult to read. We can't legally get the name that matches the account number without a court order."

"Merton something." Elizabeth narrowed her eyes at the glass-encased deposit slip. "The last name begins with 'St.' "

"Staples," Victoria said promptly. "Meatloaf Staples." Domingo raised his eyebrows at her.

"It is Meatloaf, isn't it?" Victoria looked at him.

"It could be."

"Is Meatloaf's real name Merton?" Elizabeth asked.

Domingo shrugged. "I've never heard him called anything but Meatloaf."

"If it matters, we can look up voter registration, I guess," Elizabeth said.

Domingo turned to Victoria. "Tell me, sweetheart, why do you think these bank papers are Meatloaf's?"

"When I was in the van today, he wrote something on a slip of paper." Victoria leaned closer to look at the papers under the glass. "It might have been checkbook entries."

"As if he'd misplaced his checkbook." Domingo extended his chunky hand to Victoria, who shook it gravely.

"How much did he deposit? And when?" Victoria leaned over the papers under glass.

"Look." Domingo pointed to the figures on the receipt.

Elizabeth put her hands flat on the table and leaned over. "Ten thousand dollars. Cash."

"The same day Bernie Marble was killed," Victoria said. "Did someone pay him to kill Bernie? Ten thousand down and the rest when he did the job?"

"I don't think so." Domingo smiled. "But you'd have made a good cop, sweetheart."

Victoria looked down at her skirt and smoothed it across her lap. She crossed her ankles, one shoe with the hole for her toe over the other shoe. Then she told him about the trip to Boston.

"Why do you suppose he's taking dirty laundry off-Island in the medi-van? There's no need to."

"Laundry." Domingo drummed his fingers on the table.

"He's hiding something in it, isn't he?" Victoria said. "And bringing something back in the clean laundry."

Domingo lit a cigarette.

"What would he be hiding?" Victoria gazed beyond the plants hanging in the window. "A body. Stolen goods. Something he wants to sell off-Island."

Domingo nodded as she ticked off each thought.

"Antiques. Books. Papers. Has to be something illegal. Stolen jewels." She looked over at Domingo suddenly. "Drugs. That's what it is, isn't it? Drugs."

Domingo looked at her with a slight smile. "Don't go jumping to conclusions."

"Of course that's what it is," she said. "It makes perfect sense. Something smallish and valuable."

"Sweetheart, drug smuggling is big trouble."

"Where do we go from here?" Victoria said.

Domingo stood at the window, his hands in his pockets, jingling coins. "Watch ourselves," Domingo said. "And wait."

~ ~ ~

CHAPTER NINE

On the Dawn Chorus

THE CAPTAIN'S white uniform was so sharply creased it looked as if he had not moved after putting it on. Victoria looked with admiration at the black shoulder boards on his shirt, each with four glittering gold stripes. The shiny black visor of his cap was almost covered in gold thread with an intricate design of oak leaves and ivy. He stood at the foot of the wooden steps that led from the fuel dock to the deck of *Dawn Chorus.*

"Captain Harold Jones, ma'am." He touched his cap.

"How do you do. I'm Victoria Trumbull." She nodded regally, tilting her floppy-brimmed straw hat to him. They went up the wide steps together, Victoria holding the captain's arm with one hand, the railing with her other. When she reached the deck, Rocky was waiting. "Welcome aboard, Victoria Trumbull."

Victoria leaned her head back to look up at him. "Thank you so much." She took his extended hand and stepped over the low rail. She gazed at the scrubbed teak deck, varnished railings and brightwork, polished brass, the neat coils of white line on deck, and the pennants fluttering from the masthead above her.

"How beautiful!" She held her hand on the top of her hat as she looked up at the rigging.

"I'm glad it pleases you." Rocky was nautical in a blue blazer with gold buttons, white trousers, and white deck shoes. "It's such a fine day, I thought we might like to go for a sail." He smiled at Victoria's expression of joy. "I invited Howland and Selectman Tate. Let me show you around before they arrive."

He opened a varnished wooden door and held out his hand for Victoria to go first. She descended the five steps that led into a saloon as wide as the yacht.

The interior of the yacht looked like one of the great liners she and Jonathan, her husband, had taken to Europe years ago. At one end, there was a fireplace, at the other a grand piano, its legs held in metal braces bolted to the deck. Around the edges of the polished wood floor were dark wood inlays of diving whales and porpoises. The floor (Victoria found it difficult to think of it as a deck) was covered with an Oriental rug in red, black, and gray.

Victoria took it all in — the fireplace, piano, couch and armchairs, the large mahogany table secured to the deck, the oil paintings in gilt frames fastened to the bulkhead, the inlaid designs on the floor, the rug. The polished brass portholes were the only indication that this was a boat.

She pulled her hat off and patted her white hair into place. The creases of her face formed a sunburst of pleasure.

They walked across the carpet toward the bow, and Rocky opened a door into a spotless galley with stainless-steel refrigerator, sink, and stove. He showed her the captain's quarters forward of the galley, a stateroom large enough to hold a tightly made bunk bed, a built-in bureau, and a small desk with a lamp fastened to the bulkhead above it.

"How tidy it all is." Victoria ran her hand over the shiny fixtures and patted the neatly folded towels.

"Anyone living on a boat has to be tidy." Rocky led the way back through the galley, through the elegant saloon, into the master stateroom in the stern. A king-size bed strewn with a dozen soft pillows in shades of green and rose took up most of the space. A row of windows on the slanted bulkhead above the bed ran the entire width of the stern. Standing on tiptoe, Victoria could look through the windows onto the harbor below.

Rocky turned at the sound of footsteps above them. "I hear our other guests."

As they walked back across the dark green carpet into the saloon, Victoria asked, "Did you sail the boat here?"

"I sailed as far as Bermuda from Grand Turk, then flew from there. Captain Jones and the mate brought it the rest of the way." Rocky ducked his head to go through the door.

On deck, he greeted Howland. "Good to see you," he said genially.

Victoria noticed Howland's faintly superior expression. "And our last guest, Selectperson Liz Tate." Rocky stood by the steps as the captain escorted her on board.

" 'Selectman' is fine." Liz Tate smiled. "There can be too much sensitivity."

Victoria had only seen Liz Tate from a distance. It was the first time she'd met her. Close-up, she was much younger than Victoria had thought, thirtyish, not much older than Elizabeth, and while her granddaughter usually dressed in jeans and T-shirts, Liz Tate could have been a *Vogue* model, thin, pale, with high cheekbones and a wide mouth with carmine lips. Her black hair glistened with blue highlights. Her sweater was the exact shade of her lipstick.

"Thrilled to meet you." She took Victoria's hand in both of hers, left hand on top of Victoria's right in what Victoria felt was a too-familiar gesture. "I've known of you, of course."

"Ready, sir?" the captain asked.

Rocky turned to his three guests. "If you sit on the deck chairs aft, you can see better."

The starters for the diesel engines turned, and the pressure alarms rang, then cut off as the engines kicked in, first one, then the other. Deep inside her, Victoria felt the excitement she had always felt when starting on an adventure.

The mate, a college-age boy, clambered aboard, undid the lines, and tossed them down to the green-haired dock attendant, who stood by. The yacht eased smoothly away from the dock and turned into the fairway between the moored boats in the center of the harbor and the slips along the bulkhead. They glided through the channel slowly into the Sound.

Rocky, who was standing next to the wheel, turned to Howland.

Victoria saw that Howland's sweater, a nondescript greenish thing, had a moth hole in the back. Next to Rocky, Howland looked like what Victoria's grandmother had called "an unfortunate."

"The channel has silted up," Rocky said. *"Dawn Chorus* is at her depth limit. A few inches more on her keel and we'd have to anchor outside the harbor."

Victoria stood by the rail as they passed the harbor master's shack, and she waved when she saw her granddaughter on the deck.

From this angle, the shack looked especially small and rickety, projecting into the harbor on its slender pilings. She looked from the shack across the harbor to the East Chop dock, where they'd taken Bernie Marble's body the night they'd found it, less than a week ago. She noticed Rocky was watching her with an expression she couldn't decipher, a kind of wariness. He smiled suddenly when she looked at him. Such beautiful teeth, Victoria thought, set off so nicely by his dark, full mustache.

"I thought you might enjoy sailing across the Sound to Tarpaulin Cove. We can have lunch there, and be home by five."

Liz Tate sat next to Victoria and asked her about her childhood. Victoria found herself telling the selectman how her grandfather had sailed to far places from the Vineyard.

"From Arctic waters to the Antarctic," she told Liz Tate, who listened intently, red-nailed hands folded in her lap.

They cleared the harbor entrance. To the right, Nantucket Sound stretched as far as they could see. Ahead of them, the mainland formed a thin line of white beach, with a thicker line of gray buildings and green trees. Victoria could make out a church spire and a water tower above the trees. To their left, low cliffs obscured their view to the west, but as they moved, the cliffs receded and Vineyard Sound opened before them.

The mate climbed onto the cabin roof and untied the white ribbons that held the neatly flaked mainsail onto the boom.

Victoria leaned back, her hand shading her eyes.

"Wonderful," she said to Liz Tate. "Just wonderful."

The mate uncleated the mainsheet and hauled the sail smartly up the mast.

Victoria watched every movement.

"You don't miss a thing, do you?" Liz Tate said.

"I try not to."

Liz Tate studied her. "I've known people half your age who are not as alert as you."

"Years of practice." Victoria tried to look modest.

The sail fluttered and snapped loudly, a giant sheet on a clothesline in the stiff breeze, rising smoothly to the top of the mast, until no wrinkles showed along its edge.

"I'm sure you must be a keen observer, to write the way you do."

"Thank you." Victoria straightened her lavender slacks over her knees. "There's so much to witness in the world today, to see and hear and feel."

"Speaking of witnessing, I understand you witnessed the murder last week."

Howland turned sharply and looked from Victoria to Liz Tate.

"Not exactly witnessed. I heard something on the other side of the harbor, that's all."

The yacht turned away from the wind, the sails filled, and the midmorning sun shone into Victoria's face. She put her straw hat on again and tied it under her chin.

The boat heeled with a gust of wind.

"Didn't that frighten you?" Liz Tate had her back to the sun. Though her face was shaded, Victoria could see her wide eyes.

"Things like that don't frighten me." Victoria, who was on the high side of the yacht, leaned back as the deck tilted, as if her weight would counterbalance the wind in the sails. "Domingo — the harbor master — and my granddaughter took me over to where I'd heard the commotion, and we found the body, floating."

"I suppose you heard voices?" Liz Tate said. "People talking or shouting? You must have heard a scream."

Howland, behind Liz Tate, was staring at the back of her head. Again, Victoria wondered what was wrong with him.

Victoria was aware, too, that Rocky was listening to their conversation, even though he seemed to be talking to the captain.

She went back in her mind over that evening. What exactly had she heard?

"It sounded like three men's voices. I suppose one was Bernie's. I could almost make out the words. I could tell they were disagreeing violently."

Liz Tate nodded sympathetically. "Must have been terrible."

"It must have been terrible for Bernie Marble."

"Yes, yes. Of course. Such an awful way to die. Gutted like a fish." Liz Tate shook her head. Her silky blue-black hair swirled around her face, back-lighted by the late-morning sun.

"You knew him, didn't you?" Victoria tugged the brim of her hat over her eyes so she could see Liz Tate's face better.

"Not well. He was the chair of the Harbor Advisory Committee," she answered. "I saw him often at meetings. He was not the sort I socialized with, of course."

"Of course," Victoria agreed.

They had almost reached the Elizabeth Islands when there was a flurry of activity. The captain called out to the mate and swung the wheel rapidly to port. The yacht tacked into the wind, the sail swung to the opposite side, filled, and the yacht pointed toward the Vineyard's North Shore. When they were close to shore, they tacked again.

"Such a smooth operation," Victoria marveled.

"We'll turn into the cove in a few minutes," Rocky said. "We'll anchor without the engine. Ideal sailing weather."

Victoria's eyes sparkled. She dabbed at a drip at the end of her nose with a paper napkin. "I never dreamed we'd go out today."

The captain let out the sail, turned the boat away from the wind, and headed into the cove.

Victoria knew Tarpaulin Cove well from sailing with her grandfather as a girl. The cove was on the south shore of Naushon, one of the Elizabeth Islands. Elizabeth and she often drove to Gay Head, on the western end of the Vineyard, where they could see the islands, a sparsely populated chain that hung from the elbow of Cape Cod. She stood up to see better, holding the back of the deck chair. She could feel the same thrill she'd felt as a girl. She hadn't been here for more than a half century. Surely it wasn't three-quarters of a century? A century had once seemed an eternity. Now she'd almost lived through that eternity. How short a time it had been! She gazed shoreward. She held the brim of her hat to shade her eyes from the glare of sun on water, and held the back of the chair with her other hand. Nothing seemed to have changed. The cove was still cupped by low grassy bluffs, pale gold in the sun. Sheep grazed, as she remembered they had always grazed. She had the eerie feeling they were the same sheep, like the ones they put under the Christmas tree year after year after year. She could hear them bleat mournfully. She remembered standing next to her grandfather in this same spot, listening to that same sound, with the same breeze blowing over them. She remembered the big house with its gables and chimneys, half-hidden by a low hill. The house seemed to be in the same state of disrepair it had been in when she was a child. Her grandfather had said someone should reshingle the roof, or the weather would destroy the house. The roof seemed the same. She could see the tree line beyond the big house, stunted scrub oak and pine. It looked exactly like the tree line of her childhood. She recalled two large trees that rose above the other trees, their configuration looking like an elephant. She'd told her grandfather that. The elephant was still there, unchanged. The island was enchanted. Time had stopped for it, while she continued to pass through days and months and years.

The boat swung into the wind. Sails luffed, slapped loudly.

Victoria snapped back into the present. She turned, to see Howland staring at her with concern, Liz Tate watching her.

The anchor went over the bow, and the wind carried the boat back on the anchor line.

"Are you all right, Mrs. Trumbull?" Liz Tate asked.

"Yes. It's bringing back memories I didn't know I had."

"It's a beautiful spot." Rocky looked around at the sheep grazing and the tall grass rippling in the soft wind.

The sail slithered down the mast and was caught in the Lazy Jack, a net of lines. The mate lowered the jib, tucked it into a sail bag, and then tied everything with white ribbons.

"Well done," Rocky said. "I'll bring lunch out on deck — lobster rolls."

"I'll help." Liz Tate followed Rocky into the saloon. They returned with a platter of sandwiches garnished with nasturtium flowers, along with bottles of champagne and crystal champagne flutes.

Howland raised his eyebrows when he saw the champagne. "There can't be too many bottles of Rothschild '57 around." Rocky bowed slightly. "I can't think of a better occasion to share a bottle or two of this."

The sheep bleated softly, one to another. The boat rocked gently on anchor. The smell of sweet fern wafted from shore. Waves lapped on the beach.

During lunch, Victoria chatted politely with Liz Tate. She talked (and flirted) with Rocky, who complimented her on her pantoums. She was pleasantly surprised that he had recognized the unusual rhyme scheme of the Malay poetry form.

Liz brought up the subject of the murder again. They speculated on the effect of the president's visit on the investigation. Victoria was impressed with Liz's knowledge of politics, and told her so. Liz said that was because she lived in Oak Bluffs. She asked Victoria again about finding the body, then listened as Victoria repeated what she'd seen and heard. Rocky had come up quietly behind Victoria. She saw his shadow on the deck and could smell the faint scent of his cologne.

She was going to tell Liz about finding the broken bottle, but before she could, Howland clumsily knocked over one of the delicate champagne glasses.

"Damn it, you ox!" Rocky snapped. Victoria turned in astonishment and saw that Rocky's face was scarlet. He apologized immediately. "I beg your pardon, Victoria." He turned to the others, who were also staring at him in surprise. "I do beg your pardon, everyone. I was so interested in what Victoria was saying, I was startled."

The mate cleaned up the fine splinters of broken glass, amid Howland's profuse apologies and offers to replace it.

"No, no, please, Howland. I'm not in the least concerned about the glass," Rocky said.

Once the flap over the broken glass was past, Rocky said, "I was interested in what you were about to say, Victoria. Please continue."

As Victoria resumed her recollections, Howland suddenly pointed to a flurry of gulls on the water not far from them.

Victoria stopped talking and stood up. Everyone started to speculate on whether the flurry of gulls meant a school of bluefish or not.

Victoria saw Rocky stare at Howland with a faint smile.

"Looks as though you won't be able to tell us your adventures after all, Victoria." He turned to the others. "Would anyone like me to bring out the fishing tackle?" he asked.

Once they had finished lunch and Liz and the mate had made an unsuccessful attempt to hook a bluefish, Howland offered to help the mate carry the dishes back to the galley, but he was turned down with some civilized teasing about how clumsy he was.

Victoria reminisced about her childhood with her whaling captain grandfather, and Rocky and Liz listened intently. All told, Victoria had had a marvelous day. The champagne, the lobster, the conversation, the warm sun, the soothing motion of the yacht, and the hay-scented breeze and bleating lamb sounds drifting out over the water had all combined to make her feel mellow.

"I'm afraid we have to start for home now if we want to get back before dark," Rocky said.

"I wouldn't mind staying here for an entire week." Victoria stood and gazed shoreward, taking in the sheep, the grasses moving like waves, the old house, everything bathed in the golden light.

As the sun settled over Gay Head, across the Sound from Tarpaulin Cove, they weighed anchor and headed home, the wind behind them.

Howland sat with her, leaving her only long enough to get a wool blanket from below, which he draped around her shoulders. By the time they rounded West Chop, Victoria had nodded off.

She awakened as they pulled up to the dock. The sun was disappearing behind the low bluffs of East Chop, and the air had become chilly. Clouds had formed while she was dozing, and they promised a spectacular sunset.

She heard Allison, the dock attendant, and the mate call instructions back and forth as he tossed lines ashore; then she heard the scrape of the steps pushed across the dock to the side of the yacht. She listened as the throb of the engines slowed to a soft rumble.

She folded the blanket and got up stiffly from her deck chair. Several people stood at the foot of the steps, Elizabeth and Allison and the young man who pumped fuel. The other two took her by surprise, Police Chief Medeiros and Meatloaf.

Liz Tate's behavior surprised her, too. Victoria had walked over to the rail, expecting to be the first one off. Instead, Liz pushed by her, almost rudely, and leapt onto the steps before they had fully tied up. She scooted down the steps and confronted the police chief. She spoke to him in a low voice, so Victoria couldn't hear what she was saying, but Victoria could hear the selectman's icy tone and see her anger. The chief's face turned red. He looked up at Howland and Rocky and Victoria gathered at the rail, then at Meatloaf, then back at Liz Tate.

Victoria heard her say, "Don't ever let me see . . ." and then the one-way conversation drifted off on the breeze coming off the harbor. The chief jerked his head at Meatloaf, who stood at the bottom of the steps, and the two men sauntered off the fuel dock. Victoria watched them get into a police cruiser, the chief on the driver's side, Meatloaf on the passenger's. The cruiser backed out of its space and turned, the sound of tires skidding on sand clearly audible. She glanced around the parking lot and saw a familiar gray van. She could see a hairy head with wild eyes staring through the grimy windshield at Meatloaf and the chief.

Liz Tate bustled up the steps and back on board. The lines had been secured while Victoria watched the small drama.

"Sorry about that," Liz Tate said to Victoria with an apologetic smile. "Chief Medeiros was supposed to be elsewhere, doing some business for the selectmen, not hanging around the dock like some boat-crazy kid."

Victoria looked thoughtfully at Liz Tate. "I don't suppose they see this kind of yacht in the harbor often."

Liz stared at Victoria for a moment before answering. "They see this one often enough."

~ ~ ~

CHAPTER TEN

Someone's Watching

"WHY WAS Meatloaf waiting for us on the dock yesterday?" Victoria sat next to Domingo at the glass-topped table. "It was a perfect day until we tied up, and there he was, waiting."

Victoria and Elizabeth had stopped on their way into Oak Bluffs. Early-afternoon sunlight filtered through the plants hanging in the window, casting dappled shadows on the table. Domingo was wearing his blue plaid pajamas and was drinking coffee out of a mug marked I LOVE GRANDPA.

"I don't know, sweetheart. He's mixed up in this, but I don't know how."

"It was odd to see Chief Medeiros there, too."

"Chief Medeiros was there?" Domingo paused, his cigarette halfway to his lips. "That's interesting."

"Who's running the hotel now that Bernie is gone?" Elizabeth asked.

Victoria toyed with the place mat in front of her. "The chief, I would imagine. Bernie and he were partners."

"Maybe he wanted to invite us to take showers." Victoria's face wrinkled into a smile. "Five dollars each."

Noreen came through the sliding door into the living room with armloads of groceries. "Can't you get dressed, Domingo?" She brushed past him. "It's already afternoon."

"Why should I get dressed now? It's almost time for bed."

"What a slob," Noreen said from the kitchen. "Make some fresh coffee for Mrs. Trumbull, Domingo."

" 'Please, honey.' " He pushed himself away from the table and went up the step into the kitchen. Victoria saw him kiss Noreen on the side of the cheek, heard her say softly, "Go along with you." She heard the rattle of the aluminum measure against the coffee tin, the splash of water, the gurgle of the coffeemaker.

When he returned to the table, he asked Victoria, "Did those two seem surprised to see you? Meatloaf and the chief?"

"I don't think so. They wanted to talk with Liz Tate. She was upset when she saw them, sent them both away."

"Interesting."

"Howland was on the cruise, too." Victoria leaned back in the wicker chair.

"He made a fool of himself, dropping one of those expensive Waterford glasses."

"Oh?"

"I was telling Liz Tate about finding the body. Just as I started to tell her about the broken bottle, Howland dropped his glass."

Domingo raised his eyebrows slightly.

"Then, as I was about to resume, he interrupted me, quite rudely, to point out a school of fish."

Noreen pulled up a chair between Victoria and Domingo.

"They're playing some kind of weird game," Noreen said. "Meatloaf and Liz Tate and Bernie Marble, God rest his soul," she said, crossing herself, "and the police chief and Rocky."

"And Howland," Victoria added. "He's certainly acting odd."

"No one knows about the broken bottle but us." Domingo scowled. "There's no need for anyone else to know, either. The broken bottle may have nothing to do with the murder."

"But we're sure it does," Victoria said.

Domingo shrugged, then scratched his chest under his pajama top. "Don't tell anyone any more than you have to. They don't need to know everything we know."

"I can give you a ride home, if you'd like, Mrs. Trumbull," Noreen said.

"Thanks, but I'm giving a reading at the Oak Bluffs Senior Center." Victoria looked at her watch. "One of the board members will drop me off at the harbor, and I'll go home with Elizabeth."

The ship's clock rang five bells. "We'd better get going," Elizabeth said, pushing her chair back and unfolding her long legs. "It's two-thirty now."

~~~

The late-night shift had been quiet. Elizabeth had caught up with much of the paperwork in the shack and was now sorting through the day's receipts. Outside, the night was clear and windless. The tidal current moved against the pilings of the shack and gurgled gently. Inside, the overhead lights made it bright.

"Hey, missy, I brought you two lobsters."

Elizabeth jolted to her feet, knocking over the chair.

"Scared you, didn't I?" Dojan stood at the harborside window. Again, she hadn't heard him or felt his footsteps on the rickety catwalk.

"Good heavens, yes." She went to the window.

"The sheik is bringing another vessel tonight," Dojan said, and then grinned. He wore the same outfit, black jeans, black mesh muscle shirt, black scarf imprinted with skulls, and his necklaces of bones and shells. "I hope you have a place for him this time."

"Yes," Elizabeth said. "Yes, I think we can find a place for the sheik. How big is his yacht this time?"

"Two hundred feet." Dojan's grin exposed the missing front tooth. "Where's Mrs. Trumbull?"

"She had a meeting this afternoon. Then one of the board members invited her to dinner. He's bringing her here afterward." Elizabeth looked at her watch. "She should be here any minute now. It's after ten."

"The sheik sends Mrs. Trumbull his regards." Dojan put his hands on the windowsill. Elizabeth noticed the grimy bitten nails and drew back involuntarily. He'd added a black crow feather to the osprey feather he'd worn before in his hair. It looked as if he had not changed his clothes since she had first seen him.

"Did she really know my great-grandmother?"

Elizabeth nodded.

Dojan shook his head; the feathers quivered, the bones rattled, and the scarf swirled around his neck. "I got two lobsters in a bucket. Want me to put them inside the shack?"

"You can leave them out there," Elizabeth said. "I'll get them later."

"Scared of letting me in?" Dojan bared his teeth. "*She's* not scared." He moved back from the window. "I'll sit here until she comes." Elizabeth heard the bucket clank on the deck. The darkness closed around the shack, and she heard a night heron squawk, the current swish against the pilings, carrying harbor water out to sea. The silent Wampanoag waited outside.

After that, she gave up trying to do any real work until Victoria came. She organized papers and straightened the shack.

In a few minutes, she heard Victoria's deep, firm voice. "It's here somewhere. Let's go into the shack, where there's light."

"I brought you lobsters," Dojan said.

Elizabeth opened the door, and Dojan stepped aside so Victoria could enter.

Victoria fumbled through her leather bag and brought out a slim gray paper-bound book. "This is the long poem I wrote about your great-grandmother. We kept in touch through the years. Our lives were quite different." Victoria looked up at him. "I wrote this before you were born."

"For me?" Dojan's eyes swam in their pools of white. "You're giving this to me?"

"I'll sign the book for you, if you'd like." Victoria found a pen in her pocketbook and looked up at him. "I'll say, 'To Dojan Minnowfish from his friend — and his great-grandmother's friend — Victoria Trumbull.' Does that sound all right?"

Dojan's mouth and eyes formed round circles in his hairy face, and he nodded.

"I'll put today's date on it." She wrote in the book.

Elizabeth looked from her grandmother to the Wampanoag.

"Miz Trumbull" — Dojan held his hand next to his ear, palm toward Victoria — "I'll watch out for you. Don't you worry. No one can get at you with me watching." He picked up the bucket of lobsters. "I'll put these in your car." He disappeared down the catwalk into the dark night.

Victoria and Elizabeth stared at each other.

"What was that all about?" Elizabeth asked her grandmother.

Victoria shook her head. "He's not as strange as he'd like people to think. I have no idea what's on his mind. Something, obviously."

The next couple of hours were quiet. Victoria wrote while Elizabeth worked on the computer. At midnight Elizabeth closed up the shack and deposited the bank bags in the night drop. Then they headed home. They had passed the head of the harbor when Victoria looked in the side mirror.

"There's a car behind us."

"Dojan?"

"I can't tell. Its lights are on high."

Elizabeth looked in the rearview mirror. "A second car just turned out of the side road."

"You hardly expect to see so much traffic this time of night," Victoria said. "It's after midnight."

"Should we stop at Domingo's? It's creepy to have two cars following us."

"Let's go straight home," Victoria said.

Elizabeth turned past the hospital and crossed the bridge between the harbor and the lagoon. The car behind them followed. Shortly before Five Corners, the second car dropped back, and they no longer saw its lights.

At Five Corners, Elizabeth made a sudden left turn.

Victoria adjusted the side mirror so she could see better. "They're still following us."

They passed the marine store on the left, passed the turnoff onto Skiff Avenue on the right, and continued straight ahead.

"This is a dead end." Victoria looked in the mirror. "We'll get trapped."

"There's a dirt road that leads into Weaver Lane and back onto the Edgartown Road," Elizabeth said. "I can't believe they'll follow us along that. It's only an old cow path."

"They're still there." Victoria turned to look out of the rear window, as if the mirror might have been mistaken.

"I don't like it." Elizabeth had slowed to twenty miles per hour on the narrow road. The trees on either side closed in. Branches slapped the side of the car. Their headlights picked out individual leaves on the huckleberry bushes on both sides. The sweet fern brushed against them, releasing its sweet, musky scent.

"I hope you're right about the side road." Victoria smoothed her green plaid skirt over her knees. "They're right behind us."

Elizabeth picked up speed, going twenty-two now, then twenty-three. The VW jounced on the ancient paved road.

"What are they thinking?" Victoria peered into the mirror.

"I don't like this." Elizabeth pressed her foot on the accelerator, gripped the steering wheel. The car leapt over a bump and bottomed out on a pothole in the old macadam.

"Ouch!" Victoria winced as her elbow slammed into the door handle.

"Sorry."

The headlights picked out an open white gate and Elizabeth made an abrupt right turn onto a rutted dirt road with protruding tree roots and low brush in the middle. "Hold on!" she said.

The car skidded on a patch of sand, straightened out, and roared up the hill.

"We should have stopped at Domingo's," Victoria said, patting her hair. "I feel a bit out of my element."

The headlights behind them swerved and wobbled as the pursuing car hit roots and holes and bounced off rocks. "Pray we don't get a flat tire," Elizabeth said.

The road rose steeply and turned, first to the left, then to the right. Small trees growing in the middle of the road scraped the underside of the VW. Their headlights revealed a pair of luminous eyes in the undergrowth. The pair of eyes became five pairs, and a skunk and four rat-size babies shambled out of the huckleberry bushes and into the road.

"Shit!" said Elizabeth, jamming on the brakes.

"How cute!" Victoria braced her hand on the dashboard. The VW stalled. "Look at that littlest one!"

"I should never have come this way." Elizabeth turned the starter grimly, and the VW coughed and the engine started.

Victoria looked in the side mirror. The headlights behind them swerved and jounced. They smelled the sudden pungent aroma of skunk.

"I hope it wasn't the mother," Victoria said.

"Didn't even slow them." Elizabeth's hands tightened.

Victoria peered into the night ahead of them.

"Look out! There's a deer in the road."

"Damn!" Elizabeth leaned on the horn, and the deer bounded into the underbrush.

The cow track leveled off at the top of the hill.

Elizabeth sped up. "We're near the main road now."

The car behind closed in fast. Elizabeth gunned the VW and it shot ahead, the speedometer climbing in increments. Victoria wiped the steamed-up inside of the windshield with a paper napkin. "Do we have enough gas?"

"It reads empty, but there's always another half gallon or so," Elizabeth said, looking straight ahead.

A house appeared in the headlights, then another. A light shone in an upstairs window. A side road joined theirs, and Elizabeth pushed down on the accelerator, straightened her back, and gripped the wheel higher up.

"I hope you have your seat belt on," she said. "They're closing on us."

Victoria cranked the window all the way down and put her head out, holding her fuzzy tan hat with one hand. She gazed at the ground speeding under them.

"Hang on," Elizabeth shouted. "We're turning onto the main road."

"I'm right here," Victoria said. "You don't need to shout."

Suddenly, headlights flashed on behind the pursuing car. Victoria looked into the side mirror as the new car, a van, moved into the left lane, drew up next to the car behind them, and cut in front of it. Brakes squealed as the van wedged the other car off the road.

The van made a U-turn and sped off.

"What the devil was that all about?" Victoria said, settling her hat in place.

"Let's get on home and pour ourselves a stiff drink."

A few minutes later, they sat in the living room, sipping rum and cranberry juice. The cat settled himself on the rug in front of the fire, lifted one of his hind legs, and began the long cleaning process. They talked until the fire died down to coals. McCavity finished his bath, then sprawled on his back, paws up in the air, soft belly fur exposed.

~ ~ ~

Domingo listened solemnly as Victoria described the car chase. It was a bright, cool morning, smelling of autumn and leaves and damp earth. Elizabeth had parked in front of Domingo's garage, leaving room for Noreen, whose car was out.

"Could you tell what kind of vehicles they were?" he asked. "Was either of them the one that followed you the other night?"

"I couldn't tell what the one behind us was. The one that saved us was a van."

Domingo said, "I've been afraid of this. Someone's been watching your house since we found the body. Evidently, we need someone watching you, wherever you go."

"No, thank you. I've seen what happens with the president. No privacy." Victoria sat down in the wicker chair by the table.

"You," Domingo said to Elizabeth. "Bring your grandmother some coffee." He turned back to Victoria. "Privacy is not the issue, sweetheart," he said with exaggerated patience. "The issue is, Who is trying to stop you, and why? I think I know why."

"Because someone thinks she saw something or heard something the night of the murder." Elizabeth stepped down from the kitchen and put a mug of coffee in front of her grandmother.

"Correct."

"And thinks she may be able to identify someone who doesn't want to be identified."

"And thinks she may put two and two together. Sweetheart, someone needs to be with you twenty-four hours a day until this is over."

"Elizabeth is with me all night."

"What would you have done if that car had forced you off the road last night? They'd find your bodies tomorrow or next week." Domingo placed his hand on the table. "No one uses that road."

"Domingo, you're being overly dramatic," Victoria said. A car door slammed and then Noreen came through the sliding door.

Elizabeth rose. "I'll help carry the rest in."

"Thanks, Domingo!" Noreen shouted over her shoulder as she and Elizabeth went to the car.

Domingo shrugged. "See what I have to put up with?"

Victoria straightened out the woven placemat in front of her on the table and smoothed its fringed edges.

"What do we know so far?" Domingo said.

"Someone killed Bernie Marble."

"Yas."

"With the broken rum bottle we found?"

Domingo sipped his coffee without answering.

"We found Meatloaf's checkbook cover with receipts showing he deposited ten thousand dollars in cash the day Bernie was killed."

"Correct."

"Does it fit together somehow?" Victoria stopped toying with the place mat and looked up at Domingo.

He shrugged and gazed out the window.

"Seems like too much of a coincidence, doesn't it?" Victoria, too, looked out the window, noticing the toys in the scuffed yard, the cars flicking by on the other side of the fence. A cardinal landed on the bird feeder, snatched a few seeds, and flew off in a flash of bright red.

Noreen and Elizabeth returned with armfuls of brown grocery bags.

"Coincidences happen." Domingo stood, went to the door, and slid it shut.

"Domingo, we're going right out again," Noreen said. "If you're not going to help, at least don't hinder us."

Domingo made a kissing sound and sat again.

"But you think a coincidence like that is unlikely," Victoria said.

"It's unlikely that Meatloaf dropped his checkbook close to where Bernie was killed and that the two aren't related."

"And the ten-thousand-dollar deposit?" Victoria insisted. "On the same date?" She sipped her coffee, eyes on Domingo.

"That, I can't tell you," Domingo said. "Maybe he deposited his Social Security check."

Victoria laughed. "He's not old enough."

They drank their coffee quietly. Victoria heard a jet plane overhead. A car door slammed. The cardinal called from the lilac bush. She heard Noreen and

Elizabeth laugh, the rustle of more grocery bags as they came to the door.

Domingo broke their silence. "Everyone knows you were the one who heard something in the harbor that evening, is that correct?" His look was intense.

"Yes."

"Doesn't it seem reasonable that whoever was at the scene does not want you to recall what you heard? You know how things come back to you when you hear a sound or smell, remind you of something you didn't realize you knew."

Victoria stared at him. "When Chief Medeiros pulled out of the parking lot after Liz Tate scolded him, I had a feeling I'd heard that same sound of tires on sand before."

"Did you tell anyone that?"

"I thought of it just this minute."

"Honey!" he called to Noreen, who was talking with Elizabeth in the kitchen as they unloaded groceries.

"I hear you, Domingo." She started into the living room, when the telephone rang.

Domingo answered.

"No!" He stamped his cigarette out in the ashtray. "Not Joe!" He looked up at Noreen with a stricken expression. "How'd it happen?"

Elizabeth and Victoria turned to Noreen.

"Joe Palma," Noreen said, watching Domingo with concern. "Domingo's partner in New York."

Domingo listened, his head down, chunky hands cradling the phone. "Two months before retirement," he said into the phone. "He thought he'd beat the odds."

"Oh shit!" Noreen said. "Another cop killed."

Domingo took one hand away from the phone, picked up the pen lying on the table, and doodled on the paper in front of him.

"How's Gloria taking it?" he said.

Noreen put her hands up to her face. Victoria and Elizabeth watched Domingo.

"Wake tomorrow." He looked up at Noreen. "Funeral day after tomorrow. The cathedral?"

Noreen stood frozen, hands still up at her face.

Domingo listened. He wrote something on the paper.

"Thanks. We'd appreciate that. Any room is okay." He put the pen down and ran his hand over his face. "We'll be there. Noreen and me." His gaze went from Victoria to Elizabeth to Noreen, and stopped on Noreen's face. "You got enough to think about." He looked away again.

"My condolences to Gloria."

He hung up the phone and gazed at Noreen with a look of desolation that made Victoria hurt.

"Joe Palma down," Noreen said. "That's what it was?" Domingo nodded.

Noreen dropped to her knees. She threw her arms around Domingo and cradled him. Victoria looked away.

"He was helping with a drug bust," Domingo said. "He wasn't even with the drug force. Just like him, helping out."

"Can we do anything?" Victoria asked Noreen.

"You could do me a big favor, Mrs. Trumbull," Noreen said. "I told my daughter I'd sit with my grandson tomorrow morning."

"What time?" Victoria asked.

"I have the morning shift, Gram. I can drop you off around seven, pick you up whenever," Elizabeth said.

Victoria looked questioningly at Noreen.

"The school bus comes by around ten."

"Ten?" Elizabeth asked. "That's late, isn't it?"

"Kindergarten," Noreen said.

"I'll be here," Victoria replied.

"Do you need a ride to the airport?" Elizabeth asked.

"Ernesto will take us," Noreen said.

"Leave the dock attendants in charge of the harbor when you pick up your grandmother," Domingo said. "Meatloaf is supposed to stop by tomorrow to pick up some papers that need to be signed. He can wait."

"Maybe I'll be here when he comes by?" Victoria's voice rose in a question.

Domingo gave a short laugh. "You can handle him if he does."

"Let me give you some phone numbers where you can reach us in an emergency." Noreen got up from the floor.

"Don't worry about us." Victoria accepted the paper with the phone numbers, and she and Elizabeth started for the door.

"Watch yourself while I'm gone," Domingo said. "I'll get back when I can." Noreen put her arm around his waist, her blond head on his chest.

"Call Chief O'Neill in West Tisbury and tell her everything we know," Domingo said. "Everything. We have to trust her."

~ ~ ~

CHAPTER ELEVEN

The Harpoon

VICTORIA WAS on her hands and knees, picking up the toys Baby Mingo had strewn around his room before he'd dashed off to catch the school bus, when she heard a knock on the door. It took her a few moments to get to her feet. She braced herself against the small bed and chair next to it and slowly straightened her legs.

She heard the knock again, more impatient-sounding.

She tossed the dump truck she was holding into the toy box and walked stiffly into the kitchen, her knees not yet adjusted from kneeling to walking. When she reached the kitchen, she could see past the table in the living room through the sliding door.

Meatloaf was pacing the small patio between the house and garage, glaring at his watch. Even though Domingo had warned her, she still had a jolt of apprehension when she saw him.

"It's after ten-thirty, for God's sake," he muttered, loudly enough for Victoria to hear. He returned to the door, cupped his hands around his face, and peered in at the same moment Victoria slid the door open.

Meatloaf stepped back. "What the hell are you doing here, lady? Where's Mingo?"

"He went to a funeral." Victoria was reluctant to say more.

"He was to leave something for me to get signed." Meatloaf was wearing his sunglasses, and Victoria realized she had never seen his eyes.

"It's there on the table," Victoria said, not moving.

He lumbered over from the doorway, shuffled through some papers at Domingo's usual place, and picked up a pile with a note clipped to the top sheet. He read the note.

"I'm supposed to bring this back when Liz Tate signs it. You going to be here this evening?"

Victoria shook her head. "I'll leave the door unlocked."

Meatloaf straightened the papers by smacking the edges on the table, picked up the manila folder that had been under them, put the papers in the folder, and headed for the door. He stopped before he got there, then turned around. Victoria was still standing in the same place, glaring at him, eyes half-closed.

"Whose funeral?" he asked.

"His partner," Victoria answered. "A New York policeman."

"His partner," Meatloaf repeated. He shook his head. "That's tough on a man, partner and all." He paused. Victoria waited.

"Killed?" he asked finally.

Victoria nodded.

"I'm sorry." Meatloaf shook his head again, pushed his sunglasses back up on his nose, and slid the door open. "I'll be by this evening. I'll leave the signed papers on his table."

Victoria remained standing until she heard his van start up and pull away. She went back to Baby Mingo's room and picked up more toys and some clothing until Elizabeth came to take her home.

~~~

"Where's Meatloaf?" Dotty asked the regulars at the ArtCliff corner table. "Haven't seen him for several days." She chunked mugs of steaming coffee in front of Beanie, Red, and Shipyard, then swiped the vinyl tablecloth with a damp rag.

"Who knows?" Beanie said. "Last time I seen him was here. After his medivan run." He reached for the sugar bowl.

"Probably laid up with indigestion again," Shipyard said.

"Someone ought to call his wife, find out if he's okay." Dotty reached into a rack on the wall and brought out plastic-covered menus. "Want to see the specials?"

"His wife's visiting her mother in Scranton," Red said. "Any excuse to get away from him," said Beanie.

"Maybe someone should call his house?" Dotty suggested. "He might be sick or something."

"He's sick all right," Beanie said.

Shipyard laughed. "Sick in the head."

"You guys lay off him. He's not so bad," Dotty said.

Shipyard brayed. "He's bad, all right."

"Yeah, we want to see the menu," Red said. "Not that there's anything different on it."

"Take your time." Dotty slapped menus on the table and, before she bustled back into the kitchen, said over her shoulder, "One of you guys, *his friends*, ought to check up on him, make sure he's okay."

~ ~ ~

"It's good to be home again." Noreen kicked off her high heels. "Funerals depress me."

"He was a good cop, a good partner." Domingo stood next to the table and stared blankly at his harpoons. "I'll miss him."

"New York does cop funerals the way they ought to be done," Noreen said.

"He was going to visit this fall," Domingo said. "Kept promising me."

"I'll invite Gloria to come. Once she's had a little time," Noreen said. "She'll need to get away."

Domingo stared at the wall.

"You still look pretty good in your uniform, Domingo," Noreen said softly. "It still fits you and everything. You still got the ladies making eyes at you."

"A harpoon is missing." Domingo focused on the display.

"Cops were lined up from the station house to the cathedral. Must have been three blocks. Solid blue."

"It was there when we left three days ago."

"Maybe Ernesto took it." Noreen shrugged out of her rumpled linen jacket.

Domingo, standing in the middle of the living room floor, examined the harpoons, the couch, the floor, the table.

"Something's not right," he said.

"Because of the harpoon?" Noreen picked up her shoes.

"Yes, among other things."

"You never told Meatloaf you couldn't meet with him, did you?" said Noreen. "Maybe he came by."

"He came by all right," Domingo said. "He got the papers signed and returned them. They're on the table."

"Maybe he took your harpoon." Noreen pulled off her panty hose and twisted them around her hand. "I gotta change."

When she returned, in jeans and a blue sweatshirt emblazoned with "Martha's Vineyard, Presidential Retreat" across the front, Domingo was on the phone talking to Victoria.

"You're saying, sweetheart, all he did was take the papers and leave, is that correct?" Domingo said. "You weren't here when he returned them, were you?" He paced the length of the living room with the cordless phone held against his ear. "Did he say anything out of the ordinary to you?" Domingo laughed and repeated, "Polite!" He laughed again, then got serious. "Did he say anything about a harpoon?" While he talked, he faced the wall. "One's missing. Was it there when you came by in the morning, sweetheart? Did you notice?" Victoria responded, and he grinned suddenly. "You'd have made a good cop, sweetheart."

After he hung up, Domingo stood, feet apart, his thumbs hooked in the pockets of his good trousers, his blazer open, his tie askew, his eyes studying the harpoons, the couch, the floor.

Noreen looked closely at her husband. "What's bothering you, Domingo? Is it more than the harpoon?"

"Somebody wrenched the harpoon out of the display. See how the edge of the wooden bracket is chipped?" He pointed with two fingers of his right hand, an unlighted cigarette between them.

Noreen leaned over the couch and found the broken-off piece. "You can fix it, can't you?"

Domingo continued as if he hadn't heard. "There was another person here. See the marks on the rug? The rug nap is twisted."

"Not Victoria wrestling with Baby Mingo, was it?"

Domingo grinned. "I don't think so, honey."

"Want to call Meatloaf? Find out if he took it?"

"Not particularly. I'll ask him when I see him at the next selectmen's meeting. I'm in no hurry to talk to him."

~ ~ ~

The whale-watch boat left Vineyard Haven at seven, heading southeast on Nantucket Sound toward Georges Bank. Some twenty people were on board, including several families with small children. The morning sun shone on puffy clouds, the sky was a brilliant blue, and a brisk wind kicked up whitecaps on the Sound.

"We've seen quite a few pods of whales during the last week," the marine mammals student observer announced over the loudspeaker. "We're still too close to the Island, but within the next hour, we should begin to see them. While we cruise out to the whale grounds, there are sodas and hot dogs for sale in the galley. You'll find displays on marine mammals there, too." The loudspeaker gave out a shriek of static. "The first person to spot a whale gets a free cup of coffee. Or, if you're under twelve, a free soda."

There was a general movement of people toward the galley.

The boat headed toward Cape Pogue, a recurved spit at the tip of Chappaquiddick, an island connected to the Vineyard by a narrow sandbar with a lighthouse on the point. The boat's engine thrummed; the wake curled behind them.

A trail of seagulls followed, diving after small fish stirred up by the boat's passing, arguing raucously over their catch.

A cluster of children in orange life vests stood on tiptoe on the anchor in the bow so they could look over the railing.

The bow dipped into a wave and sent a spray of salt water high into the air, and a bright rainbow sparkled, then faded.

"Mama! I see a whale!" a small girl with a baseball cap on backward called out.

"A whale, a whale!" The children pointed and looked around for their parents.

The skipper had already slowed the boat. Ahead and off to port, barely visible to the naked eye, was a large floating object. It dipped beneath the surface for several seconds and rose again, turning slowly in the current.

"Ladies and gentlemen, there is something to the port, or left side, of the boat," the announcer said over the loudspeaker. "It's unusual to see a whale this close to the Island, but maybe today's our lucky day."

The boat eased closer and whitecaps slapped against the bow.

"That's no whale," a man in a purple-and-green windbreaker growled. "Looks more like a dead cow."

The children stood on tiptoe on the anchor, holding the flat varnished railing to lift themselves higher.

The bow rose toward the sky, then slapped a wave, and the boat shuddered.

The cowlike object sank beneath the surface again, and the skipper slowed the boat to bare headway as they neared the place they had last seen it. Suddenly, it popped to the surface again, close by, and revolved slowly.

A woman screamed.

"Holy shit!" A man leaned over the rail. "A corpse!"

"Get back, kids. Get away from the bow." The mate scrambled down from the pilothouse and herded the children into the galley. "Come on, kids, free soda, on the house."

The floating corpse turned slowly in the current. Protruding from its swollen belly was the shaft of a harpoon. The corpse was bloated and green, barely recognizable as once human. Fishes, gulls, and crabs had eaten away at its flesh. An almost-intact windbreaker drifted around it like a translucent caul. As the waves washed over it, the windbreaker wafted gently, making the hideous corpse seem to have a vestige of life.

The captain's voice came over the loudspeaker.

"Ladies and gentlemen. My apologies for the delay. The Coast Guard is on its way, and we will resume the whale watch as soon as they get here."

"I wanna go home!" a little girl in pink-and-lavender jeans and matching T-shirt wailed.

The whale-watch boat, idling broadside near the floating corpse, pitched and heaved with an oily circular roll.

"1 feel sick, Mommy!" a small boy with his jeans hiked up almost to his chest cried.

In a short time, the flashing blue strobe lights of a Coast Guard cutter appeared in the distance from the direction of Woods Hole, and within minutes it pulled alongside.

The radio in the pilothouse crackled with instructions. The blue light on the Coast Guard cutter rotated. One vessel rose on the crest of a wave; the other dropped into a trough. The sky was the only stable fix, and that seemed to move in a crazy circle.

"Do we have a consensus in favor of returning to Vineyard Haven?" the student observer asked.

Passengers lined up at the rail to watch the Coast Guard crew, in orange life vests, bring the corpse next to the cutter.

"Complimentary passes for another day's trip will be available at the office when you disembark," the voice on the loudspeaker said.

The boat rolled from side to side. Its bow dipped toward the whitecaps and cycled toward the sky.

"I'm gonna throw up, Daddy!" cried a boy in tan shorts and green T-shirt printed with "Llamas Are Llovely."

The port side rolled into a wave trough, lifted, rolled toward the sky. A deck chair skidded to one side, then back to the other with a metallic scrape.

"I don't feel so good, Mommy!" a boy with greenish freckles on an even greener face said.

"Get over to the other side of the boat, quick!"

The railing lifted toward the sky, dropped toward the water. The boat rolled; its bow corkscrewed.

"Jesus, I just had these pants cleaned."

When the whale-watch boat returned to the harbor, earlier than scheduled, Victoria was walking along the beach near the harbor entrance, flicking over mats of seaweed with her walking stick, looking for shells and lucky stones. She glanced up in surprise. It was too nice a day for the trip to have been canceled because of weather. None of the passengers seemed to be smiling. Instead of laughter, or at least the sound of voices over the engine noise, there was an uneasy silence.

Victoria hustled back to the harbor master's shack as fast as she could move, along the beach, up the steep wooden steps that led to the top of the low bluff, holding the railing tightly. She walked through the parking lot, lifting her feet so she wouldn't trip, and stepped onto the catwalk that led to the shack.

By the time she reached the shack, the whale-watch boat was tied up to the bulkhead where the passenger ferry usually docked.

Elizabeth was standing on the deck outside the shack, looking toward the boat, her hands in the pockets of her shorts, her feet slightly apart.

She greeted Victoria. "Did you hear what happened?" Passengers were walking slowly down the gangplank, not looking around the way debarking passengers usually did.

"Something serious, from the look of it," Victoria said.

"They found a body."

Victoria sat down on the bench to catch her breath. "In the Sound?" she asked. "Anybody local?"

"Nobody knows yet. The body has been in the water a couple of days. They know it was a man, but that's about all."

"Was it a fisherman?"

"I don't think they can tell, Gram."

"I suppose he wasn't wearing a life jacket." Victoria shook her head. "Accidents happen so quickly on a boat."

"This wasn't an accident." Elizabeth looked down at her feet and thrust her hands more deeply into her pockets. "Somebody killed him."

"How could they tell?" Victoria continued to shade her eyes with her hand as she studied Elizabeth.

"The weapon was still in the body," Elizabeth said.

"Weapon?" Victoria said blankly.

"A harpoon," Elizabeth replied finally. "He was harpooned."

Victoria stood up abruptly, and the bench fell against the side of the shack. "Harpooned? Are you sure?"

"I listened to the whole thing on the marine radio. The whale-watch boat found the body and called the Coast Guard. I heard the whole thing in detail."

"I've got to call Domingo." Victoria stepped over the high sill into the shack and reached for the wall phone. "I've got to let him know immediately."

"He probably knows already," Elizabeth said, following her grandmother into the shack. "He and Noreen have a scanner."

"Not a marine radio, though," Victoria said as she dialed. "I don't believe they can pick up ship-to-ship transmissions."

It took several rings before Domingo answered sleepily. "Yas," he said.

"You were napping," Victoria said.

Domingo yawned. "What is it, sweetheart?"

"They found your harpoon," Victoria said.

"What are you talking about?" Domingo's voice was instantly alert. "Where? Who's 'they'?"

Victoria told him what Elizabeth had said.

"I'll be right there. No idea whose body it is?"

"Elizabeth said it had been in the water several days."

By the time Domingo arrived at the harbor in Ernesto's truck, the passengers from the whale-watch boat had left. Elizabeth repeated what she'd heard on the marine VHF radio. Domingo paced back and forth on the deck in front of the shack.

"The Coast Guard will take the body to Falmouth," he said almost to himself. "I'll find out from the state police whose body it is, when they identify it. Two killings in two weeks."

"You think they're related?" Victoria was sitting on the bench again, her back to the shingled wall, wearing her straw hat. The yellow ribbons drifted around her. She pulled down the brim to shade her eyes, then rubbed her neck.

Domingo paced back and forth before he answered. "I don't like to speculate," he said.

~ ~ ~

CHAPTER TWELVE

In Custody

"MINGO. You don't mind if I come in." A statement, not a question. Police Chief Medeiros, creased motorcycle pants tucked into polished leather boots, a shiny Sam Browne belt across his slightly bulging uniform shirt, slid the door open and strode in, a uniformed patrolman behind him. The visor of the chief's garrison cap was pulled low on his brow, touching the rims of his reflective sunglasses, its flat top bent sharply up in front. His glance stopped at the display rack.

"I see you're missing one of your harpoons." The chief set his knuckles on his hips near the gun on his belt, arms akimbo.

"Yas." Domingo had come from the kitchen when the chief entered. He stood at the top of the step and waited.

The patrolman slid the door shut behind him.

"Hate to do this, Mingo, but I'm taking you in."

"May I ask why?"

"You know why." The chief moved his feet apart with a thump.

"Why don't you tell me?"

"We found your harpoon, Mingo."

"Mind telling me where you found it?" Domingo said.

"Don't play dumb with me." The chief stepped closer to Domingo, hands still on his hips.

Domingo stared at the reflective lenses of the chief's sunglasses and saw himself.

"Funny guy, aren't you, Mingo," the chief said. "The Coast Guard found it. Rather, a bunch of whale-watchers found it."

"Oh?"

"Real pleasant thing for kids to find. Real pleasant." The chief lowered his arms, held them slightly away from his sides. "Come along, Mingo."

"You're not taking me anywhere until you tell me what you're talking about."

"They found the body, Mingo. The body. With your harpoon stuck in its gut."

Domingo stared at his reflection in the chief's glasses. "Whose body was it?"

"You know goddamned well who it was, Mingo." The chief rocked onto his toes and loomed over the shorter man.

"Tell me anyway."

"Your good friend, Mingo. That's who it was." The chief rocked from his toes to his heels and back to his toes. "Meatloaf."

"Meatloaf," Domingo said. "You think I had something to do with it?"

"Riiight. We think you had something to do with it."

"And you're taking me to the Dukes County House of Corrections on suspicion, right?"

"Riiight again, Mingo," the chief said. "You coming along of your own volition? Or do we take you in?"

"Let me tell my wife."

"Go with him, Bobby." The chief nodded to the patrolman, his sunglasses fixed on Domingo. "Don't try anything funny, Mingo."

"Yeah, sure." Domingo turned his back on the chief and went through the kitchen to find Noreen.

~ ~ ~

Elizabeth and Howland were working in the harbor master's shack when the news came over the scanner that Chief Medeiros was taking Domingo into custody for Meatloaf's murder.

"So!" Howland looked up from the computer. "The whale-watch corpse was Meatloaf's. That figures."

"What do you mean by that?" Elizabeth turned in her chair to stare at Howland. "Domingo couldn't have killed Meatloaf. He and Noreen were off-Island for Joe's funeral."

"Joe?" Howland questioned.

"His partner when he was a New York cop."

By now, everyone on the Island knew about the whale-watch discovery, and everyone knew about the harpoon. Before long, everyone would know whose body it was, and everyone would know Domingo had been arrested on suspicion of murder.

"They'll have him out soon enough." Howland moved a pile of receipts next to him and began to enter data into the computer. "As soon as he can verify where he's been the past few days, they'll release him."

The catwalk swayed, and Elizabeth looked up, to see the skipper of one of the fishing boats docked in the harbor. She went to the window, tugging down her shorts as she did.

"Here's my monthly dockage check." The fisherman opened an atlas-size checkbook, signed a check with a flourish, tore it out of the book, and handed it to Elizabeth. "What's happening with the boss? Hear he harpooned Meatloaf."

Elizabeth shook her head. "No way."

"If he needs defense money, legal fees, you know, there are a bunch of us ready to contribute."

"Thanks. I'll tell him." Elizabeth stamped the back of the check and put it in the drawer.

"Tell him he's done the Island a service." The fisherman gave her a kind of salute, fingertips touching the visor of his cap.

Elizabeth slapped the windowsill. "He didn't do it!"

The fisherman grinned at her. "Whatever you say, lady." She slammed the window shut and went back to the desk.

"Ghoul," she muttered.

"Who had access to the harpoons?" Howland asked her.

"Everyone. They don't lock their doors unless Domingo's taking a siesta." She put away the receipt book. "By the way, do you know anything about the broken railing?"

"What broken railing?"

"On the far side of the shack. It's broken off, splintered."

"Let's take a look."

They stepped onto the deck and around to the side facing the Sound, where the railing was hidden by the shack.

"Someone could get hurt on those jagged ends." Elizabeth braced her hands on either side of the gap in the railing and examined the fresh break.

"Looks as if someone's already been hurt." Howland knelt on the deck and examined it. "Looks like blood on the broken end. As if someone grabbed at it and got a fistful of splinters."

"I'll bet it was those dock attendants. They're like animals, always throwing punches and wrestling."

"Strange. Very strange." Howland leaned out over the water, holding the unbroken part of the railing for support as he examined the back side.

"What are you thinking?" Elizabeth stood up straight, her hands braced on the flat top rail, and watched Howland.

"I'm not sure what I'm thinking. An idea came to me, and I lost it again."

"Something to do with this broken section?" Elizabeth moved away from the gap and leaned against the side of the shack.

Howland nodded. "It couldn't have been the kids."

"Why not?"

"They're not heavy enough, any of them."

"Even if one gave a good shove?"

Howland shook his head. "Something heavy went through this."

"Like what?" Elizabeth tilted her head. "A Harley-Davidson? I mean, you don't get something heavy down the catwalk unless it's on wheels, or walks." She stopped. "Or walks," she repeated.

"Yeah," said Howland.

"Someone big and heavy." She pushed herself away from the side of the shack. "Like Meatloaf."

"Yeah." Howland got to his feet and faced her.

Elizabeth looked down and saw a school of small fish swimming around the pilings, nibbling microscopic food that washed past. She could see the bottom through the clear water.

"The whale-watch boat found his body somewhere around Cape Pogue." Howland indicated the water eddying around the pilings. A long streamer of seaweed wafted toward the channel that led into the Sound. "If he'd been killed here before the tide turned, the current would have carried his body out."

Elizabeth started toward the shack door, then stopped abruptly and turned to Howland. "You know, the night we found Bernie Marble's corpse, Domingo remarked that the tide was about to change." She gazed across the harbor, past the channel, past the osprey pole, to the dock on the far side.

Howland, one hand on the unbroken section, waited.

Elizabeth continued after a pause. A breeze lifted her hair, flicked the collar on her shirt. "The chief said something that seemed odd at the time." She jammed both hands in her pockets.

"What did he say?" Howland asked sharply.

"Something like, 'What bad timing.' Words to that effect."

"Possibly referring to finding Bernie's body before the tide carried it out of the harbor?" Howland said almost to himself. "Two murders, almost the same. Kill the guy, dump the body in the harbor on an outgoing tide."

"The railing seems like such blatant evidence," Elizabeth said. "Whatever happened must have been on the spur of the moment."

"Whoever did it would hardly be likely to fix it," Howland said. "Of course, it took several days for us to notice it."

"Domingo would have seen it right away. This is where he comes to pee when no one's looking."

Howland ignored her and looked again at the underside of the railing. "What possible connection did Meatloaf have to Domingo's harpoon?" He peered into the water.

"Meatloaf was supposed to stop by Domingo's with some papers the day after the call about Joe."

"That would give Meatloaf access to it. But how did it end up in him?" Howland rubbed his chin. "It throws suspicion on Domingo, whether we like it or not. Do we know he was off-Island?"

"Of course we do," Elizabeth said hotly. "If Domingo is going to murder someone, it won't be with his own harpoon."

Howland changed the subject. "We need to make some kind of temporary repair to the railing."

"I've got some yellow tape." Elizabeth stepped inside and opened one of the desk drawers. "Until Domingo gets out of jail, I guess I'm in charge. I'll call the town maintenance guy."

Once they had strung the fluorescent yellow tape across the gap in the railing, Howland returned to the computer, and Elizabeth made her phone call.

"They'll have someone here first thing tomorrow." She picked up the stack of receipts and dealt them into separate piles.

After a few minutes, Howland said, "Meatloaf had plenty of enemies, but he also had some allies."

"Victoria thinks Meatloaf killed Bernie. Do you suppose the same person killed them both?" Elizabeth paused to look over her shoulder at Howland.

"Could be. Same modus. Violent death by a nasty weapon. Both bodies in the harbor. Meatloaf worked with Bernie at the hotel. There may be some connection we don't know about." Howland continued to enter data while he talked.

"At least we won't have to worry about my grandmother anymore. She was convinced Meatloaf was following her."

Elizabeth went back to the receipts, dealing them onto piles on the desk.

"He probably was." Howland was quiet for a few minutes. The computer keys clicked softly. Finally, he said, "We have all the more reason to worry about Victoria. Meatloaf was probably trying to frighten her. He didn't try to harm her."

"My grandmother isn't about to be frightened by some bully."

"They know that now. Next, they're likely to try to stop her from talking, period." Howland shifted the monitor slightly to shade it from the glare coming off the water.

"Who is 'they'?" Elizabeth asked. "Victoria thinks Meatloaf and the chief were in cahoots."

"Quite possibly." Howland tilted his head at the screen. "She likes Rocky and Liz Tate."

He shook his head without looking at her. "Bad choice."

"She has her doubts about you. Your chocolate caper really threw her."

"I know." Howland leaned back in his chair.

"Don't lean in that chair. It can't take it."

He set the front two legs back on the floor with a thunk.

"What is your problem, anyway?" Elizabeth said. "You think Domingo is faking the funeral trip. That Domingo killed Meatloaf with his own harpoon. You suspect Rocky of poisoning Victoria. Did you test the chocolates? Feed them to your white mice?"

"Very funny."

"So what did you do with the poisoned chocolates?"

"There was nothing wrong with them." He looked over at her, hands still held above the keyboard.

"What a surprise. How did you determine that?" Elizabeth had turned in her chair to face him.

"I sent them to the lab for tests." He continued to stare at the computer screen, hands above the keys.

"Lab?" Elizabeth said. "What lab?"

"The FBI lab in Washington."

"What?" Elizabeth gathered up the unsorted receipts and stood up. "The FBI lab?" She stared at him. "Not just anybody can get the FBI lab to test a box of chocolates on a whim."

Howland said nothing. He stared at the screen.

"I've known you since I was a little kid and you were a big wheel in college. But I have no idea what you've been up to since then. I used to watch you play softball in Doane's pasture. I had such a crush on you. I must have been six."

Howland smiled. "You were a cute kid. I remember you with bare feet and a dirty freckled face. You still look the same."

"I haven't seen much of you for the past twenty years. Almost thirty years?" Elizabeth wrinkled her nose. "I don't even know what you do for a living."

Howland said nothing.

"I figured you retired early. On investments or something," Elizabeth said. "I mean, you don't spend valuable time designing a computer program for free out of the goodness of your heart. If you have to earn a living, that is."

Howland smiled. "Domingo thinks it will earn me a million dollars."

"But you don't. So how do you make your living?" Elizabeth continued to stare at him, one hand holding the receipts, the other hand clenched in a fist on her hip. "What are you, anyway?"

Howland pushed his chair back, and the metal legs grated against the sandy floor. Elizabeth winced at the sound.

He reached into his back pocket, brought out a black leather folder, and flipped it open. On one side was a gold badge, on the other an ID photo. Elizabeth took the folder and studied it.

"DEA." She looked from the badge to Howland and back at the badge. "Drug Enforcement Administration? What does this mean? What are you doing here? Does Domingo know about this?"

"No." Howland stood with his hands at his sides.

"Why not? He's a cop. A retired cop." She handed the folder back to Howland, who put it in his pocket.

Howland said nothing.

"Why not?" Elizabeth insisted. "Why tell me and not him?"

"I wasn't sure I could trust him, that's why."

"Why trust me and not him?" Elizabeth glared at him.

Howland averted his eyes. "You don't fit the profile."

"Profile!" Elizabeth sputtered. "Profile! Domingo's a mouthy black guy who puts on a dumb act, so he fits your profile?" Her face reddened, her freckles stood out on her nose. "I'm not a suspected drug pusher, but Domingo is, because of your profile?"

"Hey." Howland put up both hands as if to ward her off. "Profiles are a valid place to start. Otherwise, the list of persons suspected of drug trafficking would be unwieldy."

"My God! You sound like a bureaucrat. 'Unwieldy' indeed. You're talking about human beings."

"Exactly," Howland said. "Traffickers destroy human beings, fry their brains, impoverish them." He thrust his hands into his pants pockets. "And you're in a dither because we narrow down a list of suspects by using a profile? You think we're trespassing on people's rights? Get real, Elizabeth."

" 'Get real'?" Elizabeth flung the pack of receipts she had been holding at Howland. "Get real yourself, you fascist!" Receipts flew onto the counter, splayed out on the floor. One landed on Howland's shoe. He wriggled his toe, and the receipt slid off. Elizabeth wrenched the door open. A gust of wind coming through it tossed the papers into the air, spiraled them down onto the floor in a blizzard of receipts.

She turned. "Fascist!" she said again, and slammed the door behind her. She pounded down the catwalk.

Allison was coming up the catwalk toward her, and Elizabeth brushed past her, spinning her around. Allison was wearing a knit orange halter that exposed her navel, the pierced flesh sporting a gold ring. Her ragged cutoff jeans exposed as much bare skin as a bikini bottom. Elizabeth didn't see her.

"Hey!" Allison said. "What do you think you're doing?"

"Get lost," Elizabeth snapped.

Allison watched, wide-eyed, as Elizabeth got into her car, started it, and skidded out of the lot. Allison flipped her long curls out of her face with one hand and opened the shack door.

"What's with her?" she said to Howland, who was standing in the middle of the floor.

Howland focused on her suddenly. He pointed to the receipts strewn around the shack. "Pick those up," he ordered.

"Hey!" Allison said.

"Pick them up," Howland said again.

"You're not my — "

Howland turned on her. "Do it."

"But it's not my — "

He glared at her.

"Okay, okay. I'll pick them up." Allison knelt on the floor and gathered up the loose receipts, scooped them off the counter, and evened them on the desktop.

"Get busy," Howland growled. "Sort."

"But — "

"Sort!"

She sat at the desk, her back to Howland, and fiddled with the receipts. He worked furiously at the computer. The only sounds were the soft clicking of his keyboard, the gurgling of the water around the pilings, the cry of the osprey returning to its nest, and the hum of a boat engine in the distance.

After some minutes, Allison turned and said, "I just stopped by to see how Mr. D is doing. I heard about him being picked up, you know?"

"What do you care about Mr. D?" Howland said curtly. "As I recall, you have a suit pending against him."

"Mr. D didn't do anything funny. He just yelled at me."

"Tell it to the judge."

"My aunt Liz filed it. I told her it wasn't nothing." She bent her head over the piles on the desk. "She made me sign it."

"Yeah, yeah," Howland said. "Sort the receipts."

"Am I getting paid for doing this? I'm not supposed to work today, you know?"

"No," Howland said. "Tell that to your auntie."

"Her and me don't get along too good," Allison said. "I don't tell her much." She worked quietly for a few minutes. "Who's in charge of the harbor today? Mr. D is in jail, and Elizabeth looks as if she just quit. You in charge?"

"Ask your auntie," Howland said grimly.

~ ~ ~

CHAPTER THIRTEEN

Darkening Skies

VICTORIA stopped in front of the Harbor House, perspiring and out of breath. She could see Domingo across the water, leaning over the rail of the shack, smoking. By the time she reached the end of the catwalk, he was waiting for her.

"I don't know when I've been so hot." Victoria flapped the sides of her light jacket to air herself. "Where's Elizabeth?"

"She's not here yet." Domingo flicked his cigarette into the water and offered her his arm, which she took.

"I really came to hear about your prison experience."

"That's the first time I have ever been locked up. It's not something I want to do again, sweetheart."

"It's such a nice jail." Victoria stopped to catch her breath. "Whew! It's muggy. How do you manage to look so cool?"

Domingo raised his eyebrows quizzically. His shirt was rumpled. Sweaty dark patches stuck to his back and under his arms. "Cool?" He pulled his shirt away from his stomach.

Across the Sound, thunderheads were building over the mainland, their tops towering into the sky, flattened by winds aloft. The heavy cloud bottoms were dark and ominous.

"Not many jails are white clapboard like ours," Victoria continued. "Black shutters, pink roses growing on a wrought-iron fence. It's really quite a lovely jail."

"It's a place of incarceration." Domingo stood aside at the door to let her enter first. "A long time ago, I had a career choice: Be a crook and get rich or — "

"You'd have made a good crook."

"Or become a cop. Cops usually don't get locked up. I didn't want to get locked up again, ever."

"Does the chief think you murdered Meatloaf?" Victoria sat in one of the aluminum chairs and fanned herself with a "Say No to Drugs!" pamphlet that was lying on the desk.

"The chief suspects I used my own harpoon because no one would think

I could be that stupid. He's convinced I conjured up an alibi. Joe, my partner, shot and killed." Domingo crossed himself, looked skyward, and changed the subject abruptly. "Your buddy shared the holding cell with me."

"My buddy?" Victoria stopped fanning herself.

"Dojan."

"What was he doing in jail?"

"They picked him up for creating a disturbance. Dojan was doing a war dance in the middle of Circuit Avenue. Traffic couldn't get around him."

"Instead of tossing him into jail, why didn't they simply escort him to the sidewalk? He's such a gentle person."

A muggy breeze eddied through the open door. Victoria ran her hand around the back of her neck. "Think what it must be like on the mainland. I hope we get a thunderstorm soon."

"They're calling for heavy showers later this evening." Domingo studied the clouds building over the mainland. "The police tried, unsuccessfully, to escort Dojan out of the middle of the street. In fact, several officers were on the scene. Dojan took exception to their escorting him. He blackened a few eyes and noses, loosened a few teeth, broke a couple of ribs, and, in general, left a trail of other people's blood behind him."

"Something must have upset him."

"I believe he'd stopped at the Sand Bar." Domingo stepped to the door, his thumbs hooked in his pockets. The surface of the harbor was an oily calm; the air felt heavy. Cicadas shrilled on the shore and the osprey soared high over the nesting pole.

"I didn't think he drank."

Domingo turned to her. "He doesn't." He shrugged, walked to the end of the deck, and turned. His glance stopped at the broken railing festooned with yellow tape. "What happened here?"

"Elizabeth said they were supposed to have fixed it. She was going to ask if you knew."

Domingo leaned down and inspected the splintered ends. "I have a good idea about what happened." He checked his watch. "Where is she?"

"What time is it?"

"Three-thirty. She was scheduled for three." He paced the small deck. "She's a half hour late."

"I wonder if she had car trouble."

"She can always get to a phone." Domingo paced. "Did she say anything about a meeting? Or errands? Getting her car fixed? That VW of hers is a piece of junk."

"She didn't say anything to me about being late."

"Call home, sweetheart. See if she's left." He handed the telephone to Victoria, who dialed and let it ring several times. The answering machine picked up.

"No answer." Victoria handed the phone back to him. "Was she coming directly from home?"

Victoria shook her head. "I have no idea."

"What route does she usually take to get here?"

"It varies," Victoria said. "Usually, she goes past the airport."

Domingo tugged the visor of his cap down over his brows. "I'm calling Chief O'Neill. Have her check your house." He took down the telephone book that was hanging on a string under the phone, wet his finger, and paged through the W listings.

"West Tisbury Police Department," he mumbled to himself. He held the phone book at arm's length, grunted, then tugged his glasses out of his pocket and set them on his nose. "I'll ask her to see if they spot your granddaughter on the road."

"This isn't like her at all." Victoria stood to get a better view of the road and the cars on it. "She hates being late."

Domingo dialed.

"Wait, Domingo, I think I see her car now." Victoria stepped out onto the deck.

Domingo slammed the phone back on the wall. "She'd better have a good excuse." He looked at his watch.

When Elizabeth came up the catwalk, her face was flushed. Her usually crisp shirt was rumpled and soiled. Domingo met her at the door of the shack, his thumbs hooked on his pockets.

"Well?"

"Am I glad to be here!"

"What happened?" Victoria said. "We were worried."

Elizabeth pushed past Domingo, went into the shack, and flopped into a chair. "I've had a horrible afternoon, so far. It can't get any worse."

"This had better be good." Domingo leaned his elbows on the railing. He pushed his cap back on his forehead and glared through the door at Elizabeth.

"I got held up by a bunch of small accidents. First, there was a big branch down in the drive that I had to move. Then I skidded on a patch of oil on Barnes Road, turned a hundred and eighty degrees. Fortunately, there was no traffic coming the other way."

"How frightening," Victoria said.

"Then the road was blocked by a pickup with two flat tires."

"You might have called," Domingo said.

Victoria was aware of the sound of water below them, swishing past the pilings of the shack.

"I thought I'd better get here as soon as I could. The nearest public phone is almost at the harbor, anyway."

Domingo looked steadily at Elizabeth. "Interesting." He glanced from Victoria to Elizabeth. "I'm calling in an extra dock attendant to be on duty tonight. I don't like what's going on."

"I don't have any problem handling the evening shift," Elizabeth said defensively.

"I'm sure you don't. But until this is over, I don't want you working alone at night." Domingo stepped over the sill and checked the list of phone numbers posted on the wall.

Elizabeth snorted. "Thanks a whole lot."

"Where is Howland?" Victoria asked Domingo. "Couldn't he come in tonight?"

Domingo dialed a number, and while it was ringing he muttered to Victoria, "Howland went on a business trip." He turned back to the phone and spoke to someone.

"Allison is coming in shortly." He hung up the phone.

"Liz Tate's niece?" Victoria had been fanning herself with the pamphlet again, but now she stopped. Domingo nodded.

"She's the last person I want working with me on the night shift." Elizabeth went inside and flipped through some papers on the desk, her back to Domingo. Her shoulders were stiff and straight. "I don't like her. I don't trust her."

"Tough." Domingo's jaw was set. "She'll be here in a half hour. Your grandmother and I are going to the jail."

Victoria got to her feet. "To visit Dojan," she said.

When Elizabeth looked up in surprise, Domingo explained about the war dance.

She laughed. "It's not funny, I know. But I can just see him with his hair and eyes and skull scarf and feathers."

"I'd like to take something to him," Victoria said to Domingo. "Maybe candy."

Domingo nodded and turned to Elizabeth. "I'll be by later."

After he and Victoria settled into the leather seats of the white Corniche, hot from baking in the closed car, he turned on the air conditioner and a blast of hot air blew around them.

"Let's put the top down. I'd much prefer hot fresh air to that hot recycled stuff." Victoria fastened the yellow ribbon of her hat under her chin, as Domingo obliged. Hazy sunlight poured into the open car.

They stopped at the store, and Domingo returned with a bag of candy. "That should hold him." He handed the paper sack to Victoria, who opened it, looked in, and smiled.

They turned right onto the shore road and followed the curve of low bluffs facing Nantucket Sound. The water was bright turquoise in the eerie light of building storm clouds. Sailboats, all headed for shelter, dotted the Sound, moving slowly in the light breeze. Victoria saw an occasional flicker of lightning in the roiling tops of clouds that billowed upward and outward, and she could hear a distant grumble of thunder. A fishing smack, its net spreaders high in the air, chugged toward Georges Bank, trailed by a flock of seagulls.

Most of the large shingled summer houses that faced the water had been converted to inns and bed-and-breakfasts. On the large porches, wooden rocking chairs sat empty. As they passed, Victoria could see flickering television screens inside the houses.

"Why on earth do they spend their vacation watching TV?"

Domingo shrugged. "There's a game on."

"You'd think they could stay home in their New York apartments for that."

"They wouldn't be on Martha's Vineyard if they stayed home. They're vacationing with the president."

A car came toward them in the opposite lane; the driver lifted his hand from the wheel, and Domingo did the same. Victoria held the top of her straw hat and waved, too, ribbons fluttering as Domingo accelerated and the Rolls made its own breeze.

"Who was that?" Victoria asked.

"I have no idea." Domingo grinned.

They passed the golf club where the president would play. A car was parked by the side of the road, and a man sat next to it in a beach chair, earphones shutting him off from the sounds around him.

"Secret Service." Domingo lifted his hand from the wheel as they drove past, and the man raised his hand in return. "Aren't you going to wave to him?" he said.

The road ran along the slender barrier bar that separated Sengekontacket Pond from the Sound and formed the bathing beach Islanders called "the Bend," a smooth arc of white sand that sloped gently into the sheltered waters of the Sound. Usually, the water shaded from transparent yellow, to green, then to deep blue. Today, though, the water was an almost tropical aqua, contrasted against the blackening sky over the mainland.

As they passed, bathers were gathering up towels and children and hurrying up paths that cut through patches of thorny wild roses to cars that were parked in an almost-solid line along the road. Even this late in the season, the roses were in bloom, some white, some red. The darkening sky accentuated the bright colors of roses and water and beach umbrellas, which bathers were rapidly taking down as the building clouds covered more and more of the northern sky.

They crossed Anthiers Bridge, which spanned one of the tidal outlets from Sengekontacket Pond. The bridge had been a setting for the movie *Jaws* more than twenty-five years earlier. Victoria and Jonathan had been extras in the movie, as had most of their friends and neighbors. Their scene had been filmed on a chilly, bright June day, and, Victoria recalled, Jonathan had gotten a painful sunburn on his insteps. She thought of Jonathan and the filming of *Jaws* every time she crossed Anthiers.

As they approached Edgartown, the slender beach widened, and the waters of Sengekontacket on their right shoaled into a broad salt marsh. Scrub oak and pine closed in on the left. They reached the outskirts of town, went past the A&P and Cannonball Park.

The jail was on Main Street, near the end of the West Tisbury — Edgartown Road, in the block before the house in which Victoria had been born. The white clapboard jail building blended in with the town's tidy architecture. Domingo parked behind it.

They went up the brick walk to the jail entrance.

Inside, the jail looked much more the way Victoria thought it should, dark and barred, with locked doors and a uniformed jailer with a gun.

"How ya doing, Mingo?" The jailer greeted him as if he were an old friend. "Long time no see." He laughed heartily and slapped Domingo on the back.

"Yo, Elmo." Domingo put his hand on the larger man's shoulder. Elmo gave Victoria a fistful of papers. She seated herself in an institutional metal armchair and signed where Elmo told her to.

Domingo gave Elmo the paper bag. "For Dojan," he said.

"Mars bars. Milky Ways. Snickers." Elmo pawed through the assortment. "Not bad. Three Musketeers. No file?" He laughed at his joke. "I thought you already gave the Injun a box of candy. Some sweet tooth that guy must have."

Victoria, puzzled, looked from Elmo to Domingo, who was standing next to him.

"A box of candy from me? Who brought it?"

"The kid with green hair." Elmo moved some papers onto a high shelf behind him.

"Louie," Domingo said. "One of the dock attendants. Did he say who the candy came from?"

Elmo jerked his thumb toward Victoria. "Her. A box of homemade fudge. The card's here somewheres." He shuffled through a heap of papers on his desk. "Yeah. 'From Victoria Trumbull,' it says." He handed the card to Domingo.

"I didn't send him candy." Victoria stretched her neck to look at the card in Domingo's hand. "And that's not my writing."

"When did he bring the candy?" Domingo handed the card back to Elmo.

"A couple of hours ago. I took it up to him. He didn't want none. Feeling squeamish, he said." Elmo retrieved the forms and the logbook from Victoria, who'd finished writing the required information. "Heavy-duty hangover, if you ask me. He really tied one on."

"Where is the fudge now?" Domingo asked.

"In the rec room. He told the other guys they could have it." Elmo moved behind the high counter again and put the logbook on a shelf next to the barred window.

"Can we get the box back?"

Elmo came out from behind the counter. "Indian giver, huh?" He nudged Domingo. "Get it?" He winked at Victoria. "It ain't evidence, that's for sure. I'll send someone up for it." He called up to the second floor and turned back to Domingo. "Don't want those jailbirds rotting their pretty teeth because of too much sweets here at the country club." A couple of minutes later, a young sandy-haired, acne-faced officer came down to the front desk with the open box. Four pieces of fudge were missing.

"Who ate the candy?" Domingo looked from the box to Elmo.

"What's with you, Mingo?" Elmo said. "There's plenty left for you. He'p yourself."

"Find out who ate the four missing pieces — right away," Domingo said sharply.

"Howie!" Elmo shouted, and the sandy-haired kid clattered down the stairs. "Find out who ate the fudge."

"Sir!" Howie saluted, then turned on his heel. He returned a few seconds later. "Fatso ate three, Jernegan one. If you ask me, those two guys are acting weird, high on something."

"Get the medics here — right away," Domingo barked as if he were still a New York cop. "Call nine-one-one. Call the hospital. Tell Dr. Erickson we have a case of suspected poisoning."

"Come on, Mingo, what in hell's your problem?"

"Do it. Get Fatso and Jernegan ready to go."

"Okay, okay. Druggies, both of them. If she," Elmo said, jerking his head at Victoria, "poisoned them, she should get a medal."

"Call the sheriff. Tell him to treat this box of candy as evidence. It needs to go to the forensics lab." As Elmo stood motionless, Domingo said, "Move!"

When Elmo got off the phone, Domingo said, "I need to speak with Dojan."

He and Victoria followed Howie up the narrow wooden stairs to a long, high-ceilinged room, almost completely taken up by a scarred wooden conference table. Dojan sat at the table, hands in front of him, shaggy head bowed. He looked up when Victoria entered the room, and his bleak expression brightened.

"My friend! You came to see me!"

"How are you?" Victoria put out her hand, and Dojan took it in his grimy paws.

Howie, who had settled into a chair in the hall, scraped the chair back and stood up.

"No contact with the prisoner." He sat down again.

"I don't feel so good," Dojan said.

"I brought you some candy."

Dojan paled and shook his head. "Let the guys have it."

"I need to warn you, Dojan," Domingo said. "Don't eat anything until we get you out of here, not even jail food."

"I'm not hungry."

"And don't tell anyone what you told me this morning." Victoria looked at Domingo in surprise. "What . . ." she started to say. Domingo put his hand on top of hers.

"The spirits got to me." Dojan's eyes were rimmed with red.

"Spirits is right," Domingo said. "Stay away from booze."

"I had to talk with the spirits ..."

"Don't talk to anyone, especially spirits!"

Victoria looked quizzically from one to the other. Howie sat at the doorway, within hearing. He leaned back in the chair, the front legs off the floor, the back against the banister. He began to clean his fingernails with his penknife.

"No one's pressing any charges against you," Domingo said.

"I ... I ..." Dojan looked around, wild-eyed.

"We'll get you out this afternoon, you understand? Don't say anything to anybody. Understand me?"

"Yes." Dojan looked down at his hands. "Yes," he said again.

Victoria put her gnarled hands on top of Dojan's. Howie tipped his chair back onto all four legs with a thump.

Victoria pulled her hands away. "When you get out, will you bring me more lobsters? I want to pay."

"Yes, ma'am." Dojan looked at her bleakly. "I'll bring you lobsters. You don't owe me nothing."

Howie stood, pulling up his uniform trousers by his gun belt, which was dragging them down around his slim hips. "Time's up."

"Take care, Dojan." Domingo rose to his feet.

Dojan's eyes wobbled from Domingo's face to Victoria's. "Maybe sometime you'll show me your boat," Victoria said.

Dojan cracked a small smile. "I can take you out in my boat. I can take you lobstering. You can help me pull my lobster pots."

Domingo's eyes went from Dojan to Victoria. He started to say something, then seemed to think better of it.

"Yes," Victoria said. "I'd like that."

When they were out on the brick walk that led away from the jail, Domingo took her elbow. "You don't want to go out in that leaky bucket of his."

"I don't know why not," Victoria said tartly, her mouth a firm line. "I'm perfectly capable of hauling lobster pots."

"I guess you are," Domingo said. "Yes. I guess you are."

~ ~ ~

When they arrived at the hospital, the ambulance had already pulled up in the emergency room bay. Domingo glanced at the sky and put the top back up on his Rolls. Victoria watched as the EMTs unloaded Fatso and Jernegan from the ambulance, and she and Domingo followed them through the wide doors. Both men were strapped onto wheeled stretchers. A uniformed man stood to one side of the stretchers, and Victoria recognized Howie, the freckle-faced jail attendant.

As they entered the emergency room, Victoria heard an orderly say, "They're both on something, that's for sure."

Fatso was straining to get to a sitting position. His eyes were wide open, and the irises were so huge, Victoria couldn't tell what color they were.

"Let me outta this fucking straitjacket before I beat the shit out of all of youse." Fatso gasped for air, and the straps creaked.

"Chill it, man," the orderly said.

"Jesus Christ, get them fucking spiders offa me!" Fatso screamed and strained against the straps. The stretcher flexed and creaked with his movements.

On the other stretcher, Jernegan, whose eyes were shut, kept gasping in a weak voice, "Water! Water!"

Victoria watched in awe from a safe distance.

Domingo took her arm and led her to the row of seats in the waiting section. "Sit here, sweetheart, until we know what this is all about."

It seemed a long time before Dr. Erickson came out of the examining room. He was shaking his head.

"Domingo, we got to contact their families. They're sick puppies, both of them."

Victoria left the *Vogue* magazine she had been thumbing through on the table next to her seat.

"Are they going to be all right?" She joined Dr. Erickson and Domingo by the examining room's door.

"One probably will. The other" — Dr. Erickson waggled his hand, palm down — "I'm not so sure about." He took off his glasses and slipped them into the pocket of his white lab coat. "We've pumped both stomachs. Flushing them with a weak solution of tannic acid now. Found remains of chocolate in both."

"Any idea what poison?" Domingo reached unconsciously for his cigarettes, and patted his shirt pocket instead.

"We're analyzing stomach contents now, as we speak," Dr. Erickson said. "Don't know yet."

"You got a best guess?" Domingo put his hands in his trouser pockets and paced a couple of steps from the doctor and back again.

"Well ..." Dr. Erickson said, drawing the word out. "Dilated eyes. Rapid pulse. Aggressive behavior. Hallucinations. Thirst. Flushed skin. Could be several things." He unbuttoned his lab coat and put his hands in the pockets of his tan slacks, flipping his coat behind him. "You think it might have been administered in the fudge, eh? Not something they had for lunch that might already be digested?"

"Fudge," Domingo said.

"How long ago?"

"Couple of hours at most."

"Well . . ." Dr. Erickson drew the word out again. "An easy poison to acquire, the right symptoms, same time frame from time of administration to appearance of symptoms would be atropine." He stuck his jaw out and nibbled at his pale mustache with slightly crooked ivory-colored lower teeth.

"Atropine?" Domingo said thoughtfully. "Belladonna. Deadly nightshade."

Victoria made a choking sound and put her hand to her mouth. Domingo stopped his pacing, scowled at her, then turned back to the doctor.

"Easy to acquire?"

"Deadly nightshade grows everywhere on this Island. Every part of it is poisonous — roots, leaves, flowers, berries."

Dr. Erickson glanced at Victoria, who seemed to be about to say something. He continued: "Easy to make an infusion and doctor whatever you want to doctor. Inject it into mashed potatoes. Chop up the berries and mix them into fudge. Add it to someone's drink. Doesn't take much. One berry can be fatal to a child. Surprising it isn't used more."

"They use atropine to dilate eyes for examinations, don't they?" Victoria asked.

"They used to. In minuscule quantities." Dr. Erickson turned to an orderly who'd come out of the examining room. "Yes?"

The orderly looked at Victoria, at Domingo, then back at the doctor.

Outside, the sky had turned a greenish black. Newly planted trees in the small garden outside the waiting room windows whipped back and forth against their supports. The trickle of water in the fountain blew to one side. Leaves and small branches whirled across the grass and pelted the large windows.

"Speak up," Dr. Erickson said. "Problems?"

"The larger man" — the orderly consulted his clipboard — "Medeiros, has lapsed into coma. Vital signs are weak and getting weaker. His heartbeat is loud, but erratic."

"Still flushing his stomach?"

"Yes. It's clear solution."

"Discontinue it. Get their families here immediately."

Rain suddenly began to hammer against the windows. Lightning illuminated the small garden in the courtyard outside. Thunder rattled the windows.

"Medeiros?" Domingo said. "What's his first name?"

The orderly consulted the clipboard again. "Manuel."

Domingo patted his shirt pocket and paced. Victoria stood there, feet slightly apart, her arched-up toe protruding through the hole in her shoe, hands hanging quietly at her sides. Domingo stopped pacing abruptly.

"How old is Medeiros?"

Dr. Erickson consulted the clipboard the orderly held. "Twenty-two."

"Which Medeiros is he?"

"I don't know," Dr. Erickson said. "A hell of a lot of Medeiroses on this Island." He turned to the orderly, who was standing beside him. "The jail will have the number for his folks. Get them here right away."

The lightning flashed. Rain beat against the windows. Thunder crashed. A nurse walked past with a sheaf of green forms in her hand, her shoes squeaking on the linoleum. In the waiting room around the corner, a baby cried. Victoria sat down again and picked up the magazine she'd been looking through. A soft voice came over the speaker, "Dr. Montrowl to Obstetrics. Dr. Montrowl to Obstetrics." The rain slashed outside the windows.

The wide emergency room doors were flung open, and Chief Medeiros strode into the room, yellow foul-weather jacket glistening and dripping rainwater. His boots left wet puddles on the linoleum floor. He threw back the hood of his jacket. His garrison cap was in place, visor straight on his brow, flat top curved sharply up in front. He pulled open his jacket with the ripping sound of Velcro disconnecting.

"What's this all about, Doc?"

Dr. Erickson looked up at the much taller man. "You have a son, Manny?"

"I got a son Manny," the chief said. "In jail at the moment. What's the kid done now?"

Victoria's eyes widened.

Domingo stopped pacing and stared from the chief to Dr. Erickson and back at the chief.

"Bad news," Dr. Erickson said. "Your son is here, and it doesn't look good."

"What happened? He was in jail, safe."

"Suspected poisoning." Dr. Erickson looked down at the floor and rocked onto his toes. "Administered in jail."

"How in hell did he get hold of poison?"

"You'd better see him right away. What about his mother?"

The chief winced. "She's on the West Coast somewhere. She has nothing to do with the kid. Where's he at?"

Dr. Erickson led the chief into the curtained-off examining room. Medeiros's boots squished on the floor. He came out almost immediately.

"He doesn't know me." The chief whirled on Dr. Erickson. "Don't stand there! You, Mingo. Who slipped drugs to him? Who?"

Domingo turned and gazed out the window at the storm pelting the little garden.

The chief glared at Domingo's back. "My kid's a pothead. This isn't pot." He marched back and forth, his boots squishing. "What did you have to do with this, Mingo?"

Domingo said nothing.

The chief turned to Dr. Erickson. "Save that kid of mine, whatever it takes." He poked his forefinger into Dr. Erickson's madras-clad chest.

"We're doing everything we can." Dr. Erickson hunched his shoulders, hands back in the pockets of his chino slacks, lab coat behind him. "We can't do much at this point."

The chief marched back into the examining room and out again.

"Helicopter him to Boston. Get the Coast Guard here. If anything happens to that kid of mine, you'll never practice medicine again. Anywhere. You get me?"

A jagged fork of lightning slammed into the fountain in the patio garden outside the window, turning it for an instant into a fluorescent yellow-green torch. Thunder exploded, rattling windows. A woman in the waiting room screamed and put her hands over her ears. The hospital lights dimmed and went out, then came back on almost instantaneously with the sound of a generator kicking on. Rain beat against the building, slammed the roof, poured down the windows, flowed in wide lakes of water, mud, and gravel across the concrete walkway on the other side of the garden.

A few minutes later, an orderly reported to Dr. Erickson. Victoria heard him say quietly, "The medevac helicopter can't get to the Island. They'd route it through Providence, but the wind is too strong."

"Shit!" The chief slammed his hand onto the admitting desk.

"If the substance he ingested is what I think it is, atropine," Dr. Erickson told the police chief, who was pacing again, "everything that can possibly be done has been done." The chief glowered as he continued. "There's no known antidote. Boston can't save him."

The chief flung off his yellow slicker, threw it onto a chair. It slid onto the floor. Victoria picked it up and put it over the back of the chair. Domingo gazed past the sheet of water that poured off the roof.

Manuel Medeiros had a series of convulsions, one after another, in the emergency treatment room, then straightened out his body, arched his back, gasped, and lay still.

Chief Medeiros was with his son at the end. He laid his hand on his dead son's chest, put his head down, and wept.

~ ~ ~

CHAPTER FOURTEEN

The Warnings

NEITHER Victoria nor Domingo had much to say on the way back to West Tisbury. The death of Chief Medeiros's son was too appalling to discuss. The storm had moved on to the southwest and was now only a distant flicker and rumble in the evening sky. Domingo drove by way of Vineyard Haven. The power was still off and houses and shops were dark; the few streetlights that marked intersections were out. They passed white ComElectric trucks parked by the side of the road. Workers in hard hats conferred with one another, looked up at transformers, pointed to lines.

"I must say, it's pleasant with the electricity off," Victoria said. "I wouldn't mind if they didn't get it back for a few days. There's too much light pollution."

As they drove up the hill by Tisbury Meadow, branches and leaves littered the road. They crossed a wash of sand and gravel, dodging football-size rocks. Near the Chicama Vineyards road, they moved over into the oncoming lane because a downed tree blocked their way.

The sun settled behind the receding storm clouds, and brilliant rays shot high into the clear sky. Scarlet and crimson edged the clouds. As Domingo negotiated Victoria's rutted driveway, the sun set over Doane's pasture, and while they watched, the vivid colors changed to muted rose and purple.

When Domingo opened the door for Victoria, McCavity flipped himself over on his back in the driveway and rolled back and forth, soft belly and paws in the air, eyes closed.

They walked to the kitchen door. In the entry, tucked under a shingle next to the "Welcome Friends" sign, was a yellow paper.

"What's that?" Domingo nodded at the paper.

"The fuel bill." She tugged the yellow slip out from under the shingle. A second folded paper fell onto the brick floor. Victoria picked it up. "Here's a note from someone."

"From Packer's Oil?" Domingo leaned over her shoulder.

Victoria unfolded the paper. "No. It's not signed." She turned it over. "I don't recognize the writing. Let's go inside. I'll turn the light on so we can read it."

"You got a generator?"

Victoria laughed. "I wasn't thinking." She set her pocketbook on the ancient captain's chair inside the door. "I suppose there are advantages to electricity. I'll get candles."

"Where is everybody?" Domingo walked into the living room and back into the kitchen. "The guy in the shack out back?"

"It's not a shack; it's a cottage. He works late."

"What about the artist in the attic. Angelo?"

"He went to Boston this morning to see the exhibit at the Fine Arts Museum." Victoria felt her way through the darkening rooms, reached the front hall, and returned to the kitchen holding two brass candlesticks with stumpy half-burned green candles. "He planned to be back on the afternoon boat, but I'm sure the ferries weren't running in that storm."

Domingo lighted the candles with his Zippo and picked up the paper that Victoria had dropped on the kitchen table.

"Lined paper. From a stenography notebook. Why don't you see what it says before I leave." Domingo walked out into the cookroom, opened the door into the bathroom, looked in, and shut it again.

Victoria held the note so the candlelight illuminated it. She read to herself, then read again.

"What does it say, sweetheart? Read it out loud."

"I can't." She handed the paper to him.

Domingo held the paper in one hand, took his glasses out of his pocket, shook them open, and put them on his nose.

" 'You like what happened to your granddaughter today?' it says. 'Better not recall too much more.' " He glanced up from the paper over his glasses and his dark eyes met Victoria's. He continued to read. " 'She could be number three.' "

" 'Number three'?" Victoria moved her pocketbook to the floor and sat down in the captain's chair.

"I suppose that's a reference to Bernie Marble and Meatloaf." He studied Victoria's solemn face before he continued. "I'm taking this note, if you don't mind." Victoria shook her head. "I want to talk to your police chief." He reached into his pocket for an envelope and examined it briefly. Victoria saw it was from the IRS. He put the note into it, then put the envelope back into his pocket.

"Those accidents that happened to Elizabeth today weren't really accidents, were they?" Victoria leaned against the back of the chair. It had grown dark outside, and the candles made an island of light in the kitchen. Her strong features were accented by light and shadow, her large nose, her deep-set eyes. She stared into the candlelight.

"Not likely," Domingo said. "Someone thinks you're getting too close, afraid you'll recall too much and put it together."

"It's true." Victoria clasped her hands around one knee of her threadbare corduroy trousers. "Things do keep coming back to me." She stared into the flickering candle flames. "I heard a boat that night, too, I'm sure."

"It's more than your good memory, sweetheart. Someone thinks you're onto something."

"But I have no idea what that something is," Victoria said.

"Let me say the same thing to you that I said to Dojan. Don't tell anyone what you remember. They tried to scare you, didn't they, spooky looks and car chases? But they didn't." On the other side of the table, Domingo's dark face blended into the shadows. Only his eyes showed, gleaming in the soft light. "Now they're attempting to hush you up by going after your granddaughter." Domingo walked over to the east door and peered out into the blackness. "They tried to kill Dojan today, and it backfired." Lights from cars passing on the road flashed across the wall, lighting the room briefly before they moved on.

Victoria picked absently at a rough spot on the back of her hand. "Why would anyone want to harm Dojan? He's not a threat to anyone. What do they have against him?"

Domingo turned away from the east door, where he'd been staring out into the darkness. "They have a good reason to get him out of the way. He talked too freely at the jail when I was in the holding tank with him."

Victoria waited for him to explain.

"I'll tell you eventually. It's as well you don't know now."

"For heaven's sake. I'm not a child."

Domingo grinned and his white teeth reflected the candlelight. "No, I guess not." He became serious again. "I'm worried about you and your granddaughter. Whether you like it or not, I want you to stay with me and the wife for a couple of days."

"We don't need to do that." Victoria's jaw was set stubbornly. "Winthrop should be home shortly. And if the boats start running again, Angelo will be home soon, too."

She pushed herself out of the captain's chair and faced Domingo across the candles. "I'm worried about Elizabeth. She wasn't happy about working with Allison tonight."

"No one will try anything as long as Allison stays there."

"Allison is hardly an ally." Victoria stood straight so she could look into Domingo's eyes. "What about her lawsuit?"

"Don't blame her for the lawsuit. It's her aunt's. But I'm more concerned about you right now. I have to talk to your police chief. I also need to check on things at the harbor." He looked out of the east door again. "I hope they get the electricity back, and soon. This is not good."

Victoria watched him for a few moments. "Can they actually carry out a threat against Elizabeth?"

"Sweetheart, we won't let them," Domingo said. "Wonder why they left that note? Stupid of them."

He picked up the phone, held it to his ear, and hung it back up. "Dead. I should have known. Come with me now. I don't want you alone in the house."

"I'll be quite all right," Victoria said testily. "It won't be the first time I've been alone in this house."

"I don't want it to be the last time, either. Get your nightie and toothbrush. And Elizabeth's. You're staying with the wife and me tonight and tomorrow."

"This is a lot of foolishness."

"Three people are dead. Someone is sending you threatening notes. No, this is not foolishness. You're coming with me."

Victoria thought a moment, then shook her head and wrote a note to Angelo or Winthrop, instructions on feeding McCavity.

She carried a lighted candle with her up to the dark bedrooms on the second floor. Domingo waited at the foot of the stairs.

Victoria remembered how, as a child, she used to watch the shadow of the railing progress along the wall when her aunt went downstairs with a candle after she'd tucked Victoria into bed.

She found her small blue Samsonite suitcase in the attic, and then packed her underwear and nightgown and Elizabeth's pajamas.

She set the suitcase down by the kitchen door and Domingo took it out to the car.

When they pulled into the two-car parking lot at the West Tisbury police station, the ducks and geese had hunkered down on the crushed oyster shells, settled for the night, their heads tucked underneath their wings. When Domingo's car lights flashed on them, they untucked their heads, got to their feet, stretched their necks, hissed, honked, and quacked.

The racket brought Chief O'Neill to the door of the police station. She was silhouetted by the light of two small emergency lamps. Behind the station, the generator throbbed. The chief escorted them inside and Victoria sat in the chair in front of her desk. Domingo took off his cap and looked around the small station house, at the two desks, the potbellied stove, the computers, a calendar on the wall that showed fluffy kittens playing with a ball of yarn. He laughed out loud.

Victoria looked questioningly at him.

"I was thinking what my partner Joe would've said if Chief Kelly had hung a kitty-cat calendar in our station house."

The windows that overlooked the Mill Pond were so dark Victoria could see only her own reflection and Domingo's and Casey's in the glass. After a moment, Domingo said, "You heard about Chief Medeiros's son?"

"I heard something on the scanner. What happened?"

"He died at the hospital this afternoon. During the storm."

"No!" Casey said.

"He was in jail. Suspected poisoning."

"What was he doing in jail?"

"DUI and possession of a controlled substance." Domingo leaned forward in the chair and laced his fingers together between his knees.

"He was poisoned by fudge I was supposed to have given to Dojan, who was also in jail," Victoria said.

Casey thumped the end of her pen on the desk. The point of the pen went in and out, in and out as she tapped.

"Is this related to that Oak Bluffs murder?" Casey asked.

"It's gotten more complicated." Domingo took Victoria's note out of his shirt pocket and handed it to the chief.

Casey read the note, frowning.

"It was stuck under a shingle in the entry," Victoria said. "And you don't think it's some crank?"

Domingo shook his head. "Victoria and her granddaughter are staying with the wife and me for a couple of days. Can you keep an eye on her house? Something should break soon."

"As soon as the phones are back, I'll talk with Ben," Casey said. "He misses police work."

Domingo stood and saluted the chief. "I know all about it."

~ ~ ~

The afternoon shift had been busier than Elizabeth expected. A fleet of powerboats had come over from the Padanarum Yacht Club, and the boaters had a hundred requests — liquor store, bar, action, best restaurant, girls, car rentals, hotels. Elizabeth was fed up with powerboats and potbellied men and their doll-women. She didn't want to admit, even to herself, that she resented all the tips Allison was amassing. Twenty dollars, ten, fifty, even a hundred-dollar bill. Allison had made, in one sultry afternoon, more than Elizabeth, her boss, earned in a week. On top of it all, Allison was a sullen brat, and Elizabeth had not wanted to work with her on this shift. Damn Domingo!

She tucked her shirt into her shorts, leaned down and retied the leather laces of her boat shoes, and ran her fingers through her hair.

As the storm clouds billowed out of the north, Elizabeth looked up at the sky with concern. She strode down the ramp to the floating dock, then started up the motor on the harbor master's launch that was tied to the dock.

"Get in," she ordered Allison, who stepped gingerly into the bow, brushed sand and dried seaweed off the seat, and sat.

Elizabeth steered the boat toward the sailboats moored in the center of the harbor. Allison trailed her hand in the water.

"Cut that out," Elizabeth snapped. Allison quickly withdrew her hand and put it in her lap, where it made a wet spot on the thighs of her tan shorts.

"When I get alongside this boat, get aboard and check the bow lines. Take this chafing gear with you." She handed Allison a bundle of thin canvas strips and waxed twine. "Do you have a knife?"

Allison nodded.

"What did you say?" Elizabeth snapped.

"Yes, ma'am."

"Hurry up," Elizabeth said sharply as Allison balanced herself in the launch. "We have a dozen boats to check."

Elizabeth wheeled the launch from one sailboat to another. Allison scrambled aboard each to check lines, double them up where necessary. She replaced the canvas strips that protected lines from the sawing motion of a boat riding on a mooring in wind. Allison worked faster and more surely as the storm clouds moved toward them and the wind picked up. Footing on the boats was treacherous. At one point, Allison caught her finger between the bow of a boat and its mooring line. Elizabeth saw her grab her hand and double up in pain, saw her reach into her pocket, take out a tissue, and wrap it around her bleeding finger. Allison, hair blowing back from her face in the steadily increasing wind, didn't even look at Elizabeth. She continued to knot waxed line around the canvas strip.

They finished checking the moored boats, not speaking to each other, and put the launch away in a slip beside the shack.

"Put extra lines on it," Elizabeth said. "Then let me see your finger."

"It's okay." Allison held her hand behind her back.

As soon as they were inside, Elizabeth opened the first-aid cabinet that hung on the wall next to the radio.

"Let's see it." Allison held out her finger reluctantly. The paper she had wrapped around it was blood-soaked. Elizabeth clipped it off and examined the crushed finger. "It doesn't look too bad. I'll soak it with peroxide and bandage it. You might want to check it with Doc Erickson."

Allison shook her head, then bit her lip as Elizabeth poured the peroxide over her finger.

Elizabeth looked down at her. "The town has medical coverage. If it still hurts tomorrow, you'd better go."

The wind picked up, whirling sand and seaweed and kicking up whitecaps in the sheltered harbor. Elizabeth and Allison went out again, heads down in the wind, and walked rapidly along the bulkhead, moving from one boat to another, checking lines, warning skippers, fending off flirtations. By the time the storm hit, the boats were secure, and they were back in the shack.

Lightning, thunder, and pelting rain assaulted the small building. The usually calm harbor was a furious mass of breaking waves that crashed against the pilings and shook everything. Sailboats on the moorings bucked like terrified horses. The electricity went out, and with it the computers, the lights, and the telephone. Elizabeth picked up the radio mike, but it was dead.

"Shit," she said.

"I brought a flashlight," Allison said. "There's a battery lantern in one of the cabinets."

"Great," Elizabeth said sourly.

"There's a deck of cards. We could play gin," Allison said. "Or hearts."

"How about Go Fish?"

"I know how to play that, too."

"Gin, then," Elizabeth said. "For play money, we can use twenty-dollar bills from the bank bags."

By the time the storm passed, Allison owed Elizabeth more than she'd made in tips that afternoon.

The storm rumbled in the distance and the sun came out. Water dripped from the eaves of the shack and off the deck into the now-calm harbor. The yachters

8

Cynthia Riggs

from Padanarum emerged and wiped off the brightwork and stainless-steel trim of their yachts and laughed and shouted to one another. Elizabeth smelled cigar smoke, heard men talk. The sun dipped behind the storm clouds beyond the osprey pole.

Allison stood up and took her tip money out of her pocket, counting out the bills she owed Elizabeth.

"Forget it," Elizabeth said, waving the money aside. "That was a learning experience. Pick up the mail in town and we'll call it even."

During the storm, the two had reached a sort of truce. "Okay. I'll be back in ten minutes. Fifteen."

"Get us a pizza, if the place is open. I think they cook with gas. Here's some money." Elizabeth opened her wallet.

"It's on me this time," Allison said. "I, like, owe you guys, you know?"

Elizabeth looked at her doubtfully.

"I'm sorry about that lawsuit, you know? I didn't want to file it. Mr. D is okay."

"Yeah?" Elizabeth took a couple of bills out of her pocket. "Pick up the mail. Take this money, not yours. Anything but anchovies for me. We'll talk about it later."

Allison tossed her hair back from her face, left the shack, and disappeared around one of the gingerbread buildings that lined the harbor. Elizabeth wiped off the bench outside the shack and sat down. She watched the brilliant sunset fade. She thought about Domingo being taken to jail, about Dojan's war dance on Circuit Avenue, about her grandmother's hearing Bernie's scream, and their finding his body, about the whale-watch boat finding Meatloaf's body.

She watched the first stars come out in the evening sky. Then she stood, stretched her arms above her head, leaned over and touched her toes, yawned, and went into the shack. She set the battery lantern on the counter and was opening a drawer to see if she could find something she could work on until the electricity came back on when someone knocked on the window frame, startling her. She turned abruptly, stumbled against one of the chairs in the dim lantern light, tripped, recovered herself, and opened the door.

No one was there.

She looked down the length of the catwalk, but it was so dark she couldn't see anything. She stepped out onto the deck and looked. No one was there, either.

"Hello?" she called out into the night.

145

No answer. She went back inside and locked the door.

The window had been opened a crack for air during the storm. She started to slide it wide open when she saw a folded paper wedged into the frame. She tugged it out. The corner, soaked from rainwater accumulated in the frame, ripped off as she worked the paper out.

She unfolded it under the lantern light. She could barely read the writing in the dim light, pencil on lined paper torn from a stenography notebook. Part of the message was on the corner that had torn off in the window. She unfolded it carefully, pieced it together, and smoothed it on the desktop.

"Tell your grandmother she better lay off," the message said. "Or she knows what will happen."

Elizabeth sat down abruptly. That sneaky Allison, she said to herself, just as I was beginning to think I'd misjudged her. What does she think she's doing? Why drag my grandmother into this? She put her elbows on the desk, her chin on her hands, and stared at the paper. It figures, she thought. A kid who wants the attention she'll get from the lawsuit will do anything.

She was so angered by what she figured was Allison's sick joke that she had to work off steam. She found another flashlight in one of the desk drawers, tested it to make sure it worked, slammed the door behind her, locked it, and went out into the night. There wasn't much she could do inside anyway. In the meantime, she could make her rounds of the harbor to see if the storm had caused any major damage.

She walked along the bulkhead and shone her light on the lines tied off on cleats. Candles and kerosene lamps flickered in the cabins of the boats. The Padanarum yachters, whose boats were tied up next to one another, bows out, squared-off sterns facing the bulkhead, were partying on one of the larger cruisers, and as she approached, the noise level grew. She heard drunken male banter, the words indistinct. She heard a woman laugh, and a man's response. Hope they don't decide to go for a ride, she thought. I need Domingo to deal with this.

A large sloop, *Clotho*, its home port Saint Croix, Virgin Islands, had tied up alongside the fuel dock. She could see a kerosene lamp through the porthole. A dock line had frayed, and she reached over the rail and rapped on the side of the cabin.

"Anyone aboard?"

"Righto!" The cabin door opened and a stocky man stepped out into the cockpit, dark against the light from below.

"I'm the assistant harbor master. You need to replace one of your lines." Elizabeth directed her flashlight at it. Several strands had chafed through.

The man swung his legs over the rail and leapt lightly onto the dock. He was several inches shorter than Elizabeth. She noticed he was barefoot and was wearing cutoff jeans and no shirt. She turned her light onto his face. He had sunbleached hair and a full blond beard. He was in his early thirties, younger than she had first thought, about her age.

"Thanks, mate." He pronounced the word *mite*. He took the light and examined the line. "She'll hold tonight. I'll take care of it in the morning. Is there a ship's store around?"

"There's a small one behind the butterfly exhibit," Elizabeth said, waving the flashlight toward that side of the harbor. "It doesn't have everything. I'll run you down to the shipyard in Vineyard Haven tomorrow, if you'd like."

"That's kind of you." He handed the flashlight back to her and leaned his hand against the glossy white side of his boat. "Horace Chadwick's my name." He pronounced it *nime*.

"I'm Elizabeth Trumbull."

He stood up straight and held out a massive hand, twice the size of hers, and they shook.

"Trumbull," Horace mused. "Good name."

"Where are you from?"

"I'm a Kiwi. From New Zealand."

"You're here for about a week, aren't you?"

"At least a week." Horace nodded. "I have personal business to attend to. I've been searching for someone. I won't leave until I've found him."

"Shouldn't be too difficult if he's on the Island," Elizabeth said. "It's a pretty small place, actually."

"He's here, all right."

Above them, the rigging of *Clotho* stood out against the Milky Way. The storm had washed the sky, and the night was clear and bright.

"Did you sail alone from New Zealand?"

"I've been batting around the world for a couple of years. With someone at first." He paused. "Bought this in the Virgin Islands." He gestured behind him at *Clotho*. "Came into a spot of money there. I single-handed it from there."

"As long as you're staying, perhaps you'd like to come to my grandmother's for beans on Saturday night?" Elizabeth asked.

"Beans?" Horace said blankly.

"Boston baked beans for supper on Saturday night. A New England tradition. My grandmother likes to invite all sorts of interesting people."

"That's kind of you."

"She'll feel as if you're practically related. Her grandmother came from Australia."

Elizabeth heard footsteps on the dock and turned. "Nice evening," a man said. "Right," said Horace. "Yes, beautiful," said Elizabeth.

"I'd be delighted to come for beans on Saturday," Horace said when the man had passed. "Shall I bring anything?"

"Bring wine, and I'll pick you up around six."

Before she left to return to the shack, Elizabeth arranged to go with him to the shipyard the next day.

She walked lightly back to the shack, her anger washed away. She'd forgotten about Allison and the letter.

When she returned to the shack, Allison was sitting on the bench outside, a flat pizza box in her hand.

Allison looked up at her. "It's gotten cold. Where were you?"

Elizabeth returned to reality with a nasty thud. "Your note was not amusing." She unlocked the door.

"What note?" Allison got to her feet and went inside, where she laid the box on the table.

"Don't play dumb. It wasn't funny."

"I didn't leave a note, honest." Allison sounded perplexed.

"Here. Let me switch on the lantern." The note lay flat on the desk in a circle of weak light.

"That's not mine," Allison said when she saw it. "It's not even my writing. It's not my paper. It's not mine, honest!"

"You didn't stick this in the window right after you left? You didn't knock on the side of the shack and then run?"

"No. Honest!"

Allison sounded genuinely baffled.

"Here, read it," Elizabeth said.

" 'Tell your grandmother she better lay off. Or she knows what will happen.' What's that all about?" Allison looked up at Elizabeth, whose cheekbones were highlighted by the lantern light below her.

"You have no idea what this is?"

"No. I don't know nothing about it."

"Anything," Elizabeth said, correcting her automatically. She lifted the phone off the wall. "Damn. I forgot the phones are out. I've got to talk to Domingo. Go ahead and eat the pizza before it gets any colder. I'm not hungry."

"I bought us Cokes, too."

"Thanks anyway."

"There wasn't much mail in the harbor box," Allison said. "Stuff for Mr. D, catalogs, ads, memos from the selectmen."

"Put it on the counter. We can look at it later. Don't get pizza on it."

When Domingo and Victoria came up the catwalk, Allison was eating pepperoni pizza, sipping a Coke, and selecting toys from a catalog to match the dock attendants' personalities, and Elizabeth was pacing back and forth inside the shack.

Allison opened the door for them.

"How's it going?" Domingo stepped into the shack behind Victoria.

"She got a note," Allison said, nodding at Elizabeth.

"Note?" Domingo said. "What kind of note?"

Elizabeth moved to the desk. "Under the lantern." She adjusted the light so the writing showed up better.

Domingo put on his glasses and leaned over it. He grunted. "The same note?" Victoria asked.

"Same notebook paper. Same pencil writing. Says about the same thing," Domingo said. "Slightly different wording." He took off his glasses and looked at Elizabeth. "How did you get it?"

She told him.

"She thought I left it," Allison said.

"Allison didn't write it," Domingo said. "But I don't know who did." He spotted the mail on the counter. "Anything in today's mail?" He shuffled through the envelopes.

"Memo from the chief about parking. Dated yesterday."

"Before his son died," Victoria said quietly.

"Died?" Allison said. "Fatso died? Are you kidding?"

"No." Domingo folded his glasses and put them in his pocket.

"When? What happened?" Allison sat suddenly in the empty chair. "I just seen him day before yesterday."

" 'Saw,' " Elizabeth said.

"Died this afternoon in jail," Domingo said. "Friend of yours?"

"Nothing like that," Allison said sullenly. "There wasn't nothing wrong with him two days ago."

Allison glanced up at the three people in the shack, Victoria, who was seated on the edge of the table, and Domingo and Elizabeth, standing next to the lantern on the desk.

"He told me he was doing some security stuff he couldn't talk about. I thought he was just, you know, bullshittin'."

Domingo studied her. "He was poisoned."

Allison's face was hidden in the shadows. She put her hand up to her throat. "He runs — he used to run — messages for my aunt. He tried to make out with me couple of times, you know? Only he's not my type."

"He was in jail for possession. Where did he get drugs?" Allison shrugged. "Do you know?"

"I don't know, honest. He tried to give me some stuff one time, but I don't, you know, touch dope."

"What kind of messages did he deliver for your aunt?"

"Like he picked up packages from the Harbor House, delivered stuff there. You know." She shrugged again.

"Do you know about a package Louie delivered to jail today?" Domingo stood as still as a post. Victoria watched silently.

"Yeah. Louie told me some old guy gave him a package to take to that crazy Indian in the jail. Gave him twenty bucks."

"Do you have any idea who the old guy was?" Domingo said.

"No. Louie seen him around, but he didn't know him, neither."

"Would Louie recognize him if he saw him again?"

"He said he was an old guy, you know, with greasy long gray hair and earrings and really, really filthy clothes."

"Sounds like the guy who's always going through the Dumpsters to collect bottles," Elizabeth said to Domingo.

"Leo Wolfe," Domingo said. "Louie say anything else?"

"I don't think so," Allison said.

"When does Louie come on duty next?" Domingo asked.

Elizabeth took a flashlight and shone it on the schedule posted on the wall. "First thing tomorrow morning."

"We'll have to wait, then. We can't call until the phones are back in service."

"Okay if I go now?"

Domingo nodded.

Allison went off into the night, past the darkened buildings, her flashlight making a cone of light in front of her.

~ ~ ~

CHAPTER FIFTEEN

What Dojan Told Domingo

VICTORIA awoke to the smell of coffee and to sunshine streaming through the skylights in Noreen's sewing room. It took her a moment to recall where she was. She got out of bed, dressed quickly, and found Domingo cooking bacon and scrambled eggs.

"Good morning, sweetheart."

"I don't usually sleep so late. Any news?"

"I've seen the lab report. It's a miracle both men didn't die. Coffee?"

"Yes, thank you. Did they find out what was in the fudge?"

"Atropine — nasty stuff. As Doc Erickson said, there's no known antidote." Domingo lifted bacon slices out of the pan and laid them on a paper towel on the counter.

"Atropine in the fudge I was supposed to have given Dojan." She watched Domingo pour bacon fat into a glass dish.

"Easy to get hold of," Domingo said. "Deadly nightshade grows all over the place. I'm willing to bet I can find some plants in my backyard now." He held out the coffeepot. "Refill?"

"Thank you." Victoria pulled a stool up to the kitchen counter. "Deadly nightshade," she murmured. "Elizabeth and I were weeding it out of the garden a few days ago."

Domingo stirred the eggs as he spoke. "All of it is poisonous, especially the berries. A couple can be fatal."

Victoria thought about her aunt warning her, years ago, against eating nightshade berries, even against touching the plant without washing her hands afterward.

"The berries are supposed to be sweet," she said. "You wonder how anybody discovered that. Manny and the other boy probably didn't realize anything was wrong."

"Manny must have ingested seven or eight berries in those three pieces of fudge." Domingo lowered the heat under the eggs and continued to stir.

Victoria sipped her coffee, squinting her eyes against the steam. "Why would anyone want to harm Dojan?"

"You don't want to know, sweetheart."

"Of course I want to know. Stop sheltering me. Why is someone after Dojan?"

Noreen came into the kitchen, brushing her blond hair. "Sleep okay, Mrs. Trumbull?"

"Wonderfully, thank you. Where's Elizabeth?"

"Still getting her beauty sleep." Noreen patted Domingo on the shoulder and kissed his cheek. "Thanks, honey."

"For what? I'm doing my usual morning routine."

"Usual! You haven't touched that stove since we bought it seven years ago. I'm surprised you know how it works." Victoria laughed.

Domingo turned to her. "You see how much my woman appreciates me?"

"Domingo." Victoria returned to their conversation. "I want to know what is going on."

Domingo brushed eggshells into his hand from the countertop and dropped them into a plastic basket in the sink.

"She's right, you know," Noreen said. "You and your macho shit, protecting us little women. You think Mrs. Trumbull is stupid or something?"

"No, honey. The fact is someone is trying to silence her because she knows too much. Somebody thinks she's meddling. I don't want her to have any more knowledge than is necessary."

Noreen laughed. "Come off it, Domingo. You think you're God or something? You think you have the right to decide what Mrs. Trumbull needs to know?"

"I'm thinking about her safety." Domingo spooned salsa from a jar labeled VOLCANO! into the eggs and stirred.

"Domingo! At least ask her if she likes that hot stuff in her eggs."

"Who's cooking, you or me?"

"I want to know what's going on." Victoria slapped her hand on the table. The saltshaker fell over, and she righted it.

"Morning, Gram. Morning, Noreen, Domingo." Elizabeth appeared in the kitchen door, hair tousled, eyes puffy. She sat next to her grandmother at the counter. Noreen poured coffee.

Victoria curbed her irritation with Domingo long enough to greet Elizabeth, who looked, at the moment, like the sleepy six-year-old Victoria remembered from a quarter century ago.

She turned again to Domingo and slapped her gnarled hand on the counter-top with each word. "What is going on, Domingo?"

"It's too early in the morning for this, Grammy." Elizabeth reached for a paper towel and mopped up spilled coffee.

Domingo dished out eggs and placed rashers of bacon on the side without answering, then set the plates on the kitchen table.

"You witnessed Bernie's murder, you heard a vehicle leave the scene, and you heard a boat. But we don't know why Bernie was killed. It's possible it was connected with drug trafficking; we don't know for certain." Domingo reached across the table for a piece of toast. "Pass the marmalade," he said to Noreen.

"Say 'please,' " Noreen said.

"Please, honey."

"Maybe some woman's father decided to get even with him," Elizabeth said.

Domingo turned to Elizabeth. "Someone is concerned about how much your grandmother knows." Domingo's heavy brows were drawn together in a frown. "They are also concerned with how much your grandmother is involved."

"I'm not involved at all," Victoria said hotly. "I don't know any more than what I've already told the police." She sloshed orange juice into her empty glass.

"Don't forget," said Domingo, pushing eggs onto his fork with his toast while he spoke, "you found that broken bottle and the checkbook cover. You haven't told the police that." He shoveled eggs into his mouth and swallowed. "Of course, we have no reason to think those may be evidence. Also, you recognized the police chief's car as the one you heard the night Bernie was killed."

"I don't know that I recognized it. All cars sound alike skidding on sand."

"Next, someone followed you, quite possibly Meatloaf, at least twice, maybe more, possibly only trying to frighten you."

"Well, he didn't." Victoria scraped up the hot salsa from the edge of her plate, heaped it on top of her eggs, took a bite, and wiped her watering eyes.

"Someone else followed us," Elizabeth said. "Dojan?"

"Most likely. Dojan is feeling protective of your grandmother." Domingo bared his white teeth in a wolfish grin.

"I feel like the president," Victoria said.

Domingo got serious again. "At first, I assumed that Meatloaf killed Bernie. Meatloaf would have done it that way — crude."

"That's what I think, too." Victoria toyed with her glass.

"Not so, sweetheart. Meatloaf was trying to hush you, but not because he was the killer. He was trying to protect someone else. He was trying to protect his boss, the one who paid him."

"Then who killed Meatloaf?" Elizabeth put her toast back onto her plate. "And who was the boss he was trying to protect? Who tried to kill Dojan?"

Victoria interrupted with her own questions. "Who hoped to stop Elizabeth with the fallen tree limb and the oil slick? And who wrote those threatening notes to both of us?"

"One thing at a time." Domingo pushed his chair back. "I don't know everything. However, when I was in the cell with Dojan, he told me things he should have kept to himself."

"What did he tell you?" Victoria folded her napkin and set it beside her plate.

"The day Bernie was killed, Dojan told me, he'd gone out in his boat to pull his lobster traps on the Sound. When he came back into the harbor, he had engine trouble, so he pulled his boat up onto the beach near the osprey pole, in that small bay. He landed, fixed his motor, and watched the sunset."

"I remember how spectacular it was that night," Victoria said.

"Dojan sat on the beach in the shelter of a wild rosebush. He could see the dock, but unless someone knew he was there, they wouldn't have seen him. He saw the police car pull up and Bernie and Chief Medeiros get out. He watched them walk to the end of the dock. They argued, loudly enough so he could hear what they were saying. While they were arguing, Dojan saw Meatloaf scull a dinghy over from the dock by the liquor store. He did it so quietly Dojan didn't see him at first."

Noreen got up and brought a fresh pot of coffee to the table. Victoria watched Domingo through hooded eyes. "Then what?"

"Meatloaf tied up at the foot of the dock and waited. The argument got louder. Bernie grabbed a liquor bottle out of the chief's hand, broke it against the metal ring on the piling, and started after the chief, who whisked out that razor-sharp bayonet he wears in his boot. At that point, Meatloaf climbed the ladder. Dojan saw him twist Bernie's arms behind him. He couldn't see what the chief was doing, but he saw him jab the knife into Bernie, heard Bernie scream, saw Meatloaf cover his mouth. Dojan witnessed the whole thing."

Elizabeth grunted.

"So Chief Medeiros killed Bernie," Victoria whispered, her hand at her throat.

"That's what Dojan said. Meatloaf started up the motor on the dinghy and landed on the beach where you found the bottle and the checkbook cover. Then he returned to the liquor store dock."

"That must have been the motor I heard," Victoria said.

"Dojan told me other things he saw. He hung around for some time before he left. In fact, he saw Victoria and me go out in the launch ..."

"Hey, I was there too," Elizabeth said.

"Yas. He told me he saw Ms. Elizabeth, Victoria, and me searching; then he heard me call in. And after that, he saw the chief's car return to the scene."

"Why didn't Dojan say anything?" Victoria frowned.

"Who would he report the killing to, Chief Medeiros?" Victoria gave Domingo a tight smile. "You said there was something else Dojan talked about."

"Yas."

Victoria said, "What else?"

Domingo set his elbows on the table and looked intently from Elizabeth to Victoria to Noreen.

"What else?" Victoria said again.

"Dojan claimed he killed Meatloaf."

"What!" Elizabeth stared at him.

Noreen shook her head.

"Everything is backward and upside down." Elizabeth stood suddenly.

"Why?" Victoria asked, puzzled.

"Dojan had been tailing Meatloaf in an attempt to protect you, sweetheart. When the wife and I were in New York, Meatloaf came by to pick up the papers."

"That was while I was watching Baby Mingo," Victoria said.

"Later, that same evening, around eleven, eleven-thirty, Meatloaf returned with the signed papers. Dojan was following him and told me what happened."

The room was quiet. Victoria heard the coffeepot burble, a car pass on the road.

"Dojan saw him open the sliding door into the living room; Meatloaf was carrying a folder. He picked up a paper from the table and read it, then put the folder down and set a coffee mug on top. Dojan followed him into the house, here." Domingo pointed down at the floor. "He must have been quiet, because Meatloaf apparently didn't see him at first. When he finally looked up, he was startled. He called Dojan a 'crazy Indian,' and asked him what the hell he was doing here."

"What did Dojan say?" Elizabeth asked.

"Nothing. He said he stared at Meatloaf."

"I can just see him, with those wobbly eyes like boiled eggs, only black, and those feathers quivering in his hair, and his dark clothes blending into the night," Elizabeth said. "He'd spook anybody."

"Go on, Domingo," said Victoria.

"Meatloaf went over to the couch, sat down, and put his sunglasses on."

"At midnight?" Elizabeth said.

Domingo shrugged. "That's what Dojan said. He said he walked toward the couch where Meatloaf was sitting. The telephone rang, and Dojan didn't know whether he should answer it or not. He didn't, and it finally stopped ringing. He told Meatloaf he'd been watching him, and he asked him why he'd been following you." He nodded at Victoria.

"Then what?" Victoria said.

"Meatloaf said, 'Get outta here, you crazy Indian.' Dojan stepped closer and told him to stay away from his friend. Meatloaf half-rose from the couch and twisted one of my harpoons out of the rack and threatened Dojan with it. Dojan backed away, and Meatloaf went out of the door, still holding the harpoon. When Meatloaf got into his van, Dojan went after him, followed him to the harbor. Apparently, Meatloaf expected to see someone on duty at the shack, but it was midnight by then, and no one was there."

"I wasn't on duty that night," Elizabeth said.

"Go on, Domingo," said Victoria.

"Meatloaf was carrying the harpoon in one hand, banging on the door of the shack with the other. He turned when Dojan came up next to him, and he pointed the harpoon at Dojan. Dojan grabbed it and twisted it out of his hands. Meatloaf then pulled a switchblade on him, tried to slash his hands. Meatloaf yelled at him to keep away, but Dojan shoved him against the railing with the shaft of the harpoon. Meatloaf kept trying to slash him with the knife. Dojan could see the sweat pouring down his face. Suddenly, the railing gave way and Meatloaf dropped his knife, which skidded off the deck and fell into the water. He tried to grab the harpoon as he lost his balance, then tried to grab the broken railing, but his hands slid off. He tumbled, arms flailing to the sides, his feet bicycling in the air, and hit with a splash that sent water up the sides of the shack. He surfaced, blowing water out of his mouth in a spume, his cap and dark glasses gone, his hair plastered on his scalp, his windbreaker translucent and filled with water. He paddled frantically with both hands. Dojan stood above him with the harpoon in his hand and flung it."

"My God!" said Noreen.

Victoria looked down at her plate. "And after that, Dojan went to the Sand Bar and had a drink or two."

"More like five or six," Domingo replied. "But not right away. He built himself a sweat lodge on top of the Gay Head cliffs and tried to sweat out the evil."

"It's not Gay Head anymore," Elizabeth said. "The name's Aquinnah now."

"He's attempting to get back to his roots," Victoria said, toying with her fork. "I suppose when that didn't work, he went on his binge."

All of them were silent.

Finally, Victoria pushed her chair away from the table. "This is awful. Shouldn't we notify the police?"

"Chief Medeiros?" Domingo said, raising his eyebrows. "I don't think so."

"If he hadn't been so hung-over, he'd probably have eaten the fudge," Elizabeth said.

Domingo nodded.

"Why did he tell you? Was he afraid they were going to charge you with Meatloaf's murder?" Victoria asked.

"He needed to get it off his chest, sweetheart."

"Did anyone overhear him?" Victoria asked.

"While we were talking, I saw Howie tiptoe past the cell. I don't know how long he'd been listening. When I went to the door and rattled the bars and shouted obscenities at him, he left."

"You think Howie reported what he heard to someone? To Chief Medeiros, maybe?" Victoria asked. "Surely the chief would want to silence anyone who knew what had happened."

"Before I became aware that Howie was listening, Dojan told me that he was on the beach fixing his motor the night of the killing."

"Whom would Howie have reported the conversation to?" Victoria said.

"Probably Elmo, the jailer, who undoubtedly told the sheriff, who told the chief over coffee at Linda Jean's."

Victoria took an envelope and pen out of her pocket. "What do we know so far?" She held the end of the pen to her mouth. "We suspect a drug ring might be operating out of the Oak Bluffs Harbor."

"But we don't *know* that."

"Has Howland said anything to you lately, Domingo?" Elizabeth said abruptly.

Victoria was startled by the change of subject. She noticed Domingo dart a quick look at Elizabeth and shake his head very slightly. She looked from her granddaughter to Domingo. Elizabeth studiously avoided her eyes.

Noreen didn't seem to have noticed the small exchange. "It fits with everything that's happened," she said. "A drug ring."

Victoria smoothed her trousers over her knees with the hand holding the pen. She thought about Domingo's oddly secret shake of the head. "It would explain everything if we assume Bernie Marble's murder was a drug deal gone wrong," Victoria said finally. "We thought Meatloaf killed him, when it was actually Chief Medeiros who did. Over drugs."

"Let me caution you." Domingo stood and hiked up his trousers by his belt. "We have no evidence that drugs are involved. As yet."

"We'll get that evidence," Victoria said with assurance. "Chief Medeiros is obviously the ringleader of a drug-smuggling operation."

"We don't *know* that, either," Domingo said. "In fact, I don't believe he is the ringleader."

"So who tried to kill Dojan?" Victoria put her envelope and pen next to her plate. "And who is sending the notes?"

"It would appear to be two different people," Domingo said. "A killer and a blackmailer. The killer thinks Dojan knows something. I don't know what the blackmailer is after."

"What about Liz Tate?" Victoria asked. "She certainly was acting strange that day we came back to the dock on Rocky's yacht, bawling out the chief for being there."

"I wouldn't put it past the bitch," said Noreen.

~ ~ ~

CHAPTER SIXTEEN

Confrontation

CHIEF MEDEIROS was standing on the steps of the Town Hall, staring off into space, unread mail in his hand, when Domingo, Victoria, and Howland pulled up in the white Rolls Royce.

The bright, clear morning, crisp and rare, was what Victoria called "typical Vineyard weather." The sultry heat had moved off-Island, leaving everything clean and new.

The chief was in uniform: navy blue motorcycle pants with a light blue stripe on the sides, polished black boots with a knife hilt showing at the top, navy shirt with leather belt, a strap across his chest, his gun, radio, club, keys slung from the belt. His dark glasses touched the brim of his garrison cap. He shifted his gaze to the car and his mouth pursed.

Domingo stepped out of the car, slammed the door, and stood on the sidewalk, looking up at the chief at the top of the steps. Victoria waited in the front seat, Howland in back. Domingo hitched his pants up and walked toward the steps.

"You got some nerve showing up here, Mingo," the chief said.

"My condolences on the passing of your son," Domingo said, and took his cap off. "I'm very sorry."

"Yeah. I bet you are." The chief shifted his gaze to the mail in his hand.

"I know this is a bad time for you, but we need to talk."

"You can talk to me right here." Without looking up, the chief shuffled envelopes, top onto bottom, the next, the next.

"In private." Domingo stood still, hands in his pockets.

"I got nothing to say to you, public or private."

"We have something to say to you. I think you're going to want a more private place," Domingo said.

"What the hell do you have to say to me in private? I don't want to talk to you, period."

"Have it your way." Domingo shrugged. He put his cap back on and turned to the car. "Atherton?"

Howland unfolded himself from the back seat of the Corniche and walked deliberately up the brick steps. The chief inclined his head to look up at him.

Howland reached into his back pocket, brought out his black leather folder, and flipped it open. Victoria saw a flash of reflected sunlight on a gold shield.

The chief took the folder from Howland and studied it. Howland started to say something, but before he could, the chief said, "Where do you want to talk?"

"We can go to your office, if you'd like." Howland waited.

The chief stared across the street. "No, not there."

"The Harbor House?" Howland said. "Perhaps you have a private room, a small conference room there?"

"I don't think so." The chief returned Howland's leather folder to him.

"This is unofficial, at least at this stage." Howland put the folder with his shield and ID in his back pocket and crossed his arms over his chest.

"Mingo's place?" The chief turned to Domingo, who was facing away from them. A young man in splotched painter's overalls was walking toward him with an athlete's springy step.

"How ya doing, Mitch?" Domingo greeted him.

"Pretty good, Mr. D. And you?"

"Can't complain. How's the wife and baby? A boy, was it?"

"Yessir, Mr. D, both fine. Mitch junior, nine pounds two ounces."

"All right!" Domingo jabbed an emphatic fist at the ground.

Mitch went up the steps of the Town Hall two at a time, brushed past Howland and the police chief. "Pardon me." He pushed open the screen door, which slapped a couple of times before it shut.

"Your place, Domingo?" Howland said.

"Fine." Domingo swung around to face them.

"We can talk over a cup of coffee," Howland said to the chief, who gathered up a lot of something in his cheek and spit it into the privet hedge that surrounded the Town Hall.

"We'll see you there." Domingo got back into the driver's seat. Howland seated himself again in back.

The chief flexed his legs one at a time, as though his muscles had stiffened, and clumped down the steps of the Town Hall. Victoria could hear his boots squeak.

Domingo parked in front of his house and left a space for the police cruiser. The chief pulled into it.

Once inside, Victoria lowered herself onto the couch, Domingo sat at the glass-topped table, and Howland and the chief stood.

"She sitting in on this?" The chief jerked his head at her.

"Yas." Domingo lighted a cigarette, snapped his Zippo shut, and laid it on the table with a small clink.

"As I said, this is unofficial." Howland indicated one of the wicker chairs around the table. "Won't you have a seat?"

The chief hesitated before he sat. "Where's the wife?"

"My wife has taken my grandson to see the fire station."

Howland stepped up into the kitchen, and Victoria heard him open the cupboard where Noreen kept the coffee, heard him fill the pot with water, heard the clatter of mugs as Howland took them from the rack next to the stove.

While the coffee brewed, Howland sat at the table. Victoria attempted to break the awkward silence with small talk, but she gave up after a few tries. Chief Medeiros sat with his arms folded, staring sullenly at the tabletop in front of him. Domingo looked out the window. Howland toyed with the place mat. Victoria watched all three from her seat on the couch.

When the coffee had finished brewing, Howland went up into the kitchen and poured. "How does everyone take it?" he asked.

"Black, thank you," Victoria said.

"Cream, milk. Double sugar," the chief muttered.

Once Howland was seated again, Domingo spoke first, turning to the chief with an unsettling, calm stare. "We suggest you admit to the murder," he said quietly, gazing at the chief.

The chief started, his eyes twitched. He stared back at Domingo, his mouth seeming to form words that never emerged.

"Murder," he said in a choked voice. He brought the coffee mug to his mouth.

Domingo watched the chief steadily. After a pause, he said, "Of Meatloaf Staples."

The chief, who had that moment taken a sip of coffee, spewed it across the table with a convulsive movement and got to his feet. Domingo blotted the tabletop with the paper napkin Howland had given him with his coffee.

"What in hell! You're crazy." The chief rose out of his seat, grabbed his cap, which he had placed on the table, jammed it on his head, plucked his sunglasses out of his pocket, and strode toward the door. He turned. "You know goddamned well I had nothing to do with killing Meatloaf." He slammed the door open, and it bounced on the track. "Trying to cover your own ass, are you? You're more of a fool than I thought, Mingo."

Domingo sat serenely, his hands folded over his stomach, cigarette smoldering in the ashtray. "We know for a fact you didn't kill Meatloaf."

Howland said nothing. He'd put his elbows on the table and had both hands around his coffee mug. He gazed absently through the hanging plants into the bright, sunny garden outside, where Baby Mingo's plastic toys lay where he'd left them. Victoria leaned back and watched through half-shut eyes.

"You're out of your minds." The chief paused in the doorway. "I have nothing to say to you."

"However," Domingo said, "we know the person you did kill. And how you killed him."

"Whaaat!"

"We have a witness to Bernie Marble's death." Domingo said it softly. "An eyewitness."

The chief froze and glanced at Victoria.

"Not her," Howland said.

The chief moved back into the room.

"Shut the door, please." Victoria looked over her shoulder. "You're letting in flies."

The chief lifted the door back onto its track and slid it shut. He took off his sunglasses and glanced quickly at Victoria, then from Domingo to Howland and back again at Domingo.

"What in hell? Come out with it."

Howland continued to stare out at the garden. "Why don't you sit," he said. "You might want to hear what we have to say."

The chief sat, took his cap off, and, after a few moments' silence, put it under the chair. He took his glasses off and put them back in his pocket, leaned forward, hands clasped on the table, and looked around.

"There's no one else here," Domingo said.

"Yeah?" the chief said.

"We are not recording this," Howland said. "Victoria Trumbull is here as an observer."

"What's on your mind, Mingo?"

"We'll talk, if you don't mind," Howland said politely. The chief glared at him.

Victoria sneezed three times in a row.

"God bless you." The chief glanced at her.

"Domingo?" Howland said. "Care to continue?"

"As I said, we think you might want to admit to killing Meatloaf Staples."

"Jee-sus," the chief said.

"Or, if you prefer, we can produce the individual who actually witnessed what happened to Bernie Marble."

"What in hell is this?" The chief was beginning to sweat. Howland handed him a paper napkin, and the chief mopped his forehead with it.

"You'll say you killed Meatloaf in self-defense, of course," Domingo continued. "Better than a charge of first-degree murder."

The chief wiped his forehead again, crumpled up the napkin, and tossed it onto the table. "You're crazy, both of you."

"I don't think so," Howland said.

"What do you expect to get out of this?" The chief pushed his coffee mug away from him and stared at Domingo.

Domingo nodded his head at Howland. "Atherton, take over."

"Once upon a time," Howland said, "there was an elder son of a wealthy New England family, blue-blood stock. A difficult kid, brilliant, charming, and shifty. Summers on Martha's Vineyard, winters in the Caribbean, private boarding schools. Father was a great philanthropist, mother a patron of the arts, that sort of thing. The son dabbled in drugs during his preteen Caribbean winters, not as a user — he was too smart for that — but as a courier. By the time he entered college, he had built up his own network of sources, distributors, and dealers."

From where Victoria sat, she could see the chief's profile. He sat motionless, his face expressionless.

"Are you still with me?" Howland asked.

The chief said nothing.

Victoria saw Domingo's dark eyes through a blue haze of cigarette smoke.

"To continue," Howland said. "Daddy, who never did trust his son, got suspicious, hired a private investigator, found out what the son was up to, and disowned him. The son finished college on an academic scholarship, went on to graduate school on a fellowship, got a Ph.D. in astrophysics, and won a professorship at MIT. A professor's salary being what it is, he maintained his drug contacts at a low-key level, enough to support his lifestyle without arousing undue suspicion."

The chief shifted in his seat. Domingo stubbed out his cigarette. Victoria saw a vein or artery pulsing in the chief's temple, a muscle twitching in his jaw.

"Our professor," Howland went on, "developed a computer program under a university grant from the Defense Department to track electromagnetic pulses. He did much of his research in Puerto Rico, on the giant radio telescope. He believed, however, that the university was not giving him his share of the royalties for the very successful program. He felt he had a right to appropriate a portion of the grant money for his own purposes. When the university found out about what they considered his misuse of the grant money, they ousted him. Since much of his research had been in the Caribbean, he had, quite naturally, maintained his contacts there.

"To make up for his lost income, he switched into high gear with his drug business. Importing high-profit goods from South America by way of the Caribbean. Are you with me?"

Victoria sneezed again.

"God bless you," the chief said. "Go on."

Domingo watched the chief.

The chief stared at Howland, the throbbing in his temple the only sign that he was listening.

"He learned that vessels putting in at the Vineyard after a long sea voyage seldom go through U.S. Customs." Howland took a sip of coffee, his eyes on the chief. "He knew he could enlist yachting adventurers heading north from the Caribbean, delighted to carry goods for him for a small fee. The Oak Bluffs Harbor was ideal for his purposes."

"Where are you going with this?" the chief said finally. "What does this have to do with my 'killing' Meatloaf?"

Victoria blew her nose.

The chief glared at Howland.

"He decided he could easily explain his high living by capitalizing, so to speak, on his software invention. Few people understand university policies, few people would question his involvement with the university, and few people are going to wonder how lucrative an astrophysics software program can be."

He glanced at Domingo, who was playing with his Zippo, snapping it open and shut.

Victoria shifted on the couch, crossed one ankle over the other, put her hand-kerchief back in her pocket.

"You're not catching cold, are you, sweetheart?" Domingo looked over at her with concern.

She shook her head.

"To continue," Howland said. "Our professor needed three things: a depository, where he could keep his goods temporarily until he could move them to their point of sale; a means of transporting them safely off-Island; and, most important, a team he could trust." He looked up at the chief. "Are you still with me?"

The chief lowered his head and looked at his clasped hands.

A cardinal flashed by in the garden outside. Victoria heard the melodic call of a Carolina wren. A car passed on the road, and her view of it was chopped up by Domingo's tall wooden fence.

Howland continued. "Our professor needed to bring his goods into a place where the record keeping was haphazard, and where no one asked questions." He looked from the chief to Domingo. "Oak Bluffs was ideal. The harbor takes in half a million dollars over a three-month period. A lot of boaters pay cash. The former harbor master had a little cash slush fund he used to supplement his salary, pay for favors, that sort of thing."

Domingo cranked the window open slightly.

"Our professor did his homework," Howland continued. "He found, to his delight, that one of the town's selectmen and the two owners of the major hotel — one owner a convicted criminal on probation, the other the town's police chief — were benefiting from the sloppy management of the harbor.

"Now our professor hoped, ideally, to distance himself as much as possible from day-to-day operations of his business. So he enlisted this particular select-man to act as his right-hand person, to keep records and deal with subordinates." He stopped talking. "You still with me?"

"Go on," the chief growled.

"Our story's hotel was situated at the head of the harbor, and it was the only place where showers were available for boaters. What could be better, our professor must have said to himself. The imported goods came in small packages, one kilo each, something the size of two pounds of butter. What could be simpler than asking his Caribbean adventurers, sailors who were about to take their first hot freshwater showers in some time, to carry a small parcel into the shower room and 'accidentally' leave it behind when they were through. The parcels were small enough to be unnoticed among towels, soap, and clean and dirty clothes. Later, a trusted minion could retrieve the parcels when he, or she, cleaned the shower room. The minion took the parcels to the hotel's lost and found, conveniently near the shower rooms. This way, the minion was absolved of any responsibility for taking part in the business transactions. From the lost and found, the parcels found their way to the hotel's hamper for soiled laundry. Probably a specially marked hamper, wouldn't you say, Chief?"

The chief said nothing. He picked at a loose flap of skin on his finger.

Howland went on. "The goods were indeed laundered. The soiled linen would then go to Boston, taken by a trustworthy, low-echelon member of the team, and be returned to the hotel as clean towels, sheets, and *voila!* Laundered money."

Victoria laid her right arm along the back of the couch.

The chief continued to pick at his finger.

"In addition," Howland went on, "the selectmen had hired what they thought was a dumb black guy who would take orders from them without question." He turned to look at Domingo and his mouth turned down in a smile. "To go on: In our story, the imaginary selectman takes her, or his, orders from our professor. How can our professor guarantee her, or his, loyalty? That's critical, don't you think?" He paused and looked at the chief, who said nothing. "I myself can think of several ways. One, or a combination, would do the trick. Affection, greed, and fear come to mind. Or a certain sense of adventure. I'm sure you can think of others."

The chief unfolded his hands and looked at his watch. Howland smiled. "We're taking your valuable time, aren't we? Shall I stop?"

"Jesus Christ," the chief said. "Go on."

"Why kill Bernie Marble?" Howland continued. "We can only guess that Marble began to realize how much money was involved. He may have felt he was being shortchanged. Perhaps Bernie got greedy. Maybe he threatened to divulge this elegant scheme. Bernie was already on probation for his behavior to a female employee of the hotel. Had that gotten out of hand?"

Chief Medeiros shifted in his chair. "What do you expect me to do about all this garbage you're feeding me?"

"Ah!" Howland said. "As with much fiction, this is grounded in reality. Now let me tell you about Bernie's death. Tell me if I'm mistaken on some fine point. This was — let's see — about two weeks ago now."

He turned suddenly to face Chief Medeiros and his voice no longer had its polite edge.

"Okay, Medeiros. You summoned Meatloaf to your office at the Harbor House, told him you couldn't talk on the phone. 'Get your ass in here,' you said."

The chief stared at Howland.

"Meatloaf lumbered into that office of yours that looks out over the parking lot in back of the hotel, right?"

The chief said nothing.

"Meatloaf was probably breathing heavily and sweating, although, as I recall, it was not a hot afternoon. He plopped himself into that wooden armchair in front of your desk where the light from your window must have shone in his face. A cop technique, right?"

The chief stared at Howland.

"I can imagine the conversation," Howland continued. "You probably made him cool his heels for a long time. Then you leaned forward across the desk. 'I'm having a slight problem with Bernie,' you may have said. I suppose Meatloaf, who was sure you'd found out something he didn't want you to know, was relieved. Just as you intended. Maybe you said something like, 'He seems to have forgotten who's boss. He's getting greedy. Wants a bigger cut.' I can hear you now, playing the good-cop/bad-cop routine all by yourself, and Meatloaf, who was not the brightest, fell for it, didn't he?"

The chief looked down at his hands. Domingo sat motionless. Victoria shifted slightly on the couch.

"Meatloaf couldn't see your face, backlighted the way it undoubtedly was. He had to guess how he was supposed to react, probably squinting into the light, trying to see your expression. 'I'd say he's had a pretty generous cut,' you may have said.

" 'Damn right. Want me to talk to him?' Is that what Meatloaf said? Did he make a fist of his right hand and smack it into the palm of his left? I've seen him do that. He probably glared like a thug for your benefit.

"Then I can imagine you saying, 'He thinks he can cut a couple of middlemen out of the operation, delusions of grandeur.'

"I'll bet Meatloaf agreed with you. 'Not good,' or something like that.

"To really hit home, you might have said, 'Bernie's letting his prick do his thinking for him. Not smart in this business.'"

The chief glanced nervously at Victoria, who was studying the backs of her hands.

"You undoubtedly reminded Meatloaf of the way Bernie bought off one woman who threatened to file charges against him. Followed her all the way to Ireland, right? You said to Meatloaf, 'We don't need this kind of publicity.'

"Were Meatloaf's eyes watering from the bright light? Probably. You planned it that way, didn't you? I know that gesture he had, reaching into his pocket for that blue bandanna, lifting his glasses, and wiping his eyes."

The room was still except for a fly buzzing at the sliding door. Sounds filtered in from outdoors. Two boys rode past the house on bicycles, calling to each other and laughing. The chief sat motionless.

" 'He thinks we need him more than he needs us,' I suppose you said. 'Plenty of other places to store stuff. They don't have to use this hotel.' The way I imagine it," Howland continued, "you stood up, stuck your hands into your pockets, and probably jingled change, the way you do. Did you look out the window at the parking lot? From your office, you can see the Camp Meeting Ground, can't you? Quite a contrast, those quaint gingerbread houses painted in pastel colors, the oak leaves rustling in the breeze.

"You probably stood at the window for some time, letting Meatloaf wonder. Did you rock back and forth on those squeaky leather boots of yours? Good way to make someone nervous, isn't it? I can hear you saying, once you decided Meatloaf was softened up, 'He needs to be taught a lesson. We need to take care of him, permanently.' Did you say that?"

The chief swallowed. His neck quivered.

"I suppose you told Meatloaf that you were meeting Bernie at the East Chop dock around dark. Did you check the tide table? Figure out that dead high tide was around seven-thirty? I'm sure you did."

Victoria noticed that the chief had crossed his feet and was rubbing one against the other. Except for that, the muscle in his jaw, and the pulse in his temple, he was motionless. Domingo, too, was absolutely still.

"I suppose you told him to scull a dinghy from the dock by the liquor store to the East Chop dock, and to get there before seven-thirty. You didn't want any noise, did you? Maybe you told him he could use the exercise." Howland smiled. "Did you tell him to wait at the foot of the ladder until you needed him?"

The chief said nothing. The fly buzzed and bumped against the glass door.

"I suppose Meatloaf was wearing those pointed Italian shoes he was so vain about. You probably gave him that steely cop look and asked him if he could get his fat self up the ladder in a hurry, right?"

The chief said nothing.

"Then you must have jerked your head at him. 'Okay,' I imagine you said, 'get outta here. We never had this discussion.' "

Howland stopped. Domingo's clock rang six bells. Victoria checked her watch.

"Eleven o'clock, sweetheart," Domingo said.

"Have you heard enough?" Howland asked the chief.

"Shit," said the chief, then turned to Victoria. "Excuse me, ma'am."

"Go on, Howland," Victoria said.

"I imagine when Meatloaf left, you got on the phone to Bernie. 'Bernie,' you probably said, 'how's it going?' And while Bernie talked, I'll bet you doodled those square boxes on your desk calendar, right?"

The chief stared without expression at Howland.

"How did you get him to agree to meet you, Medeiros? You tell him one of the couriers was getting too big for his britches? Tell him you were not sure who? That you figured he was taping goods to the underside of the dock to come back for them in his own sweet time? I can see you now, doodling, probably connecting those boxes you'd drawn with lines so they looked three-dimensional."

The chief blinked.

"I've seen your calendar, Medeiros. Boxes with arrows shooting into them. You probably suggested that the courier would be at the dock at high tide so he could reach the underside of the dock, didn't you? Seven-thirty, you said. Then, to allay suspicion — Bernie was a suspicious guy, right? — you probably said you weren't sure it would be that night. 'We may have to wait a day or two,' I'm sure you said. Then, to make it seem like a good-time junket, you told him you'd bring a bottle, didn't you? Said you'd pick him up in the cruiser.

"I can see you now. You slammed the phone down and turned your chair to the window. Were those two kids riding their pink-and-lavendar bicycles down in the parking lot? Or did you even see them? You didn't want to be reminded of *normal,* did you?"

The chief shook his head and looked at his hands, which were still clasped in front of him on the table.

"Everything went according to plan, didn't it? At least until you learned that Victoria Trumbull had heard you and Meatloaf, had heard Bernie's screams, and found his body before the tide took it out to sea." Howland stopped and waited for the chief to say something.

Medeiros continued to look down at his hands.

"Back to my story. You and Bernie went together in the police cruiser to the dock. You took along a bottle of Caribbean rum one of your couriers gave you."

The chief looked up in surprise.

"You didn't know we found the bottle, did you?" The chief was silent.

"I suppose he put up a fight, didn't he?" Howland said. "Kicked out at you. But you've been trained to kill. Vietnam, the Marines. Or did you learn at police school?"

The chief stood up and slapped his hand on the table.

"I don't want to hear any more of this shit." He reached under his chair and snatched his cap. "I don't know where you're getting it from. Straight out of some TV show."

"First-degree murder carries life," Domingo said quietly.

"No one can pin anything on me." The chief turned to the door. "Your eyewitness is another figment of your imagination. There was nobody around. Nobody." He started to open the door.

"The witness saw Bernie break the bottle against the piling," Domingo said. "Saw you pull the knife on him. Saw Meatloaf hold him. Saw what you did next."

"Meatloaf did it, not me."

"The witness heard you order Meatloaf to drop Bernie's pants. Saw Meatloaf cover Bernie's mouth with his arm when he started to scream."

"Oh yeah?" The chief paused in the half-opened doorway.

"The witness saw what you did." Domingo stopped and looked uncomfortably at Victoria, who was regarding the chief with disgust.

"I know what he did to that man," Victoria said. "You can stop trying to shelter me." She pushed herself off the couch and pointed to the chief as if he were in fifth grade. "Come back in this minute. Shut the door. And sit down and listen."

She stood until the chief obeyed her.

"You'll listen to the rest of this nasty tale. You should be drawn and quartered. Instead, you're getting a chance you don't deserve." She sat down again. "I thoroughly disapprove of giving him that chance," she said to Howland.

Domingo avoided Victoria's bright eyes.

Howland tilted his chair against the wall and looked away. "Don't lean back in your chair," Victoria said, and Howland set it back on its legs.

"You." She nodded her head at the chief. "You cut off his testicles and stuffed them into his mouth, didn't you?"

The chief looked from Domingo to Howland. Both men were staring out the window.

"The barbarian answer to rape," Victoria said. "You have a fourteen-year-old daughter, don't you?"

The chief looked blankly at his hands on the table.

"He raped your daughter, didn't he? Melody, your only daughter."

"Stop!" The chief sagged over the table. "Yes. It wasn't money. Or drugs. I know what happens to rapists. Nothing." He looked out the window. A chickadee was picking at seed in the bird feeder that hung from a post in the garden.

"Bernie Marble." He spat out the name. "On probation for assault against a female employee. It wasn't assault. It was rape." He laid his arms on the table and put his head on his arms. "I've seen what happens to women who are raped." He lifted his head. "Girls. They're damaged for life by rape. When they go to court, what little they have left is ground into pieces by the defense lawyers and the courts. Ground up and spit out."

Victoria, Howland, and Domingo were silent.

"I wasn't going to put my daughter through that."

Birds chirped. Cars went by on the road beyond the tall board fence. The coffeemaker sputtered and stopped.

"And they say justice is done." The chief sat up straight. "My only daughter fouled by that beast, my only son killed, my wife gone."

The room was silent for several minutes. Then the chief said, "What do you want from me?"

"We have been after Folger for years," Howland said. "He's smarter than most of us put together. For the first time, we have someone who can testify against him."

"Not me!" the chief choked.

"You," Howland said. "We want you to testify against him."

"Christ! Put me away for life for Bernie. If Rocky gets me, he'll kill me by inches."

"You testify, and Rocky will be put away forever," Howland said. "He's been destroying lives for years. For years, we've been hoping he would make a mistake. He's too smart to make a mistake. But with your testimony and Liz Tate's, we've finally got him."

"You'll never get Liz Tate to talk."

"I think we will," Domingo said.

"They're thick. What have you got on her?"

Domingo and Howland spoke at the same time. "She killed someone," they said.

"Killed?" the chief said. "Killed who?"

There was a moment's silence. Finally, Victoria spoke up. "Your son." She gazed at the chief with sympathy. "I'm sorry."

~ ~ ~

CHAPTER SEVENTEEN

Liz Tate

THE CHIEF leapt to his feet, slammed his cap on his head, patted his gun holster, stuck his reflective glasses on his nose, and, in two agile steps, was at the door.

"Where do you think you're going?" Domingo asked.

"None of your fucking business." The chief wrenched the handle of the sliding door, which jounced out of its track and bounced onto the patio pavement with a crash of breaking glass.

Howland was out of his chair and through the empty doorframe before the glass shards settled, but the chief was already in the cruiser. The engine caught with a roar, the siren started with a howl, and the strobe lights began to rotate. The vehicle took off with a squeal of tires and a blast of swirling sand.

"Where's he going?" Victoria, too, had stood up.

"More to the point, what's he going to do?" Domingo said.

Howland strode back in the room. "Hand me the phone book, Domingo. I need to call Liz Tate." He already had the phone in hand and had dialed the first three digits.

"I'll look it up for you." Victoria reached for the phone book as Domingo searched through his pockets for his glasses. She read the number to Howland.

"Seems to me it would solve the problem if we let things take their natural course," she said to Domingo as Howland waited for someone to answer the phone.

Howland put his hand over the mouthpiece. "We can't afford to lose her as a witness. We've finally got something on one of the biggest drug operations in the Northeast."

"I can't believe Rocky is involved in anything like this."

Domingo snorted.

"He seems so refined," Victoria said.

"Yeah," said Domingo. "Refined."

"No answer. Not even a machine." Howland slammed the cordless phone onto the glass-topped table.

Victoria winced. "Don't break anything else."

"Look up Allison Phipps's number." Domingo pointed to the phone book.

"She has her own phone. Her aunt may be there."

Victoria paged back to the *P* listings and gave the number to Howland, who punched it in and handed the phone to Domingo.

"You talk to the kid," Howland growled.

Domingo looked from Howland to Victoria while he waited for an answer.

"Yas," he said into the phone after what seemed a long time. "This is the harbor master. I need to speak to Ms. Tate."

Victoria could hear a woman's voice come on the line.

Domingo identified himself, and Victoria heard the woman talk at a higher and higher volume, until finally Domingo interrupted her.

"Chief Medeiros is looking for you in connection with his son's death."

He listened, looking from Howland to Victoria.

"I understand. However, the chief seems to believe you had something to do with it."

He waited.

"You knew Fatso was his son, didn't you? His only son?" He listened.

"Correct." He nodded. "Yas."

He shrugged at Victoria. "That may be. However, you had better stay out of his way for the time being."

He interrupted the flow of talk. "You have no time to go home. He left here less than five minutes ago with his siren on. He'll try your niece's place when he finds you are not at home."

Long pause.

"Go to Victoria Trumbull's. It's unlikely that he'll think of her house." He looked questioningly at Victoria, who nodded. "She has room. Drive the long way around, through Edgartown. You know where she lives. He's heading into Oak Bluffs on Barnes."

Domingo showed impatience. "For God's sake, get out, now." He pressed the off button and set the phone down. "She has to argue over everything I say."

"Maybe she and the chief will have a shoot-out, and that will be that," Victoria said.

"I need both of them." Howland paced. "I can't afford to lose either one. Those two are the break we've needed."

Domingo looked at his watch.

Howland stepped carefully over the doorsill, then paused when Victoria began to speak.

"What about Dojan?" she said. "Should he get off scot-free?"

Howland came back slowly into the room and faced Victoria, who was standing by the couch, her eyes on him.

"What about Dojan?" he said.

"Dojan killed someone." Victoria looked intently at him.

"The only reason we know is because he told Domingo. We can't hang him on his own word," Howland said.

"Will he go unpunished, then?" Victoria's knobby hands hung by her side.

Howland sat down again, and Victoria did, too.

"You know how much I care for Dojan," she said. "But he did kill Meatloaf, by his own admission. Shouldn't he be tried? I would be if I'd harpooned somebody."

Howland and Domingo were silent. Domingo looked out the window where his grandson's tricycle lay on its side in the trampled grass. Howland studied his fingernails.

Finally, Howland said, "The government has been after Rocky for a long, long time. He's been responsible for more than a dozen deaths. Indirectly, he has probably killed three times that through drug trafficking."

"What does that have to do with Dojan?" Victoria asked.

"We can get Rocky only if someone with credibility will testify against him. Chief Medeiros and Liz Tate have that credibility."

"So you're making deals, blaming the chief for Meatloaf's death, blaming Meatloaf for Bernie's murder, and letting Dojan off entirely?"

"It's not my decision, Victoria," Howland said.

"Blame your superiors," she said. "More buck passing. I'm ashamed of you, Howland."

Howland looked down at his hands. "Victoria, if I were running the world, Rocky would be put away forever. Chief Medeiros would be put away almost forever. There were some mitigating circumstances. Dojan would be ... I don't know what I'd do with Dojan."

"But you're not running the world," Victoria said.

"You're right. My bosses tell me what to do. Presumably, they know more than I do about the Rocky Folger drug case. It's their judgment, right or wrong, to get Rocky, any way we can."

"No matter how you do it?" Victoria said. "What's happened to the justice system?"

"Rocky has wriggled and squirmed through every loophole in the system. The killings of Bernie, of Meatloaf, then of the chief's son, offer our only hope to nail him."

Victoria gazed at him steadily.

"Hear me, Victoria. Medeiros will be put away permanently. He'll have to start life all over again in the witness protection program. He's not rotten. He's weak."

"You're not listening to *me*," Victoria said. "You can't let Dojan off completely just because you have some bizarre plan to trap Rocky. You — or your superiors — have no right to judge Dojan. Maybe the courts will find him innocent by reason of self-defense or insanity, but in this country, you, some government employee, can't just let him go" — she gestured with a casual wave of her hand — "like that. That's not justice. You ought to know better. You're blaming the less horrible killing on Chief Medeiros so he'll testify against Rocky. Will you say Meatloaf killed Bernie? Meatloaf, who can't defend himself?"

"Wait one second, Victoria." Howland looked up. "We have to be concerned with the greater good here."

"None of it is good," Victoria said. "It's all rotten."

"Least bad, then," Howland responded. "We've been after Rocky for fifteen years. During that time, he has destroyed more lives than you and I can count. Kids on the street shooting up dope. Murder, prostitution, muggings, the whole panoply of crime. He's got to be stopped. For the first time, we have two people we can negotiate with in exchange for their testimony. Dojan's not a killer. His conscience will punish him."

Victoria shook her head vigorously. "Noreen said it to Domingo — neither of you is God. Nor are your superiors. What right do you have to judge Rocky and Meatloaf and Chief Medeiros and Liz Tate? And Dojan? Who gave you the right?"

"Can I say something, sweetheart?" Domingo said.

"I've heard enough." Victoria struggled to her feet.

Domingo held his hand up, palm facing her like a crossing guard. "Tell me, sweetheart, how would you make sure justice is done? What do you suggest?"

Victoria sighed and sat down again. She studied the two men, who gazed back at her intently. Domingo's clock ticked; a car went by on the road; a chickadee landed on the feeder, which swung on its hook.

Victoria hoisted herself up from the couch with dignity. She drew herself up to her full height; although she'd shrunk somewhat over the years, she was still stately. "Turn him over to the tribe," she said. "The Wampanoags will know what to do."

Domingo sat still. Without moving his head, he looked from Victoria to Howland, who was staring in astonishment at Victoria.

"He's a tribal member," Victoria said. "The tribe has jurisdiction over its members."

Domingo got up, too, and held out his hand to her. "You'd have made a great judge, sweetheart."

Victoria heard a car drive up, heard Baby Mingo's voice and then footsteps.

"Shit, Domingo. Now what have you done?" Noreen stopped and stared down at the shower of glass fragments on the patio.

"I can explain, honey," said Domingo.

"I'm leaving." Howland stepped through the open door frame and kicked at the paving of broken glass. "Let me drive you home, Victoria. If Liz Tate shows up, I want to deal with her."

They were parking beneath the Norway maple just when Liz Tate's white Mercedes pulled in beside them.

Liz stepped out of her car, slammed the door shut, and marched over to Howland's car.

"Would you mind telling me what this is about?" she said. "I gather you were at Domingo's and heard. I'm too busy for this."

Howland nodded. "You may have nothing to worry about. However, we thought you should play it safe, at least until the chief cools down."

"Come in," Victoria said. "I'll show you to your room."

"I have no intention of staying here." Liz marched back to her car and opened the door.

"At least come in for a cup of coffee. Won't take a minute to brew it," Victoria said.

After a few moments, Liz followed Victoria into the cookroom. Without a word, she sat in one of the caned chairs at the pine table and crossed her legs. McCavity followed her, looked up at her, turned, and left.

"I'm allergic to cats. If I decide to stay, it will have to remain outdoors. I hope it hasn't been in my room."

Victoria's jaw set. She opened the refrigerator door to take out the half-and-half. McCavity rose up on his hind legs.

"You've had your food, Cavvy." Victoria looked at Liz Tate sitting stiffly in the chair that Victoria considered her own. Liz placed her elbows on the red-checked tablecloth.

Howland joined her at the table.

"Do you plan on letting me know what this is all about?" she asked. She shook her foot impatiently.

"I think you have a good idea. Chief Medeiros is prepared to testify against your boss."

"What are you talking about?" Liz stopped shaking her foot.

"You didn't realize the chief's son was in jail, did you? Did you even know he had a son?"

Victoria carried two cups of coffee to the table. Liz Tate put her hands in her lap. Victoria could see they were trembling.

"Thank you, Mrs. Trumbull," Liz Tate said dismissively. "You don't need to sit in on this."

"Yes, I think I do." Victoria pulled the chair that was usually Elizabeth's up to the table and sat across from Liz.

Howland turned back to Liz. "What did you have against Dojan? Did you think you had to get rid of him because he was onto your scheme? You botched that big-time. Dojan didn't have any idea of your involvement."

Liz Tate looked from Victoria to Howland. "I came here only because Domingo was so insistent. Not to be insulted."

Victoria lifted her mug to her lips and watched Liz Tate over the rim.

"I think you know what an angry Chief Medeiros can do," Howland said. "It's not pretty. You were wise to take Domingo's advice. Stay out of the chief's way until he cools off. Perhaps you can discuss things with him then."

"This conversation is too strange." Liz Tate pushed the chair back and stood.

"Let me tell you a story. It made things much clearer to the chief." Howland reached into his back pocket, withdrew his black leather folder, flipped it open, and held the DEA badge and ID out for Liz to see.

Liz Tate examined it and sat down again.

~ ~ ~

"Where's he going in such a hurry?" Shipyard was at the corner table in the ArtCliff Diner. He stood up and went over to the window as the cruiser sped by on Beach Road.

"Who was it?" Beanie slurped his coffee. "That black cop who's been causing all the trouble?"

"The black cop didn't make the trouble. It was that jerk-off redneck patrolman." Red reached for the sugar bowl, dumped two spoonfuls of sugar into his coffee, and stirred vigorously.

Shipyard returned to the table. "It was the Oak Bluffs po-leece chief himself."

"What's he doing in this neck of the woods?" Red put the spoon on the table and took a sip.

"Who knows?" Beanie said.

"Tough about his kid. I hear he's taking it hard." Red set the mug back on the table.

"Can't blame him. The kid was a handful, but still in all ..." Shipyard studied a puckered spot on the plastic tablecloth where someone had spilled something hot.

The three were respectfully silent for a moment.

"Anything happening with the investigation into Bernie's murder?" Beanie asked. "And Meatloaf's? Haven't heard a word about that since they arrested that" — he looked up and saw Dotty, hands on her hips, glaring at him — "that Latino harbor master."

"He wasn't even on the Island when Meatloaf got it," Shipyard said. "The cops released him."

Dotty brought menus and swiped the tablecloth with her damp rag. "Want to hear today's specials?"

"Might as well."

"Meat loaf with mashed potatoes, side dish of green beans. Apple pie for dessert," she recited.

"Meatloaf." Red looked down at his knife. "Meatloaf."

"That what you want?" Dotty looked around the table. "Meat loaf? All of you?"

"No. We was just talking about him," Beanie said. "I don't feel like meat loaf. What else you got?"

"Liver and onions. Chicken-fried pork chops. Chowder."

"The chowder fresh?" Red asked.

"You know it is. Dojan Minnowfish brought me a bushel of quahogs last night."

"He outta jail?" Beanie asked Shipyard.

"He didn't do nothing. Tied one on is all. Had him in there until he dried out."

Shipyard handed the menu back to Dotty. "Chowder. As long as it's not that New York stuff you served couple years back. Watery vegetable soup was all it was."

"I made this with milk, potatoes, onions, lots of clams, and salt pork. A half cup of quahogs in every bowl."

"Yeah, I'll take that."

"Same for me," Red said.

"Same here." Beanie passed his menu to her.

Shipyard looked up as a siren sped past. "There he goes again, back the way he came. Looks like he's about to have a stroke."

"Who's he know lives this way?" Beanie said.

"That selectman — selectwoman — selectperson — whatever you call them now — has a place on Hatch Road."

"Hatch Road? Where all the beautiful people live?"

"Where does she get the money to live there?" Beanie asked. "I'm in the wrong business, that's for sure."

"They paying selectmen that much these days?"

"Could be. That town's crazy enough," Shipyard said. "Wanna run for Oak Bluffs selectman, Beanie?"

"No way. I ain't that crazy."

"Ex-husband's money, I think," Red said.

"She's a cold fish. He's lucky to be rid of her. Butter wouldn't melt in her mouth."

"She feels the same about you, Beanie," Shipyard said.

"Here you are, boys." Dotty had three heavy white china bowls of chowder lined up along her left arm, and a larger bowl of chowder crackers in her right hand. She set the bowls in front of the men, the chowder crackers in the middle of the table. "Anything else? Salad? Coleslaw? Apple pie?"

"More coffee." Beanie held out his mug.

"A slice of pie later," Red added.

~ ~ ~

Allison heard heavy footsteps on the stairs outside her third-floor room over the Sand Bar, and she opened the door a small crack to see a red-faced Chief Medeiros on the other side.

"Where's Liz Tate?" he demanded, tugging off his sunglasses.

"I don't keep track of my aunt." She held the door open a crack, one hand on the knob, the other flat against the door.

"I need to find her, kid, immediately."

"How am I supposed to know where she's at?"

"Let me in, kid." He pushed the door open against her hands, backing her into the room. Allison tossed her hair out of her eyes and set clenched fists on her hips as he strode into her space. Her aunt was the only person she'd ever let see her room.

Allison had been working at a small rickety table under the window. She had stuck a paint brush behind her ear; a daub of blue paint flecked her cheek.

A hot plate on the floor under the table was plugged into a tangle of extension cords. The Raybeez blared at top volume from the stereo. The TV blasted discordantly.

Much of her floor space was taken up by an unmade futon. Her teddy bear sat on a shelf above it.

She had taped up on the wall her watercolors and pen and ink sketches of Oak Bluffs scenes, most of them views around the harbor — boats, the Harbor House, the harbor master's shack, the gingerbread houses.

The chief stood in the middle of her floor and glanced around. "Your aunt do those?" He spoke above the cacophony, nodding at the drawings on the wall.

"They're mine." Allison kept her hands on her hips.

He looked around her room, his eyes poking into all her stuff. "I need to find her, kid. Your aunt."

"You don't see her here, do you?" She tossed her head, her hair swinging away from her face.

"I've got business with her." The chief's face flushed an unhealthy red. He spoke loudly, trying to be heard above the noise. "Where is she?"

"How am I supposed to know? Try Town Hall."

"She comes by here, call me. Understand, kid? Here's my card. That's my pager number. Reach me anytime." Allison took the card.

"You understand, call me?"

"Maybe." Allison looked down at the card.

"Maybe, nothing. Call."

"Sure, sure." Allison held the door open until he stepped into the hall and clumped down the wooden stairs to the ground floor, his footsteps shaking the building as he descended.

She made a fist and shook it at his back.

~ ~ ~

When the phone rang, Victoria answered. Howland and Liz sat silently at the table, Liz staring at her coffee mug, turning it around in circles on the cloth. Howland had gone through his act, telling Liz his tale of drug smuggling and murder. She'd protested, demurred. Acted angry and hurt and puzzled.

Howland had been courteous and distant. Victoria followed his diplomatic maneuvering, a side of him she had never seen before. The fencing had gone on for a half hour before the call came.

"Domingo, I'm glad to hear from you," Victoria said. Liz and Howland both looked up.

"Allison called you?" Victoria glanced at Liz. "Yes, she's here. Do you want to talk to her?" She waited for Domingo to finish what he was saying. She looked at her watch. "I imagine he'll stay until Elizabeth gets home." She looked questioningly at Howland, who nodded, and then she hung the phone back on the wall.

"That was Domingo. Allison called him just a few minutes ago. The chief is looking for you, Liz."

"Well, I guess that settles it." Liz Tate stood. "Show me to my room."

"After we finish our little talk," Howland said.

"I don't want to hear more." Liz moved toward the kitchen.

"Perhaps you don't want to hear more, but I have one hell of a lot more to tell you." Howland's high cheekbones had bright spots of color. "Sit down and listen to me. You're in serious trouble, lady."

Liz sat.

"You have a choice." Howland pushed his chair back slightly. "Prison, on the one hand, or the wrath of two powerful enemies you've made, Rocky, with his subtle ways of handling problems, and Chief Medeiros, who is less subtle."

"I have no problem with Rocky," Liz said sulkily, tracing a line on the table-cloth with her finger.

"You think not?" Howland fixed her with a bright stare.

"I have no problem with Rocky," Liz repeated.

"More coffee?" Victoria asked, getting up from the table.

Liz Tate shook her head. Her hair swirled around her face.

"We know where you got the atropine you put in the fudge. Nightshade berries. We collected the plants from your garden and can identify where berries were detached from the stems. The decorative swirls on your fudge are your own unique touch. The ladies who run the church fair identified the fudge as resembling yours. We've traced the chocolate, the sugar, and the cream you used to the market on Circuit Avenue, where they know you and recall your purchasing them. We found the man to whom you gave the shopping bag, the man who gave the bag with the fudge in it to Louie. Whether you intended to kill the chief's son or not, this is murder."

Liz Tate spoke softly, still tracing her fingernail along a pattern on the table-cloth. "It wasn't meant for Manny. What do you want me to do?"

"Testify against Rocky," Howland said without emphasis.

"My God! Never." Liz stopped running her fingernail along the tablecloth and looked up. "You know what he'd do to me?"

"I can imagine," Howland said dryly. "Care to think about what the chief will do to you?"

Liz Tate put her head in her hands. Her hair cascaded over her face, hiding it.

Howland said nothing.

Victoria fiddled with her cup.

McCavity stalked into the room and began to wash himself, one leg high in the air.

Victoria looked down at the cat with a faint smile.

Howland folded his arms over his chest. "Dare I say you made your own bed?" He leaned back in the chair. When he saw Victoria's expression, he set the chair back on its four legs. Liz stood, paced the small room, sat again. McCavity stopped cleaning himself long enough to stare at her. He stretched, yawned, investigated the wastebasket, leapt into it, and curled up, a ginger-colored mound.

"What do you have in mind?" Liz said in a small voice.

"I have a typed confession." Howland rummaged through his green canvas briefcase and brought it out. "In this, you explain in detail how you attempted to kill Dojan, believing that he knew you were involved in the drug-smuggling scheme, and how you killed Fatso Medeiros instead."

"I didn't mean to kill him." Liz lifted her head.

"You intended to kill Dojan, didn't you?"

Liz put her head in her hands again.

"You intended to kill, and you did kill. You killed the chief's son in a most un-pleasant way. Doesn't matter who you intended to kill; someone died as a result of your actions." He put the typed confession in front of her. "It is against the law to kill people. Read this."

She lifted her head again.

"Make whatever corrections are necessary. I'll call the notary up at Alley's store, ask her to come here to witness our signing it. You, Victoria, and I will sign."

"What are you going to do with it?" Liz looked up, face contrasting whitely with her black hair and red lipstick.

"Use it if I need to."

"What about Rocky?" Liz spoke so softly it took Victoria a second to understand what she'd said. "I would never do anything to hurt him."

"Rocky got you involved in this, didn't he?"

"He trusts me. I would never harm him, will never testify against him, no matter what."

Howland went on as if he hadn't heard her. "I have a typed affidavit explaining your relationship with Rocky, and your role in the drug operation."

"And I'm to read it, make corrections, and sign."

Howland said nothing. He held the pen out to her.

"I can't do it. He loves me." She put her head down on her arms. "And I love him. He asked me to marry him."

Victoria stared at her cup, eyes half-closed, her wrinkled face a topographic map of disapproval. "He's not likely to marry you if you're in prison for murder."

Liz lifted her head. "What do you plan to do with this affidavit?"

"We use it in court with other evidence to lock up Rocky for a long, long time."

"My God!" Liz paled.

"I can recommend a lesser sentence for you on the basis of your cooperation."

"When I get out, my life won't be worth a damn."

"Probably not," Howland said. "However, it's likely that Rocky will get a life sentence. The chief will be spirited away to some unknown place in a witness protection program."

The kitchen door opened and Elizabeth came in. The American flag stood out sharply on her starched uniform sleeve. She stopped when she reached the cookroom door.

"Sorry. I didn't mean to interrupt."

Victoria saw Elizabeth's puzzled expression as she glanced from Howland, whose face was grim, to Liz, who was staring, white-faced, at her folded hands, and then to Victoria.

Victoria pushed herself away from the table, got slowly to her feet, and said to her granddaughter, "We need to get the downstairs room made up."

~ ~ ~

CHAPTER EIGHTEEN

Victoria Goes Lobstering

"MR. D trusts you alone in this place?" Louie had come into the shack where Allison was working with a pile of receipts.

"He put me in charge for a couple hours. I'm hardly alone. Have you looked around the harbor lately?"

"I'll be glad when the president's outta here." Louie slapped a handful of receipts on the desk in front of Allison. "Here are some more."

Allison shuffled through the receipts Louie had given her. "When are you going to learn how to write? I can't read any of this stuff, you know?"

"So what?" Louie slumped into the chair in front of the computer, entered something, and moved the mouse around. "They forgot to take off the games when they installed the harbor stuff. I'll bet Mr. D plays Minesweeper when no one's here."

"Leave it alone," Allison said sharply.

"Listen to you now. Little Miss Lawsuit."

The radio crackled. Louie answered, gave the skipper a slip number, then hung up the mike.

An angular man wearing an earphone and a button in the lapel of his blazer came to the window. "I need to use your radio," he said to Louie.

"I'm in charge here, not him," Allison said.

"Sure," Louie said. "Anything for the president."

The man turned his back on Louie and Allison while he talked in semicode to a vessel. Then he hung up the mike and left.

"You could say thank you," Allison shouted after him, but he was already off the catwalk.

An elderly woman came to the window. "Would you know, miss, when the president will be arriving?"

"No, ma'am. Today or tomorrow, I guess."

"Will he come here to Oak Bluffs?"

"I'm sorry, ma'am, I don't know what his plans are. Maybe for the fireworks tomorrow."

"Thank you so much, miss."

"At least I been doing important stuff." Louie wadded up a piece of paper and tossed it at the wastepaper basket. It missed and fell on the floor. Allison kicked it.

"Yeah? Like what?"

"I did stuff for Meatloaf. He paid me. A lot."

"So what are you doing for Meatloaf now? Planting grass?"

"I don't know why I bother to talk to you." Louie clicked the mouse on the game. "I been doing stuff for the selectmen."

"My aunt, I suppose. Her errand boy."

The phone rang. Allison answered, took a message for Domingo, and hung up.

A sailboat came in through the channel, and Allison went out on the deck with her clipboard. She called out a slip number and pointed; the skipper nodded thanks.

She stepped back inside the shack, finished sorting the receipts, and took them over to the computer. "Mind if I do some real work?"

Louie's face flushed. He exited from the games program, stood up, and stretched. Allison took the seat he'd vacated and opened up the reservations program.

"You're wasting your time. You know that, don't you?"

"So?" Allison continued to enter data.

"Mr. D thinks he's so smart, computerizing everything." Louie put his hands in his pockets and sauntered over to the window that overlooked the parking lot. "He's making a lot of enemies is what he's doing."

"Why don't you shut up and let me do my work, you know?"

"You wouldn't talk so smart if you knew what I been doing."

"What've you been doing? You're just dying to tell me, aren't you?"

A call came over the radio. The phone rang. Allison took the radio call while Louie answered the phone.

"You know that big tree limb that came down in Elizabeth's driveway?" Louie said when it was quiet again.

"Yeah?"

"I did that."

"Well, whatever you were trying to do, it didn't work."

"Yeah, it did."

"I'm not impressed." Allison held up a receipt and stared at it. "What does this say? What's this boat name?"

Louie looked at it. *"Night Hawk?* I don't know. *Right Stuff?"*

"Is the boat still here?"

"Probably."

"Go back and write the name so we can read it, will you?"

"Furthermore, that accident she had? On Barnes Road? I set that up."

"Let me work, will you?" Allison pushed her hair away from her face with her shoulder. "I don't want to hear this stuff."

"It scared her shitless. Scared her old lady, too."

"Mrs. Trumbull scared? I don't think so." Allison waved her hand in front of her face. "I suppose you left those notes, too?"

"That's right."

"Whoever thought that up was stupid."

"I thought that up." Louie stood. "That was hardly stupid. Mr. D was pretty worried about that, too. Still is."

"Not really. You finished bragging? How about going away and doing your job, you know? Here are a couple more receipts no one can read."

When Louie sauntered off, whistling, batting his receipt book against the railing as he went, Allison called Domingo and told him what Louie had said.

~ ~ ~

Dojan pulled his lobster boat up to the floating dock at the foot of the harbor master's shack, where Victoria waited, sitting on a chair Elizabeth had put there for her.

Dojan's wooden boat was not large, maybe eighteen feet long, had a small cabin forward, a large cockpit aft, and an outboard motor patched with black vinyl tape and shiny aluminum duct tape. A long tiller led from a large red-painted rudder dotted with barnacles. The rudder had a cutout near the stern of the boat for the outboard motor. Most of the boat's paint had flaked off, and what remained was mostly green, with touches of black and red. The flat, broad gunwales were worn and splintery, as if over the seasons Dojan had pulled his lobster pots aboard there.

He shut off the motor, tied the lines to dock cleats, and leapt nimbly onto the dock. His bare feet splayed out.

"You came!" His grin showed his missing tooth.

"Did you think I wouldn't?" Victoria rose, holding on to the railing, and picked up a basket that was next to her. "I brought lunch, roast chicken and hard-boiled eggs."

Dojan rolled his eyes.

"Napkins and orange juice." She looked up at him and smiled. "I decided not to bring fudge for dessert."

His mouth formed a pink O in the middle of his beard. "You gonna be warm enough?"

"I'm layered." Victoria showed him the windbreaker Howland had lent her. Under that was the heavy Canadian sweater from Fiona's parents, then the gray moth-eaten sweater of Elizabeth's, under that a down vest that didn't quite close, and then a stretched-out red turtleneck shirt. She started to lift that, and Dojan hurriedly held up his hand. "If you get cold, I have jackets and blankets and hats."

"I have leather work gloves so I can haul pots." Victoria held up her gardening gloves, a hole in the thumb mended with masking tape.

Elizabeth came down the ramp to the dock. "For heaven's sake, Gram, you'd think it was February."

"I expect to be outside working, not idling."

"Don't fall overboard. With all those clothes, you'll sink like a stone."

"They'll be full of air, buoy me up."

"Bring home a lot of lobsters. I'll get your lines."

Dojan helped the bulky Victoria aboard and leapt into the boat after her. She sat on a box he'd brought for her. He started the engine, Elizabeth tossed the lines aboard, and Dojan steered slowly out of the channel. Victoria, still seated, coiled his lines neatly.

When they were clear of the buoys at the mouth of the channel, Dojan opened up the throttle, and the boat lifted in the water, the engine humming. Victoria noticed him cock his head toward the sound of the motor, as if listening to it, watched him steer with the slightest movement of the long tiller. The wind ruffled his hair, blew his beard away from his face, and sent his skull scarf streaming behind him. His bare arms, tattooed with eagles and roses, were dark brown, sun and dirt combined.

Victoria shed some of her layers. First the windbreaker, which she rolled up and tossed into the cabin, then the heavy sweater. Soon she was down to the red turtleneck, and the cabin floor had a heap of clothing on it. Dojan nodded. His eyes were clear; his mouth was open in a wide smile.

They turned right toward Cape Pogue, the same route the whale-watch boat had taken. Gulls trailed after them, mewing. The motor hummed quietly, and small waves slapped against the bow. Before they reached the cape, Dojan slowed. Victoria could see the line of low shore and the lighthouse on the tip. Dojan pointed, and she saw his lobster-pot buoys bobbing in the water, yellow, with two blue stripes around them. He steered next to the first buoy, reached into the water, and pulled it on board. He hauled up the line fastened to the buoy, and Victoria saw the trap rising through the clear green water.

"Couple of keepers there." Dojan dumped the lobsters onto the deck and tossed the lobster pot overboard.

"Only a couple? It looks like a dozen to me, Dojan."

"See those marks on the gunwale? They gotta be that long."

Victoria moved her feet out of the way as lobsters scurried around the deck, claws clashing. Dojan grabbed the littlest ones by their backs and dropped them overboard. He reached into a coffee can for a handful of wide yellow rubber bands and fitted them over the claws of the two largest lobsters, then dropped them into a white plastic bucket of seawater. He shaded the bucket with a piece of dirty gray canvas.

The boat rocked gently. Dojan pulled his pots, dumped out lobsters, and dropped the pots overboard with a smooth rhythm. Victoria sorted out the smallest lobsters and tossed them overboard. Her work gloves were soon wet and coated with slimy green algae. The masking tape disintegrated, exposing her thumb.

Gulls cried and dived at schools of small fish; the sun wheeled overhead. Neither Victoria nor Dojan spoke.

Finally, Dojan stood erect, stretched his arms out to the side, and said, "That's all."

Victoria counted the lobsters. "We have a nice mess, at least fifteen."

Dojan grinned.

Victoria looked at him. "It's a nice picnic spot."

They tossed their gnawed-on chicken bones into the Sound. They cracked the eggs against the gunwale and flicked the shells overboard, where large fish rose to the surface to snap at the remains. Gulls fought and squabbled and cried over their picnic leftovers. Victoria dipped her hands into the water, washed off the chicken fat, reached into her pocket for a napkin, and dried her face. She grinned happily at Dojan, who grinned back. The boat rocked gently, waves lapping against its wooden sides.

"When does the tide change?" Victoria had been watching trees on the shore pass them as the boat drifted slowly toward the arc of Cape Pogue.

"Full flood now." Dojan's mouth was full of chicken, his beard full of crumbs and dripping fat. He tossed the bone he'd been gnawing overboard, and a fish snatched it and dived with a silver flash. "Slack tide in two hours. Change, a half hour after that." He wiped his forearm across his mouth.

Victoria watched the shoreline drift past. The near trees seemed to move faster than the distant ones. Dim objects approached, became rocks or boats pulled up on the shore, or tree trunks washed in from far places. The objects faded behind them as they drifted slowly. When they neared Cape Pogue, she could see what looked like an array of slender poles. At first, she thought they were fishing rods stuck in the sand, but as they came closer, she saw they were tall masts on the other side of the spit. They drifted toward the cape. There were six or seven large sailboats clustered together beyond the breaking surf along the straight east shore.

"Are they at anchor?"

Dojan turned and stood up. "They're big."

"Are they rafted up? Seems like an out-of-the-way place for an overnight stay."

Dojan ducked into the cabin and came out with a pair of binoculars. He held them to his eyes and adjusted the focus.

"They're not from here. Saint Croix, Saint Thomas, Grand Turk. I can't read them all."

"That's unusual, isn't it? After making a long cruise, don't boats like that come into the harbor?"

Dojan scratched his stomach and burped.

"May I look?" She held out her hand for the binoculars, and Dojan passed them to her. They were greasy where he had held them. "There's only one anchor out. No, two. They're rafted together. They must know each other."

"Not much room in the harbor. Full of law vessels."

"If there's no room in the harbor, why wouldn't they anchor outside, where they can row their dinghies into shore? There's nothing here. No houses, no stores, no people, no nothing. Even the lighthouse is automated, no lighthouse keepers." She handed the binoculars back to Dojan.

"My great-grandfather was the Gay Head lighthouse keeper," Dojan said. "He lighted the kerosene lamp every night. He used to wind the clockwork that made the light go around. He lived in a house next to the light."

"That would have been your father's grandfather, wouldn't it? I didn't know him, but my big sister did."

"They didn't have electricity then. My grandmother remembered when the electricity came Up Island."

"I remember, too, Dojan. That wasn't so long ago."

Dojan gazed at her. "I wasn't born."

He stood in the stern, next to the tiller. The wind had picked up and his hair blew back from his face.

"Dojan." Victoria settled herself on her box seat with her back to the cabin. "I want you to do something for me." She looked up at him soberly.

"Yes, ma'am. I'll move the sun and the moon for you."

"As I recall, you're the Wind and the Rain."

Dojan grinned. "Yes, ma'am."

"What do you think of the tribal council?" Victoria put her hands beside her, her right hand resting on the coiled line.

"The tribal council." Dojan scratched under his arm and thought. "Good people."

"If you did something wrong, would you tell the council?"

Dojan stared at her, motionless. "Yes, ma'am."

"Would you tell them even if you knew they would punish you and the punishment would be harsh?"

"I am a Wampanoag from Aquinnah." Dojan stood up straight, his hand on the tiller. His eyes settled firmly on Victoria's somber face. "I can take what's due me."

Victoria took a deep breath. "You know it was wrong to harpoon that man."

Dojan swallowed. He looked over at the large boats anchored behind the curve of the spit. "Yes, ma'am." He swallowed again and looked at Victoria. "There was nobody I could tell. I couldn't tell the police chief, after I saw what he'd done."

"You could have told me," Victoria said quietly.

"Yes, ma'am. I trusted you. I should have told you. I was ashamed." He slapped his hands on his stomach. "There's been a thing growing inside me since that night. I tried to sweat it out. I tried drowning it out. I told Domingo." He lowered his head. "I keep seeing that man fall into the water. I still remember that red-hot anger I felt. I hurt bad."

"Who's the head of the tribal council now?" Victoria asked.

"Chief Hawkbill," Dojan said.

"He's your father's second cousin, isn't he?"

"Yes, ma'am."

"Go to him tomorrow and tell him what you told Domingo. The tribal council will deal out the punishment they believe is right. Will you do that?"

"Yes, ma'am." Dojan bowed his head.

"We'd better go. The breeze is picking up."

Dojan pulled the starter cord, the motor cut on smoothly, he steered the boat into the wind, and they headed home. The wind had stirred up whitecaps. Waves slapped the bow, spraying salt water over Victoria, whose back was to it. She blinked the spray out of her eyes. Her eyebrows and eyelashes were crusted with salt.

"We need to tell Domingo about those sailboats." Victoria reached into the cabin for her warm clothes. She put on the down vest and Elizabeth's gray sweater over it. "It seems strange to have boats from such a distance clustered so far from anything."

Dojan steered with the tiller tilted up so he could stand. His black beard, his hair, his eyebrows had turned white, rimed with salt. He had aged. Victoria laughed. She had not.

"Will you go with me?" Dojan asked.

"I will if you give me a ride and take me home again."

Dojan nodded his white-tipped head.

They cut straight from Cape Pogue to Oak Bluffs, crossing the wide-open bay that surrounded the beach. Whitecaps sparkled as far as they could see. Dojan stood straight, his shoulders thrown back, his head up, and began to sing a sea chantey that Victoria knew. She joined in the chorus with her strong voice: "Look away! Look away, you jolly, jolly boys, look away!"

When they reached the lee of East Chop, the water was calm. Dojan turned into the channel and slowed to bare headway.

Elizabeth came down the ramp to the floating dock. The long muscles in her slim tan legs flexed smoothly as she walked.

"See what I brought back for our supper." Victoria held up two lobsters for her granddaughter's inspection.

"Did you have a good time, Gram? Was it rough out there? Were you warm enough?"

"I was glad I was prepared. You never know, on the water."

Elizabeth helped her grandmother out of the boat, and Dojan took off again toward the liquor store. He turned to Victoria as he left the dock. "Tomorrow morning." He held up his hand to her, and she returned his salute.

"What was that all about?" Elizabeth asked.

"They buy his lobsters at the liquor store," Victoria said.

"But — " Elizabeth started to say.

"Domingo!" Victoria interrupted. "I'm back."

"So his boat didn't sink after all." Domingo was waiting at the door of the shack.

"I'll be right back," Elizabeth said, striding up the ramp. "I need to help that sailboat with lines."

Victoria paused at the top of the ramp, out of breath, and watched Elizabeth run toward a boat that was pulling into a slip. Victoria carried the two lobsters by their backs; they flipped their tails and flailed the air with their unbound legs.

Once she had seated herself on the chair in the shack and had taken a couple of deep breaths, she turned to Domingo, who was leaning on the railing outside the shack.

"Before Elizabeth gets back, I wanted to tell you that Dojan is going to the tribal council tomorrow. It's poisoning him. He needs to get it out of his system."

"You did the right thing, sweetheart. You're a better man than either Howland or me."

"Something else," Victoria said. "What would you say if someone told you there were seven boats anchored on the other side of Cape Pogue, all big boats, all from the Caribbean?"

Domingo gazed at her.

"When the harbor is teeming with police of all kinds?"

"Sweetheart, I'd say you found another piece of the puzzle." He reached around inside the door for the phone. "Atherton needs to know about this."

~ ~ ~

Howland was walking his dogs on the beach below his house when his cell phone rang. It was Domingo, telling him about the sailboats off Cape Pogue.

Howland immediately contacted the DEA and the Coast Guard. They dispatched the two Coast Guard cutters from the Oak Bluffs Harbor to the far side of Cape Pogue, along with two spotter planes and a DEA helicopter from Otis National Guard Base on Cape Cod.

The pilots reported activity on the deck of one of the sailboats. The crews from all seven boats seemed to be baiting and setting a dozen or so lobster pots.

The aircraft pilot reported this back to her lieutenant, who reported back to Howland, who told them to photograph everything. He requested that the Coast Guard cutters circle the sailboats until the DEA paperwork and people were in place.

"They're not likely to run for it," Howland said to the lieutenant. "Top speed for those sailboats is six or seven knots. They may try to jettison drug packages. Get the pilot to spot where they drift, if she can. They probably plan to hold the drugs in lobster pots until someone can retrieve them."

"When you're ready, we'll escort the boats to the harbor," the lieutenant told him, "and you guys can take over."

"There are at least two dozen law-enforcement officers there. This will give them something to do." Howland disconnected and headed for home with his dogs.

~ ~ ~

Elizabeth dropped her grandmother off at Domingo's on her way to work the next afternoon, and Victoria met with Domingo and Howland.

"Chief Medeiros is going to get away with committing Bernie's murder, isn't he?" Victoria asked Domingo. "I'm sorry for him, in a way, and somewhat sympathetic, but justice won't be served if he gets off."

"Sweetheart, Chief Medeiros is going to have the worst-possible punishment." Domingo gazed out the window. "He is going into the witness protection program. His daughter will go to live with her mother and the diesel salesman out west, and he may never see her again." Domingo turned slightly, and Victoria examined his profile, curved nose, large lower lip, bright eyes. "He will lose his identity completely as a police officer. He'll lose his roots. He will never again be able to be with family on birthdays or Christmases. He will start a new life in a place he probably doesn't want to be. If he breaks free of the program, Rocky's people will get him. If they don't, the DEA will."

"He didn't kill Meatloaf. Dojan did. I don't want to see Dojan put away somewhere, but ..." Victoria left the rest of her sentence unfinished.

"You went with him to the tribal council?" Domingo asked.

"This morning. He wanted me to go with him while he talked to Chief Hawkbill, and I did."

Howland whistled. "Nice job, Victoria."

"The tribal council knows how to deal with this." Domingo took out a cigarette and lit it.

"He's not as crazy as he appears," Howland said.

"Of course not," Victoria retorted. "He and I went to the tribal chief. Dojan told him everything, the murder he witnessed, his fight with Meatloaf. Dojan is wild with guilt. The chief is going to discuss it with the tribal elders."

"I wonder what their idea of punishment is," Howland murmured.

"I don't know." Victoria looked down at her hands, green-streaked from pulling weeds. "Chief Hawkbill said something about sending Dojan to Washington as tribal representative."

Howland put his hand on top of Victoria's, a strong square hand on top of her knobby one.

~ ~ ~

CHAPTER NINETEEN

Vineyard Fireworks

THE FOG bank held offshore for most of the day, a thick ominous gray mass that loomed on the horizon. Late in the afternoon, it began to move. From the beach, the fog looked as if it was rolling steadily toward the Island across the water, a woolly fleece, sucked inland by the rising warm air in the center of the Island. Tendrils and wisps of fog drifted across the sun, veiling it, making it a pinkish yellow disk.

On the beaches, the last of the sunbathers and swimmers tugged sweatshirts over their heads, wrapped towels or terry cloth robes around them, gathered up the remaining children, and headed back to rented cottages and hotel rooms.

In the Sound, foghorns intermittently wailed a mournful warning of shoals and rocks. The ferries sounded their higher-pitched whistles as they inched their way toward the Island.

Streamers of fog wafted past the harbor master's shack. A boater came to the window, his hair and yellow slicker beaded with moisture, and Elizabeth slid the window open.

The boater wiped his face with the back of his hand. "It's thick out there." He unzipped his jacket and took his wallet from an inside pocket. "Any slips available?"

"The slips are all taken. There are a few moorings still." Elizabeth waved a hand toward the center of the harbor, which neither of them could see. "Are you at the fuel dock now?"

He nodded.

Domingo was standing with his back to Elizabeth and the sailor. "There should be two or three places left. Four boats to a mooring." He turned. "Think you can find it okay?"

"Yeah. We came over for the fireworks last year." The sailor laughed and indicated the thick fog.

"It might clear a little by this evening." Domingo shrugged. "You never know with Island weather."

The sailor took a bill out of his wallet and handed it to Elizabeth. "One night."

She filled out a receipt, gave him change, and watched him disappear into the murky cloud. Another figure materialized.

"Damn, Domingo. Here's that arrogant Secret Service guy again." She turned away from the window. "You deal with him."

The agent came into the shack without knocking and propped himself against the edge of the desk, folded his arms across his chest, and stared sullenly at Elizabeth. He was a tall, hefty, dark-haired man.

Domingo started to say something to the agent, but Elizabeth interrupted, flushed with irritation. "Don't you guys believe in manners?"

"May I please come into the harbor master's office, ma'am?" he said without unfolding his arms. "So I can guard the president of the United States, if you don't mind."

"Funny," Elizabeth said sourly.

He was there for only a few minutes when a state trooper came in. "Need to use the radio." Domingo pointed to it. While the trooper was talking on the radio, a Coast Guardsman showed up at the door. "I'm supposed to check your radio against ours."

"As soon as that guy gets off," Domingo said.

Two women in yellow rain slickers came to the window. The phone rang. A voice on the radio asked to talk to the trooper. The Coast Guardsman picked up the mike and responded. The Secret Service agent crossed one ankle over the other, unfolded his arms long enough to take a pack of gum out of his pocket, unwrapped a stick, tossed the rolled-up wrapper toward the wastebasket, fed the stick into his mouth, and refolded his arms over his chest.

"You know, guys, we need to use our radio, too," Elizabeth said. "Believe it or not."

"Won't be a minute," the Coast Guardsman said apologetically.

Elizabeth went over to the desk, where the Secret Service agent lolled. "Move out of my way, buster. I need to get into that drawer."

He slid over, arms still folded. She opened the drawer, took the receipt book to the counter, and started to thumb through pages.

"Where's your grandmother?" Domingo asked her.

"Reading to the elderly at the hospital. . . . Sixteen, seventeen, eighteen . . ."

"Don't you think you should pick her up?" Domingo put his hands in his pockets and stared out at the grayness.

Elizabeth held her place in the book. "She'll be fine." She went back to counting. "Twenty-five, twenty-six, twen — "

"It's hazardous driving."

"She'll be fine, Domingo. Really. She's a big girl. Thirty-two, thirty-three . ."

"She going to watch the fireworks tonight?"

"Yes. Thirty-four, thirty-five . ."

"With this pea soup, there won't be much to see. Only a lot of racket. We'll shoehorn her in with the boys." Domingo nodded at the crowded shack.

Elizabeth slapped the book shut. "Damnation, Domingo. I lost count. Noreen's driving my grandmother here to the harbor. You, Domingo, are driving me crazy." She looked around at the law-enforcement people cluttering the small office.

Domingo turned from the window. "When's she due here?"

Elizabeth sighed and looked at her watch. "She'll be here any minute."

"I don't like her out alone." Domingo stared at the fog.

"Come on, Domingo. She's with Noreen."

Domingo stepped outside, lighted a cigarette, and paced. He tossed the cigarette overboard. "I'm going to look for them."

"Give them another couple of minutes."

The parking lot had disappeared. The catwalk seemed to be suspended in space over a bottomless void. The planks of the walk appeared and disappeared in eddies of fog.

"You there, Mike?" A second Coast Guardsman rapped on the door frame and entered the shack.

"Yes, sir. I'm waiting to use the radio."

The trooper, who was speaking into the mike, held up his hand in acknowledgment.

Domingo checked his watch. "Something may have happened."

A diver in a blue-and-black wetsuit with scuba tanks on his back and swim fins on his feet slapped into the shack.

"Why don't you guys have your own radios?" Elizabeth snapped.

"Ma'am, I wondered if you had a Band-Aid?" the diver asked.

Elizabeth opened the first-aid kit and handed a couple to the diver. He took off one of his swim fins and looked up sheepishly at her. "Blister."

"Here they come now, Domingo." Elizabeth straightened up and peered through the fog.

They could hear Noreen's high voice, Victoria's deeper one, and then the two women appeared out of the silvery mist. Victoria's white hair glistened with droplets of moisture.

Cynthia Riggs

Victoria leaned over the railing. "You can barely see the harbor master's launch through the fog." The launch was tied to the shack's pilings. Beyond it, Elizabeth could vaguely make out the shape of a Coast Guard cutter with its diagonal red slash across the bow.

"What kept you?" Domingo said crossly.

"Nothing kept us." Noreen looked around. "Jesus, this is like a commuter bus."

Victoria wiped moisture off her face with a napkin from her pocket and sat down. "Will they still have the fireworks?"

"It's on the president's schedule. It will take more than fog for them to cancel," Domingo answered.

"You guys hanging around all night?" Noreen asked the agent leaning against the desk.

"Yep."

Elizabeth scowled at him.

The phone rang. Elizabeth pawed people aside to answer it. The agent's beeper went off. He looked at the number on it.

"Let me have the phone," he said to Elizabeth, who was taking a reservation. "Hang up."

Elizabeth glared at him, excused herself to the caller, and handed the phone to the agent. A customer had come up to the window, and she pushed past the state trooper, who, in stepping aside, bumped into her.

"Sorry, ma'am."

Elizabeth snapped. "Clear out, all of you! You." She pointed to the agent, who had hung up the phone. "Outside. Guard the president from that bench out there. Out!"

The shack cleared, and Domingo looked at Elizabeth with respect.

A powerboat entered the harbor, cruised around slowly, and departed again.

"Who let them in?" Elizabeth said. "I thought someone was keeping boats out of the harbor."

"That's a police cruiser making its rounds," Domingo told her. "As we speak, divers are checking the harbor for anything out of the ordinary."

"Like explosive devices stuck on boats," Victoria said.

The radio on the Coast Guard cutter came on with a crackle of static and an announcement that consisted mostly of numbers.

Elizabeth put her hands over her ears. "I'll be glad when this day is over."

Deadly Nightshade

Domingo went out onto the deck, and Elizabeth heard the click of his Zippo. He took a few puffs and tossed his cigarette over the railing, then went back inside. On his way, he patted the shoulder of the Secret Service agent, who was sitting outside on the bench, his collar turned up against the steady drip of condensed fog spilling off the eaves onto his back.

Darkness crept in, filtered by the fog. As soon as Elizabeth hung up the phone from one call, it rang again. The scanning radio locked onto Channel 16, then Channel 22. Somewhere out in the foggy night, the Coast Guard was trying to assist a disabled vessel and an injured crew member.

"There seem to be a lot of people gathering," Victoria said. "You can hear them, even if you can't see them."

Elizabeth was aware of the soft murmur of voices, heard an occasional word she could almost identify.

By 8:30, the activity on the radio had quieted, and a half hour later, they heard the opening salvo of the fireworks.

Each time a rocket was shot off, the entire sky lighted up with a glow that lingered for a few seconds before the next was set off. Fog droplets reflected and refracted the light in a milky way that left no shadows and lit up the night softly. It was more magical than the displays would have been on a clear night.

Victoria turned to Elizabeth and gestured to the Secret Service agent sitting on the bench outside. "He looks miserable. He's welcome to have my seat."

Elizabeth rolled her eyes, then invited the agent back into the shack. He rose from the bench and shambled inside. The back of his jacket was wet.

With each detonation, the shack shuddered. No one talked over the noise. The display went on and on, lighting up the fog, blue, yellow, red, gold, green. Combinations of color were enhanced by the eerie drifting fog. It was difficult to tell where the explosions came from. Sound seemed to surround them; color engulfed them in swirls and eddies, the inside of a light bulb, the inside of a milk bottle.

"This must be the finale," Victoria said as the fog was pierced with galaxies of light, explosions of color and sound, a tattoo of quick reports, a thunderous blast, a series of pops like firecrackers, the smell of gunpowder. Then everything seemed to be detonated at once. Red and orange flashed in the fog to the west, yellow and green overhead, blue and purple to the south. A rainbow of soft colors shimmered in the opalescent sky. And then it was over.

Victoria applauded. So did the Secret Service agent.

"My name's Joshua." He offered Victoria his large hand, which she shook firmly. Elizabeth stared in astonishment as he stood and politely told Victoria, "It was real nice meeting you, ma'am. I'm afraid I've got to get back to the boss. He'll be leaving before the crowd does."

Car horns and boat horns honked, and boaters blasted their canned air horns. Hundreds of footsteps swished on the bulkhead. Elizabeth heard the single voice of a pleased crowd.

"They were smart not to cancel it." Victoria turned to one of the men next to her. "This was one of the most beautiful displays I've ever seen."

"You must have seen quite a few, ma'am."

"We used to burn punk sticks when I was a child. The only fireworks I remember were all white, like white rockets."

"I'll make the rounds of the harbor," Elizabeth said. "Where did you put the launch, Domingo?"

"Right there." Domingo went outside and pointed to where he'd tied the launch to the piling. The boat was gone.

"I'm sure it was there. I saw it when we came back from the hospital." Victoria was puzzled.

"Some watchdogs," Elizabeth muttered. "Two Coast Guard cutters, the Secret Service, the marine police, the state police, a conservation officer, the Oak Bluffs police, and visiting firemen. And someone walks off with the harbor master's launch. I hope you do a better job of watching the president."

She looked up as she heard pounding footsteps on the catwalk, and one of the dock attendants stumbled into the shack.

"Liz Tate," he gasped.

Domingo looked up. "What about Liz Tate?"

"She was parked," the kid said in between gasps for air, "Harbor House."

Domingo grabbed him by the arm. "What about it?"

"It's gone!"

"What are you talking about, the launch?"

"No, no," the dock attendant said. "Liz Tate!"

"Out with it." Domingo released his arm.

"Let him catch his breath, will you?" Elizabeth barked.

Domingo cut his eyes at Elizabeth. "You sound like my wife."

"Sure, Domingo," Noreen said from her seat on top of the desk, where she'd been sitting throughout the fireworks.

Domingo stepped back. He stared at the teenager. "Well?"

"She parked in front of the Harbor House." He was shivering. "She was watching the fireworks from her car with Louie."

"Who?" Domingo demanded.

"Louie, the dock attendant. The kid with green hair. I seen them sitting in the car, and the next second it disappeared."

"What!"

"There ain't nothing left," the kid said. "A hole is all."

"It exploded?" Victoria asked.

"Yes, ma'am. It blew up. Like a fireball. I seen them sitting there, and I seen it blow up."

"How long ago?"

"Right at the end. The finale. When the fireworks were going crazy. At the end. It vaporized."

"Did you report it to the police?"

"Somebody musta. There was a cop car there before I left to come here."

"You said Liz Tate and Louie were in the car when the explosion took place?"

The kid nodded.

Victoria stood up. "Let's go."

When they reached the Harbor House, both lanes were blocked with cars and people leaving after the fireworks. No one seemed to be concerned about an explosion involving a car.

The fire truck was held up by the stream of cars flowing away from town. Someone had witnessed the blast; someone had called 911. A small crowd was gathered around the space between a truck and a rusty Volvo, but no one in the passing cars seemed to notice the space in the line of parked cars or the pit where a car had been, or the damaged cars on either side.

It made no difference that the equipment could not get through. There was nothing anyone could do. The dock attendant was right: The car had vanished, leaving strewn debris, a deep pothole, a blue pickup truck with its bed blackened, and a rust red Volvo with its snout skewed.

While Victoria and Domingo were standing to one side, Howland arrived, disheveled from running.

"Heard it on the scanner," Howland said. "Who was it?"

"The dock attendant, Huey or Dewey, said it was Liz Tate's car. She was in it at the time of the explosion," Domingo informed him. "With Louie."

"Hell." Howland slammed his hand against the blue truck. "There goes my case. My chief witness. All I've got now is Medeiros. I should have anticipated something like that. Goddamn!"

"Liz was still at your house, wasn't she, sweetheart?" While he spoke, Domingo stood with his feet slightly apart, hands in his pockets, staring down at the hole. To Victoria, the hole didn't seem big enough for what had happened.

"She was staying in the downstairs room."

Howland paced. The small crowd of people looked and pointed and moved on, one by one or in groups of two or three.

"Should someone get yellow tape from the shack?" Victoria finally asked. "We need to keep sightseers away, don't we?"

Domingo shrugged. "It's not up to us. It's up to the police."

"Are they likely to find enough to identify anyone?" Victoria asked.

Domingo gave a macabre grin, white teeth flashing against his dark skin.

"Is it possible there was some mistake?" she said. "That there really was no one in the car?"

"I don't think so, sweetheart."

"I had invited her to supper this Saturday," Victoria said. "Boston baked beans. I'd invited Rocky, too."

"Didn't you think that might have been a bit awkward for them under the circumstances, Victoria?" Howland asked. He paced back and forth in front of the hole.

"I wouldn't do that," Domingo said, stopping him. "You'll mess up whatever evidence the Crime Unit might find."

Even in the darkness, Victoria could see Howland's scowl, the lines of his face heightened by the lights along the harbor.

"She loved him," Victoria said. "She hadn't made up her mind to sign anything, and Howland couldn't force her. She wanted to be with Rocky at least one more time."

The three stood silently for long moments. Cars streamed by slowly. An occasional passenger would lean out the window and look at the small knot of people still around the place where the car had been. Victoria could see the fire engine working its way slowly through the oncoming traffic, its red light flashing.

Howland spoke first. "When I heard it on my scanner, I called the Crime Unit. They should arrive on the next boat." He looked at his watch. "By then, the traffic should have cleared."

"What can they possibly find?" Victoria said.

"They'll vacuum up everything inside a wide circle, if our friend here" — Domingo slapped Howland on the arm — "hasn't trampled it into the ground. They'll examine every blade of grass, every grain of sand microscopically."

"Surely you don't think Rocky had anything to do with this," Victoria said, sweeping her arm around the area. "Do you?"

There was a long silence. Finally, Howland spoke. "This is the way Rocky works. We've been trying to get evidence and witnesses against him that will hold up in court, but every time we get close, witnesses disappear, evidence vanishes. This isn't the first time he's used explosives."

"How can you destroy a car, every last bit of it, without damaging everything else around it?"

"Plastique," Howland said. "You can be surgically precise with the stuff, mold it like modeling clay, and stick small pieces where you want it to go off."

"Liz and Rocky were close." Victoria wadded up the damp napkin she had been holding and put it back in her pocket. "She didn't have the least suspicion of him. Just this afternoon, he gave her a jewelry box." Victoria sighed.

"A jewelry box?" Howland said.

"He was so romantic, she said. He told her not to open it until the grand finale of the fireworks." Victoria suddenly realized what she had said, and she put a gnarled hand up to her mouth. "She thought it was an engagement ring and a necklace."

"That's how he did it," said Domingo.

"Thank goodness she didn't open the box in my house."

"Nothing would have happened," Howland said. "The box was only the detonator. The explosives were inside her car."

"So when she opened the jewelry box, the detonator set it off." Victoria stared thoughtfully at the hole. "Wonder why Louie was with her? What a pity he was killed, too."

"Apparently, he and Liz had some kind of deal going," Howland said. "She was siphoning off drugs for Louie to sell, according to my sources, and Rocky knew about it. He must have told Louie to deliver a message to Liz in her car, and to wait with her until after the fireworks were over."

Victoria thought a minute. "I'm going ahead with the bean supper," she said firmly. "He has to eat, even if he's grieving, and he won't suspect me. Perhaps he'll let something slip." Howland nodded.

"Would you like to join us for supper? Either of you?"

"No!" Howland and Domingo said together.

"Ah, wait!" Howland held up his hand. "I believe I'd like to accept. Who else will be there?"

"Rocky, Elizabeth, and me. Elizabeth invited someone she met at the harbor, so there'll be five of us, including him."

Howland shoved his hands into his pockets and stared at the grassy strip between the road and the paved walk. There was not much to be seen in the dark.

"A thousand damnations. I should have known. All we have now is the chief, and I'm not sure we've got a strong enough case with only his testimony. We have to go with it. Goddamn it to hell."

~ ~ ~

Baked Bean Supper

"SO KIND of you to ask me to dine with you." Rocky handed Victoria a large bouquet of late-summer roses. "This is a difficult time, as you can imagine."

"I'm so sorry. I knew you and Liz were close." She buried her nose in the velvety pink blossoms. "They're like the ones my grandmother used to grow. I haven't seen any like this for years." She lifted the silver teapot from the corner cabinet.

"Our gardener taught me everything I know about roses. He could make anything grow." He held out his hands. "I'll carry that. Where would you like it?"

"In the dining room." Victoria handed him the arrangement and led the way into the parlor, where she had laid a fire earlier in the day.

"There'll be only five of us tonight." She held on to the mantel and started to kneel.

Rocky quickly moved to her side. "Let me light the fire for you." He struck a match, then waited until the kindling blazed.

"Who are the five? You and Elizabeth and me, I assume."

"A friend of Elizabeth's, someone she met at the harbor."

"We can exchange sea stories, then. And the fifth person?"

"Howland. You know him, of course." Victoria glanced over at Rocky to see if his expression had changed.

He coughed and took his handkerchief from the pocket of his beige jacket. "Excuse me, Victoria, pollen. Howland and I have computers in common. This should be a most interesting evening."

"Howland can be difficult," Victoria said, gazing innocently at Rocky. "You seem to be able to handle him so tactfully. He's quite vain, although I can't imagine why."

Rocky smiled faintly and stared into the fire.

"You knew, of course, I had invited Liz. I'm so sorry." She smoothed her worn corduroys over her knees. "She was such a vibrant person. What a tragedy."

"A great tragedy," Rocky replied. He leaned forward, his hands clasped between his knees.

"Does anyone know how it happened?" Victoria asked.

"There was speculation that because she was selectman and had access to the fireworks, Liz borrowed some for a private display. They're quite dangerous, unless you're trained to handle them, I'm told."

"You must miss her terribly."

"Her loss hasn't sunk in yet," Rocky said solemnly. He looked at the flames. "So pleasant. Comforting."

"There's nothing like oak for steady burning. Locust, too, but that tends to snap."

"I read your sonnet on Prometheus, bringer of fire," Rocky said, still staring into the flickering flames. "A lovely poem."

"I'm flattered that you remember." Victoria changed the subject abruptly. "The fireworks were spectacular the other night. The fog actually enhanced the display."

"The water droplets in the fog give it a wonderful soft quality," Rocky said. "In a physicist's terms, diffraction and diffusion." He smiled.

"Do you know where they set them off?" Victoria asked.

"In one of the parks in a roped-off area. Our gardener, the one I mentioned, used to design fireworks displays for the Holy Ghost celebrations. As a child, I was fascinated. They require great skill, and a knowledge of explosives."

Elizabeth entered the room with a tray of sherry glasses and a platter of cheese and crackers and set it on the coffee table.

"Not quite as elegant as *Dawn Chorus*," Victoria said, "but the thought is there."

Rocky made a demurring sound.

"My friend should be here any minute," Elizabeth said. "I told him I'd pick him up at the harbor, but he's hitchhiking."

"Is he a local man?" Rocky asked.

"He's from New Zealand, quite nice." Elizabeth blushed.

"Ah, I see," Rocky said, smiling. "Obviously a man of discrimination." He lifted his glass of sherry to Elizabeth, who blushed even deeper, and then to Victoria, who tilted her head.

"There are quite a few New Zealanders on the Island," Victoria said. "The Vineyard seems to attract them."

"People who live on islands are great travelers," Rocky said. "Think of your whaling grandfather."

Someone knocked at the kitchen door.

"That must be Horace." Elizabeth unwound herself from the small chair she'd set next to the fire and went to the kitchen. She returned, followed by a chunky, tanned man with clear deep blue eyes, hair so blond, it was white, and a beard to match.

Rocky stood, towering over Horace. Elizabeth made the introductions.

"My grandmother."

He bowed stiffly to Victoria. "Elizabeth tells me your grandmother came from Australia. A long way, in those days."

"It's a long way today," Victoria said. "Sailing here still takes as long as it did in the whaling days."

Elizabeth introduced Rocky. "My grandmother's and my friend, Rocky. He has a boat, too."

Horace turned from Victoria, and when he saw Rocky, he looked startled. He recovered immediately, but Victoria had glimpsed the expression.

He held his hand out. "How d'ya do, Dr. Folger."

Rocky seemed surprised at being addressed by name and title. "Please, Rocky," he said.

"A nickname derived from your family name no doubt,"

Horace said. "1 understand 'Rocky' is what your students call you."

"When I was teaching," Rocky corrected. "I'm not doing much teaching these days." He seemed puzzled, as if he should know Horace but couldn't quite place him.

"I understand you're consulting," Horace said.

"You seem to know quite a bit about me," Rocky said. "I'm afraid I'm at a disadvantage."

"The disadvantage of an international reputation." Horace bared large teeth and bowed to the taller man.

Victoria sensed an undercurrent she couldn't quite pin down. Elizabeth seemed slightly embarrassed by Horace. Rocky continued to look puzzled. When there was a knock on the door and Howland entered, Victoria was relieved, but only briefly. While the tension seemed to ease between Rocky and Horace, it was even worse between Rocky and Howland. The two men faced each other like cats defending territory, Victoria thought. As she began to regret having invited Howland, Elizabeth rang the dinner bell.

Victoria made her Boston baked beans in the traditional New England manner, soaking dried beans on Friday night, boiling them Saturday morning, and baking them all day with molasses and salt pork. Her grandmother had used the same bean pot every Saturday during Victoria's childhood.

Victoria had set the table with the sterling silver, the good china, the crystal goblets. She had polished the brass candlesticks and melted new candles into place so they stood straight. The silver teapot with Rocky's roses was in the center of the old damask tablecloth. She'd ironed the heavy linen napkins that morning, and they lay next to the forks at the left of each plate.

Elizabeth poured the wine and set the bottle on the floor next to Rocky, who nodded, as if to say he'd be pleased to take care of refills.

Horace held Victoria's chair for her, and she sat at the head of the table. Elizabeth came into the dining room from the kitchen bearing a great rectangular platter heaped with steaming baked beans, hot dogs set along the side. She set them in front of Howland, who was at the end of the table, opposite Victoria.

"You have the honor of serving, I see," Rocky said to Howland, slightly easing the tension between them.

The conversation touched on world events, on boats and sea stories, on computers. It skirted the deaths of Bernie and Meatloaf. Avoided, at first, the demise of Liz Tate.

Rocky sat at Victoria's right, Horace at her left. Elizabeth sat between Horace and Howland.

It was her granddaughter who stumbled into the subject Victoria hadn't wanted to introduce herself.

Elizabeth turned to Horace. "What did you think of our fireworks?"

Victoria watched Rocky's face. He stiffened slightly.

"Marvelous good show," Horace said. "Especially the finale."

"Do you have fireworks displays in New Zealand the way we do here to celebrate nothing?"

"Christmas, the queen's birthday, that sort of occasion," Horace said. "Usually a special event, not simply for the fun of it." He looked at Rocky again. "Where they really put on a good show is in the Caribbean, isn't that so, Dr. Folger?"

"Rocky," Rocky said automatically.

"You spent quite a bit of time in the Caribbean on your astrophysical work, didn't you?" Howland asked.

"I did much of my research at the radio telescope in Puerto Rico," Rocky said carefully.

"You spent time, too, around the islands as a child, isn't that right?" Horace said.

"You seem to know a great deal about me." Rocky smiled grimly. "May I ask how you do?"

"I'm interested in the famous." Horace grinned.

"I'm hardly famous," Rocky said.

Victoria watched as if she were at a tennis match, Rocky to Horace, across the table, back and forth.

"You're famous all right," Horace said, and grinned again. Elizabeth looked from him to Rocky to her grandmother, a perplexed expression on her face. "These beans are delicious, Mrs. Trumbull," Horace said.

"An old, old recipe," Victoria replied. "Simple fare."

"Served in the most elegant manner," Rocky said, obviously relieved to have attention shift from him.

"A good traditional meal," said Howland. "It emphasizes the pleasure of good conversation."

Rocky darted a quick look at Howland. Horace smirked. Elizabeth looked uncomfortable. Victoria watched them all and wondered where this was leading.

Rocky turned back to Horace. "I gather you've spent time in the Caribbean yourself."

"Righto," Horace said.

"Did you spend much time there?" Victoria asked.

"Bought my boat there. *Clotho.*"

"Clotho," said Victoria. "One of the Fates. The one who spins the thread of life."

"That Atropos snips," Howland added.

"You sailed from New Zealand to the Caribbean with someone, didn't you?" Elizabeth said.

"Right." Horace looked down at his empty plate. "My much younger sister."

"Where in the Caribbean?" Howland asked.

"The Turks and Caicos," Horace said.

"Isn't that where you keep your boat, Rocky?" Victoria asked. "I seem to recall your saying you sailed *Dawn Chorus* up from Grand Turk."

Horace was looking at Rocky in an oddly expressionless way.

Rocky nodded. He had bitten into a piece of brown bread before Horace mentioned the Turks and Caicos, and he seemed to be having trouble swallowing it. He avoided Horace's pale eyes.

"Where's your sister now?" Elizabeth asked Horace.

"She was killed." Horace never took his eyes off Rocky.

Silence thundered in Victoria's ears. Elizabeth stared at her new friend. Rocky stopped chewing his mouthful of brown bread. Howland sat up straight, put his hands on the arms of his chair, and watched Rocky.

"Killed!" Elizabeth said weakly. "How awful!"

"What happened?" Howland turned to Horace.

"Howland . . ." Victoria began.

"She'd got into drugs in New Zealand," Horace said, his eyes fixed on Rocky's face. Rocky chewed, shifting his mouthful from one side to the other, like a cud.

"I got her away from that scene. Took her with me on my boat. She sailed with me and dried out, cold. You can't imagine the agony she went through."

The others were silent. Victoria heard the house creak. Bicyclists went by on the road in front of Victoria's house, laughing. The sound of their laughter was jarring.

"There were days and nights when I had to hold her while she screamed and thrashed. Let the boat drift. She hated me, she did. We went through nightmare storms together, when every bit of rigging shrieked and moaned and sang, high-pitched, like a banshee. Where the waves rose as high as the spreaders, breaking. Sometimes we'd ride over the tops of the waves and get caught on a steep slide on the backside, and plunge the bow into a trough and keep going down and down. Sometimes the waves would break over us, fill the cockpit, start a regular waterfall into the cabin. We'd throw the door boards off, and use a toilet plunger in the scuppers to get the water to drain out before the next wave swamped us."

Victoria stared at him, her mouth open.

"The boat would heel over fifty, sixty degrees to starboard, then in an instant whip over to port. I never knew whether it was my sister who was screaming or the wind. Or the boat, or me, or all three Furies. You know what I'm talking about, Dr. Folger?"

Rocky took a sip of wine from the goblet and swallowed. He continued to stare at Horace.

"She came out of it. The sea does that. When we reached Grand Turk, she was clean. Strong and brown and healthy. She was beautiful, wasn't she, Dr. Folger?"

Rocky stood abruptly, and his wineglass toppled over, spilling merlot over Victoria's damask cloth. "That's why you look familiar," he said in a whisper. "Arabella's brother."

"You thought you could dodge me forever, eh?"

Victoria felt the hair on the back of her neck lift.

"I must say, mate, I didn't expect to find you here at this supper table." Horace put his chunky hands on the table and looked up at Rocky, who loomed over all of them. "I'd traced you to the Island, mate, and I'd have traced you to hell."

"This is neither the time nor place to discuss this," Rocky said. "Why don't we meet tomorrow at my boat?"

"I don't think so, mate."

"What do you want of me? I never intended to harm her," Rocky said. "In fact, I didn't harm her. She did it to herself."

Horace made a strange choking noise and stood, both hands flat on the table, his back hunched like a gargoyle, his mouth twisted in a snarl.

Victoria felt the violence build.

"I'm not a fighter," Rocky said. "Come to my boat tomorrow, and we can talk like civilized people."

"Civilized!" Horace spat. "Heroin. Cocaine. Crack. Speed. Civilized?" His voice rose. "How many people have you slaughtered so you can live like a bloody emperor? Look at your fine threads." He reached across the table and seized the lapels of Rocky's cashmere blazer, knocking over the arrangement of roses in the silver teapot. One of the candlesticks fell over. Elizabeth picked it up quickly and snuffed out the flame. Howland stood at his end of the table and glanced from Rocky to Horace. He held his hands tensely at his side. Victoria lifted herself up from the table and got her grandfather's cane from beside the bookcase.

"Stop this minute!" She shouted over the two raised voices. "Stop! I won't have violence in my house."

Horace glanced at her, briefly distracted. Rocky reached under the table and brought out the half-empty bottle of merlot.

In that instant, Victoria was aware of the smells around her: the baked beans that had been cooking all day, the lavender hand lotion Elizabeth used, the camphor-wood sea chest in the front hall, the fear scent of Rocky.

Victoria moved around the dining room table, one careful foot after another, until she was in back of Rocky. Howland twisted his head slightly to look at her. His mouth turned down in his faint smile.

Rocky drew his hand back in a wide arc to avoid the low ceiling, and started to swing the bottle, full force, at Horace.

Victoria moved as quickly as she had ever moved in her life. She held her grandfather's cane by its tip and brought it down smartly with all her might on Rocky's uplifted arm. The merlot bottle dropped onto the table with a crash, rolled onto the floor, and broke, spewing shards of glass and red wine over Victoria's worn carpet. Rocky stepped back and slipped on the broken glass and the spilled wine. He grabbed at the tablecloth, which came off in his hands, scattering dishes and silverware and glasses over everything with a huge crash.

Victoria felt a surge of anger at the destruction. She lifted the cane as high as she could and thwacked Rocky on his head, stunning him.

From out of nowhere, Howland brought out handcuffs, and snapped them onto Rocky's limp wrists.

Victoria checked her grandfather's cane to make sure she hadn't damaged it.

Rocky put his tousled head in his cuffed hands. Sitting among the debris of Victoria's bean supper, his elbows on his knees, he shook his head over and over again.

Horace stood up straight. "You're a fed, eh?" Howland nodded. "I've got enough bloody documentation on that devil to seal him up live in a bloody tomb forever." He jerked his head at Rocky. "Put me on the stand. I'll testify against him if it takes the rest of my bloody life. Shake on it."

Howland thrust out his hand.

~ ~ ~

"To Washington? They're sending that crazy Indian to Washington?" Beanie pushed his baseball cap back and scratched his head.

"Hey!" said Shipyard, covering his coffee cup with a beamy hand. "Keep your cooties to yourself."

"Whose crazy idea was that?" Beanie straightened the visor of his cap and put both elbows on the table.

"The tribal council," Red said. "It was unanimous. Pass the sugar, will you?"

"Where's Dottie?" Beanie checked his watch. "I ain't got all day."

"Sorry, boys." Dottie bustled in with three bowls of chowder and chunked them down on the table. "This is the last of Dojan Minnowfish's quahogs. You heard about him going to Washington?"

"Yeah. To negotiate for a casino," Beanie said.

"No!" Dottie said.

Shipyard laughed. "Don't believe what Beanie tells you."

"What'd he do to deserve such an honor?" Red reached for a chowder cracker, broke it into his bowl, and shoveled a spoonful into his mouth.

"Musta been something bad," Beanie said.

"I can see him working over some senator." Shipyard laughed. "Scare anybody into doing anything."

"The guy's not stupid," Red said.

"Where he's going, who'll know the difference?" said Shipyard.

"Seems more like a jail sentence to me," Red said.

"Speaking of jail, I hear they nabbed the professor," Beanie said. "I told you there was something fishy about him."

"They ever find out who killed Bernie?" Red asked around his mouthful of soup and crackers.

"I hear they're trying to blame that on Meatloaf." Beanie reached for the pepper shaker and shook it over his chowder.

Dottie, who was passing the table with her hands full of an order, bent and nudged him with her elbow.

"What's the matter? Not seasoned right for you?" Beanie flung his arm over his head and ducked.

"Who are they saying killed Meatloaf?" Red asked.

"They're trying to blame that on Medeiros," Shipyard said.

"I hear he's testifying against the professor." Beanie stirred the pepper into his chowder.

"Christ, I wouldn't be in his shoes," said Shipyard.

"He's going into a witness protection program. We've seen the last of Medeiros, that's for sure," Beanie said.

"Surprised the hell out of me when Atherton turned out to be a drug agent. I thought he was a computer nerd." Red reached for another cracker.

"Speaking of that, you heard some company offered to buy his computer program? Pass the crackers, will you?" Shipyard took one and spread butter on it.

Dottie, on her way back with dirty dishes, scowled at him. "You guys are animals."

Shipyard brayed.

"The harbor program?" Red said. "No kidding."

"How much they offering him?" Beanie asked, potatoes showing in his full mouth.

"I hear it's a million dollars," replied Shipyard.

"No shit!" said Beanie.

"How'd you find out about it?" Red asked.

"He got a registered letter from some computer company." Shipyard bit into the buttered cracker, and flaky crumbs dropped onto his shirt front.

"You reading other people's mail again?" Beanie asked.

"Wasn't me. It was my wife's sister," said Shipyard.

"A million dollars?" Red shook his head.

"That's what she said," Shipyard said. "He turned it down."

"What!" Red and Beanie said together.

"Says he developed it on government time."

"Jee-sus," Beanie murmured.

"I hear Mrs. Trumbull beat shit out of the professor," Red said.

"Broke his arm with her grandfather's gold-headed cane."

"Teach him not to mess with our senior citizens," Red said.

"They don't make old ladies like they used to," Shipyard added.

~ ~ ~

THE END

The
Cranefly Orchid
Murders

by Cynthia Riggs

CHAPTER ONE

Sachem's Rock

WHEN she heard a knock on her door right after Christmas, Phoebe Eldredge was ready to invite the missionaries in for tea and cookies. The only people who called on her without telephoning first, especially this time of year, were Jehovah's Witnesses or the Mormons. They usually were young, usually came in pairs and usually were dressed nicely, not in the Vineyard chic of torn jeans and ratty sweaters that Islanders, young and old, favored.

Phoebe lived alone at the end of a dirt road off Tea Lane. Her house was on the bare rock-strewn top of a wooded hill, surrounded by two hundred acres of woods, fields, marshes, and hills. Her property included the great Sachem's Rock.

She was disappointed when the caller turned out to be a slim, small woman, much too stylishly dressed in a dark red coat, matching hat, and black high-heeled boots, and carrying a briefcase. The woman had parked her large gray car in front of Phoebe's herb garden, blocking the view from the parlor windows of the ice pond at the foot of the hill.

"Yes?" Phoebe's voice didn't hold the warmth she would have used for young missionaries.

"Phoebe Eldredge?" The woman held out her black-gloved hand.

Phoebe put hers under the apron she was wearing and the woman withdrew her hand and clutched the briefcase instead.

"Yes, I'm Mrs. Eldredge." Phoebe waited.

"My name is Karen Underwood, and I'm from CARP." She smiled, showing small white teeth with a smear of lipstick on them.

Phoebe waited, her hands still clasped under the apron, a frilly thing her daughter Janice had given her years ago, when they were still on speaking terms.

"Have you heard of CARP, Phoebe?"

"I'm Mrs. Eldredge."

"I'm sorry, Mrs. Eldredge." The woman had the grace to blush. "Have you heard of CARP, Mrs. Eldredge?" She remained standing on the granite step at Phoebe's door.

Phoebe stared at the woman without answering. Her pale eyes squinted in the sunshine. Her white hair made a wispy frame around her face.

"CARP is 'Conservation Acres Real Property,' a new concept in land preservation," Karen said.

Phoebe waited. She had a hunch this was another slick real estate person trying to buy her land. She had already talked with Josiah Coffin about a conservation restriction on the property, and Josiah and his assistant, Zachariah West, were working on it.

Taxes had gone up so high she could no longer afford to keep the old place. Thirteen generations on this land and it looked as if she would be the unlucky one who would lose it.

"I'd like to talk with you, Mrs. Eldredge."

"May I ask what about?" Phoebe stood in her doorway.

"CARP would like to make a presentation to you on innovative ways to preserve your land. May I come in?"

"I'm not interested," Phoebe said.

"You're not interested in preserving your land?" The woman looked and sounded appalled.

Phoebe was silent.

"There's no obligation." Karen shifted her briefcase in front of her and held it with both gloved hands.

"I said I'm not interested."

"It will take only about fifteen minutes of your time, and it's really quite a fascinating presentation." The woman's voice quavered slightly.

"I don't have fifteen minutes to spare."

"I've come all the way from Boston today to see you."

Phoebe started to close her door, right in the face of Karen Underwood. "Next time call first."

As the door closed, Phoebe saw with astonishment that Karen's chin was trembling, and realized she was about to cry.

Phoebe opened the door again. "Come in," she said gruffly.

"Thank you." Karen stepped over the front doorsill into Phoebe's parlor, pulled off her black gloves, drew a white hanky out of her coat pocket, and dabbed carefully at her eyes, patting around the dark eyeliner.

"What's this presentation you have?" Phoebe muttered.

"Let me show you," Karen said more brightly than Phoebe had expected, and set her briefcase on Phoebe's mahogany table.

"Not there. Not on my table."

"I'm so sorry." Karen looked around the small parlor and finally laid the briefcase on the ancient carpet, its Oriental nap worn through to burlap backing.

Phoebe wiped the tabletop with her apron. This Boston woman was too stylish, too rapidly recovered. Phoebe remained standing and clasped her hands underneath her apron again. "Get on with it. I don't have all day."

Karen Underwood perched on the couch and bent over her open briefcase, angling her booted feet away from her body as if she were posing for some fashion magazine. Her hair, too black and too curly and too long, fell in front of her face. She brushed it back behind her shoulders.

"It's so kind of you to let me intrude like this." Karen looked up, brown eyes bright. "It was rude of me not to call first. I'm so sorry."

"Yes. Well."

Karen brought out glossy colored brochures and laid them on the couch next to her. She brought out a plastic-covered report with a title in large letters that Phoebe could read from this distance. "Sachem's Rock Property," and her name, "Phoebe Eldredge" underneath.

Phoebe felt as if she had let a skunk into her hen house. This slick presentation with her name on it must have cost a pretty penny. "Look, Miz Underwood, I'm not interested after all." Phoebe went to the door and opened it. "Please leave."

Karen looked up in apparent consternation. "But Mrs. Eldredge, I've come all this way."

"Next time call first. I'm in the phone book." Phoebe held the door open.

"Won't you even listen to me?" The woman was beginning to look and sound more and more like Phoebe's daughter, and Phoebe had wanted nothing to do with Janice for the past twelve years.

"Please leave. You're letting cold air in."

Karen Underwood carefully placed her brochures back in her briefcase and got to her feet. "I'm so sorry, Mrs. Eldredge. Apparently I've offended you in some way."

Phoebe remained silent, remained by the open door.

Karen crossed the room, stepped down onto the large granite entrance stone, got into the big gray car, started it up with a puff of transparent blue vapor, and drove away. The car bounced over rocks in the rutted road. Phoebe watched it disappear into the trees below the crest of the hill.

Then she called Josiah Coffin's number at the Conservation Trust. She got the answering machine, and hung up.

~ ~ ~

In Santa Barbara several weeks later Phoebe Eldredge's granddaughter Melissa learned through an item in the weekly *Island Enquirer,* to which she subscribed, that her grandmother was negotiating with a conservation group to sell the family land. Melissa's first thought was to call an attorney, since she and her grandmother weren't on the best of terms. The only Island attorney whose name she could remember was a Montgomery Mausz. She debated with herself for a couple of hours before she finally called the long distance operator and got the number. When Mr. Mausz turned out to be a sympathetic listener, Melissa talked to him for almost an hour.

She was sitting on the unmade futon on the floor of the room she shared with Butch on East Victoria Street, her legs crossed under her, the receiver tucked against her shoulder. She played with the silver rings on her bare toes, twisting them around and around as she talked.

Mr. Mausz murmured understandingly when she told him her father and aunt were estranged from her grandmother and that she was probably the only one in the family on speaking terms with the old lady, and just barely. She was probably her grandmother's heir, she told Mr. Mausz.

She got up from the futon, the cordless telephone still held against her shoulder, took a bottle of nail polish from the bathroom cabinet, and sat at the spindly table she'd bought at the flea market. She opened the bottle and put her foot up on the other chair. She stuffed cotton between her toes and began to paint her nails, a nice glittery dark blue.

Mr. Mausz was such a sensitive listener she found herself telling him family stuff, like how her grandmother and Aunt Janice had quarreled over her aunt's third marriage to a Nigerian taxi driver, and how weird her father was after Vietnam.

She finished painting the toes of one foot, set the foot on the floor, and started on the toes of the other foot.

She found herself telling Mr. Mausz something she had never told anyone else, not even Butch. She told him how her father and her mother had gotten into an argument after her father had come home from the war. She had been three years old, and now, almost twenty-five years later, she still remembered that argument as clearly as though she was seeing it on a movie screen. Her father had hit her mother, over and over and over, awful, sickening thuds of fist against flesh. Her mother screamed until she had no scream left in her. Melissa could still remember, as clearly as when it happened, how her mother's screams turned into whimpers and then silence. She remembered the sound of her father's boots in the downstairs hall, how the door slammed. She still could see the upstairs hall mirror bounce on the wall over her head when he slammed the door. She remembered his footsteps on the porch, the squeak of the loose step, the crunch of his boots on the concrete sidewalk, his steps fading away. Her father had walked out of their lives. She had never seen him again.

Melissa was crying now, feeling sorrier for herself than she had for some time. Mr. Mausz listened attentively three thousand miles away. Melissa tugged a tissue out of a box on the windowsill and blotted her nose, careful not to snag the tissue on the two gold studs on the left side of her nostril.

What about her mother, Attorney Mausz had asked.

The neighbors had come to the house when they heard the screams, she told him. They took her mother to the hospital and found Melissa, huddled in the upstairs closet under coats that smelled like stale cigarette smoke. Whenever she smelled stale smoke or worn shoes she remembered that closet and that day.

She stood, now that the toenail polish had set, and moved the curtain aside so she could look down onto the street, still holding the phone against her shoulder. She and Butch lived on the second floor of a Spanish-style house where they had one big room, a kitchenette, and a bath.

Melissa told Mr. Mausz about Butch, and how she made jewelry to sell at the Saturday street fair under the tall palm trees. She told him her dreams about returning to Martha's Vineyard, where she used to go summers. Her mother had never divorced her father, Melissa said. She told Mr. Mausz she was the only one in the family who knew that her mother was still in Santa Barbara, living with an abalone fisherman on a boat in the city harbor marina.

Mr. Mausz mentioned something she'd often thought about, and that was tracing her father. Her mother didn't want to. Vietnam had done a number on a lot of the guys who'd fought in it, Mr. Mausz said. But Melissa didn't have the kind of money a search like that would cost. Besides, she wasn't sure she wanted to find the bastard who'd beaten up her mother and then walked away from them like that. Yet she wondered sometimes what had happened to him. Did he ever think of his wife and daughter? Did he ever feel sorry he'd walked out on them years ago? Mostly, though, when it came to her father, she didn't give a shit.

She didn't realize until after she'd hung up that Mr. Mausz had said nothing about the possible sale of the family land and what she could do about it, the reason she had called him.

She reread the item in the *Island Enquirer* and got still more concerned. She would have to see for herself what her grandmother was up to. This didn't seem to her something she could discuss with the old lady over the phone, since they usually argued within the first minute. She hadn't seen her grandmother for a couple of years. Even though this was February, perhaps it was a good time to visit, to talk to her in person. Melissa decided to wait until she got to Martha's Vineyard before she called, so her grandmother couldn't talk her out of the trip.

Melissa threw stuff into her backpack — her ski parka, underclothes, and a couple of sweaters — and caught the shuttle to Los Angeles, the red-eye to Boston, took the bus to Woods Hole, the ferry to Vineyard Haven. It was a lot colder in New England than she had remembered. The wind coming off the water brought tears to her eyes. She was wearing the gray sweatshirt with UCSB in large block letters across the front that had been plenty warm for California. Once she was on the ferry she went up the metal stairs into the snack bar, bought a cup of herbal tea, sat at one of the tables, took her down jacket out of her back-pack, shook it out, and snuggled into it.

When they docked, she called her grandmother. There was no answer. Melissa hadn't eaten since yesterday noon, so she walked the short distance to the ArtCliff Diner to get some breakfast or lunch, she wasn't sure which. Time was all screwed up. Once she'd had something to eat she would hitchhike to her grandmother's.

When she entered the ArtCliff, Dottie, who'd been the waitress ever since Melissa could remember, greeted her, and Melissa sat at one of the small tables against the wall.

"How you doing, honey? Haven't seen you for some time." Dottie dropped a plastic-covered menu in front of her.

"I just got in from California," Melissa said. "I guess I want some lunch. I'm still on Pacific Time."

"The quahog chowder's fresh today. Pork chops, meatloaf, chicken-fried steak. You need something solid, cold day like today. They're calling for snow later."

"A salad," Melissa said. "No meat."

"I forgot you're one of those California gals now, alfalfa sprouts and tofu. Hope you brought warm clothes." Dottie scooped up the menu. "Visiting your grandma up-Island? I hear she's thinking of selling that property of hers."

"That's why I'm here. I was talking to Mr. Mausz about it just yesterday," Melissa said.

"Him!" Dottie practically spat out the word. "Why were you talking to him, for crying out loud? He represents the real estate guy who's been hounding your grandma."

Melissa felt blood drain out of her face. "He does? Harry Ness? Mr. Mausz represents Harry Ness?"

"That's what I hear," Dottie said. "Are you okay, honey? I didn't mean to give you a shock."

"He never told me he was representing that sleaze." Melissa looked up at Dottie, who was tucking a pencil behind his ear. "I told him all this stuff I shouldn't have."

Melissa was dimly aware of several men sitting at a round table in the corner, the same men who always gathered there. She heard the bray-like laugh of one of them. Heard male banter.

Dottie shook her head. "Mausz is a full-blooded sleaze himself, honey," she said. "Want Roquefort, Ranch, French, Italian, or Lemon Dill dressing on your salad?"

"I can't believe I told him all the stuff I did. And he listened! And he didn't say a thing."

"You could report him to the Board of Bar Overseers," Dottie said. "Only trouble is, they're all part of the same good-ole-boy network." She wrote something on her pad. "The Lemon Dill is nice. I'll give you that. And a couple of poppy-seed rolls."

While Melissa was eating, halfway listening to the kidding at the corner table, she noticed the sky had clouded over. A few flakes of snow drifted in front of the window.

Dottie came by with the check. "They say it's going down to the twenties for the next couple of days," she said. "Dress warm! Tell your grandma I was asking for her."

Melissa hadn't thought to pack gloves. When she stepped outside, her breath steamed around her face. A cold wind blew off the harbor. Back home, people who'd bought stuff from the nursery a couple of blocks from her place were probably planting their six-packs of flowers. She shivered, pushed her free hand deep into her pocket, and thrust her thumb out. Almost immediately, a red Volvo station wagon driven by an elderly woman stopped.

"Awfully cold to be standing out here," the woman said. "We can take you as far as North Road."

"Thanks," Melissa said. "That'll be great." Melissa climbed into the back seat. By now the snow was falling thickly.

"Where are you heading?" the man in the front seat asked.

"I'm going to my grandmother's," Melissa answered. "She lives off Tea Lane, Sachem's Rock."

"You must be Phoebe Eldredge's granddaughter," the man said. "Don't you live in California?"

"Santa Barbara." Melissa set her backpack on the seat.

"Bet you don't see weather like this often," the man said.

The woman turned on the windshield wipers, and hunched tensely over the wheel. Melissa found herself just as tense, waiting for a skid on the now-slick pavement. No one spoke. The five-mile drive seemed interminable.

When they got to the big oak tree where North Road branched off, the woman slowed cautiously.

"Be careful now," the woman said. "It's awfully slippery."

Melissa lifted her backpack off the seat. "Bye. And thanks."

After the car had gone, Melissa got a ride in a pickup truck driven by a guy about her own age. She climbed in and blew on her chilled hands to warm them up.

"How far you going?" he asked as he started up again.

"Tea Lane?" Melissa made it a question. "Mrs. Eldredge's?"

"I know the place," he said. "Nice property." He pronounced it *propahty*. "Be glad to take you right there."

"That's okay. I need the walk."

"You sure? It's a long hike."

He let her off where Tea Lane joined the main road. She thanked him and set off down the lane.

Tea Lane looked the same as it always had. Except for the trees that now overhung it, the lane had probably not changed much since before the Revolutionary War, when the tea smuggler lived along here somewhere. It was a sandy cart track with high banks lined with tufts of brown poverty grass. Sheep had once grazed on either side of the lane. Melissa still remembered hidden stone walls that once had fenced open pastures. When she was little she used to explore old cellar holes that were remnants of a small settlement. Her grandmother's was the only house still standing.

She turned left onto a narrow road that led up the hill toward the house. Melissa's were the first tracks in the snow. She had called her grandmother before she left the diner, but again there had been no answer. Her grandmother might be digging up parsnips this time of year, or who knows what.

At one point Melissa thought she heard voices but decided it was the wind. No one would be around here this time of year, especially not on a day like this. She could remember wind-voices from her childhood that sounded exactly like people at a cocktail party. She had heard laughter and even distinct words. Now the wind-voices sounded like people arguing. She shivered and tucked her hands deeper into the pockets of her parka.

She came out of the oak woods into a clearing and there was the house, a curl of smoke coming out of the chimney. It was a typical old Vineyard farmhouse, gray-shingled, with a roof that sloped down to the first-floor windows, and a second-floor window at each end. She took a deep breath, not sure how her grandmother would receive her, and tried to walk confidently the hundred yards or so to the front door. She stepped up on the snow-covered granite stone and knocked.

Her grandmother came to the door, frail-looking in a large brown cardigan with sagging pockets and a soiled apron. One hand held a checked dishtowel; the other hand was braced against the doorframe as if to keep intruders out. She looked down at Melissa from where she stood in the doorway.

"Hi, Grandma, it's me, Melissa. From California." Steam puffed out of her nose and mouth. She smiled brightly.

"So I see." Her grandmother moved aside for Melissa to step up from the granite stone, and closed the door behind her.

"May I ask what brings you here? I suppose you just happened to be passing through?"

"I thought it was time I came to visit you," Melissa said. The two faced each other just inside the front door.

"In February?" Her grandmother's expression was pure disapproval.

"Well, it seemed like a good time, you know."

"No, I don't know," her grandmother said. "It wouldn't have anything to do with that item in last week's *Enquirer*, would it?"

"What do you mean?" Melissa avoided her grandmother's eyes.

"Never mind. Are you planning to stay here in this house? And for how long, if I may be so bold as to ask?"

"Well, I had thought so, you know, if it's okay with you."

"It's not convenient, if that's what you're asking, but I don't see that I have much choice, do I? And for how long?"

Melissa said nothing, simply stood there in the parlor with her backpack in her hand, her down jacket partly unzipped. The parlor looked the same, with its horsehair sofa, worn carpet, and mahogany table. Her grandmother moved into the parlor and flicked the surface of the table with her dishtowel.

"I don't suppose you've had anything to eat, have you?" Her grandmother clasped her hands together under her apron.

"I ate something at the ArtCliff. Dottie asked for you."

"That place. Well, put your things upstairs in your old room. It's not made up. I wasn't expecting company."

Once Melissa had swept away the cobwebs that hung from the bedposts, from the curtains, across the mirror, and from the sloping ceiling in the chilly room; once she had changed her clothes, put her things away, and made up her bed, she decided she should confront her grandmother directly.

"Are you really thinking of selling the land to that conservation group?" she asked when she found her grandmother in the kitchen scraping carrots.

"I don't see that's any concern of yours." Her grandmother continued to scrape.

"It's part of my heritage too." Melissa leaned against the kitchen doorframe.

"Oh? What makes you think that?"

"My father was the fourteenth generation on this land. I'm the fifteenth."

"Your father? Hah! Don't mention his name in this house."

"But I'm your granddaughter, you know. Your only grandkid."

"You are, eh? Fifteenth generation on this land? I don't think so. Look at you. Nose rings and tattoos like some Fiji Islander. Hair colored like a parrot. That may be the way they do things in California, but not in my house. You think I'd claim you as granddaughter? A greedy tart who comes to see me when she thinks she'll get something out of me, hey? You and your father."

"My father." Melissa said softly. "Have you seen my father?"

Her grandmother ignored her. "Don't think I don't know all about your mother living on some derelict boat with a fisherman. Whore! And still married to that man she calls your father."

"Where did you get that from?" Melissa asked, but she knew.

"I have my sources." Her grandmother brushed her wispy hair out of her eyes with the back of her wrist, the knotted veins of her hand standing out like cords. "I suppose you want this land so you can start an artists' colony with that so-called tattoo artist you live with."

Melissa had a sick feeling in her stomach. What else had she told Montgomery Mausz? What had he told her grandmother? What could she do to stop him? Or was it too late?

~ ~ ~

CHAPTER TWO

Victoria's Discovery

WHEN Victoria Trumbull heard the crows, it was almost a month after Melissa's visit to her grandmother, Phoebe Eldredge. Victoria was hiking along the trail to Sachem's Rock, carrying in her gnarled hand an oak branch that she'd picked up to use as a walking stick. In her other hand she held a cloth bag with an orange, a notebook, and her navy blue baseball cap. Spring was in the air and she wanted to be out in it, writing poetry by the big rock. Victoria shifted the stick into her left hand and brushed her white hair off her forehead.

It was odd to hear crows so far from the hayfields where they usually gathered.

Tree roots stretched across the steep path where it wound among oaks and beech trees. Victoria put her feet down carefully, watching the ground beneath her, sandy soil with a covering of pine needles, acorns, and twisted rope-like roots. The beech trees still wore the bright gold leaves they'd kept all winter. Spring growth would push them off in a few weeks.

Sunlight filtered through the oaks and touched a bed of brilliant green moss, almost fluorescent in the drab brown and gray woods, a contrast to the tree trunks and rocks splotched with gray lichen. Victoria stopped to catch her breath and leaned on her stick.

The crows continued to squabble over something.

Above her, bare branches formed a lacework against the bright sky. Somewhere below her she heard a redwing blackbird carol in the wetlands. Another called in response.

Victoria had started up the path again, walking slowly, flicking acorns with her stick, when she saw the crows, a flock of them on the ground ahead of her and up to her right. They were worrying over something — carrion, she supposed, a dead skunk, or, when she got closer and the crows flew up in a raucous flurry, something much bigger. A deer, perhaps.

She moved slowly. At ninety-two Victoria was not as agile as she had been a few years earlier. She did not intend to fall and break something and have her granddaughter fuss about her walking in the woods by herself. As it was, Elizabeth was going to be upset because she had hitchhiked to the place where the overgrown path to the rock began.

More people should hitchhike on the Island, Victoria mused as she approached whatever it was the crows had found. All she had to do was stand by the side of the road, smile, and point her thumb in the direction she wanted to go. It was usually Islanders who picked her up, often someone she knew. This morning it had been a pickup truck, and the driver had gone out of his way to drop her off on North Road.

Perhaps she'd find a pair of antlers on the deer, if that's what it was. She would take them home in the cloth bag.

Victoria had to climb to reach the spot. She slid the bag up her arm to free her left hand, pushed aside the huckleberry bushes with her stick, and grabbed hold of a sassafras sapling to hoist herself up the bank. Thank goodness for her sturdy hiking shoes. Elizabeth had cut a hole in the top for her arched-up toe.

She noticed mayflower leaves underfoot, and thought how nonsensical it was to call them an endangered species. If you knew where to look, they were all over the place. She and Elizabeth would have to come back in another month when the sweet-scented delicate pink flowers would be in bloom.

Before she could identify what it was the crows had found, she smelled it, a putrid stench that drove the remembered sweet scent of mayflowers out of her mind and made her gag. Victoria reached into the pocket of her gray corduroy trousers and brought out a flowered napkin from Thursday's senior center luncheon. She held it over her nose. She hadn't realized dead game smelled quite so horrid. She wasn't so sure, after all, that she wanted to detach the antlers, even if they were perfect ones. But she would investigate what it was before she returned to the path.

When she reached the spot, a clearing floored with reindeer moss and wild cranberry, she didn't immediately absorb what she was seeing. What had appeared to be gray lichen, green moss, and brown twigs turned out to have unnaturally straight lines. As she focused on it she realized it was a plaid wool shirt. What had at first glance seemed to be moss-covered rock became tweed trousers. And at the bottom of the trousers were hiking boots with new-looking lugged soles. Only after she'd finished examining the shirt and what was below it did she dare look at what must have been the face, the part on which the crows had been feeding.

Victoria hustled back to the road, her oak stick thrust in front of her, her feet stumbling over pine needles and across roots. She flagged down the first car that came along.

The girl in the passenger seat looked at her uncertainly.

"I need a ride into West Tisbury." Victoria was out of breath. She didn't know either the girl or the boy who was driving, but they seemed nice enough.

"Are you okay?" The girl opened the passenger door and moved over to let her slide in.

"I found something up in the woods," Victoria said. "I need to get to the police station, quickly. Can you take me there?"

"Yes, ma'am." The boy reached across the girl to fasten Victoria's seat belt, and reached out still more to slam the car door shut.

The girl looked at Victoria with concern. "What did you find?" she asked.

"I'm not sure," said Victoria. "It's something I need to tell the police chief about, though."

The boy pulled away from the side of the road with a squeal of tires on sand. The green cardboard pine tree hanging from the rearview mirror swung back and forth. Victoria held on to the window crank.

"Is there anything we can do?" the girl asked.

"No, thank you. I think it's a police matter."

The car's wide front seat was covered with furry material, patterned in black and white like a Holstein cow. Victoria took a deep breath. She would put out of her mind what she'd seen up at the rock until she talked to the police chief.

They flew down North Road toward town until they were slowed by a tractor inching along in front of them. The boy honked his horn, and the tractor driver, without looking around, held up his left hand in a gesture that clearly said, "What's your hurry?"

At a wide place in the road, the tractor pulled off to the side and the boy swerved around it. Victoria waved at the driver, Asa Bodman's oldest son, Ira. He returned her wave before they rounded the curve by the old ice pond and were out of sight of him.

On the left the hayfield at Seven Gates Farm was showing spring green through winter stubble, and the trees beyond were touched with a haze of pink. The hayfield was dotted with black crows. One flew up in a flurry of wings and settled back on the field again as they passed. Victoria wondered if the crows were the same ones she'd disturbed up on the hill.

She didn't feel like talking and the boy and girl were silent too. The car sped around the road's tight curves and plunged into the dappled lattice-like shade of overhanging bare trees. The girl sat with one hand on the boy's thigh, looking straight ahead except for an occasional worried glance at Victoria. Victoria shifted slightly in her seat.

"Do you have enough room?" the girl asked. She brushed her mop of curly hair away from her face and moved closer to the boy. Victoria nodded.

They crossed the narrow bridge over Mill Brook. Victoria could see the early hooded shoots of skunk cabbage, bright green fingers poking up along the marshy edges of the brook. She did not want to think about what she'd found near the big rock.

The boy slowed for the curve around the cemetery and sped up again on the straight stretch where the road tunneled under arching maples.

At Brandy Brow he turned left, passed between the millpond and the old mill, and pulled into the oyster-shell parking area in front of the police station.

"Want us to wait?" The boy held the car door for Victoria, and helped her out.

"No, thank you," she said. "The police chief will give me a ride home."

Two Muscovy ducks nipped at her feet as Victoria hustled past, their mottled red and black heads outstretched. At the station house steps she turned and waved to the boy and girl.

The police station was a small shingled building that, years ago, had served as a one-room school. The front door faced the old mill across the road; the west windows overlooked the millpond. Swans were feeding on something under the surface, their tails up in the air like white elfin caps.

Victoria opened the door. "Anybody home?" she called in. When she didn't see the chief, she went outside again. Chief Mary Kathleen O'Neill was behind the station house, scooping cracked corn out of a plastic trash barrel. She hurled a scoop full of corn toward the flock of ducks and geese that had gathered around her. Victoria watched the creatures flutter around the chief's stocky figure, honking, quacking, and hissing.

The chief, who was called Casey, dusted off her hands, wiped her boots on the back of her uniform trousers, and looked up with a pleased smile.

"Hey, there, Victoria. What's up?"

Victoria knew the chief well enough to come right to the point. "I think we have a problem at Sachem's Rock, Casey." Her voice was solemn.

Casey's smile faded. "Serious?"

Victoria nodded.

"Come inside." Casey climbed the wooden steps, two at a time, opened the door for Victoria, and followed her into the small office. Victoria sat primly in the wooden chair in front of the chief's desk, hung her cloth bag from the arm of the chair, and unbuttoned her blue quilted coat.

She told Casey what she'd found, the crows, the smell, and the plaid shirt. Casey listened, both elbows on her desk, hands clasped in front of her.

"We'll go there right away," Casey said when Victoria finished. "First I need to call the medical examiner." She ran her finger down a list thumbtacked to the wall under the calendar. "Doc Jeffers is on duty at the hospital this week." She picked up the phone. "Once I see what's up there, I'll radio him from the Bronco. If it's human remains, he needs to see them in place."

Victoria stood and buttoned her coat again. She fished her blue baseball cap out of her cloth bag and walked over to the small mirror on the closet door. She settled the cap on her hair and tilted her head until she was satisfied with the way it looked. Gold stitched lettering across the front read, "West Tisbury Police, Deputy."

"Looking good." The chief smiled at her ancient deputy and hung up the phone. She lifted her red-gold hair out from the neck of the Navy sweater she'd pulled on, and fastened her heavy equipment belt around her waist. She wrote a note for her sergeant, Junior Norton, and left it under a rounded beach stone on the tidy desk he shared with the two patrolmen. She followed Victoria out the door, pulled it shut behind them, and pushed it to make sure it was latched.

"The selectmen still haven't decided to install locks," Casey said. "Anybody can walk in."

At Victoria's puzzled expression Casey added, "You've got to remember I come from the city where cops lock stuff up. I'm not used to people walking in any old time."

Once Victoria had settled herself into the passenger seat of the Bronco, Casey took off. Past the millpond, past the cemetery, past Whiting's fields, onto North Road. Asa's son was turning the tractor in at the entrance to Seven Gates.

Casey parked the Bronco on the left side of the road near the path. She locked both doors, and Victoria laughed.

"I intend to lock up stuff, Victoria, whether you do or not," Casey said defensively.

They retraced Victoria's route next to the brook, past the overgrown field, and up the hill. The crows were still feeding. The stench was still awful.

Victoria waited beside the path. She sat on a fallen tree while Casey climbed to where the crows were assembled. When she approached they flew up in an angry black cloud, cawing curses at the chief.

Casey was gone what seemed to Victoria a long time. When she finally climbed back down the slope to the path, her boots slipping on the wet leaves under the huckleberry, her face was pale. She and Victoria walked back to the Bronco without speaking. Victoria lifted herself up into the passenger seat, and Casey called the hospital's emergency room on the radio.

"I need to talk with Doc Jeffers." She turned to Victoria. "I have to watch what I say. Half the people on the Island have scanners."

When Doc Jeffers responded, Casey said into the mike, "I'm where I told you I'd be. You better have a look."

"I'll be there, twenty minutes, a half hour."

While they waited, Victoria stared out of the passenger side window at the stone wall on the other side of the road and the grapevine that formed a twisted network behind it. She didn't want to think about why they were here. She thought instead about wild grapes. There would be a good crop this fall. She would come back in October and pick some for jelly.

Finally Casey broke the silence. "There's not much left of his face. A lot of fuzzy gray hair, beard, sideburns. His hair and beard must have stuck out five to six inches from his face and head. He's dressed in expensive clothes, Pendleton wool shirt, Irish tweed trousers, handmade leather boots."

Victoria thought for a while. "You know who fits that description, fuzzy hair and beard? Montgomery Mausz, the attorney for the real estate developer, Harry Ness."

" 'Loch' Ness?"

Victoria nodded. "Mr. Mausz lived on North Water Street in Edgartown up until a month or so ago. His wife tossed him out because of another woman."

"Yeah?" Casey looked at Victoria with interest.

"Someone said he's in Aruba with the other woman."

"Maybe not," said Casey.

There was a roar on the road behind them. Victoria looked in the rearview mirror and saw a huge motorcycle, its metallic blue finish glittering in the sun. The biker himself was encased in black leather and wore a helmet that matched the bike. Tiny blue lights across the top of the helmet blinked like Christmas tree ornaments. Two small white wings stuck out on either side. The biker pulled over, cut his engine, lifted his right leg over the seat of the bike, kicked down the stand with his booted foot, and pulled off his helmet to expose a thatch of white hair, rimless glasses, and a jutting jaw.

"Where's the corpse, Chief?" He detached a black leather medical bag from the carrier on the back of the bike and unzipped his jacket. Beneath it he wore a light green hospital scrub shirt with curls of white hair in the V of its neck.

Casey stepped out of the Bronco and strode over to Doc Jeffers, who was much taller than the chief. Victoria looked at his feet. His boots were festooned with steel chains.

Victoria led the way at first, then let Casey and Doc Jeffers go on ahead of her. She sat on a fallen log and waited until they returned.

"It looks like Mickey Mausz, all right," Doc Jeffers announced. "Whacked on the side of the head. Been dead awhile. Several weeks, I'd guess. Maybe a month." He sighed. "Would be the week I'm on duty."

"Not natural causes, I gather?" Victoria said.

Doc Jeffers shook his head. "Not unless he happened to hit the side of his head hard on something like a rock. I didn't see any rocks up there."

~ ~ ~

"I need to take some papers to Junior," Casey told Victoria, as she held the Bronco door for the older woman. Junior Norton lived down one of the unmarked roads that branched off the sandy Quansoo road.

"I must say, I'm glad to have you along to help me find places, Victoria. Without you it would take me months — years — to learn who lives where."

Victoria settled herself in the passenger seat and adjusted her cap with a faint smile. "What do you suppose Montgomery Mausz was doing at Sachem's Rock? He wasn't even near the path."

Doc Jeffers had examined the corpse. Casey called in the state police, who brought in the state forensics people, and they, in turn, had gone over the scene. After that, Toby, the undertaker, drove the remains off-Island for an autopsy.

Casey lifted her shoulders in a shrug. Victoria continued. "A month ago it was cold and snowy. It went down to the twenties. He wasn't wearing a jacket, was he? Only a wool shirt. Did he have a hat on? Or gloves?"

"Good question." Casey pulled off the road into the huckleberry brush to let a Jeep pass them. The driver waved. Casey waved back.

"Who was that?" she asked Victoria.

Victoria turned to look at the Jeep that was disappearing in a swirl of dust. "One of the women from the garden club."

Casey eased back onto the road. It had not rained for more than a week. Dust kicked up in the one-lane road settled on the Bronco and drifted in through the half-open windows. Victoria sneezed and blew her nose on the napkin from her pocket, then looked out at the undergrowth along the sides of the road.

"Stop!" she suddenly cried out.

Casey jammed on the brakes with a squeal. The Bronco bucked and stalled. She looked at Victoria, alarmed. "What's up?"

"Boxberries grow here. We should be able to find berries this time of year, if the pheasants haven't eaten them all."

Casey put her head down on the steering wheel in dismay, and her hair fell over her face. "Don't do this to me, Victoria," she muttered. "You're going to give me a heart attack."

Victoria opened the passenger door and slid out. "One doesn't usually get heart attacks at your age."

Dark red-green boxberry leaves carpeted the ground under the oak trees. Victoria brushed aside the leathery leaves and picked a handful of the red berries that dangled like miniature Japanese lanterns underneath.

"Better get back in, someone's behind us." Casey started the engine. Victoria turned and waved at the car behind.

She offered the berries to Casey, who looked away from the road briefly, took one and nibbled it. "Wintergreen. Nice." She looked in the rearview mirror. "Who's *that?*"

Victoria turned to look. "Zack West. He lives on this road not far from Junior. He's a biologist with the Conservation Trust." Victoria eyed Casey. "He's single. About your age."

"I'm not interested, Victoria. Once was enough."

Victoria settled her blue quilted coat underneath her. "I'll have you and Zack over for baked beans some Saturday night."

"No, no, no, Victoria. You tried that before, and the guy was gay."

Victoria changed the subject. "I haven't been down this road all winter." She cranked down her window.

"Junior probably isn't home, Victoria. It's his day off."

"I'm sure he doesn't lock his door." Victoria looked sideways at the chief, who smiled.

When Junior's father, Ben Norton, had retired as police chief, the selectmen, instead of promoting Junior, advertised off-Island and hired Casey O'Neill. After a few tense weeks things settled down, and Junior had adjusted to working as Casey's sergeant.

Casey slowed and turned into a rutted road with a grassy hump in the middle. Ahead of them the Great Pond spread out like a sheet of blue-gray glass.

"He told me he'd be fishing at the opening when the tide changes," Casey said. "Can you tell what it's doing now?"

Victoria sat up straight in the passenger seat so she could see across the Pond to the opposite shore. "It looks as though the tide has started to turn. It's beginning to run out."

"I'll leave the papers on his kitchen table, then."

Junior's camp was a one-story shack cobbled together with driftwood and scrounged lumber from construction jobs around the Island. It was on a low bluff overlooking the Great Pond. From the bluff Victoria could see Junior's father's place on the opposite shore. On clear days, Ben's gray-shingled house stood out distinctly against the trees. Victoria could even make out Ben Norton's figure walking from house to barn. By boat, she thought, his house was about three-quarters of a mile from Junior's. By road it must be about seven miles.

Casey slammed the vehicle door and swished through the long brown grass to Junior's side door and knocked.

Victoria walked to the edge of the bluff. She could see, out of Ben's sight around the point and close to the opposite shore, someone working in a dory. She couldn't quite make out what the person was doing. From this distance she couldn't even tell whether it was a man or a woman. The figure was bundled up in a navy blue coverall and was wearing a brown knit cap. As Victoria watched, the dory moved from the cove into the main body of the Pond, and she saw the person drop something overboard. She couldn't tell what it was, nets or pots, something bulky. Shellfishing hours were over for the day, so he — or she — wasn't shellfishing. Not legally, anyway.

While Victoria was thinking about the figure in the boat, she turned to watch Casey, who knocked on Junior's door a second time, then, when there was no answer, opened it and went inside with the papers.

To her right, Victoria could see the grand sweep of the Atlantic. Over the narrow barrier bar that separated ocean from pond, breakers tossed foaming crests into the air before they curled and crashed onto the beach. She could smell the clam-flats exposed by the outgoing tide, a sulphurous smell that reminded her of greasy mud squishing up between her toes. She could feel the rumble of pounding surf, could hear above the roar gulls quarreling near the opening, a cut in the barrier bar that let tidal waters flow in and out to nourish the Great Pond's oyster beds.

She sat on an overturned rowboat at the edge of the bluff and watched the dory, which had moved almost as far as the opening. While she watched, it turned and headed back toward the cove, rounded the point, and disappeared from sight. She heard the putt-putt of its motor echoing against the shore.

The sun was warm on her back. She could work the subtle late-winter colors into a poem, a sonnet perhaps. Contrast the brown and beige of grasses, dark green of cedars, black of wild rose and bayberry with the changing blue of sky and sea and pond. Maybe use the image of sleep. Winter was certainly not death, the way so many poets saw it. Dig into the ground a bit and you would see life burgeoning. For the final couplet, she might put in something about the person in the boat, the ambiguity of gender and purpose. She found an envelope and pen in her pocket.

When she was a child, Victoria had hunted arrowheads along the edges of the Great Pond. Junior's camp, or at least part of it, was here, even then. His great-grandfather had built it as a duck hunting blind before Victoria was born.

She was pondering on the figure in the dory when Junior's door shut with a wooden thump and Casey strode through the grass.

"Sorry I took so long. I left Junior a note to explain what he was supposed to do."

"I don't mind the wait." Victoria lifted her wrinkled face to the sun.

Casey stood next to her at the bluff's edge. "It's clearer than I've ever seen it."

"This is the kind of day old-timers called 'a weather breeder,' " Victoria said. "We'll have a storm in a day or so. The surf sounds as if there's heavy weather offshore."

"I can feel it through my boots."

"I saw Ben heading to the barn, and I saw someone out in a dory." Victoria pointed to the cove. "The boat went around the point a few minutes ago."

"A fisherman?"

"I couldn't tell. The person was dropping something overboard, maybe bags of oyster cultch." Victoria got stiffly to her feet, holding a bayberry bush for support. "It could be the right time of year, I guess."

Casey stared at her. "Victoria, I have no idea what you're talking about. I'm a city girl. Remember?"

"Cultch is what oysters attach themselves to." Victoria picked up a driftwood stick near the rowboat to use for support. "Newly hatched oysters drift around in the water. After a bit they attach themselves onto something hard, like rocks or shells. That's 'cultch.' "

"Why *bags* of shells?"

"The bottom is muddy here. If you drop loose shells into the water, they'll sink into the mud. So they put scallop shells in bags of wide netting. The bags stay on top of the mud. The shells increase the surface for the oyster spawn to attach themselves."

Casey shook her head. "I have a lot to learn."

As they walked to the Bronco, Victoria poked at dried grass and leaves with her stick. "Signs of spring everywhere." She pointed to a small cluster of green leaves she'd uncovered. "Birdfoot violet. It won't bloom for another couple of months, but you can see it's getting ready." She covered the plant with leaves again.

As they headed home, thick clouds were beginning to move in. The few cars coming toward them had turned on headlights. Casey slowed going down Brandy Brow, passed the police station, and continued to Victoria's house, a quarter-mile beyond.

Victoria got down from the Bronco and glanced up. "I thought the weather would hold off a day or two but it's likely to storm tonight." She slammed the car's door shut with a heavy thunk. "From the looks of it, a bad storm. Well, good night, Chief."

"Good night, Deputy."

As she went up the stone steps to the entry, Victoria held the railing tightly. Elizabeth had turned on the kitchen lights, and was waiting in the doorway, tall and wiry in worn jeans and gray sweater.

She's so much like her grandfather, Victoria thought. Jonathan would have been standing here, just like this, worried about me, but not wanting it to show.

"You had a phone call, Gram," Elizabeth said when Victoria had taken off her coat. "Zack from the Conservation Trust. Said it involved Mr. Mausz. He wants you to call back."

McCavity, the ginger cat, stalked in from the living room, where, Victoria assumed, he had been napping all day on the couch. He rubbed up against her corduroy legs and stretched, opening his mouth in a wide yawn to show his splendid teeth.

Elizabeth filled the teakettle and put it on the stove. "That cat brought you a present today. I have no idea what it was, something disgusting."

"Nice Cavvy," Victoria crooned. The yellow cat closed his eyes and purred.

~ ~ ~

CHAPTER THREE

A Storm in the Night

WHEN the phone rang later that evening, Victoria and Elizabeth were eating supper. "Zack will be right over," Victoria said after she hung up. "Casey and I passed him on the Quansoo road this afternoon."

"What's he coming for, Gram?"

"Phoebe's sold her land. To developers."

"Oh no! What a shame. I thought the Conservation Trust was hoping to buy it."

"Apparently the developer got to her first."

"What does Zack expect you to do about it, Gram?"

Victoria dabbed at her mouth with her napkin before she replied. "I'm sure he thinks I can be of some help."

Rain was starting to ping against the windows of the cookroom, the room that had been the summer kitchen in Victoria's childhood. The small room, filled with hanging green plants and baskets, was where Victoria wrote her poetry and her weekly column for the *Island Enquirer.*

Elizabeth cut into her chicken, then put her fork down. "Phoebe's family has had that land for ages. How could she ever think of selling out?"

"They offered her a million dollars, according to Zack."

"For two hundred acres of prime land on Martha's Vineyard? That's not much."

"It seems like a lot of money to me." Victoria helped herself to more salad.

The wind wailed through the loose window frame in the kitchen and rain began to slash against the glass.

"Someone should put tape over that crack." Victoria looked meaningfully at Elizabeth, who grinned and left the table. Victoria heard a kitchen drawer opening.

"A hundred dollars seems like a lot of money." Victoria spoke up so Elizabeth could hear. "What is property in West Tisbury selling for these days?"

"Would you believe a hundred thousand dollars or more an acre? Someone bought a house on a three-acre lot in Edgartown last week for eleven million dollars."

Victoria heard Elizabeth rip off a piece of duct tape and putter at the window.

244

The wailing stopped. She did some quick calculating on an envelope she had retrieved from the wastepaper basket. "Two hundred acres would come to closer to ten million dollars than one million."

"Twenty million, Gram." Elizabeth returned to the table and sat again. "They took advantage of her. Developers are tearing this Island to pieces. It's just raw real estate to them, a way to make a buck."

Victoria nodded. "Apparently the deciding factor was when her granddaughter came to visit last month. Phoebe wanted to make sure neither her son nor her daughter — nor her granddaughter — would ever get the land."

"Nice family," Elizabeth murmured.

When Zack West came to the kitchen door a few minutes later, Elizabeth was clearing the table. His yellow slicker glistened with raindrops. He hung it on a nail in the entry, where it dripped water onto the brick floor.

Outside, water poured off the roof and out of the overflowing gutters and hit the stone steps in a steady cascade. Lightning flashed occasionally, distant thunder grumbled.

Zack swiped his wet hair from his forehead, kicked off his boots, and padded into the kitchen, toes and heels showing through holes in his socks.

The warm kitchen air made his glasses steam. He removed them and wiped the lenses with a red bandana he'd taken out of his pocket. Zack was about the same age as Chief O'Neill, and much too thin, in Victoria's opinion.

He blinked and put his glasses back on. "Filthy night."

"The fire's all set." Victoria handed him a box of matches. "Go ahead into the parlor and light it while I make tea."

Elizabeth loaded the dishwasher and turned it on. She yawned. "If you don't need me for anything, I'm going upstairs to read, Gram. Goodnight, both of you. Don't stay up too late."

By the time Victoria carried the tea tray into the parlor, the fire was blazing and Zack, who'd been squatting next to it, stood up and headed toward the ornately carved horsehair sofa.

"What on earth was Phoebe thinking of?" Victoria seated herself in the mouse gray wing chair and poured mugs of tea.

Zack watched the rain stream down the windows. "She was in a hurry to lock up a deal. The real estate people were nice, she told me. They were concerned about conservation."

"Hah!" said Victoria.

"She fell for it hook, line, and sinker. They sent her plants for her garden. This nice man, according to her, Roger Nordstrom, started dropping by. He was so attentive, more like a son to her than her own son." Zack paused. The wind shook the shutters and slammed against the house. "He even brought in a truckload of manure and spread it over her garden. When he gave her papers to sign, she signed them. She hasn't seen him since."

"She's along in years." Victoria smoothed her hair with her knobby hand. "Some elderly people can be quite gullible."

Zack's crooked smile showed large white teeth. "They not only offered the million dollars, but offered to pay all the taxes on the transfer." He leaned forward on the sofa. His knees, showing through torn jeans, were almost chest high.

"And they agreed to let her live there?"

"They told her the property would not be altered or touched or built on until after her death," Zack said. "Seemed like a good deal to her."

"Did she hire an attorney to go over the agreement?"

"Roger Nordstrom recommended an attorney." Zack paused and looked at Victoria.

"Surely not Montgomery Mausz?" She set her mug with a clink on the glass-topped coffee table.

McCavity came purposefully into the parlor and leapt into Victoria's lap. Victoria squinted as he kneaded his front paws on her thigh. "Ouch!"

"You okay, Victoria?"

"Yes, yes." She unhooked McCavity's claws. "You were saying Mr. Mausz represented Phoebe in the real estate transaction?"

"He was killed before the final closing, but he'd already done all the necessary paperwork. Did you know that Harry Ness was the principal owner of CARP, the real estate company? The developer? Phoebe didn't realize Ness was involved."

Victoria absently stroked McCavity, who purred.

"Don't tell me Mr. Mausz represented Harry Ness as well as Phoebe?"

"Yes." Zack stirred a spoonful of sugar into his tea.

Victoria shook her head. "It sounds as though Mausz had a serious conflict of interest."

Zack nodded.

"The deal went through?"

"The deed is signed and registered at the Court House."

"Weren't you and what's-his-name negotiating with Phoebe to purchase her land for the Conservation Trust?"

"Josiah Coffin. Yes. Loch Ness slipped in before we could get the money together. As I said, Phoebe was in a hurry. Ness's real estate agents sweet-talked her into believing that they were working in the best interests of both her and the Island. The Conservation Trust wasn't able to act fast enough."

"What happens now?" Victoria shifted McCavity slightly in her lap.

"He's filed a development plan with the Planning Board."

"Oh?"

"Ness intends to build sixty houses on the property."

"Sixty!"

The cat, startled, bounded off Victoria's lap, sat in front of the fire, and began to clean himself. He licked a front paw and scrubbed behind an ear.

"Sixty trophy houses, monuments to money, each on a three-acre lot. Each is to sell for three million dollars."

"Each house will bring in more than he paid for the entire property. Let's see." She scribbled on the clean side of an envelope. "Sixty houses times three million dollars comes to eighteen million dollars, am I right?"

"More like one hundred eighty million. Minus costs, of course."

Victoria was silent for long seconds.

"Are you still with us?" Zack said.

"I'm recalculating." Victoria scratched with her pen. "One hundred and eighty million dollars. Eighteen million dollars. It doesn't matter, does it? It's all the same, too much money."

"The entire development — called Ocean Zephyr Estates, by the way ..."

"Ooze." Victoria worked it out on her envelope. "Oz. N for Ness would make it Noze."

"... will be surrounded by a chain-link fence with barbed wire on top, and will have a gate with a security guard."

"I thought you said they agreed to wait until after Phoebe dies before they did anything with her land."

"Buddie Keene on the zoning board called Phoebe to tell her Loch Ness had filed the plan. That's how she found out. They didn't honor what she thought was their agreement. She called me. Upset, of course."

"Can she do anything?"

"I'm not sure. The contract didn't state what Nordstrom had told Phoebe it did. She didn't read it, you know. All that fine print. Nordstrom said he had asked Mausz to read it and she trusted both of them. If we can prove somehow that she was deliberately misled, we might be able to delay things."

"But that's hard to prove, I suppose. You'd have to have documentation, and she's not likely to have any."

A fork of lightning lit up the room. Thunder rattled the windows. Victoria's mind flashed back to finding the lawyer's body. She remembered the awful stench, and shuddered.

"Storm's practically on top of us now," Zack said.

Victoria stared into the fire. "Was Mr. Mausz involved in anything else?"

"Who knows. Mausz had his fingers in so many pies he'd made enemies in every one of the six towns. I can name a half-dozen people who are glad to see him out of the way."

"Me, too," said Victoria. "I mean, I can name a half-dozen people, too."

"The fact that you found his body near Sachem's Rock seems to point to a connection. There's enough money and power at stake over the property to make people do crazy things."

Victoria gazed at Zack for several moments before she said finally, "Why are you coming to me?"

Zack shifted on the hard sofa. "I have a couple of ideas."

"Oh?" Victoria sat forward.

"You know Island plants better than anyone." He pushed his glasses back on the nose. His thick eyebrows almost met over the tops of the frame. He looked, Victoria thought, like a red-tailed hawk, with his large curved beak, his magnified eyes glittering fiercely, and his shoulders hunched as if he were about to pounce on prey.

"I suspect I know what you're about to suggest," Victoria said. "What do you want me to find?"

Zack focused his eyes on her and grinned. "That property must have at least a couple of endangered species on it."

McCavity finished cleaning himself and stretched out on the hearth rug so his soft belly fur faced the warmth of the fire. With each gust of wind, the curtains billowed, the fire blazed.

'I shouldn't be surprised to find a half-dozen rare plants," Victoria said. "They're putting everything on the endangered species list these days. Dandelions will be next."

"If we could only find one endangered plant or animal on the property ..." Zack sat forward. He pushed his hair off his forehead with a quick gesture.

"We could stop them," Victoria finished. "They can't bulldoze rare plant habitats." She turned to Zack. "Well, I could take a look, if that's what you're about to ask me to do."

Zack settled back on the sofa and nodded.

"Will you come with me?" Victoria asked.

He shook his head. "I can't be seen on the property. The caretakers know me."

"Give me a checklist, then." Victoria's hooded eyes were bright. "A list that tells me what leaves of endangered species show this time of year. That sort of thing."

"We have a volunteer at the Trust, Robin White, an eleven-year-old, who can go with you weekends or afternoons when he's not in school."

Victoria heard a noise in the kitchen and got stiffly out of her wing chair to investigate. Zack unfolded like a carpenter's rule and followed. Water was dripping off the beam in the kitchen ceiling. Victoria put a saucepan underneath. "I asked Warren to fix that leak two months ago." She laid dishtowels in the rivulet that ran along the floor.

When they returned to the living room Victoria said, "Several ancient ways cross the property. Those are public rights-of-way. By law anyone can use them."

"You're right. Of course."

"Old cart roads and stage roads and sheep paths. I know most of them. Loch Ness can't stop me from walking on them."

Blinding lightning hit close by, with a simultaneous crash of thunder. The lights flickered. Victoria heard a long, drawn-out cracking sound and a dull thud.

She and Zack looked at each other blankly, and both rose. Victoria grabbed the flashlight she kept next to the black bowl where Elizabeth put the bills, and they went to the kitchen door. Zack swung his yellow slicker over his shoulders and slipped his own flashlight, a long four-cell one, out of the pocket.

"Wait in the entry where it's dry, Victoria."

He flipped the hood of his jacket over his head and stepped out into the pouring rain. Lightning strobed. Thunder growled. In the brief flashes, Victoria could see a vague massive object on the ground.

Zack had gone only as far as the bottom stone step, moving his light around, when Victoria saw that the large silver poplar in the turnaround had toppled, completely blocking the drive.

Zack returned to the entry and took off his wet slicker. The storm had already moved farther away. The pause between lightning and thunder had lengthened.

"Looks as if you'd better spend the night," Victoria said. "There's no way you can get your truck out tonight."

"Thanks. I will. In the morning I'll cut the tree, if you have a chain saw. Clear your drive."

They returned to the living room, where the fire was dying. Zack added a log, and then folded himself onto the sofa again.

Victoria listened to the storm as it faded into the distance. "Sometimes the wind sounds almost human the way it moans around the windows."

"It's not surprising. These old houses are supposed to be haunted. A night like tonight I can imagine ghosts in your attic."

"A lot of nonsense." Victoria changed the subject. "Did you have supper?"

"I forgot."

"Put the screen over the fire and come into the kitchen. We have some leftover chicken."

After Victoria had made up the bed in the East Chamber for Zack and had gone to bed herself, she had trouble falling asleep. The storm had moved far off to the west, but she continued to hear a low moaning. At one point she started to get up to check around the house, then scolded herself for letting Zack's talk of ghosts bother her. It was the wind, she was sure.

~ ~ ~

The next morning Zack and Victoria were up before dawn. He set three places — one for Elizabeth, who had not come downstairs yet. Victoria cooked bacon and eggs, pancakes and toast.

"Wonderful!" Zack said, his plate clean, his mouth full.

Victoria passed the platter of pancakes and eggs. He helped himself to thirds, poured more orange juice. When Victoria saw the way the food was disappearing, she brought out a large box of Shredded Wheat and Zack ate two helpings and a fourth piece of toast with beach plum jam spread thickly on it.

"Don't you eat at home?" Victoria couldn't help asking.

"Not like this." Zack shoveled cereal into his mouth. "You said you have a chain saw?" Strands of Shredded Wheat stuck out like hay from a horse's mouth.

"It's in the cellar," Victoria said. "Open the bulkhead doors next to the fuel oil tank. There's gasoline in the shed."

The eastern sky still had the ragged dark remains of last night's storm clouds. The sun rose over the maple trees, late winter skeletons silhouetted against the sky. The gray scud lighted up with dawn colors — pink, lavender, red, and gold.

Zack filled the old chain saw with gasoline and started it up. It coughed a couple of times, spit out gray smoke, and whined into a ragged rhythm that gradually steadied. Victoria followed him out to the fallen tree.

She stooped down and picked something up. "Are these your spectacles, Zack?"

He shook his head and pointed to his own glasses. "I can't see two feet without them."

"Gold frames," Victoria said. "Bifocals. Someone's going to miss them. I wonder whose they are?" She wiped them off carefully with a napkin and put them in her pocket.

"I hardly know where to begin," Zack shouted above the noise of the saw. "That was one huge tree." He examined the top branches that filled the angle between the main house and the kitchen wing. "Ten feet in either direction, and you'd have had some major house repairs."

Victoria was behind him when he suddenly stopped the saw.

"Holy mackerel!"

Victoria hurried toward him.

"Call 911. Someone's pinned underneath the tree. Alive, I think."

"Good Lord," Victoria gasped. "That moaning I heard last night ..." She hustled into the house and dialed. Zack started up the chain saw again.

By the time Casey and Junior arrived and the EMTs came with the ambulance, Zack had cut most of the smaller branches that pinned the unconscious man — nobody Victoria had ever seen before.

Zack carved away the thick tree trunk, careful not to shift more weight onto the man underneath, while Casey, Junior, and the EMTs held as much of the weight of the trunk off the man as they could. It looked to Victoria as if the tree had knocked him sideways. He was lying on his back with the heavy trunk across his chest. When they lifted it, he looked caved-in. Victoria put her hand on her own chest and took a deep breath. *I heard him,* she thought. *And I did nothing.*

Neither Victoria nor Zack could answer any of Casey's questions about the man, who he was or what he was doing there. They knew only that the tree had come down during the storm around nine-thirty the previous night.

"He lay there all night in the rain," Victoria whispered, her hand still on her chest.

"Don't think like that, Victoria," Zack said sharply. "What do you suppose he was doing there, anyway?" He set the saw down on the stone step.

Nobody answered.

The EMTs eased the stretcher under the man and gently moved him into the ambulance. Casey radioed the emergency room. This time Doc Erickson answered the call. "Lucky it was mild last night. Bring him in. I'll be ready when you get here."

The ambulance rushed out of the drive, siren wailing, lights flashing, and sped toward the hospital along the Edgartown Road.

By the time Elizabeth appeared, rubbing sleep out of her eyes, the ambulance had gone. "What was all the commotion, Gram?"

Victoria told her what she knew. "He was standing under the tree in that thunderstorm for some reason. I wonder why. Who can he be? These must be his spectacles I found." She took the glasses out of her pocket and examined them.

Victoria, Zack, and Elizabeth stood around uncertainly. Normal activities somehow seemed inappropriate.

"I guess we have to take care of the tree," Victoria said finally.

Zack returned to work with the chain saw. Victoria pulled on her leather gloves and wheeled the garden cart next to him. The saw buzzed like a swarm of bees, too loud for conversation. Zack stopped occasionally to chuck fireplace lengths into Victoria's cart. Then he'd pull the cord to start the saw up again, and it roared and bit and chewed and whined. Chips flew.

The early clouds had cleared and the sky was a bright washed blue. Redwing blackbirds called from the wooded area behind the compost heap. On the south side of the house, green snouts of snowdrops poked up through the ground underneath the fuel oil tank. Perhaps this year her snowdrops would be the first in town to bloom, Victoria thought. Then she thought again about the man crushed under her tree.

Who was he and what was he doing there? She could think of no explanation. He had been dressed in new-looking foul weather gear, so he didn't seem to be a homeless man needing a place to stay out of the storm. He appeared to be in his early fifties, not a young person playing some game. He wasn't a suitor of Elizabeth's, as far as she knew.

She trundled the cart of green logs to the woodpile where Elizabeth unloaded them and piled them where they would season. Elizabeth was wearing an old plaid flannel shirt of her grandfather's. It still had the angular tear she had never mended. Jonathan wouldn't let her put his shirt in the ragbag. She could see him now in his granddaughter, tall and slender, independent, stubborn, and decent.

The sound of surf on the south shore was gentler than it had been yesterday before the storm. She could still feel its vibration under her feet and in her chest, the ever-present surf, cresting and combing and tumbling onto the shore as it had for centuries. She wondered if that man would be able to feel anything in his chest ever again. He had looked so crushed.

~ ~ ~

CHAPTER FOUR

The Conservation Trust

JOSIAH Coffin stood at a window of the small Conservation Trust office and looked down at the old cranberry bog at the foot of the hill, half-hidden in a rising ground mist. He thrust his hands into the pockets of his jeans. Zack leaned back in Josiah's swivel chair. The chair squealed. A lock of hair had fallen over Zack's forehead, and he peered out from under it through thick glasses and saw discouragement in his boss's slanted shoulders.

"We have so little to fight with." Josiah turned from the window. His large nose cast a shadow on the side of his pale face. His auburn hair needed trimming. He was about the same age as Zack, mid-thirties. "Loch Ness can buy off anyone who gets in his way. Damn Phoebe Eldredge. We were so close to getting that conservation restriction."

"It was her granddaughter's visit that triggered it," Zack said. "The granddaughter apparently swooped in like a vulture scenting a kill. Phoebe hadn't heard from her for at least two years. The granddaughter showed up with rainbow-colored hair, nose studs, and tattoos."

"So she was afraid the kid — how old is she, anyway?"

"Late twenties. She's not a kid."

"Afraid the granddaughter would end up with the property before we could get the conservation restriction on it."

Zack flicked his hair out of his eyes, pushed his glasses back onto his nose, and peered at Josiah. There was nothing he could think to say.

Josiah broke the silence. "Everybody was after Phoebe's land. For a golf course. For a millionaire's enclave. For a campground. The Wampanoags want it for a casino. Tom More still hopes to get it for a Utopian housing complex. Ness got to Phoebe first. Damnation." Josiah stared out of the window again. "If she could only have waited another three weeks." He shoved his hands deeper into his pockets. "You wonder if it's worth it. Are we the only people on the Island willing to fight to preserve some small part of it? Does it even matter?"

Zack leaned back and the chair squealed.

"Well, hell." Josiah turned again and straightened his shoulders. "Let's look at the map and talk."

Zack unwound his legs from the base of the chair and stood up.

He was a full head taller than Josiah.

The Island map Josiah referred to covered an entire wall of his office, twelve feet long and seven feet high. Parts of it were shaded in different colors, and it was stuck all over with colored pins.

Zack was responsible for about half the pins, which marked the locations of plants on the state's endangered species list. For ten years he had scoured the hills and moors and marshes and woodlands and grasslands and shores of the Island making an inventory of plants and animals and birds.

Josiah pointed to the area of Sachem's Rock. "The endangered species act is our only weapon. It would be a loss to the Island to have the two hundred acres around the rock developed. Sixty trophy houses."

"What do they say up at the tribal office?" Zack asked.

"I haven't spoken to Chief Hawkbill. I don't know how they can help. A casino would be worse than sixty homes."

Sachem's Rock was a house-size boulder that overlooked the two-hundred-acre property below it. It was a glacial erratic, dropped on top of a morainal hill by glaciers twenty thousand years before. It had been called Sachem's Rock long before white settlers came to the Island. The rock jutted out of the ground like a sperm whale broaching, split at the bottom to form what looked like a jaw. For generations, the Island's Wampanoags had come to the rock for ceremonial occasions, had revered it as a whale, and had named it "Sachem," the title of a tribal chieftain.

Zack leaned down to peer at the part of the map that showed the property, a large chunk almost in the center of the Island.

"Not many pins there," Josiah went on.

"I never had a chance to survey it," Zack said defensively.

"I didn't mean to fault you." Josiah turned from the map and gripped Zack's arm with a calloused hand. "It's so frustrating. No one expected Phoebe to sell out." He dropped his hand and turned back to the window. Swirls and tendrils of mist rose over the bog outside. "Ness has posted the land. He's hardly likely to give us permission to make a survey of rare species now. He knows that if we find anything on the land, it will, at a minimum, delay him."

Zack sat in the swivel chair again and rocked back and forth. He laced his hands behind his head. "You knew I was at Victoria Trumbull's the other day?"

"During the storm. The tree came down on that guy. How is he, by the way?" Josiah continued to stare out the window.

"Still alive, but still in a coma. The doctors think he'll recover okay."

Josiah shook his head. "What were you about to say?"

"I mentioned the subject of finding rare plants on the property to Victoria. She picked right up on it. She volunteered to help."

"She's ninety, for God's sake. I know she's tough, but still, we can hardly ask a ninety-year-old lady to tramp around the way we do."

"She's ninety-two, not ninety," Zack said. He thought of Victoria's bright eyes and her pleased smile, the multitude of creases in her face that, strangely, made her look like a young girl. "She's related to you, isn't she?"

"Everyone on the Island is related to Victoria."

Zack waited.

Josiah stared out of the window. He jingled change in his pocket. At last he said, "I see what you mean, I guess. It's in the blood. Should we go to her place to talk to her, or bring her here?"

"I imagine she'd like to come here. We can show her maps and pictures, make copies of stuff she needs," Zack said.

"We've got nothing to lose." Josiah turned to Zack. "Who knows."

"I told her Robin White would go with her."

"A ninety-two-year-old and an eleven-year-old." Josiah laughed for the first time that morning. "I guess that averages out to fifty-one or so. Fifty-one isn't exactly combat age." He was quiet for several minutes.

Zack waited.

"What about transportation?" Josiah said finally.

"She hitchhikes." Zack pushed his hair off his forehead and linked hands behind his head again.

Josiah laughed again. For the first time in several days, Zack saw his boss's mood lift.

Zack went on. "When she's not hitching, she rides with Chief O'Neill in the police Bronco. The chief appointed her a deputy police officer, you know. After Victoria fingered that serial killer."

Josiah shook his head. "They don't make 'em like that anymore." He paced from the window to the wall map, glanced at it, and paced back to the window again. "She can ride with one of us. We have to be careful, though, not to let Ness's people associate her with the Trust."

"Harmless old lady strolling on the ancient ways with a little boy." Zack grinned and leaned forward.

"I must say, I'm concerned about her safety." Josiah became serious again. "We don't know why Montgomery Mausz was killed, and not far from the rock. Was it something personal against him? His wife or mistress? Why there? Was he mixed up in some way with Ness? Double-crossing him, maybe? Does one of the Wampanoags feel their sacred rock has been violated? I don't know how Mausz's killer is going to feel about Victoria Trumbull innocently hiking the old trails."

Zack shook his head. "It didn't look like an accident, that's for sure."

"Did a stranger kill him, a tramp, maybe? A psycho? In which case, it's irresponsible of us to let an old woman walk around there on her own. She can hardly protect herself." Josiah's hands were in his jean pockets again, jingling coins.

"She can take care of herself," Zack said. "Maybe the killer is one of the doctors who hopes to build a golf course." Zack bared his teeth in a grin. "Half the members of the Park and Rec committee are crazy enough to murder someone over swings and slides and monkey bars. Tom More is a religious fanatic about his commune. Maybe one of the Indians — Native Americans — brained him. Maybe Mausz's mistress killed him. His wife."

"His wife had probable cause, I guess," Josiah said. "He wasn't exactly discreet about his fooling around. What was he doing on the property, anyway?"

"He was the attorney for the land transaction."

"I know. But that was no reason for his being there. Unless he was with Ness or one of his agents."

"You knew he was also the attorney for Phoebe?"

"No. I didn't know that. That's wildly unethical."

Zack shrugged. "That's our boy, Mausz. Maybe he liked to walk by himself and ran into a low branch."

Josiah went back to the window. "The medics in Falmouth say he was killed around the time of that hard freeze last month. Around the first week of February. They couldn't be definite about the time of death because of the cold." Josiah stared out the window. "If you recall, it got down into the twenties."

"Could they tell what killed him?"

"They couldn't be definite about that, either. Or at least, they wouldn't tell me. They said it looked like he'd been hit with something heavy and hard, like a stone or a chunk of metal. A tire iron, maybe."

"I don't see that Victoria's in any danger," Zack said. "Tramping around up there is nothing new for her." He got up from the chair and started toward the office door. "She certainly isn't afraid of a mere murderer. She was the one who found the body, after all."

"Well, we're desperate." Josiah left the window. "We've got to do all we can to prevent Ness from going ahead with that development. If Victoria can help, we'll put her to work."

"I'll give her a copy of the state's endangered species list." Zack ducked his head to go through the low door.

"She actually might find mountain cranberry on the property; it's the right habitat. Or goldenseal. If she could find a cranefly orchid, that would really stop Ness dead." Josiah reached up and brought down a thick book from the shelf in the hall outside his office. "I'm sure she knows the cranberry and goldenseal, but cranefly orchid is so rare she's probably never seen it. It may not even be on the property." He put the book on a small table and thumbed through it until he came to a picture and a brief description of the rare orchid. "She should be able to recognize the plants this time of year. The leaves will be green now. The Vineyard is the only place in New England where they've been found. There are a few specimens on Seven Gates, one near the Great Pond, but nowhere else in the eastern U.S. until you get to North Carolina. The Great Smoky Mountains. If we could find one plant on that property, just one, it would be enough to trigger a cease and desist order."

Zack grinned. "And one hell of a lot of trouble."

~ ~ ~

Victoria unzipped her yellow slicker, unbuttoned her heavy sweater, peeled both of them off, and sat down with a plop in the chair next to Casey's desk.

"Whew!" Her white hair sparkled with droplets of condensed fog. She had walked the quarter mile from her house to the police station.

"Yesterday was quite a day!" She laid her coat and sweater over the back of the wooden chair. Her face was rosy from yesterday's sun and wind, and from this morning's hike.

From the station house window she could see the swans sail in and out of the eddying mist that rose over the millpond.

"You should have called me, Victoria. I'd have given you a lift." Casey stood up and went to the window. "The fog seems to be getting thicker. What's the weather going to do?"

"It'll burn off by afternoon," Victoria said with assurance. "Have you heard any more about the man under my tree, Spencer Kirschmeyer?"

Casey shook her head. "He's still in intensive care. Hasn't regained conscious-ness yet. The new surgeon repaired everything she could. It's out of her hands now, she said."

"Do they know anything about him besides his name?"

"He's a licensed private investigator from Bridgeport, Connecticut." Casey leaned down and brushed a speck of dust off her sharply creased uniform trou-sers.

"Investigating my house? How strange."

"He had a rental Jeep he'd parked on New Lane. He picked it up at the air-port three days ago, rented it for a week. He'd put a hundred twenty-seven miles on it."

"Did he leave anything in the car?"

"Receipts. He was staying at the Harbor View in Edgartown. A briefcase with some electronic gear in it, a tape recorder, earphones. A couple of lined legal pads. Chewing gum wrappers. An empty Diet Pepsi can. Nothing else."

"Electronics," Victoria mused. "I don't know anything about electronics. Could he have been bugging my house?"

"Surely not you," Casey said with a smile.

"It's conceivable that someone might want to listen to my conversations." Victoria's mouth turned down.

"Yes, yes, of course. I meant ... I don't know what I meant." Casey went to the small closet and took her jacket off a hook. "Let's go. I need to make my rounds. We can check your house for bugs at the same time."

She shut the station house door, gave it a small push to make sure it had latched, and shook her head at it.

"I'm tempted to invest my own money in a lock."

"The police station doesn't need a lock. It's a public building," Victoria said.

Casey glared at her.

Victoria waited while the chief unlocked the Bronco's doors.

Casey backed out of the small parking lot and turned toward Victoria's house. On the way they passed the rock on the corner of Old County Road in front of Mabel Johnson's house. Mabel Johnson had been dead for at least fifty years, but no one called the house by the new owner's name, even though the new owner's children had grown children by now.

The vehicle tires swished on the wet road. The fog drifted in long ribbons with clear patches in between. As they passed New Lane, they saw a Jeep parked by the side of the road.

"Island Auto Rental was supposed to pick it up. I'll give them another call." Casey turned into Victoria's drive. "It looks bare without your tree."

"I remember when my grandfather planted it. Uncle Dan was cutting the horse and wagon too close to my grandmother's flowerbed. The tree would stop him, Grandpa said."

"So the tree was eighty-five, eighty-six years old?"

"About that."

"It was huge." Casey parked under the Norway maple. "I can't imagine what Mr. Kirschmeyer was doing here. Electronic bugging is about the only thing that makes sense. But I can't imagine why."

"Zack was working all around the tree. If there was a bugging instrument, you'd think he would have seen it."

"Maybe not. He didn't expect to find electronic devices. If he had seen something like that, he probably would think it was some electronic game of your great-grandkids. GameBoy or Pokémon."

The tree's roots had come out of the ground in a ball the size of a small car, leaving a gaping hole. Where Zack had cut up the fallen tree, there were heaps of fresh sawdust. The driveway was littered with leaves and small branches.

"I'll get the rake," Victoria said.

"Let me check the house first. Where were you the night the tree came down?"

"In the parlor."

From the main road Victoria's two-hundred-and-fifty-year-old house seemed neatly symmetrical. But from the back, it rambled off in a jumble of additions, ells, and crazy roof angles.

Victoria led Casey to the side of the main house. They started with the stone foundation, examining it carefully. Then the brick foundation on top of the stones, then up the weathered gray shingles toward the window.

"Who was here the night before last, just you and Zack?" Casey asked.

Victoria nodded. "Elizabeth had gone to bed."

"Were you in the living room — parlor — most of the time?"

"Yes. That's the window right above you."

Casey searched along the bottom edge of the window frame with her hand.

The window itself was above her head, just within her reach.

"Aha! Look at this, Victoria." She pointed to a small black box the size of a cigarette pack attached to the lowest pane of glass by a suction cup. She stood on tiptoe, pried the suction cup loose with her fingernail, and turned the box over. "It's a transmitter." She stepped out of the garden and away from the house. "Get the rake. We'll see if we can find the receiver under the debris. It wasn't in the rental car."

Victoria returned from the shed with two rakes and they cleared the ground around the stump.

"Here we are!" Casey held up what looked like a small tape recorder. "Let's take it back to the station house and see what we have."

"What was he listening for?" Victoria stared at the small black box. "Why? I certainly don't have any secrets."

~ ~ ~

CHAPTER FIVE

Robin Comes Along

THAT afternoon Victoria met Robin White, her eleven-year-old assistant, for the first time. Zack and she picked him up after school. He seemed small, frail, and surly.

"Are you going to be warm enough?" she asked him.

The boy nodded without speaking.

Zack had let them off at the Sachem's Rock trailhead with a promise to pick them up in two hours. It was now about three o'clock. Days were noticeably longer, but the air was chilly and getting chillier as the sun dropped lower on the other side of the high ground.

Robin was wearing a brown baseball cap turned backwards so the band was across his forehead, almost touching his glasses. Above the band, a tuft of sandy-red hair stuck out in several directions. The front of the cap read "UPS" in yellow stitching. He was wearing jeans with the knees worn through to horizontal threads, and a dirty gray sweatshirt printed with a dog's skeleton and bold black lettering that read, "Dead Dog."

"Where on earth did you get that shirt?" Victoria asked, hoping to find some common ground so she could talk to this boy.

He shrugged and pushed his hands deeper into his pockets.

"It must be a collector's item," she said.

He shrugged again, shoulders lifting up and down.

"You don't have to go with me, if you don't want."

He looked at her through his glasses and grinned, showing big new teeth. "They're paying me."

"Who's paying you?" Victoria asked indignantly.

He shrugged again and looked down at his feet.

"Look at me, Robin White," Victoria ordered. "I don't want you to go with me any more than you do. You can sit there," she pointed to a rock beside the path, "and wait until I come back."

He shook his head. "I told them I'd go with you."

"For pay." Victoria frowned. "Who's paying you, Zack?"

He shook his head. "Mr. Coffin."

"How much is he paying you?" Victoria stood, feet apart, and leaned on her walking stick.

The boy hung his head. He thrust his hands still deeper into his pockets, shoulders up like the wings of a half-grown chicken. He looked down at his running shoes.

"Tie your shoelaces," Victoria ordered. "How much is Mr. Coffin paying you?"

He brought one hand out of his pocket. In it he held a deck of cards.

"Well?" Victoria demanded.

"Pokémon." He handed the cards to her, and she took them. He bent down and tied his shoelaces.

"You sold out for Pokémon cards?" she asked him.

He stood up again and nodded.

"If you're getting paid to guard me, I should think it would be worth more."

The boy glanced up with a worried look.

"Well, come on, then. We've got work to do." She handed the cards back to him.

They started up the path that led to the wooded area and high ground. Victoria walked carefully, making sure her footing was firm. Robin bounded ahead of her, then circled back. At one point Victoria stopped and opened out the folded topographic map. Robin loped back and looked over her arm.

"We're here." Victoria pointed with the hand that held her stick. "One of the ancient ways branches off and follows the low land, you see here?"

Robin nodded, wrinkling his nose to lift his glasses into place.

A redwing blackbird caroled from the nearby marsh. Another answered.

"We're looking for any of five different rare plants," Victoria said. "Pay attention, Robin. Stop that." Robin had scooped up a handful of acorns and was flinging them at the trees next to the path. The acorns hit the trunks with a thunk.

"I'm listening."

"Mountain cranberry likes high ground. It's an alpine plant that's been here on the Vineyard since the Ice Age."

"Yeah?" Robin flung another acorn. Thunk! "Woolly mammoths lived here then."

"I suppose," said Victoria.

"Maybe they ate mountain cranberries. That's why they're rare." Thunk!

"We'll start with this path." She indicated it on the map. "You mark off the places we've been." Victoria handed him the map and a pencil.

He jabbed the pencil at the spot on the map she indicated, and the pencil point broke.

Victoria set her cloth bag on the ground with exasperation. "This partnership is not going to work. I can do this survey better without your assistance. I can't imagine what Josiah is thinking." She reached into the bag and handed Robin a small pencil sharpener shaped like a mouse.

"Wow!" Robin took the mouse sharpener, gazed at it in awe, and grinned. "Pikachu! Where'd you get it?"

"I have my sources," Victoria said tartly. "I suppose we're stuck with each other for the next two hours."

Robin was grinding the pencil round and round in the mouth of the plastic mouse. Pencil shavings curled off and dropped onto the ground.

"Isn't that sharp enough?"

"It works good," Robin answered.

" 'Well'," Victoria corrected. "You may keep it. Come along, now. This path goes past a vernal pool, a damp place that's a pond in spring. In another month we should be able to find a lot of different plants there." For a brief stretch she led the way along the narrow path, then Robin ran ahead again.

Victoria stopped frequently and gently poked at the earth with her stick. She saw the bright green hoods of skunk cabbage at the edge of the marsh, and tight fiddlehead curls of ferns. Unkempt cattail heads showed white fluff beneath their brown velvet coatings. A breeze riffled the tall dry grasses on the other side of the wetland.

"What are we looking for, anyway?" Robin called out.

"The best discovery of all would be a cranefly orchid," Victoria told him. "If there are any here — and this is the kind of place they like — we should be able to find green leaves lying flat on the ground. They might have purple dots on top. The undersides of the leaves are purple." She stopped as Robin leaped up to catch an overhanging branch. "Pay attention."

"I am. Purple dots. What's the big deal?"

"They're endangered. The Vineyard is the only place they've been found in all of New England."

"Yeah?" He leaped into the air and slapped at a branch. A shower of dry red berries dropped around their feet.

"There used to be cranefly orchids on Cape Cod, but when developers built houses there, they destroyed the orchid's habitat. That was only about twenty years ago."

"That was in the olden days. Before I was born."

Victoria glanced at him. "That was only yesterday. Not even a hairline in geologic time."

Robin shrugged. He picked up a small rounded stone and flung it into the marsh, where it landed with a plop. "How do they know they're here, in this spot?"

"They don't. That's why we're looking. But they've found a few plants in other places on the Island, so it's possible there may be some, or at least one, here."

"Mr. Coffin wants us to find them so nobody can build houses here?"

"I suppose so."

They continued along the old trail. In places it was marshy, and Victoria stepped carefully from one tuft of dry grass to another. A stand of beetlebung trees arched over the path.

"What kind of plants are these, Mrs. Trumbull?" Robin pointed to a clump of bushes with dry seeds in clusters like miniature upright bunches of grapes.

Victoria glanced over. She had been watching the ground to make sure of her footing. "Clethra," she said. "Sweet pepperbush. When it blooms in the summer, it's one of the most wonderful scents on earth, spicy and clean."

"Oh," Robin said.

They passed swamp maples and oak trees, sassafras and viburnum. Victoria recognized their winter skeletons.

"Look!" Robin shouted. "Holly! I know holly."

Victoria nodded. "Look under it for green leaves."

"With purple spots," said the boy.

They stopped under a beech tree, the gold-brown leaves of last autumn still clinging to the branches, and they searched the ground carefully, pushing through catbrier, bright green with wickedly sharp thorns, to get a better look.

"I don't see anything," Victoria said finally. "But this is the sort of place they like."

Robin looked up suddenly. "What's that noise?"

Victoria stood still and listened. She had heard a rustling that only nudged at her mind, a scratching in the dry leaves, perhaps a noise that didn't really register. When you stood still, the sound she wasn't sure she'd heard stopped. They waited, both of them holding their breath.

"Perhaps it was a deer," Victoria whispered.

"Maybe it was a person. That's why Mr. Coffin said I should guard you. Some person might try to attack you, he said."

"He said that? That someone might attack me?"

"Not exactly, but that's what he meant, I know."

Victoria looked at her watch. "We have only a half hour left before we need to turn back."

"I bet it was a person we heard. Sneaking up on us." Robin ran on ahead. Victoria followed slowly.

The ancient way skirted the hill of the great rock, wound slowly up between beech trees and oaks, rising gently, an old cart path, away from the wetlands where the beeetlebungs and catbrier kept their feet wet. Bright green moss contrasted with the golden beech leaves and the austere browns and grays of early March.

"I heard it again," Robin said. "I think he's following us."

Victoria listened and heard nothing, not even the remembrance of hearing something. The sun was settling behind the hill, and the path was in deep shadow. She shivered.

"You cold, Mrs. Trumbull?" Robin sounded anxious.

"Not really, but we should be getting back. Mark the map. Carefully now. No more pencil holes."

"I can't help it."

"Here, lean on my notebook." Victoria stopped walking and brought her notebook out of her cloth bag. As she did, she heard the sound, a stealthy rustling of dry leaves that stopped an instant after she did. It wasn't the leaping sound of a deer. Nor the scratching, rustling of a chewink, hunting for something in the fallen leaves. Nor did it sound like a dog or a skunk following along with them. It was the sound a person might make if he wanted to see without being seen.

"Let's go back," Victoria said abruptly. "Right now. It's getting dark and cold. Come on, now."

"You think he's going to attack us, Mrs. Trumbull?"

"Don't be silly." Victoria stepped along as fast as she could, holding her stick in front of her like a blind person to feel the roots and stones that were hidden now in shadow.

"I've got a weapon." Robin held up a large oak branch that he'd picked up.

"That won't do. It's rotten. You'll simply enrage him if you hit him with it and it smashes. Come along." She had heard the sound again, and it did sound like footsteps. An occasional snap of a dead stick. A rustle of leaves. She looked up quickly in the direction the sound came from, thought she saw a flick of movement in the dusky woods. They came out of the shadow to the marshy place where they'd searched for the orchid. Victoria was slowed by having to step carefully from one grass tuft to another. She heard the rustling now, almost steadily. It was as if the stalker no longer needed to be stealthy. Would he come out into the open, she wondered? There wasn't much she could do to defend herself if he did. Perhaps Robin could run for help; she certainly couldn't. She moved faster, tripped over a grass tuft. Robin reached his scrawny arm out as if it were spring-loaded, and she fell against it. His arm gave like a sapling, and he helped her to stand upright again.

"Well." Victoria caught her breath. "Well. Maybe you *are* earning your pay. Thank you."

He looked around behind them. "We better keep moving. Want to hold my arm?"

Victoria heard the rustling, closer now. "Yes. I'd better."

~ ~ ~

While Victoria and Robin were scouting for an orchid that might not exist, the gang on Alley's porch was basking in the warm spring sunshine.

Joe unzipped his windbreaker and shoved his grimy hands into his pants pockets. "Where's Donald at?" He was standing at the edge of the porch, pelvis thrust out, rocking back and forth. He shifted a wad of something from one side of his mouth to the other.

"Down at the boatyard," said Lincoln, bending and straightening his long legs to scratch his back on the doorframe.

Sarah had unbuttoned her coat, exposing a black T-shirt printed with a slogan for the Two Braves Trucking Company in Day-Glo pink and orange. She was sitting on the bench, drinking a Diet Coke. She wore her hair in an inch-high crew cut.

Joe jerked his head toward the T-shirt. His hair curled in dark ringlets that

Sarah envied. "How come you're always wearing that Indian shit? You ain't no Indian."

"'Native American,'" Sarah said primly. "I work for the Tribe, in case you forgot."

Joe shook his head.

"Anybody heard any more about the Mausz murder?" Lincoln stopped scratching his back and straightened up. He had a long, horsy face topped by blond hair that was beginning to gray. "It's been mighty quiet."

A black pickup truck pulled up in front of the store and a short bearded man in jeans and a jeans jacket got out. He nodded at the three on the porch and went into the store. The door banged shut.

"Who's the short guy in the high-heeled cowboy boots?" Lincoln indicated the door with his thumb.

"Tom More," said Sarah. "The one who wants to build that commune at Sachem's Rock."

"I thought Ness had that locked up."

Sarah shrugged. "You never know."

"You was saying about Mickey Mausz." Joe turned back to Sarah.

"Toby took his body off-Island in the hearse and they did an autopsy in Falmouth." Sarah took a sip of her Diet Coke. "All they found out was what everybody already knows. He was hit on the head with something, and he'd been dead about three, four weeks. A month maybe."

A red Volvo went past headed toward Chilmark. The driver waved. Lincoln nodded.

"How's his wife taking it?" Lincoln said. "They weren't getting along too good, last I heard."

"That's putting it mildly." Sarah finished the last of her soda and set the empty can on the bench beside her. "She was suing him for divorce."

"Yeah?" Joe looked at Sarah with interest. "Because of his girlfriend?"

"'Woman friend,'" Sarah corrected.

"Who's the woman friend, anybody we know?" Lincoln started rubbing his back against the doorframe again.

"Get a splinter, doing that," Joe said.

Lincoln ignored him. "I heard she was someone from the Island. A mystery lady."

"He must be about the first person on this Island who kept his girlfriend's name a secret," said Joe.

Sarah brushed a speck off her black trousers. "If you've got money, you can always fly to the Caribbean. That's where his wife thought they'd gone. At least that's what she's saying."

"Did his wife know who the other woman was?" Lincoln asked.

"Who knows what she knew," Joe wriggled his hips. "Minerva Peabody is Edgartown Yacht Club, dahling. Tennis. Sailing. Pink shirts and flowered drawers. Mausz married her for her money."

"Yeah?" Lincoln leaned forward. " 'Peabody?' "

"She kept her maiden name," Sarah explained.

Joe guffawed. "Wouldn't you if you was her? Minerva Mausz?"

Lincoln shrugged. "Where's her money come from?"

"Old money," said Sarah. "Railroads or oil or mergers or something."

Joe spit off to one side again and wiped his mouth with the back of his hand.

"That's disgusting, Joe." Sarah shifted on the bench as if to distance herself from him.

"Want me to swallow it instead?"

Sarah shuddered. "Animal."

Joe guffawed. "You got that right, lady."

"Any more news about the guy Miz Trumbull's tree fell on?" Lincoln asked.

"They say he's still in a coma," Sarah replied.

"What's her and that nerdy kid doing?" Joe took his penknife out of his pocket and began to clean his fingernails. "They been walking up to Sachem's Rock."

Sarah set the soda can down again. "She's always walking places. That's why she's in such good shape."

"Probably scouting for something." Joe rocked, heel to toe.

"Everybody wants that land," Lincoln said. "The golfing docs. The tribe."

"Well, it's Ness's land. He bought it," Sarah said.

"Don't mean he's going to keep it." Joe finished cleaning the nails on one hand and started on the other. "Park and Rec wants the town to buy it for a kiddie park and campground."

"How'd you hear that?" Lincoln asked.

"My wife's cousin is on the Park and Rec. And then there's that religious freak in there." Joe jerked his head toward the interior of the store, where Tom More had gone. "Alfalfa sprouts cooked by solar energy in a community kitchen. Red plot."

"It's not communist, it's communal," Sarah said.

"Same thing."

"Don't forget the Conservation Trust. That quiet guy has something up his sleeve, too," Lincoln added.

"Josiah Coffin?" Sarah raised her eyebrows. "What about him?"

"Mark my words. Coffin is going to tangle with Loch Ness," Lincoln said.

"Coffin don't have two cents to rub together." Joe started down the steps. "I gotta get back to work."

"Want to take bets on what happens next?" Sarah asked.

"Only thing I'm betting on is Old Lady Trumbull," Joe said over his shoulder. "She's some smart, for an old bird."

~ ~ ~

CHAPTER SIX

Pinkletink Time, and Discoveries

WHEN they got back to the Conservation Trust office, Victoria sat heavily in the armchair at the head of the conference room table. "Someone was following us," she said to Josiah. "At least it sounded that way."

Josiah turned to Zack, who was standing behind Victoria. "This is foolish. We have no idea who's out there. Maybe it's Ness's caretaker or maybe not. Until they determine who killed Mausz we shouldn't send anyone out there. I'm calling this off. We'll have to find another way."

Robin, who was circling the table, stopped. "You mean you won't let us go back there?"

Josiah shook his head. "I don't think it's wise."

Victoria drummed her fingers on the table. "If Robin and I stay together, there's no danger to either of us. The person who was following us this afternoon could easily have attacked one of us today and didn't."

Zack turned to Josiah. "Suppose I go along with them?"

"We've got to come up with some other plan," Josiah said, still shaking his head. "You'd be a dead give away, Zack. Everyone on the Island knows you're with the Trust. It won't work for you to go along."

Robin had stopped by the bookcase and was running his fingers along the backs of the books. He turned around. "That's not fair," he said to Josiah. "You promised ..."

Josiah glowered at him and Robin didn't finish.

"It seems to me," Victoria said, "since I'm the one involved, since it's my safety you're worried about, that it's my decision whether to continue or not. You've told me your concerns, and I thank you. But I intend to continue my survey of the property. I have no right to speak for Robin, of course."

"Me, too," Robin said quickly.

"That's not up to me," Victoria said.

Josiah stared down at the map in front of him. Zack looked out at the cranberry bog. From the window the bog was a dark red blanket below them. Victoria continued to drum on the table. Robin's glasses had slipped down to the end of his nose.

"It's not your decision," Victoria repeated. "It's mine. If you won't take me, I'll get Elizabeth to take me. Or Casey."

"Me, too," said Robin.

Victoria turned her head. "That's up to your mother."

Josiah stood. "All right, Victoria. We need your help, that's for sure. And you're the only person I can think of who can get away with the search. You and Robin, that is."

Zack leaned against the bookcase. "What about letting her take a handheld radio, Josiah?"

"I've never worked one of those," Victoria said.

Zack grinned. "You can learn."

"I don't need a radio," Victoria insisted.

"Can we take a radio, Mrs. Trumbull? Can we? I can work it for you."

" 'May' we," Victoria said. "Not 'can.' "

And so it was decided. Josiah showed Victoria and Robin, both of them, how to work the radio, and from then on, Victoria carried it with her in her cloth bag.

On their second day out, Victoria and Robin went beyond the marsh, followed the gentle slope of the old cart path, and came out of the woods into a clearing. Boulders the size of automobiles dotted the overgrown field, left there by the glacier. The grass moved in the breeze like russet and tan ocean waves. A song sparrow sang a snatch of an almost recognizable aria. Victoria unbuttoned her heavy sweater, the one Fiona's parents had given her. She was still too warm.

"Hey," Robin shouted. "Here comes a dog." He held out his hand. "Here, dog!"

A large black and white dog trotted toward them, tongue hanging out. It stopped a few yards from them and growled.

"What's the matter, dog?" Robin kept his hand out.

The dog growled.

"Here's a piece of bread." Victoria gave Robin a crust from their sandwiches, and he held it out to the dog.

The dog growled.

"He doesn't seem very friendly," Victoria said.

Suddenly, the dog started to move, and moved swiftly toward Victoria. Taken by surprise, she stepped back, and the dog leaped at her, grabbed her open sweater in his teeth and snarled. Robin snatched up a fallen branch from the ground and clobbered the dog on the head. The dog, still growling and snarling, let go of Victoria's sweater, and turned on Robin, who swung the stick at him again and again until the dog backed away, teeth and gums showing. It finally turned and slunk away, looking over its shoulders at Victoria and the boy.

"Are you okay, Mrs. Trumbull?"

"Yes. Thanks to you. And you?"

"He didn't scare me."

"Was he wearing a collar?" Victoria asked. "It happened so quickly, I didn't see."

"A red collar," the boy said, "with metal tags."

"It wasn't a feral dog then. It must be somebody's pet. It must think we're trespassing on its territory."

"Do you think his owners are around here someplace?"

"Perhaps they're hiking," Victoria said.

"Maybe they're camping out. Maybe they built a cabin and live here and no-body knows about them. Maybe that's who we heard the other day. Maybe it's like that man who lived in an underground house, and nobody knew about him until one day somebody tripped over his stove pipe."

"Hmmm," Victoria said.

Robin paused. "I didn't hurt him, I don't think."

"I'm sure you didn't."

~ ~ ~

Later that afternoon, when they sat around the table in the Trust office with the map spread out in front of them, Victoria told Josiah how the dog with the red collar had attacked her.

"That's strange." Josiah leaned his elbows on the table. "The caretaker has a dog, but it's a black lab. Doesn't sound like his."

Robin said, "I bet somebody's camping out. That's what I think." He ran his hand along the polished surface of the table.

"Sit down," Victoria said. "We can't think with you doing that."

Robin sat in a chair in front of the window that looked out over the cran-berry bog. He immediately jumped up again. "Look, Mrs. Trumbull. Cedar waxwings. That's what you told me they were. There's a million of them in that tree!" He pointed.

Both Victoria and Josiah got to their feet and looked at the birds in a red cedar to one side of the bog.

Josiah patted the top of the boy's baseball cap. "You're absolutely right. That's what they are."

Robin knelt in the chair and stared out the window. Victoria and Josiah returned to the table and the open map.

"There are only a few more places I can think to search," Victoria said. "Here," she pointed with her gnarled finger, "and here. And over here."

"That's precisely where Ness wants to put several of the houses." Josiah circled the area lightly with his pencil. "It would be great if you found something there."

"When we got this far today," Victoria pointed, "the way was blocked by a fence."

"A fence?" Josiah sounded puzzled. "Those ancient ways are public rights-of-way. They're not supposed to be blocked."

"It's a new board fence, about six feet tall. We turned back when we came to it."

"Try to get around it if you can," Josiah said. "That area should be good orchid habitat. If it's anywhere on the property, that seems like a probable place."

~ ~ ~

The next day was rainy.

"Are you sure you want to go walking today, Victoria?" Zack took off his glasses and wiped them with his bandana. "It's nasty out."

"It's not going to rain hard." Victoria walked outside to Zack's truck and looked up at the sky. In the driveway a robin hopped three or four times, stopped and cocked his head, hopped again, cocked his head. Victoria watched. The robin darted at something, leaned back on his tail, the end of an earthworm in his bill, and tugged. The worm was anchored in the ground.

"March showers," Victoria said. "They don't amount to anything." The worm was stretching, longer and longer. Suddenly, it let go, and the robin flopped back onto its tail, shook itself, and flew off with the worm.

"That slicker looks as if it will keep you dry unless it's pouring, Victoria. If it starts to rain hard, I'll come back early for you."

They drove to the school. Robin was waiting for them where the yellow school buses lined up. A sea of kids in yellow and blue and red slickers were milling around the school entrance, throwing punches at each other, shouting, running, pushing.

"'Bye, Robin," said a girl Robin's size in a shiny powder blue slicker. "Call me this afternoon!"

"Maybe," Robin said.

Zack looked over at the boy. He had climbed into the passenger side next to Victoria, who slid to the middle. "Girlfriend?" said Zack.

"She's a dork. A retard. A nerd. She's ugly and she's a psycho."

"Sounds as if you like her," Victoria said.

Robin made a gurgling noise.

"How was school?" Zack asked, and Robin chattered on about Magic cards and GameBoy and Pokémon. Victoria felt as if she were in a time warp.

Robin pulled something out of his book bag and turned to Zack. "See what Mrs. Trumbull gave me?" He held out the mouse-shaped pencil sharpener.

Zack, who was just turning onto State Road from Old County Road, took a quick look and grunted. "A mouse."

"Not a mouse," Robin said. "Pikachu. Jeez, even Mrs. Trumbull knows who Pikachu is."

Victoria smiled faintly.

The sky was blotchy gray and overcast. It had sprinkled off and on during the morning, and looked now as though it might rain again. The air smelled fresh, of wet earth and germinating seeds and plants ready to emerge.

After they turned onto State Road it started to sprinkle again. Zack turned on the windshield wipers and looked questioningly at Victoria.

"This won't last long."

The rain let up and Zack turned off the wipers.

He dropped them off at the usual place and agreed to meet in two hours. Victoria checked her watch before she moved across the passenger seat behind Robin, and, holding the sides of the door, slid off the seat until her feet touched the ground.

Robin and she had gone along the trail several times now and were familiar with its branches. Only once had they seen anyone — the caretaker, with his black Lab. He'd greeted them pleasantly. Victoria had asked how his new grand-baby was doing, said she was showing her young friend, Robin, Audrey White's grandson, some of the places she'd known as a child, hoped it was all right if they walked the ancient ways. She promised to be careful. He'd tipped his cap, lifted the visor slightly, and said sure, any time she wanted to walk the place, it was okay with him. Robin had patted the black Lab, whose name was Pepper, and they went on their way.

They walked past the marsh, where the tiny tree frogs Vineyarders called "pinkletinks" had started shrilling in the past day or two. The tufts of dry grass where Victoria stepped to keep her feet dry showed green shoots close to the ground. She hated the thought of crushing the fragile new growth. The trail wound around the base of the hill, then branched off onto the path that was blocked farther along by the new fence.

Rain had softened the crisp fallen leaves and turned the pale new wood of the fence a reddish gold. Victoria sniffed the vanilla scent of the new lumber and the rich smell of wet leaves and earth.

She suddenly sensed that someone was watching them. She stopped and listened. She could hear Robin walking carelessly through the undergrowth, the squish of damp leaves and the slap of branches. She heard the sound of water dripping from wet limbs, the distant rumble of surf on the south shore. Far away and below them she heard a car go by on North Road. A crow called. She heard the sleighbell sound of pinkletinks in the marsh. Was she simply imagining a sound that did not belong?

They stopped at the fence and Victoria said to Robin, "I'll wait here while you see how far it goes." She looked around for something she could sit on and found a lichen-covered rock. "See if there's a way around it."

Robin darted off through the huckleberry and catbrier that grew next to the fence. The briers snatched at his jeans with a sound like fabric ripping.

While she waited, Victoria took out her notebook and pen, alert for sounds and smells. The gray sky and gray trees, the gray of the rocks around her, and the gray lichen formed a silvery grayness that was broken by patches of green moss and golden beech leaves. She heard only the sounds of the woods and the sea. Within a few minutes Robin returned along the fence, running a stick along the new boards with a clacking sound.

"It stops at the brook, Mrs. Trumbull. You can get around okay. I'll help. There are big stepping stones."

He held the briers aside so they wouldn't slap across her corduroy-clad legs and they walked beside the new fence.

Before she saw the brook she heard it burble over its rough bed. The brook was narrow, only five or six feet across. Four large stones led from the end of the fence to the other side of the brook. On the upstream side was a thick growth of bright green watercress.

"On the way back, we'll pick some for your mother and Elizabeth." Victoria pinched off the tip of one of the plants and nibbled it.

"You can eat those leaves?" Robin turned up his nose.

"Ladies serve watercress sandwiches at tea parties."

On the downstream side of the rocks, long streamers of green grass-like weeds trailed and waved in the current.

"Hey, an eel!" Robin said, leaning out over the rock he was standing on.

Victoria bent over to look. "It's a lamprey," she said. "I think that's supposed to be rare. Be sure to tell Zack."

"It looks like an eel."

"It's not. Its mouth is a sucker. Some kinds of lampreys latch onto other fish and drink their blood, but I don't think this kind does."

"Vampires!" Robin hopped across the stepping stones to the other side and back. "Sweet!"

Victoria held one hand on the post that supported the fence, set her stick in the brook, and stepped cautiously onto the closest rock. Robin was beside her instantly, and held his arm out to her in case she wanted to take it. Victoria set her feet firmly on the mossy bank, took a few steps, and sat on a fallen log to catch her breath.

"Do you really think those vampire fish are rare?" Robin asked. "Will you tell them I was the one who found it?"

"Yes, yes," Victoria said in between breaths. She stood up again. "Let's go."

They heard the soft patter of rain on the beech leaves off to one side, and felt a sprinkling. Before they reached the path where it continued on the other side of the fence the rain had stopped again.

As they walked, Victoria kept listening for the sound she thought she had heard, but there was only rainwater dripping from trees, the frog chorus, the sea. She concentrated on searching for the elusive leaves with purple spots.

Then, as if it were quite ordinary, just another green leaf on the ground, she saw it. The leaf was under an old oak tree that spread long low branches far out from its trunk, and next to a large beech tree. A single dark green leaf lying flat on top of last autumn's fallen oak leaves. The leaf, which was only an inch or so long, was spotted with dark purple blotches. Its edges were slightly ruffled.

"Look, Robin. We've found it!"

Robin dashed over to her, and when he saw it he jumped up and down.

"Careful!" Victoria cautioned. "Don't trample it." She got down onto her knees carefully, holding her stick for support, and gently turned one of the leaves over. "Look at this."

"It's purple. Just like Mr. Coffin said. Just like you said. Cool!"

"We need to mark this exactly." She handed a pencil and the folded map to Robin with her notebook for backing.

A few feet on, near a cluster of clethra, she found three more leaves. And a quarter mile up the path she found another single leaf. Then it was time to turn back.

They hurried down the trail, skirted the fence, carefully went around it at the brook. The lamprey still clung to a rock on the bottom of the brook, looking much like the green weeds that pointed downstream. Its eely tail waved in the current.

They followed the fence back to the path.

Then Victoria heard something again. Her neck hairs lifted. She looked over at Robin, and held a finger to her lips. His eyes opened wide.

She whispered, without making a sound. "Do you hear anything?" and raised her eyebrows in question.

He shook his head.

They moved steadily along the path. At one point Robin veered off to the right to follow a deer trail, and came bouncing back holding a box turtle about eight inches long with a high domed shell. The turtle had drawn in its head and feet and closed its hinged lower shell.

"Hey, Mrs. Trumbull! Look what I found on the path!"

He put the turtle down on the ground, and they watched while it gradually stuck its head out. Its eyes were a fierce red, its beak turned down in a sort of sneer. It ventured its feet out, one after another, four toes on each. Its dark brown shell was boldly patterned with yellow and orange streaks and splotches that matched streaks on its legs.

"Pretty," Victoria said with admiration. "I shouldn't be surprised if you haven't found another special creature. They're calling everything rare these days."

"Can I take him home?" Robin asked, picking the turtle up again. The turtle immediately withdrew its head and feet and snapped its lower shell shut.

"Leave him here. He probably has a family somewhere."

"Turtles? Families? They lay eggs and bury them. That's not a family."

"Leave him alone," Victoria said more sharply than she intended. She had heard a distinct sound on the other side of the path. "Come along." She reached into her cloth bag to make sure the handheld radio was where she could get it easily, and moved as rapidly as she could.

"Hey," Robin said. "Wait for me!"

They rushed along the path, Victoria watching where she put her feet, Robin matching her speed silently. Down the gentle hill, where she felt, rather than heard, the presence of someone. Over the grass tuft steps next to the pinkletink marsh. Across the open meadow, over the stone wall, to the road, where Zack waited for them.

Victoria was out of breath and leaned against the truck for several minutes while Robin chatted excitedly.

"I found a vampire fish that Mrs. Trumbull said is rare."

Zack looked out from under the fall of straight hair, through his thick glasses. "Vampire fish?"

"An eel in the brook. It was holding on to a rock or something with a suction cup. Mrs. Trumbull said they drink blood."

"A lamprey?" Zack asked.

"Yeah! That was it!" Robin jumped up and down and then stopped. "And I found a turtle, but Mrs. Trumbull said I had to leave it there."

"How big was it? Did it have a high shell?"

"That big." Robin held out his hands. "And this high."

"Orange and yellow and red splotches?"

Robin nodded.

"Think you can remember where you saw him?"

Robin nodded.

"If you've found a brook lamprey and an Eastern box turtle, that was great work for today."

Victoria was leaning against the fender of the truck, listening. She breathed deeply. "Tell Zack what else we found."

"Oh, yeah. Mrs. Trumbull found a whole bunch of cranefly orchids."

~ ~ ~

CHAPTER SEVEN

Everybody's Talking

IN the senior center later that afternoon, the heavy-set woman in the flowing black-and-brown caftan was knitting, making a clicking sound that was irritating to Tom More. "Is there any chance of buying the Sachem's Rock property from Harry Ness?" she asked, without looking up from her work. Tom studied her before he answered. Her white hair, worn long and loose, floated part way down her back. Her gold-rimmed granny glasses rested on her nose. When she finished speaking she finally looked up and her knitting needles paused. She was knitting the bulky sweater of speckled brown wool she had been working on as long as Tom More had known her, a year now.

Tom More had called this meeting of investors in Cranberry Fields, his co-operative housing project. Twenty of his investors were seated on folding chairs arranged around him in a semicircle in the senior center's basement.

Tom More himself was sitting in an armchair under a large watercolor of geese standing by the millpond. Members of his group were talking to each other and the noise level had grown to a low roar with an occasional tinkle of laughter.

"I'm hopeful, Marguerite." Tom More's eyes fixed on her intently before he looked from one to another member of the group. He stood up, a short stocky man in blue jeans, a jeans jacket, and cowboy boots that gave him an additional two inches in height, and held up his hands for silence. On one wrist he wore a heavy Rolex watch, on the other a thin copper bracelet. The flock stilled.

"I have an announcement to make." He waited until all eyes were on him, then waited a few moments more, gazing from one face to another with hypnotic eyes. "An anonymous donor has offered to put up a considerable sum of money if we can get Mr. Ness to sell Sachem's Rock to us." There was a soft murmur from the group. Individuals looked at each other, then back at Tom More.

"What's Ness's price?" a young man with untidy dark hair and farm-grimy hands asked.

The knitting needles clicked.

"As you know, Sanders, Mr. Ness bought the property for one million dollars." Tom More sat down again. He leaned forward, elbows on the arms of the chair, hands clasped in front of him. His hair waved thickly around his face and hung down to his shoulders. His beard covered the lower half of his face. His glasses magnified his intense eyes. "We had offered Phoebe Eldredge one point five million."

"How come she turned it down, sir?" asked a blond young man in white painters' overalls standing by the far wall.

Before Tom More could answer, a balding middle-aged man sitting on the far side said, "She told me she thought Cranberry Fields was a hippie commune."

"How ridiculous." Marguerite twitched a length of speckled yarn out of a tapestry bag on the floor beside her chair.

"How much would we need to offer Ness to get the property, do you think?" Sanders asked again.

Tom More unclasped his hands and held them out, palms up. "It's anyone's guess. I'm prepared to offer him two and a half million."

"That's a sizeable profit for Ness," the balding man said.

Marguerite's knitting needles clicked. Tom More considered asking her to stop, and decided not to.

"How much will each of us have to ante up?" Sanders asked.

"Our donor has offered to contribute one million dollars to the Cranberry Fields project." Tom More looked over the group until his eyes met those of a lean, tan woman wearing a cashmere blazer that matched the sun-streaked blonde of her hair. She smiled at him. He leaned back in his chair and waited.

The group was silent. Then there were murmurs. A young woman in the back row of chairs raised her hand.

"Deborah," Tom More acknowledged her. A small girl, probably two years old, clung to Deborah's jeans-clad legs.

"One of us? Offered a million dollars?"

Tom More nodded.

"Thank you, somebody," Deborah said.

"Yes! Yes!"

The tan blonde in cashmere folded her hands in her lap.

"Are there any conditions on the grant?" Sanders shuffled his boots, and a chunk of dried mud fell onto the floor.

"Only that we acquire the land and build our community." Tom More looked around the group, which had started murmuring again. "This individual believes in Cranberry Fields." He stood again and raised his hands. The group quieted. "This person believes in a simple life, as do we." His deep voice was growing louder. "Believes in a community of brothers and sisters. Believes in family. Believes we have the only lifestyle that can survive on this frail planet in this new millennium."

"Yes! Yes!" said several voices.

"We will live in harmony with the earth, as Native Americans did before white settlers came. We will not waste the earth's precious resources. Cranberry Fields will be a life of harmony."

"Yes! Yes!"

Tom More's voice dropped down from its preaching level. "Does anyone want to ask any further questions before we get down to business?"

"Will this discovery of the endangered orchid affect Cranberry Fields?" a thin, almost scrawny, fortyish woman asked.

"You mean the layout of our houses, Evie, community center, and carpentry shop?"

Evie nodded.

"Good question," Tom More said. "It should help us, actually. We believe in maintaining the existing ecosystems. We intend to keep human intrusion to a minimum. Cranberry Fields concentrates our houses in one small area, and leaves the rest of the property untouched. Ness's plan subdivides the property into three-acre lots with a large house on each lot. You can imagine how that would disturb the ecosystem. A septic system for each house. Swimming pools. Lawns. Gardens. Garages. Our community will not be built on the sacrificed corpses of other species."

"Suppose they find another orchid, or some other rare plant, on our site?" Evie asked.

"That's not likely," Tom More said shortly. "Any other questions?"

There was a general head-shaking.

"We're going ahead with our plans for Cranberry Fields as if Sachem's Rock is ours. Positive thinking, guys and gals?" He raised both hands in a sort of bene-diction.

"Yes! Yes!" the group responded.

"To business, then." Tom More reached behind his armchair and brought out rolls of maps and charts and blueprints. Sanders got to his feet and clumped to Tom More's side, leaving a trail of dirt. Together, they unrolled charts and taped them over the paintings on the wall.

That done, Tom More turned back to the group. "Harmony. We could almost call our new community 'Harmony,' rather than Cranberry Fields."

"Someone already did that," the balding man said and laughed. "That one didn't work."

Tom More ignored him. "Here's the overall plan." He turned back to the charts and blueprints taped to the wall. "Here's the carpentry shop, off to one side where no one will be disturbed by the sound of saws and hammers. About half of the people who have signed up for Cranberry Fields already work in the old carpentry shop. They'll be able to walk to work, walk home to the community center for lunch, take a quick nap or whatever, and go back to work."

There were titters and smiles.

"Here's the community center." He placed his hand flat on the schematic. "This is where we'll want to spend most of our free time. On this side is a community kitchen with a commercial-size stove and refrigerator. We'll take turns preparing food. Here's the dining room. We'll eat family style. And over here," he pointed, "is the community recreation room. We'll have a fireplace with couches arranged around it, and over on this side a place to set up tables for writing letters or playing bridge or board games. And over here" — he moved to the other side of the chart on the wall — "we'll have a teen center, where the kids can do their homework or do their thing without bothering the rest of us."

"Is there a place where I can keep my sewing machine?" one of the women asked.

"Over here" — Tom More pointed — "we'll have a hobby area for sewing or working on stamp collections or making models or whatever. Big work surfaces, unlike what most of you have at home now, right?" He turned to the group.

"Right! Yes!"

"Any questions about this so far? I know we're going over some of this for the third or fourth time for some of you, but for others, this is new."

"Have you assigned any of our homes yet?" the bald man asked.

"I'm getting to that." Tom More turned to a second drawing taped to the wall. "Our homes are simplicity itself. A comfortable bedroom or, in the case of those of you with children," he nodded to Deborah and her child, "more than one bedroom. A place to sleep. A lavatory with composting toilet. Showers and baths will be in the community center. A small kitchenette for preparing breakfast or snacks. Simplify, simplify." He slapped his hand against the sketch taped to the wall.

"Laundry?" someone asked.

"Washing machines will be here, in the community center. No dryers. We'll have a drying yard over here, where our clothes and bed linens will get plenty of sun and the good west wind." He turned back to the group. "I'm sure you want to know where you'll be living."

"Yes! Yes!" said the group.

"The houses are arranged in a square around the community center, so no one has too far to walk for dinner. Or a shower."

General smiles.

"Jeff, you and your wife and kids have a three bedroom. Here, on the northwest corner of the square. And Marguerite, yours is a single bedroom next to Jeff."

"Tom, is it all right to be totally frank and open?" Marguerite stopped knitting.

"Of course. Now's the time."

"This is a bit uncomfortable to say," said Marguerite, "and I realize it's my problem, not anyone else's. But I don't like being around small children."

Jeff's wife made a choking sound. "Then why did you sign up for Cranberry Fields? We're supposed to be a family, and families have small children. Even if you don't remember, that's how you started."

"I know, I know." Marguerite looked down at the pile of knitting in her lap. "I realize this is my problem. I don't mind being three or four houses away, or on the other side of the community center, but I really don't want to be right next door to children. That's one reason I signed up. The brochures said this would be a wonderful place for older single people."

"We'll see what we can do," Tom More said soothingly. "Perhaps you'll feel differently once we're all settled. Older members of our community have so much richness to bring to our younger members. We envision surrogate grandmothers reading to and playing with the little ones. And baby-sitting. Older people are a truly wasted resource."

"That's not my vision of my life. I'm a painter. I don't want somebody else's grandchildren. I don't have any of my own and don't want them. With all those houses," she pointed with a loose knitting needle, "I should think I would have a choice whether or not to live right next door to squalling brats with sticky fingers and dirty faces."

Jeff's wife stood up abruptly and started to say something. Before she could, Tom More said, "We can work this out. Don't worry about it. Naturally we all feel a bit of pressure, especially since we don't even have a piece of land. Let me go on. I'll work on your location, Marguerite."

Marguerite took up her knitting again, her face a bright pin. Jeff's wife sat down again, her eyes glittering, her mouth a tight line. Jeff patted her knee.

"Chris, you'll have the third house — we'll decide later who'll be in Marguerite's."

"It's okay to fence my backyard, isn't it?" Chris said. "I got two German shepherds."

"Do they hate kids, too?" Jeff's wife called out.

Chris turned to her. "They're real good with kids, as long as the kids don't tease them. They may bark a little, but they're real good dogs. Fluffy and Muffin."

"Moving on," Tom More said. "Sanders, you'll be next door to Chris."

"Are your dogs going to bother my chickens?" Sanders said.

"I don't think so. You'll have them fenced in, won't you?"

"No," said Sanders. "They're free-range chickens."

"Wait one damn minute," the balding man said. "This is turning into some damn barnyard. Are we going to wake up before the sun when his damn chickens start crowing?"

"You advertised this as an environmentally aware community," Sanders said. "Birds sing. Roosters crow. If people don't want to hear country sounds, move to South Boston or Braintree. All you have to listen to there is traffic and horns blaring and rock music out of boom boxes, for crying out loud."

Marguerite's knitting needles clicked.

"We can settle all of this later," Tom More said. "This is a first cut."

~ ~ ~

That same afternoon the gray weather had lifted slightly as the sun burned through thinning clouds over Edgartown. The road in front of the Harbor View Hotel was striped with wet and dry pavement from passing cars. Three men and a woman were seated at one of the tables in The Coach House, the hotel's pub, where they could look past the wide porch with its empty rocking chairs and see the lighthouse and Chappaquiddick on the other side of the harbor.

"Will Dr. Jeffers be joining us this afternoon, Dr. Erickson?" asked the elegantly slim woman. "I'm in a bit of a time crunch."

Doc Erickson stroked his sand-colored mustache. "He should be here any minute." He adjusted the collar of the rumpled linen sports coat he wore over a pink and blue madras shirt. "What's the outlook for your crushed-chest patient?"

"Kirschmeyer. That's my chief reason for being on-Island today, to check on him. He's coming along slowly."

"Curious case," Doc Erickson said. "I can't imagine why he was standing under Mrs. Trumbull's tree in that storm."

"It's not my job to worry about motives." Dr. Gibbs placed her hand on the table and flexed her long fingers.

"Why don't we go ahead and order drinks?" Doc Erickson beckoned to a bartender, who came over to the table promptly. "I'll order for Jeffers. He takes ginger ale with a twist."

From where they sat they could see the Chappaquiddick ferry shuttling back and forth on its two-minute run across the narrow part of the harbor. A large sailboat came in while they waited, motored around the bend, and headed out of sight into the inner harbor. The Edgartown light flashed its beam, watery-looking in the late afternoon light.

"It's good to be back on the Island," said the youngest of the group, a pudgy man with a shiny bald head. "Especially out of season like this."

"You ought to come over more often, John. We could use an orthopedist at the hospital," Doc Erickson said. "More moped accidents every year. Enough broken bones to keep you happy."

"Got plenty of those on the Cape now." John turned to the woman, who was sitting on his right. "It's nice to see you again, Kate. You're looking good — as always. Last time was at the Boston AMA meeting, wasn't it?"

"On the golf course after the meeting, actually." Dr. Gibbs smiled. A sudden ray of sunlight picked out highlights in her glossy black hair. Two streaks of white fanned out from her temples, giving her a distinguished look.

"Well," said Doc Erickson, "that's why we're here, after all." He turned at a clanking sound. "Here's Jeffers now."

Dr. Gibbs's eyes opened wide.

Doc Jeffers, who was well over six feet tall, was wearing his leather motorcycle jacket and trousers. He had taken off his metallic blue helmet, and was holding it under his arm. As the others stared, he reached into an inside pocket and the small blue lights that blinked across the front of his helmet went out. He unzipped his jacket, exposing a bunch of curly white hair in the V-neck of his hospital scrub shirt.

Dr. Sawicki and the fourth person at the table, an elderly man wearing a Harris Tweed jacket over a starched white shirt and regimental tie, stood as the biker came to the table.

The biker stuck out a great paw to the white-haired man in tweed. "Jeffers," he said.

"Russ Billings," the man said.

"Kate Gibbs," the woman said, keeping her hands in her lap.

"Dr. Gibbs, the surgeon. Delighted to meet you," Doc Jeffers said. "Lucky you were on-Island that day. No one else could have saved him. Nice piece of work." He grinned, showing great strong teeth.

"Thanks. He's coming along nicely."

Doc Jeffers turned to the plump young doctor. "You must be John Sawicki. Orthopedics. I suppose Erickson has already tried to enlist you?"

Dr. Sawicki smiled, his small mouth like a dimple in bread dough.

Doc Jeffers pulled out a fifth chair and sat, with a final clank. He stowed his helmet under his chair and settled his booted feet firmly on the floor.

Dr. Gibbs looked at her watch again. "I'm afraid I have to catch the six-thirty boat. If you don't mind, perhaps we can get right down to business."

Doc Jeffers leered at her.

Doc Erickson reached down for a folder that was leaning against his chair and opened it on the table. "This is a map of the Sachem's Rock property. Ideal for an up-scale golf course. Put the clubhouse here, right behind the big rock. Nice landscaping around the rock, Island plants, that sort of thing, make it the theme for the golf course. Parking here in a circle around the rock. There's a house here presently," he pointed, and Dr. Gibbs and Dr. Sawicki leaned forward for a better look. "It belonged to the former owner, a Mrs. Eldredge. We'll raze that and on the site, which has a great view, construct a small country inn, eighteenth-century flavor, twenty-first-century conveniences. Big fireplaces at either end, a common room, a dining room, no more than ten to twelve guest rooms, each with its own bath."

"What about acquiring the property from Ness?" Dr. Billings smoothed his hair and straightened his tie with a gnarled hand.

"I don't think that will be much of a problem," Doc Erickson said, shuffling the top papers onto the bottom of the stack. "He paid one million for it. We're prepared to offer him two point five for it, maybe go as high as three million. It's probably worth ten."

"From what I hear of Ness, he's not likely to sell out at bargain rates." Dr. Sawicki pursed his lips.

"We'll turn up the heat," Doc Jeffers said. "Nothing like social pressure. We know how to apply it." He winked at Dr. Gibbs, who looked back at him stonily through almond-shaped dark eyes. "We've got, how many investors, Erickson?"

Doc Erickson peered over his half-frame glasses. "Fifty investors have already pledged two hundred thousand each for membership. We're limiting membership to five hundred, so that gives us room to grow."

"All physicians?" Dr. Sawicki placed his elbows on the table and laced his plump hands beneath his chin.

"Physicians or health care professionals." Doc Erickson looked up from the papers. "Ah, here comes the bartender."

Dr. Gibbs was making notes with a slim gold pen in a leather-bound notebook with gold edges. "Ten million. Those are firm pledges?"

The bartender set down coasters and drinks. Doc Erickson signed the tab with his illegible signature and the bartender left.

"Firm pledges," Doc Erickson said. "Acquire the land for two point five, maybe three. That leaves seven million to develop the golf course, put up the buildings. Memberships and fees, the restaurant and the inn will sustain it."

"It looks pretty good to me," Dr. Sawicki said. "Good investment, a healthy choice, not like putting up a gambling casino, which is what I understand the tribe wants to do."

"An opportunity for the physician investors to get a much-needed vacation in an unspoiled spot," Dr. Billings said. "You've done a good job, Erickson. I commend you."

"Thanks. I've been working with DufferPro," Doc Erickson said. "They get the credit. They have a track record of developing golf courses for professionals who have the money but not the time or know-how."

Blue-black highlights glinted in Dr. Gibbs's hair as she turned to Doc Erickson. The white strands were brushed carefully away from her temples. "What do you need from us? A check?"

"Not yet," Doc Erickson said. "Let me show you what else we have here."

Dr. Sawicki moved drink glasses to one side so Doc Erickson could spread out the papers, and they leaned over to see better.

"Looking good!" Doc Jeffers lifted up his glass in a toast and took a swig of his ginger ale. "The greatest selling point that I can see is that the course will be open to Islanders, at cut rates."

Doc Erickson nodded. "I agree. For years, I've been urging my patients to get out there on the links and swat at a few balls. With this — " he slapped the papers in front of him — "they won't be able to say they can't afford it."

"A grand scheme," Doc Jeffers agreed.

Doc Erickson ran his pen lightly around the map. "Another of our selling points will be this system of public paths that wind around the golf course."

"Somebody's going to get hit in the eye with a golf ball." Dr. Sawicki's bald head reflected the overhead light as he bent over the drawings. "Trying to get us more business, are you?"

"No, the paths were designed by the DufferPro people to be well away from the line of fire. No, we see this as a way to stem public criticism of an elitist golf club." Doc Erickson peered over the top of his glasses at Dr. Sawicki.

"It certainly isn't elitist if we allow the public at large to play." A frown creased Dr. Gibbs's smooth forehead. "Did I hear you say it will be open to Islanders at cut rates? I should remind you that one of the reasons I agreed to invest was to get away from the great unwashed public. I see enough of them every day at the hospital."

"I agree." Dr. Billings stretched his turkey neck out of the constrictions of white collar and tie. "This was intended, if I understood correctly, to be a retreat for overworked physicians. We all know what will happen if the general public is encouraged to join. Every hypochondriac on the Island will be asking for a free consultation. Every visiting tourist. We'll have no peace at all."

Doc Erickson put the papers back into the folder. "The only way we're going to be able to build the golf course is by getting public support. There's already a public backlash over the No Trespassing signs going up all over the Island. That plus fences and lack of access. We need public support."

"Well, go ahead and get your public support, then. Sounds as if you don't need mine." Dr. Gibbs rose to her feet. "I've got to go."

Doc Jeffers rose also.

"Don't be so hasty." Doc Erickson looked up at Dr. Gibbs. "We're still in the initial planning stages. Lots of room for negotiations and adjustments. Don't harden your position, Doctor."

"She has a point, though," Dr. Billings said. "If we're talking about a public golf course, I'm not interested, either. I can invest in a public golf course closer to home and a hell of a lot cheaper. Two hundred thousand bucks will buy me and my wife quite a few nice vacations away from it all."

"Why don't we sit on this for a week or so," Doc Erickson said. "Before we can take any further steps we have to be sure we can buy the land. I'll have the DufferPro people see what they can negotiate with Ness and then I'll get back to you."

Dr. Gibbs was still standing. She pulled on thin black leather gloves, her fingers smoothing the soft leather in a way that Doc Jeffers watched with bright moist eyes.

"How are you getting to the ferry?" he asked her.

"I'll ask the concierge to call a cab."

"I've got an extra helmet," Doc Jeffers said. "Be glad to give you a thrill ride on my Harley."

Dr. Gibbs stared at him in horror. "No, thank you. I've stitched up too many hotshot bikers. I have no intention of ruining my assets." She held up her black-gloved hands and wiggled her fingers. "Good day, gentlemen."

~ ~ ~

While the golfing doctors were meeting in Edgartown and Tom More was meeting with his community housing people downstairs in the West Tisbury senior center, the Park and Rec committee was having a heated discussion on the senior center's sun porch.

"Forget the Sachem's Rock property, kiddo. Find another site for a campground." The speaker, Julius Diamond, a recently retired gasoline dealer from New Jersey, was involving himself in the politics of his newly adopted Island town, starting with Park and Rec. "The town doesn't need two hundred acres of swings and slides and tent sites. Let Ness build his houses. It's his land. He can do what he wants with it." Julius smoothed his new L. L. Bean checked shirt over his slight paunch.

Page Bachwald, chair of the committee, was standing beside the round glass-topped table. "I can't believe you said that, Julius!" She thrust both small fists straight down by her sides and stamped a foot. "West Tisbury has a greater percentage of young children than any other Island town."

"I think Mr. Diamond is right, honey," said a sharp-nosed older woman wearing a broad-brimmed purple felt hat. "We should put up swings and slides next to the library and encourage our wonderful young people to read books."

Page turned to the fourth person at the table, a vague-looking woman with frizzy hair and round glasses. "You agree with me, don't you, Fanny, that we should get the town to purchase Sachem's Rock from that developer? I mean, we don't want another suburban development, do we?"

"Well" — Fanny looked down at the yellow-lined pad in front of her on which she was drawing a row of stars — "on the one hand, Sachem's Rock would make a nice campground, since we lost one of our two campgrounds to that golf course down-Island, so now families don't have any place to stay if they want to spend their vacation in a tent, which I don't, but many people do, and it would give families a Vineyard experience that would be unlike any other Vineyard experience, since we don't really have any low-cost places for families to stay." She stopped and took a breath. "On the other hand, we'd probably have to ask the town for more than a million dollars, since that's what Mr. Ness paid for it, and I'm not sure the taxpayers *would* want their taxes to go up that much, although if we divide a million dollars up among all the people over several years it won't be so bad, but I don't think they'll like it."

"Oh for God's sake." Julius, who had been sitting next to Fanny, wrinkled his nose and shifted away from her in his seat.

"It's a matter of saving open space," Page insisted.

"A family campground isn't open space," Julius said. "Trailers, RVs, kids, boom boxes. Look what happened to Yosemite. Ruined it. Sheets hanging on lines between campsites. People arguing about the neighbor's TV. Smoke from hamburgers grilling over those damned briquettes. You're talking about a ghetto. Muggings. Robberies, rapes. Believe me, I know."

"This isn't Yosemite with waterfalls and Half Domes and a highway that goes right to it," Fanny said. "We don't need to squash people right next to each other, Julius. We can plan nice sites that will give everybody privacy and have public trails and Page can have her swings and slides and even a jungle gym. My only problem with it is who's going to take care of it? I mean, do we have outhouses and garbage pails?"

"For God's sake," Julius said again. "That's exactly it. People urinating in the bushes. Polluted wells. Trash everywhere. Candy wrappers and used condoms."

"Please." Lucy, the older woman, shook her head. "We're getting off the subject, and Julius, I don't think what you just said was nice at all." She fixed him with a severe look.

"Nice!" Julius sputtered. "What do we need a campground for? That's ridiculous. It's not for the people in town. Except for some people's junkie kids, a place to shoot up." He looked meaningfully at Fanny, who was drawing her stars and didn't notice.

"We'll charge them twenty-five dollars a night for a tent site," Page, still standing, said. "That way we can make money for the town."

"Are you out of your mind?" Julius leaned forward in his chair. "How many tent sites are you planning on? Fifty?"

"That sounds about right," Page said. "That's a good number. Somebody multiply that out."

Fanny had her calculator out. "That comes to twelve hundred and fifty dollars a night."

Page counted something on her fingers. "So over the season, Fanny, from May through October, let's say it's a hundred and eighty days, what does that come to?"

"Two hundred twenty-five thousand." Fanny looked up from her calculator.

"How wonderful!" Lucy reached up to straighten her hat, which was slightly askew.

"See?" Page said. "We'd be putting all that money into the town's economy."

"Listen, sweetheart, you don't know beans about business." Julius shifted his chair back and crossed an ankle over his leg. "Take it from me, you'd be lucky to realize one quarter of that amount from a campground. It's not going to be occupied one hundred percent every night from May through October. You'd be lucky to have a twenty percent occupancy. On top of that, don't forget you have to pay trash pickup and maintenance, someone to man the entrance booth."

"We don't say 'man something' these days, Julius," Lucy said. "We need to be sensitive to the feelings of people." She tucked her white bangs under the brim of her hat.

"To continue," Julius said. " 'Person' the entrance booth. Security. You'll be paying more in salaries than you take in. And for what? Not a benefit for the town, that's for sure."

"It would be a benefit for the town," Page said, thrusting her fists down. "We'd have a picnic area …"

"Yeah, and swings and slides. You going to drive your kids all the way up there after school to play on the swings and slides? I don't think so." He uncrossed his leg and set both feet flat on the floor.

"He's right about that, honey," Lucy said. "It would be so much nicer to have the swings and slides right next to the library. You could walk there with your little ones after school, and when they get all rosy-cheeked and tired from swinging and playing on the jungle gym, they'll be so happy to have you take them into the library where you can read to them. Parents are not reading to their children today the way I did to my children."

"Fanny, you understand what I'm trying to do, don't you?" Page was close to tears.

"Well, yes," Fanny said. "I don't think any of us want to see that awful man Ness build all those disgusting trophy houses on one of the most beautiful pieces of land on Martha's Vineyard — with a gate and a guard — and it will be like every other expensive suburb on earth and we'll have lost what we're all about."

"Exactly." Page wiped her nose on a tissue she'd taken out of the sleeve of her pink sweater. "I want your support in asking the selectmen to put a request on the town meeting warrant to buy the Sachem's Rock property from Mr. Ness. For the benefit of future generations." She blew her nose and put the tissue in her pocket. "I need you to be on my side, Julius."

"I'll vote with you," Fanny said. "Basically it's a good idea, only I think the voters may have a problem with it, but it's up to them to decide after all, and, I mean, who are we to tell them how to vote?"

"I will too, honey, but I believe we ought to spend a little more time thinking it over." Lucy tugged on the brim of her hat. "We care so much about our town's children, and, well, I just don't know, but I'll vote with you."

"Oh, hell." Julius said. "The town will never go for it. I might as well vote with you to make it unanimous. But you're making a mistake you'll live to regret."

~ ~ ~

CHAPTER EIGHT

The Cranefly Orchids

JOSIAH opened the folded map Victoria had been carrying in her cloth bag the day before and flattened it on the conference room table. He and Zack studied the marks she and Robin had made on it.

"Hand me the aerial photo, will you, Zack?" The overhead light picked out the auburn highlights in Josiah's thick hair. He had recently shaved off his beard, and Victoria was surprised to see how strong his chin was, definitely a Coffin feature.

Zack slid the aerial photo across the table, a square of heavy paper that curled stiffly at the edges. Josiah pointed to a distinctive line on the map that marked a turn in the trail and then to the same distinctive turn, half-hidden by trees, on the same path Victoria could see on the photo.

"From your marks on the map, it looks as if the orchids are in this area." He pointed to the photos with a grease pencil.

Victoria had seated herself in front of the spread-out map. She looked carefully from map to photo, and nodded. "Yes. That looks about right."

"Victoria, can you pinpoint the place you found the plants?" Josiah leaned over, both hands flat on the table, and looked from the map to her.

"You see that large tree here on the photo," she pointed with her pencil, "and this one. It looks like the beech that was right next to the first orchid. The second orchid was over here on the other side."

Josiah circled both spots with his grease pencil. "This is great, Victoria, better than we could have wished for." He stood up straight and stroked his chin as if the beard were still there. "I want to take a look myself, confirm what you found, make some notes of my own." He flattened the folds in the map, set the photo next to it, and put a heavy book on top.

"I'm sure Robin would like to come." Victoria noticed for the first time that Josiah's eyes were hazel, almost green.

"When does he get out of school?" Josiah asked.

She looked at her watch. "School lets out at three. It's only ten o'clock now."

"I'd like to go there now," Josiah said. "I'm afraid we can't wait for him. The sooner we get this discovery on record the better. Everybody in town seems to know about it already."

"I'll stay here at the office," Zack said. "Call on the radio if you need anything."

Josiah and Victoria crossed the wooden bridge that led to the parking area hidden among the trees. Josiah helped her into the pickup truck. She moved a pair of binoculars and a bird book onto the shelf behind her, where there was a collection of shells and seedpods, and an old oriole's nest, woven with shreds of blue plastic that might have come from a tarp at a construction site. She settled her quilted coat under her and smoothed her corduroy trousers over her knees.

They jounced down the rutted dirt road until they came to the paved main road, where they turned left. They drove past the bog, overgrown now, where Victoria used to glean cranberries after the late October harvest. Grasses and shrubs had turned the old bog into a meadow.

Josiah had apparently noticed her wistful look. "One of these days we'll restore it," he said. There's so much to do and nowhere near enough people and money."

They passed the cemetery and the tiny Methodist Church, passed the path that led to the Lambert's Cove Beach, passed Uncle Seth's Pond, where parents brought their toddlers in summer to paddle in the shallow water.

They turned right onto State Road. A great spreading oak tree marked the beginning of North Road and Seven Gates Farm. One winter, a storm had split the tree almost in half, had ripped the ancient trunk, exposing raw heartwood. A host of volunteers had patched the wound, splinted the bleeding trunk, bandaged it, fed it tree delicacies, and watched it until it sent out leaf buds the following spring, more than anyone could remember.

"That tree has always been the same size, except for what the storm did to it," Victoria told Josiah. "It was a giant tree when I was a girl."

Josiah glanced over at her. "That tree is probably two hundred years old. You've known it through half its life."

"Not quite." Victoria's face creased in a smile.

They parked at the usual turnout by the trailhead.

"Aren't you worried that someone will see you with me?" Victoria said. "Zack was afraid he'd be associated with me."

"We didn't want to be seen time after time searching for plants. It won't be a problem now, one walk. You said the orchids were immediately off the ancient way?"

"Practically on it."

They retraced the route past the marsh and shrilling pinkletinks, over the tufts of grass, noticeably greener only one warm day later. Up the gentle slope, when they came to the new fence, they skirted along it to the brook.

"This is where Robin found the lamprey." Victoria pointed to one of the stepping-stones. "It looked so much like one of the weeds it was difficult to see. It seemed to be hanging on to a rock with its tail pointing downstream."

Josiah leaned over one of the big stones, his hands on his knees. "There it is now," he said. "Just where you saw it. *Lampetra appendix,* American brook lamprey. It's a threatened species that needs clear, clean running water." He had taken his notebook out of his shirt pocket and started to write. "It's sensitive to very low levels of pollution. Quite a find." He was smiling broadly. Deep creases lined his cheeks. Victoria thought how attractive his and Casey's children would be if she could only get those two together. He continued to write. "Do you need help to get around the end of the fence, Victoria?"

Just as she started to say, "No, thank you," she slipped on the slimy algae that coated the stepping-stone. Josiah caught her as she started to fall.

"That was stupid of me, showing off. By the way, it was right around here that I thought I heard someone yesterday."

"I can't even guess who that might have been," Josiah said thoughtfully. "A hiker or one of Ness's caretakers or maybe someone who was simply curious. I suppose we'll never know."

They followed the fence to where the path continued on the other side.

"I'll have to talk to Ness. He can't block this path."

They retraced Victoria and Robin's route up the path to the spot where Victoria had found the first orchid.

"It was right here," Victoria said, looking around in bewilderment. "I'm absolutely sure. I recall the clethra next to it and that distinctive beech."

"Perhaps it was farther on."

"There were other plants farther on, but this is where I found the first one, I know." She poked around the fallen leaves. "Right here. I even recall some of the individual leaves. It was here, Josiah, right here. I know it was."

Josiah brushed aside the leaves in the spot she had indicated. "Someone was digging here."

"You don't suppose they uprooted the orchid, do you? I am absolutely sure it was here."

"I believe you, Victoria." He bent down and examined the ground. "This is the right habitat. The ground has been disturbed." He stood up straight. "Someone must have heard you and Robin. Perhaps that was who was following you."

"Why?" Victoria leaned on her walking stick. "Why?"

"A very good reason. If we were to make such an important find on this property, Ness's development would be held up for months, perhaps even halted permanently."

"So it must have been Ness or one of his people?"

"That's the only thing that makes sense." The creases that had made Josiah's face look so young and happy only a few minutes earlier now made him look grim and older.

"You knew, didn't you, that I'd found other plants?"

They walked solemnly up the trail to the second site, where the cluster of leaves had been. The same thing. The plants had been dug up, and last autumn's leaves smoothed over to conceal the disturbed ground.

"This represents a huge loss. The last recorded *Tipularia* population in Massachusetts other than here on the Vineyard was on Cape Cod, and that's gone now. They're nowhere else in New England."

"For petty gain," Victoria murmured.

"To Ness, it's millions of dollars, hardly petty gain." Josiah dropped his head so far his chin rested on his chest. "I wonder what they did with the plants they dug up? I hope to hell they didn't destroy them."

"Can they be transplanted?" Victoria asked.

"Yes. But they've got specific habitat needs. Someone would have to understand what they need in order to transplant them successfully."

"I'm afraid we made a fuss about finding them. If somebody was following us, he must have heard. Robin was so excited he jumped up and down. I was afraid he might trample them."

Josiah shook his head and said nothing.

"I found two other plants farther on." Victoria said quietly.

He looked up bleakly. "We might as well look."

They walked along the path in silence.

"We'd better assume someone is watching," Josiah said. "If the plants are there still, we don't want those dug up too."

When they came to the places Victoria had found the orchids, they had to search before they saw the characteristic spotted leaves, lying flat on top of last fall's leaf litter.

"Keep walking, Victoria." Josiah scuffed dry leaves over the orchids, covering them. When they had moved up the path well away from the plants, he turned to her with a smile. "We may yet be okay on this," he said. "Let's keep going up the trail. ...."

"In case anyone is watching."

"Yes. Then we can turn around and head for home."

The way back was a gentle downhill slope, much easier for Victoria. Josiah was in an exuberant mood.

"They're odd, Victoria, not like most other plants. This time of year when other plants have died back, the cranefly orchid leaves manufacture food for the corms, which are something like gladiolus bulbs. Then in spring, when other plants are putting out new green leaves, the cranefly orchid leaf dies back, and you won't see anything for a couple of months."

"Yes, I read that in the papers you gave me," Victoria said.

"In June the orchid sends up a stalk that flowers in mid-July," Josiah continued. "It has numerous small flowers along a slender stalk."

"I read that," Victoria said.

Josiah went on. "In the South, where it's common, it may have forty blossoms."

Victoria was walking slightly ahead, flicking leaves and acorns out of the path with her stick.

"Up north it will have fewer." He paused and Victoria looked around. He was smiling.

"I've read all that," Victoria said again. She leaned on her stick, more tired than usual.

"Sorry," Josiah said. "I'm getting carried away. I was thinking about the best way to protect the last two plants that are still there."

Victoria started down the path, then stopped again to catch her breath.

Josiah was right behind her. "If you'd like to sit, there's a log not too much farther on."

"I'm fine," she said.

"They do produce seeds," he said. "The seeds are like dust."

They continued to walk down the path again. "An interesting aspect of the cranefly orchid," Josiah went on as if he were lecturing to an undergraduate botany class, "is that it's pollinated by night-flying moths ..."

"Yes, yes," said Victoria, slightly out of breath. "Noctuid moths. I read that, too."

". . . noctuid moths," Josiah went on as if he hadn't heard, "like the kind that fly into your porch light. Theoretically, the flowers could self-pollinate, but it's probably rare."

Victoria was becoming increasingly irritated. "I know all that, Josiah. About how the pollen sac the moth picks up has a thin cap over it that prevents it from adhering to the flower's stigma."

"Absolutely right, Victoria," Josiah said. "And then …"

"And," Victoria continued, somewhat louder, "a half hour after the moth picks up the pollen, the protective cap falls off, and the pollen is able to stick. You see, I've done my homework."

"Yes, well," Josiah said, "nature's way of preventing inbreeding."

"Astonishing, isn't it," Victoria said. "Our own reproductive method seems strange until you hear how other organisms reproduce themselves."

Josiah laughed.

Victoria said, "Can't you see a moth professing undying love to one orchid plant before it sweeps the pollen up on its tongue, or whatever it does, flies around for a half hour, and then transfers it to another plant? It's a wonder any survive."

While they were walking back to the truck, Victoria kept listening for the rustling she and Robin had heard before, but the woods were still except for an occasional chickadee calling its winter call, the sound of pines sighing in the light wind, the distant sound of the surf.

Apparently Josiah was too wound up to stop talking. "Actually, the orchids here on the Vineyard seem to reproduce by cloning, rather than by seed. A professor in North Carolina thinks our Vineyard cranefly orchid is related to the same species found near him, only one species spirals clockwise around the stem and the other spirals counterclockwise."

Victoria was beginning to feel ashamed of herself for trying to cut Josiah off when he was so obviously elated. "I suppose, then, you can tell by looking at the flower stalk whether they're Vineyard plants or not."

"Yes. They're common in the Southeast," he said. "But the Vineyard is their northernmost range." He stopped. "Are you all right, Victoria?"

"I think I do need to sit for a minute or two." She stopped next to a fallen log, and eased herself onto it. "Whew!"

While she caught her breath she could hear the steady bell-like sound of pinkletinks. A car hummed far away on North Road. She heard crows arguing, and thought about Montgomery Mausz. She wondered if he had been aware of someone following him. She had heard nothing this afternoon. She was sure a person had been following her and Robin. Perhaps it was the same person who had followed Mausz and had killed him. Perhaps it was the killer with no motive other than madness. She shuddered.

"Are you all right, Victoria?" Josiah sounded worried. "I'm afraid we've overdone the walk today."

Victoria got up as quickly as she could. "I just needed a moment to catch my breath." She wanted to hear Josiah's voice talking about matter-of-fact things. She was sorry she'd tried to one-up him about how much she knew. "You were thinking how we can protect the plants we found," she said.

"The best protection is to publicize it," Josiah responded. "It's a balancing act between arousing curiosity and informing the public of the value of this discovery. We have to let people know they mustn't trample it or pull it up."

"Perhaps the *Island Enquirer* will do an article," Victoria said. "I can write it up in my West Tisbury column."

"Good. I'll contact the state endangered species people. They'll want to send a botanist here to confirm the find."

~ ~ ~

Spencer Kirschmeyer regained consciousness that same afternoon. When he opened his eyes and looked around, one of the orderlies was straightening his room, and immediately called for Doc Erickson, who was on duty.

The bandages on Kirschmeyer's head covered his hair and his cheeks and his chin like a football helmet. It was difficult to tell what he looked like normally, or even how old he was.

"Where am I?" he said when Doc Erickson came into his room.

"You're in the Martha's Vineyard hospital," the doctor answered.

"Martha's Vineyard? What the hell am I doing on Martha's Vineyard?"

Doc Erickson shrugged.

"I don't remember anything."

Doc Erickson wrapped a blood pressure sleeve around his patient's upper arm, held a stethoscope in the crook of his arm, looked at his watch and listened. He nodded. He peered into Kirschmeyer's eyes and mouth. "It will come back to you. In the meantime, welcome back to the real world. You had us worried for a few days."

Kirschmeyer shook his head. "Ouch!" He put his hand up and felt the bandages. "Did a job on myself, didn't I?"

"Yep. A tree fell on you."

"Where else did I get it?"

"You have a few stitches in your chest."

Kirschmeyer moved his hands from his neck down toward his stomach. "Holy shit. I'm in a cast."

"Yep." Doc Erickson wrote something on a clipboard.

"Funny. I don't recall a thing."

"Don't worry about it. It will come back in time. Are you hungry?"

"Starved."

"We'll start you out slowly on solid food. Mashed potatoes, applesauce, and Jell-O." He noted something on the clipboard.

"How about a steak? Rare."

Doc Erickson cracked a tight smile. "If the applesauce and potatoes stay down, I'll order you a steak in a couple of days."

"Days!"

"Something to look forward to."

"Is there a TV in this place?" Kirschmeyer asked.

"I'll see that you have one." Doc Erickson made a note on the clipboard. "This afternoon, if you feel up to it, we might get you out of bed. I want you to take it easy for now."

"Wish I knew how the hell I got here."

"So do a lot of other people," said Doc Erickson.

~ ~ ~

CHAPTER NINE

Robin Is Missing

HARRY Ness had grown up in South Boston, the youngest of eleven children. When he turned sixteen he dropped out of school, got a job loading freight onto boxcars in the South Boston yards, and left home. He put every cent he could save into buying land. In ten years he had accumulated a fair amount of property.

When he made his first million, he married a long-legged Nevada showgirl, Crystal Payne, the daughter of a Mormon bigwig. She was taller than he and a lot smarter than she looked.

Harry Ness, not yet fifty years old, now saw his logo, a sea serpent twisted around a world globe, in almost every city and town east of the Mississippi. He intended to make that *every* city and town, not *almost* every. He planned to spread out from there, truly circle the globe.

He built a large house on the Vineyard for his wife, its windows paned with lead crystal in honor of her name. He built a dock and parked his sixty-five-foot seagoing motor yacht alongside, where everyone could see it. At night the lights in his house turned on automatically, one at a time like theater lights, and stayed on until midnight when they went off, one at a time. The neighbors, the entire town, complained about light pollution. Let them. It was his house and he'd damn well turn on any lights he wanted.

He bought land on the Island, more land, and more land. For several years he had been aware of the Sachem's Rock property, one of the largest tracts of undeveloped land on the Island. He knew that Phoebe Eldredge was getting along in years, knew that she wasn't speaking to either of her kids. He knew about the conservation group negotiating with her about buying a conservation restriction. What a waste that would be. Why would the town go along with that, taking the land off the tax rolls completely? Build exclusive housing on it, and the land would be as good as preserved, plus adding some heavy-duty taxpayers who would be here a month, two months, five months at most during the year. Their taxes would pay for educating the town's kids.

Whenever he thought about kids in school, he'd have a pang of regret that he and Crystal didn't have any. Crystal would have been a good mother and he thought he'd have been a hell of a lot better father than his old man. He thought sometimes that they didn't have kids because Crystal didn't want any. Well, whatever. It hadn't worked out that way.

Before he bought Sachem's Rock from Phoebe Eldredge in February, he had considered joining forces with the physicians' golf club consortium that was also looking at the property. He got hold of their prospectus, and decided the doctors were naïve, the managers incompetent.

He looked into the town's Park and Rec Committee, the group that wanted to build a campground. He had thought when he acquired Sachem's Rock he might carve off a few acres near the road and sell it to the town at a fair rate. Not only a tax write-off, but good public relations. But when he looked into the membership of the committee, he decided they were airy-fairies, well-meaning do-gooders who had no concept of politics, finances, or management. He crossed them off his list.

One of his people looked into Tom More's housing scheme. Several of the units would be set aside for affordable housing, something the Island needed. "More Homes," the company was called. The guy was a competent enough builder, had been putting up touchy-feely solar homes for ten years, long after the hippies of the sixties and seventies had become stockbrokers. Tom More wanted his commune, Cranberry Fields, to be an experiment in group living, as if that hadn't been tried before. And why, for God's sake, pick the most expensive chunk of real estate on the East Coast for an experiment in group living? Why not Maine or Vermont? Or someplace out west like Idaho or Nevada?

In case there was something he had overlooked, Ness examined everything he could find out about Tom More and his plans, and found there was a gap in his background that no one was able to penetrate. Except for that, a period of five years, the guy seemed to be exactly what he said he was, a builder out to make a buck under a cloak of environmental blarney, only More had not put it that way. Ness decided he'd better not underestimate the guy. Tom More had an almost religious following, the kind of people who would probably leave their homes and families and go off with him in a spaceship.

Ness also investigated the Conservation Trust's plan to put a conservation restriction on the entire property. Josiah Coffin was young, quiet, and idealistic. He had both a law degree and an environmental science degree. His followers were every bit as rabid as Tom More's, but they were lawyers, bankers, and investors, professors of economics and hydrogeology, practical people with brains, money, and power. After studying the reports that came back on Josiah Coffin, Ness marked him down as formidable.

After all his research, Ness felt, quite reasonably, that his plan was the wisest and best use of the Sachem's Rock property, and two months before he finally closed the deal, he had set about wooing and winning Phoebe Eldredge.

About that time his attorney, Montgomery Mausz, disappeared for what everybody thought was a Caribbean vacation.

~ ~ ~

The day after Victoria and Josiah had found the cranefly orchid missing, Elizabeth dropped her grandmother and Robin off at the trailhead.

"Have a good walk. I'd go with you, but I'm late for work. Can you get home okay?"

"Of course," Victoria said. "Josiah or Zack could pick us up. I still have the radio." She rummaged in her cloth bag and brought it out.

Victoria had not told her granddaughter that Josiah had expressly forbidden her to go to Sachem's Rock. She had done her part, Josiah had said. It was time for the state endangered species people to take over. He warned her to stay away from the property, especially since they didn't know who had been following them.

The Island spring, always so unpredictable, had finally settled in. The meadow grass was greening. A meadowlark sang.

Before she asked Elizabeth to take them to the trailhead, Victoria had told Robin about Josiah's warning. "He thinks it's not safe," she said.

"He's nothing but an old lady." Robin tugged his UPS cap off and tossed it into the air, caught it, and plopped it backwards onto his tousled hair.

"I think we need to check those plants," Victoria had said.

"I think so too."

So it was set, and Elizabeth, unsuspecting, had driven them to the trailhead.

Now, Victoria watched Robin dart across the familiar meadow, sweet-smelling in the warmth. He jumped from one green tuft of grass to another. She followed slowly, her own heart skipping and jumping with each step of Robin's. They moved up the gentle incline into the beech woods to the new fence, went around it where it ended at the brook. The lamprey seemed to have attached itself permanently to the rock, for it was still in the same spot, its tail waving in the brook's current. They edged along the other side of the fence and back onto the path.

A bird Victoria didn't recognize caroled a few notes, and Victoria, glad to be out on this glorious day, repeated the bird's notes, her mouth pursed in a whistle.

"Wow, that sounded exactly like him," Robin said with admiration and leaped into the air, slapping a high branch.

A soft breeze shook pine needles onto them and onto the path. Above them the sky was clear spring blue.

They came to the patch where Victoria had found the first orchids, where only yesterday she and Josiah had found them missing, dug up, and the ground covered over with fallen leaves.

And there, almost exactly where she had found them the first time, were two cranefly orchid leaves. The dark green leaves, splotched with purple, lay flat on top of the leaf litter as if they had always grown there.

"What do you make of this?" she asked Robin.

He shrugged. "Maybe somebody was sorry they dug it up and planted it again."

"It's a different plant."

Victoria knelt next to it.

Robin bent over her, hands on his knees. "Yeah. It's got two leaves, not one."

Victoria took out her notebook and started to write.

"I'll see if the other plants are okay," Robin said.

Victoria nodded absently. What was going on? None of this made sense. In the back of her mind she heard Robin racing up the path, heard him jump, heard him slap a tree branch overhead, heard his light-hearted whistle at a squirrel or a bird fade away down the path. She heard a quail call, "Bob white! Bob bob white!" The call of the bobwhite always sounded like summer meadows and hayfields, a nostalgic sound that brought back the scent of new-mown hay. The first call of the quail came right around haying time and the fields would echo with their whistle, "Bob white! Bob white!" She heard it again, off to the left of the path.

She returned to the new orchid plant, noted its exact position, sketched its leaves, then moved a few feet over to where she had originally found the second plant, where she and Josiah had found it missing, dug up. Sure enough, a new plant had been set in the old one's place.

Victoria tried to reason this out. Someone must have known the plants were there in the first place, must have been following her and Robin, and must have dug them up. But who set new plants in the same place? Were the woods full of people following other people, digging up and transplanting plants? And where were they getting the new plants? They were, after all, rare. At least here in New England.

With this, she thought about Robin. He should be back by now. She listened for his footsteps on dry leaves and heard nothing. There was no sound of underbrush slapping across small boy jeans, nor his whistle. She got to her feet with difficulty, hoisting herself up with her stick, and listened again.

A beech leaf fell. A hawk cried high in the blue sky. Blood pounded in her ears. But no boy noises.

"Robin?" she called.

No answer.

She started up the path again, stiffly at first from having knelt on the ground, then faster as her muscles limbered up.

"Robin?" She stopped and waited. She heard a faint echo from the woods and thought it might be Robin, but it was only her own voice coming back to her, bounced off tree trunks.

She hurried now. Where could he be? She thought of the footsteps they had heard before, Robin and she, the footsteps in the woods beside the path that had made them hurry back to where Zack had parked at the trailhead. She thought about the concern in Josiah's voice when he had warned her not to go back to Sachem's Rock.

Her breath was coming in short gasps. She stopped and rested on her stick and listened. She heard only the sounds of the woods and the call of birds and the faraway whish of tires on North Road. She heard the sound of surf everywhere around her, in her ears and in her being, the beat of surf keeping time to the beat of blood pounding through her arteries. Where could Robin be? Had he jumped up for a branch and hit his head and knocked himself out? No, she would have found him in the path. Why had she let him go off by himself? They were strong together, but so vulnerable alone, he, a very small boy, and she not as agile as she once had been. She continued up the path until she had passed the point where she and Josiah had turned back, where the gentle hill started to curve downward again. From the top of the hill, she could see over a wide area through the trees, as far as the pond and the icehouse. But there was no sign of Robin.

"Robin? Robin!" she called.

She was tired. She knew she could go no farther. She rested both knobby hands on her stick and leaned on it until she caught her breath again and could think. Her knuckles showed white through the skin of her hands, dirt-stained from gardening, the winter cracks on her fingertips that hurt so much she no longer felt the pain, the brown age blotches she didn't really mind, the prominent blue veins that coursed over the tops of the frail-looking bones.

She could not hope to find him by herself. She had to get help, and right away. She moved back down the trail until she came to the first site, where the newly transplanted orchid plants seemed as fresh as if they'd always grown there. She sat on a fallen tree on the other side of the path and scrabbled around in her bag until she found the handheld radio. She examined it. Turn this button on the right, that should switch it on. Turn it farther to the right and that will increase the volume. Turn the button on the left until you hear static, then move it back just a bit. Josiah had said the radio was set to reach him or Zack; all she had to do was press a flat bar on the side and speak into the perforations of the leather case.

Josiah had told her what to say. Identify yourself. So she held the flat bar on the side and spoke clearly into the radio. "Victoria Trumbull to the Conservation Trust." She released the bar and waited. You were supposed to wait two minutes, Josiah had said, but that seemed much too long. The second hand on her watch had ticked off one minute. She spoke into the radio again, held the flat bar and released it. No answer. Were the batteries dead? Was she too far away? Did the hills between them block reception?

Victoria left the radio on in case someone had heard and might try to call her, and moved down the trail. She paused as she came to the end of the fence. Someone had always been with her before and she hadn't worried about falling. Now, she froze. The stepping-stone looked slippery, and probably was. She had almost fallen there yesterday. But Josiah had been there to catch her. Should she take off her shoes and wade so she wouldn't have to trust the slippery rock? *No, I've got to take a chance,* she thought. *Time is critical.* She thrust her stick into the streambed and gingerly placed her foot on the rock, leaning on the stick. So far her footing was secure. *This should take two seconds,* she mumbled to herself, *and here I am, acting like an old lady, taking two entire minutes. And if I don't act boldly, it will be two hours and who knows what will happen to Robin?* She put her second foot on the rock and balanced there, holding her stick. She repositioned the stick on the other side of the rock, took a deep breath, and stretched her long leg over the space that separated the rock from the bank and the other side of the fence. She reached for the fence post, clutched it, and there she was, around the barrier, as easy as that. She was shaking. She was out of breath. She was annoyed with herself for being so tentative. She stood up straight and took a breath, tossed back her shoulders and marched ahead through the briers and huckleberry back to the path, and down the path to the trailhead. It seemed an eon ago that she had made almost the same journey, when she had heard the crows and found the body of Montgomery Mausz. But it was only a couple of weeks.

When she reached the trailhead she stopped where she could flag down a car, if she needed to, and tried the radio again.

This time the radio crackled with static and she turned the squelch down. It was Zack. "Victoria? Where are you?"

Victoria said cautiously, "In the usual place. Come as quickly as you can, and bring help."

"Roger," Zack said. "Ten minutes."

It was a long ten minutes. Victoria paced back and forth. She sat for a time on the stone wall, and picked with her ridged fingernail at the flat gray lichen that covered the surface of the rock on which she sat. A car approached, slowed. Victoria lifted her hand to wave, and the car sped up again and went on. A bicyclist passed, leaning over his handlebars, his feet alternating like pistons. The sound was the swish of oiled machinery. The bicyclist didn't seem to see her. She watched him disappear bit by bit, first his black-clad legs, then his blue jacket, then his white helmet, toward Seven Gates and the intersection where the great oak grew.

She stood again. She was stiff. She paced part of the way up the path toward the meadow, then back again, then up the path, then back. The day didn't seem as springlike and innocent as it had only an hour ago. The crows sounded sinister, not clownlike. The breeze seemed to have a bite. The sky had a milky tinge. She heard the mournful summer cry of a chickadee, "Pee-wee."

She looked at her watch. She took out the radio again. She had left it on in case she was called. She held down the flat bar and said, "Victoria Trumbull here."

Zack's voice came on immediately. "I'm rounding the bend now. Be only a second."

And within a second Victoria saw the familiar pickup, saw Zack's glasses reflecting the light, his beaklike nose, his black hair falling into his eyes, his nestlike beard. In the passenger seat next to Zack she saw Josiah, his bare chin and deep-set eyes, his thick auburn hair.

Zack pulled on the emergency brake with a squeal, turned off the ignition, opened the door, and leaped out as if he were on a spring, and Josiah followed him.

"Casey is on her way," Zack said. "I called her."

"What are you doing here, Victoria? Where's Robin?" Josiah's concern tumbled out with the questions.

"Robin's missing. He went on ahead of me. He's gone." Victoria looked up at Josiah with a pained expression.

The police Bronco pulled up behind the Conservation Trust truck, and Casey and Junior joined them.

Victoria sat on the stone wall again while Casey and the others questioned her. She fidgeted as she answered.

"We've got to know exactly what happened before we rush off in all directions, Victoria," Casey said.

Victoria picked at the skin around her nails while she answered Casey's questions. She looked at her watch. Time was going by too slowly and too fast. She would never forgive herself if Robin had gotten hurt. He was so small and so bright and such good company. His Pokémon cards. The half-dozen pencils he'd ground down with the Pikachu pencil sharpener she'd given him. She was scarcely listening.

"Let's go." Casey held out her hand to Victoria.

"Robin might be hurt or unconscious." Victoria took Casey's hand and got to her feet. "He may have fallen into an old cellar hole. He may have been attacked by that dog. He may have fallen into the brook. That person who was following us may have kidnapped him."

"We'll find Robin." Casey put her arm around Victoria's shoulders. "Don't worry. There's probably some simple explanation."

For the first quarter mile Victoria led until she began to tire and flag behind. Casey walked with her.

Victoria told Casey about finding the orchids in the first place. About finding them dug up when she returned with Josiah. About finding new plants there now.

Josiah listened. He stroked his chin as they walked. "It doesn't make sense. None of it."

They got around the fence safely. They passed the first group of newly planted orchids and reached the place where Victoria had found the second group, the ones Josiah had protected with leaves. When she had passed by earlier, Victoria had been so intent on finding Robin she had not noticed that the ground had been disturbed. Nor had she seen that the two cranefly orchid plants she and Josiah had identified and carefully covered were now gone.

Josiah bent down and ran his fingers through the leaves, and shook his head. "What in hell is going on?"

"Victoria, stay here and don't move." Casey pointed to a rock in the path. "The rest of you start searching uphill," Casey ordered. "Fan out through the woods. Keep in sight of each other."

Victoria could hear their voices fade away. At first she heard them talking to each other, could hear what they were saying. She heard them call Robin's name. Then their voices died away and she heard only the mournful cry, "Robin! Robin!" and then that, too, died away and the noises of the woods returned, a thrush, a towhee, a chickadee. Then she heard the quiet woods noise, a rustle of a leaf dropping, the whisper of pine needles falling, the sound of growing things pushing aside the winter mold.

Victoria poked the ground with her stick. What could have happened to Robin? At the time he disappeared she had been concentrating so hard on the new orchid plants she had paid no attention to him. Was there anything she could recall? A sound that didn't belong? A noise that had meant nothing to her at the time? She thought back to the call of crows, the chickadees, the bobwhites. Bobwhites? Calling this early in the spring? She didn't remember ever hearing them much before June. And, now she thought of it, the bobwhite had called from the woods on the left side of the path, not from the open meadow. Had it been a signal from Robin? She got to her feet, holding her stick for support. She turned slightly to peer through the woods to the right of the path, the uphill area that Casey and Junior, Josiah and Zack were searching. They would return and search the other side of the path, she knew. But that might be too late.

Victoria studied the ground, the undergrowth, the branches to the left. She noticed a scuffed area just off the path, where soggy leaves had been flipped over, dark undersides showing. Why had she not thought of this before?

She called, "Casey! Josiah?" and waited. Nothing. Not the sound of voices or footsteps or branches snapping.

I've got to search for Robin myself, she thought. *Time is running out. I must find him.*

Victoria laid an arrow of small branches in the path to point in the direction she intended to go, then started through the undergrowth, watching for disturbed leaves in front of her. Robin might have made those marks, bouncing through the woods, leaving broken twigs, torn briers, turned over stones. The trail was easy to follow. It moved downhill gradually, angling along the side of the gentle slope. Here, the trees were smaller than on the other side of the path, with an occasional clearing. Victoria had to stop often to rest and rather than take the effort to sit and get up again, she leaned on her stick, breathing heavily, annoyed with herself for having to rest so frequently. She broke branches to mark her route. The trail would be easy to follow. While she was resting this last time, she decided to take the trouble to sit. She examined the ground around her for a rock to sit on or a log, so she wouldn't have so far to get up.

Victoria was in a clearing where she could look through bare trees and see ahead and down the slope. The clearing was covered with reindeer moss, soft gray and plump from the recent rain. The only raised surface where she might be able to sit was a large clump of grass, a tuft that stuck up about two feet high, oddly solitary in this glen of reindeer moss, cranberry, low poverty grass, and bare blueberry plants.

Something moved down the hill. She put her hand up to her forehead to shade her eyes. It was a person, limping up the slope toward her. As the figure came closer, she could see it was Robin, covered with mud as if he had been dipped in chocolate.

Victoria called to him. Robin looked up. His glasses had slipped down his nose and his eyes were white spots in an umber mask. He moved faster and Victoria could see his limp was more pronounced.

She waited for him in the clearing. When he reached her he stood with his head down, not saying a word, until Victoria bent down to him, dropped her stick, threw both arms around him, and hugged him tightly.

"Hey," he said, snuggling against her, "you'll get all dirty."

Victoria hugged him more tightly. "Where have you been?" she said into the top of his muddy head. "We've got people searching for you."

"You didn't need to do that. I was okay," he said gruffly, still clinging to her.

"You know you shouldn't ..." Victoria stopped.

Robin nodded his head against her and she saw he was crying. Light brown streaks ran down the side of his nose through the darker coating of mud.

~ ~ ~

CHAPTER TEN

Ulysses

"TELL me what happened," Victoria said gently. Robin handed the walking stick to her and they started back up the path, side by side.

Robin put his hand in hers. "You remember the dog? The black and white dog with the red collar?"

"The one that attacked me."

Robin nodded and wiped the back of his hand under his nose, leaving a broad light stripe. His glasses were blotched with mud. Victoria handed him a paper towel from her coat pocket. He took it from her and blew his nose.

"Let me have your glasses," she said. He tugged them off, and his eyes stared myopically out of the pale mask where they'd been.

"I'll clean some of that muck off you." Victoria took the paper towel from him and rubbed it across his face. He shut his eyes and clamped his lips together. When she had finished he took the muddy paper towel from her and held it in his clenched fist. She breathed on his glasses to mist them, and lightly wiped them with a napkin from her pocket, careful not to scratch the soft glass. He put them back on.

"Now tell me what happened."

"Well, I was walking up the path to see if the second batch of orchids was okay, you know?"

Victoria nodded. "And then you saw the dog?"

"Yup. The dog came up to me, real friendly. He was wagging his tail and everything."

"Then what?"

He put his hand back in hers. "Somebody whistled to him, and he charged off into the woods."

"Was the whistle like this?" Victoria puckered her mouth and whistled, "Bob white! Bob bob white."

"Exactly like that, only loud."

"And you followed the dog?"

"Well, yeah."

"Let's rest a bit." Victoria leaned on her stick.

"I'll get something for you to sit on." Robin bounded off through the woods.

"Don't go too far away!" Victoria called after him.

She heard him drag something through the underbrush, and when he appeared he was tugging a stump that he placed upright for her. She sat, first spreading the bottom of her quilted coat over the rotted top of the stump.

"Whew! Thank you. How far did you follow the dog?"

"To right about where you were when you first saw me," Robin said. "Only farther down the hill."

"Did the dog's owner appear?"

"Nope. The dog went racing down the slope and popped into a hole." Robin hunkered down next to Victoria.

"Really?" Victoria stared at the boy, who nodded his head up and down vigorously.

"He just popped into a hole in the side of the hill."

Victoria looked closely at Robin. His shirt was coated with drying mud. His jeans were slick with mud. Where the mud had dried, it had fallen off in chunks, leaving square patches of faded blue jeans.

"If I had been you," Victoria said thoughtfully, "I probably would have found that hole and tried to follow the dog."

Robin looked up at her with awe. "That's exactly it. That's what I did."

"How far did the hole go?"

"I couldn't tell. The dog just disappeared."

"You mean it didn't open into a cave or cellar hole? How big was it?"

Robin held his arms in front of him, touching his fingers together to form a circle two feet in diameter.

"Did you get stuck?" Victoria asked.

"Yes."

"And you couldn't move forward and you couldn't move backward, and it must have been dark and scary."

He nodded and wiped his nose again. He stood again and shifted from one foot to the other in front of Victoria, who was holding her lilac-wood stick in front of her.

"Could you hear the dog ahead of you?"

"Not exactly. I thought I heard a voice, but …"

"I know," Victoria said. "It's an awful feeling to get stuck in a dark hole. You imagine things. How did you finally get out?"

"The hole kept getting smaller, so I couldn't go forward. I couldn't turn around." Robin was breathing heavily as if stuck in the hole again. "All I could do was push back with my hands and toes." He demonstrated, standing on the tips of his toes and waving his hands over his head.

"It must have been slippery," Victoria said.

"It was. I couldn't find anything to push against, just mud. Yuck!" Robin stopped and took a deep breath. "I dug my fingers in and tried to push back that way. It was really, really dark and slimy and my arms were not ahead of me. I couldn't move them back because there wasn't room for my elbows to bend."

He looked up, and Victoria realized his brown UPS cap was missing. "I kept imagining things. The earth closing down on me. Me being stuck there forever. I thought I heard the dog and I figured he might come back and chew on me and I couldn't do anything about it. I thought I heard somebody talking, like a radio or something, and I thought maybe somebody really, really small lives at the end of the tunnel in an underground house. And I thought maybe they would find me and kill me and nobody would ever know what happened to me."

Victoria reached her arm out and Robin stepped toward her and leaned against her. She tightened her arm around his narrow shoulders and he nestled against her.

"What time is it?" he asked, abruptly squirming away from her. "How long was I gone?"

Victoria looked at her watch. "I reported you missing around four and it's almost five-thirty now. We'd better get going again. They'll be worried about us."

But Victoria was thinking to herself. The dog had vanished down a narrow tunnel and had not come out again. Suppose somebody did have an underground house on the side of the hill? Maybe even used an old cellar hole and roofed it over and planted sod on top. No one would ever suspect. Perhaps the tunnel down which the dog had disappeared was for extra ventilation, or for the dog to come and go. Or for drainage. There must be another entrance, certainly. The more she thought about it, the more it made sense. But who would the dog's owner be? The person who had killed Attorney Mausz? Whoever lived like that, hidden away from the world in an underground house, would have to be a bit different from other people.

"You aren't listening to me," Robin said.

"I'm sorry, my mind was somewhere else. What did you say?"

"I said we could come back tomorrow and I'll show you the tunnel." He stopped abruptly. "I can't do it tomorrow. I have a stupid music lesson."

"Let's make it the day after tomorrow," Victoria said, and her heart lifted.

~ ~ ~

"I should have known," Casey said, when the four searchers returned to the path and found Victoria missing. "She won't listen to anybody." Casey pointed to the arrow of sticks that Victoria had laid on the ground. "Look at that."

Junior looked down at the arrow, his thumbs in his trousers pockets. The gold stitching on his baseball cap picked up glints of the low-angled sunlight filtering through the trees. The usual crinkles of good humor around his eyes and mouth drooped with concern.

"Now we have to find two people." Casey paced.

Josiah stared at the stick arrow. Zack squatted down in the path and picked up a handful of sandy earth, mixed with pine needles and shreds of dry leaves, and sifted it through his fingers.

"She thinks she's a Boy Scout or something," Casey went on. "She thinks she's a real cop." She shook her head. "Once we're done with all this she's going back to school to learn proper police procedures, and that's that."

Zack sifted the handful of dirt into his other hand. Josiah scuffed the toe of his boot into the ground. Junior tipped his cap onto the back of his head.

"Well, let's not just stand here," Casey ordered. "Let's find her."

Zack stood again and looked in the direction Victoria's arrow pointed. "She's marked her trail plainly enough."

"Zack, you come with me. Junior, you and Josiah follow to one side. Who knows what she's stumbled into?"

They had gone only a few hundred feet through the tangled brush when Casey heard a faint "Hello!" coming from below her on the slope and saw two figures trudging through the undergrowth.

"Victoria!" Casey called out.

"He's safe." Victoria and the boy stopped and Casey saw her lean on her stick.

"Are you okay?" Casey tore down the slope. Huckleberry bushes slapped against her trousers and boots. Branches stung her face.

"We're fine. You don't need to come down here. We'll be up there in a minute or two."

"Robin?" Casey slowed and waited.

"Robin needs a cup of hot cocoa and a bath. That's all." Victoria and the boy were moving up the side of the hill again, hand in hand.

When all six had assembled back on the path, Robin told them how he'd followed the dog and had gotten stuck in the tunnel.

"Could it be an entrance to a cave?" Casey asked. "Like the caves in Kentucky?"

"Not likely," Josiah said. "The Island is glacial moraine, a rubble of rocks and sand. There's no limestone to form caves like the ones in Kentucky or Indiana."

Victoria sat with a sigh on the moss-covered stone beside the path. "Cellar hole," she said.

"You could be right." Josiah turned to the others. "There was a small settlement here at Sachem's Rock in the early 1700s. Six or seven houses."

"Do we know exactly where the settlement was?" Casey asked.

"Not precisely." Josiah continued. "Phoebe Eldredge's is the only house left."

"Did the rest burn down, or what?" Casey asked.

"They burned or they were abandoned," Josiah answered.

Victoria rose to her feet. "We'd better get this young man home to clean up and do his homework."

"Awww, man!" Robin groaned.

~ ~ ~

Between the time he walked out on his wife and baby daughter in California and the time he came back to life, the man who called himself Ulysses could remember nothing but fleeting images. He'd worked on a freighter, he recalled. But what freighter and what ports he'd visited were blanks. He'd worked as a roughneck in the offshore Louisiana oil patch, as a parking lot attendant somewhere, slept on top of a steam grate in front of an art gallery in D.C., stole a shopping cart from a store in Virginia to hold his bundle of clothes. He'd built himself a shack of cardboard and hammered-flat juice cans under a bridge. He had a vision of rain pouring off the roadway above him. He scavenged for food in restaurant trash barrels and grocery store Dumpsters. He fought with wild cats and dogs for food, growling and clawing the same way they growled and clawed.

He moved, always moving, hitchhiking, riding the rails, walking, from one coast to the other, from north to south. He headed up the East Coast. Caught a ride on a freight train, sat in an aluminum lawn chair he'd scrounged from a Dumpster and looked out at scenery flying past him through the big open door. That was an image he recalled. The car shook on the rails as the train picked up speed and he had felt a motion sickness the likes of which he had never felt before, an awful jarring, curdling feeling, so awful he wanted to hurl himself out of the big open door onto anything solid. But his body wouldn't let him. The car built up a sickening rhythm as it swung and shook, faster and faster, until the train was moving so fast the sympathetic vibrations stepped up a notch and it was as if he had broken through some barrier into calmness.

He got off the train in a freight yard and heated a can of tomato soup over a fire a hobo had left burning next to the track. Nothing was connected in his mind — not his body, certainly. His body was an organism that fought for life without help from his mind. His body fed itself. It eliminated what it couldn't use. It slept. And his mind raced off into images and impressions, shattered colored glass that formed itself into focus briefly, then whirled out of focus again. He saw a cave in Nam. The freighter. Saw pieces of his buddy flying through the moist air. Blood and body parts dropped onto him. The parking lot. Rice paddies. The steam grate. Green hills and denuded hills. Rain pouring off a bridge above him.

He awoke in Vermont. It had started to snow. He was squatting on a street corner in his rags with a cup in his hand. Occasionally someone would drop coins into his cup, and he would shake the cup and mumble, "Thank you, miss" (or sir). At first the snow was only a few specks that he was not sure he saw or felt. The specks dotted the sidewalk and vanished, and the morning or afternoon, he wasn't sure which, was gray and raw and colorless and damp, and it was the first time he had felt anything for as long as he could remember, except for the sickening ride in the freight car. He looked up and snow hit his face and he blinked his eyes. He stuck out his tongue and the snow, now big fat flakes, dropped onto it with a hiss, and he heard it and felt it and tasted it. He got to his feet unsteadily and looked down at himself. Who was he? And where was he? He was disgustingly filthy. He had a long scraggly beard, his hair was a tangle almost down to his waist, his teeth felt like moss-covered stones and they hurt. His clothes were nothing he could remember acquiring; they were horrid-smelling rags that hung on his gaunt body in layers of plaids and stripes and checks and tweeds, all melded together into a uniform mud brown.

My God, how did this happen?

He stumbled along the sidewalk toward a church he saw midway down the block. The men and women he passed veered out of his path, and he suddenly felt ashamed of himself, of the way he looked and smelt. *Smelt* was a good term, he thought, rotten smelt is how he smelt, and he realized he was thinking and even making a small joke, and he held his face up to the snow that was now fall-ing in great fat flakes, and rubbed the wetness around with his black, calloused hands. How had he got those callouses? The sidewalk had a thin white coat of snow. The street was black. A car swished past. Another car. A dozen cars. He was alive again and there was hope.

He found his way to the soup kitchen in the back of the church, to the home-less shelter. Someone gave him a small wrapped bar of soap and a toothbrush and led him to a shower. He dropped his clothes outside the stall and turned the handle all the way around, and stood under the blast of hot water, soaping himself and his hair, watching rivulets of gray water and soap bubbles pour off him. He stood there, his mouth open, swishing the water around in his mouth and spitting it out again and again. He used up the small soap bar on his hair, his beard, his crotch, under his arms. The longer he stood under the stream from the showerhead the more he felt life returning, felt his mind reconnecting to his body.

They had left a towel and a comb and a razor on the bench outside the show-er for him. He scoured himself with the towel until his body was raw. He found another scrap of soap and a pair of scissors on the sink under a steamed-up mir-ror in which he could see himself only as a blur of dark hair and dark eyes, and he used the scissors to hack off his beard and shaved it off. He chopped off his hair until it stuck up like a brush all over his head, an inch tall, no longer snarled and knotted. He wiped the fog from the mirror with the end of his towel and stared. My God! He would never have recognized himself.

Someone brought him clean (and new) underwear. How long had it been since he'd had clean clothing next to his body? He couldn't even guess how much time had gone by. They brought him new tan work pants. New! Why? And a T-shirt that smelled of newness. And a jacket, a worn jacket, but a clean one.

When he first saw the calendar on the wall of the soup kitchen, he was sure he had misread it. Then he thought the calendar must be wrong. He asked every-one he met what date it was. He finally came to terms with it. It had been seven years since he had left California and his wife and daughter. Seven years.

Slowly, slowly, he'd healed. And then he got a part-time job with the sanita-tion department collecting trash and lived in the shelter at night. He worked in the soup kitchen, cutting up carrots and onions and potatoes to pay for his food. He mixed cement for a bricklayer. He hauled shingles for a roofer. He tacked up insulation. He painted. He carried boards for a carpenter. And after he had carried boards and nailed up framing and taped sheetrock, he got a job with a construction company. The other workers left him alone. He was strange, odd. That was fine with him. He didn't need or want their company.

He got himself a cheap room and started to save his money, and began to think about getting home to his family's land on Martha's Vineyard. He needed to save enough to get back there and build himself a place on the family land, and enough money to hold him over a year or so, or until he got a job.

Sometimes, not often, he thought about his wife and daughter. By now they must have forgotten him. They were only an infinitesimal part of his life, a fleeting moment. He wondered how his mother would feel about his return, and did he really care? He and his mother had never seen eye to eye.

Eventually he bought a used pickup for cash. And eventually he headed home to the Vineyard.

~ ~ ~

The morning after Robin discovered the tunnel, Victoria was reading about cranefly orchids in the Conservation Trust library when the phone rang. Josiah, who was working at the other end of the table, answered. After he hung up he made a thumbs-up gesture. "That was the state botanist, Dr. Cornelius. He's in Woods Hole now, and is catching the ten-thirty ferry."

Victoria looked at her watch. "That's less than an hour from now. Is he bringing his car?"

"No. I'm to meet the boat. Want to come? I'll leave in about a half hour."

During that time, Victoria finished writing up notes and made sketches from a photograph in a journal article she'd found.

Josiah looked over her shoulder at the drawing. "Not bad. I'm writing an article for the newsletter. Your sketches would be good illustrations."

Victoria cocked her head to one side. "I suppose I could polish them a bit." She gathered up the notes and stowed them in her pocketbook.

"They're great just as they are." Josiah headed toward his office. "I'll get my camera equipment and then we can go."

Victoria started down the steep stairs that led to the back of the building where the pickup was parked, holding the railings on either side tightly. She didn't intend to keep Josiah waiting. When she reached the truck, she turned to see if he was behind her. The building was built against a hill, two stories high in back, one story in front. As she looked up she could see into Josiah's office windows on the second floor, and thought, at first, she saw him standing next to the window, staring down at her. She couldn't make out the figure clearly because it was in shadow, but she had the impression it was deliberately staying out of sight. She had convinced herself that it was Josiah and was wondering why he would conceal himself from her when she heard the heavy metal door at the foot of the stairs clang open and Josiah strode out with his camera case and tripod.

"Sorry to keep you waiting, Victoria. Another phone call. What time do you have?"

She lifted the cuff of her blue coat to look at her watch. "Ten-twenty."

"We'll make it in time."

Josiah helped her into the passenger seat and went around to the driver's side and slammed the door shut behind him. The truck jounced down the rutted track that skirted the old cranberry bog, and turned right onto the Lambert's Cove road. Victoria forgot to ask him about the figure at the window.

They reached the steamship terminal as the ferry was pulling into its slip. Dr. Cornelius, who had been standing on the upper deck, was one of the last passengers to disembark.

He greeted Victoria with a bear hug. "This is a significant find, Mrs. Trumbull." His enthusiasm seemed at odds with his white hair and gold-rimmed glasses.

"They're quite excited about it at the Endangered Species Office," Dr. Cornelius continued as Josiah led the way to the truck. "Martha's Vineyard is getting quite a name for itself."

"I'm afraid so," Victoria said.

"I'm referring to endangered species." Dr. Cornelius sounded amused. "This is great!"

Victoria glanced at him as he helped her up into the truck. He was probably in his mid-sixties, her daughter Amelia's age, lean and leathery and distinguished looking.

"We'll go right to the site, unless you want to stop at the office first." Josiah backed out of the parking space and merged into the line of cars coming off the ferry.

"The sooner the better," Dr. Cornelius said. "Haven't been on the Island for ages. Good to see it hasn't changed much."

"It's changed," Josiah said. He waited for the Five Corners traffic to clear. "It's a constant battle to keep it from changing too much, too fast, and in the wrong direction." Traffic moved and he turned right onto State Road. "And who are we to decide what's the right direction? Harry Ness, who bought the property, isn't a demon. He thinks he's doing the right thing by building a housing development." He passed a car that was turning onto Main Street and continued up the hill. "A millionaires' housing development, true."

"I'm sure you've seen a lot of change on the Island, Mrs. Trumbull," said Dr. Cornelius. "What are your thoughts about all this development?"

Victoria, who'd been thinking of something else, namely how to get back tomorrow with Robin to explore for the tunnel, looked over at Dr. Cornelius with a smile. "I don't mind change. I'd like to be around for a while to see what happens next."

Josiah followed State Road through the outskirts of Vineyard Haven and into the rural countryside. He passed the split oak on North Road and pulled over onto the wide place where the trail to Sachem's Rock began.

It was a bright warm day. The sun was high. Birds sang. Overnight, miniature leaves had burst out of fat pink buds on the wild rose canes. Spring perfumed the air.

When they came to the brook, the lamprey had moved over to another rock, but there it was, hanging in the current, its eely tail moving with the flow of the water.

Dr. Cornelius bent low to examine it. "My God, what a find this is. Brook lamprey. It would be criminal to build on this land."

He helped Victoria across the stream. "You talked to Ness about this?" he asked Josiah.

"I have an appointment with him tomorrow," Josiah said. "I wanted to get your confirmation of Victoria's discovery before I spoke with him."

When they reached the site where Victoria had found the first group of orchids. Dr. Cornelius knelt and brought out a small magnifying glass that was on a chain around his neck.

"These are not the same plants that were here originally," Victoria said. "When I brought Josiah here to see the ones I found, they were gone. Someone had dug them up."

"And later these were planted in their place?" Dr. Cornelius asked.

"Yes."

"Very strange," he said after he had examined the new plants minutely. "I can't be sure until the orchid blooms, but I could swear this is not the same variety of cranefly orchid that occurs on the Island."

"Are these similar to ones that grow in the South?" Victoria asked.

"It's possible," Dr. Cornelius said. "I'll photograph this one and document it, take a sample of the leaf to the lab for analysis."

"Here's another plant," Victoria said, standing over the second newly transplanted orchid.

"Same thing," Dr. Cornelius said, after he had examined it. "Curious. I can understand somebody digging it up if they thought the orchid would hold up construction. But why replace it? And with a different variety?"

When he had finished writing notes and making sketches, and had photographed the plants, they moved up the path to where Victoria had found the second group, and where, just yesterday, they had found the second group dug up also. There were three new plants, looking as though they had been there always.

"I'll be damned!" Dr. Cornelius said. "What on earth is going on?"

~ ~ ~

CHAPTER ELEVEN

Six Attorneys, or Ten

WHILE Josiah and Dr. Cornelius set up the camera and adjusted lights, made notes and conferred over the newly dug-in plants, Victoria hiked up the gentle slope that led to the big rock, through the beech and oak wood that grew to the right of the path. She was still within sight of the two men when she noticed something bright orange on the trunk of a large beech tree in a clearing, a strip of fluorescent surveyors' tape. When she got closer, she saw that strips of tape fluttered from trees all around her, forming a large square.

She walked back and forth across the clearing. In a grassy spot in the dead center she saw a flat green leaf with ruffled edges and purple spots. She bent down to examine it. It was the leaf of a cranefly orchid.

She called down to Josiah and Dr. Cornelius. "Come up here and see what I've found. The trees are marked with orange tape."

"Damn," she heard Josiah mutter. "Ness doesn't let any grass grow under his feet."

"Or cranefly orchids either, apparently," said Dr. Cornelius.

"You might want to see what else I've found."

"Be right there," Josiah called back.

She heard the scraping sound of the telescoping tripod being put away and the two men came toward her through the huckleberry brush, Josiah in his worn jeans and sweater, Dr. Cornelius in his pressed tan trousers and plaid wool shirt.

"Good heavens!" Dr. Cornelius looked around the clearing at the tape-marked trees. "Does this mark the lot or is it one house?"

"One house," Josiah said after he'd looked around. "The tape is on the trees that are to be cut. The stakes for the house are over there." He pointed to orange plastic stakes ten feet beyond the largest beech tree.

"This beech is gigantic." Dr. Cornelius walked to the tree. "I hope they don't plan to cut this down. It must be two hundred years old."

"Afraid they intend to," said Josiah.

Victoria leaned on her stick while she waited for them.

"What else have you found, Mrs. Trumbull?" Dr. Cornelius strode through the grass toward her. She pointed to the leaf. He knelt down next to it. "I can hardly believe what I'm seeing. Come here, Josiah."

Josiah ambled over and stared. "Damn!"

"It's not the normal habitat, would you say?" Dr. Cornelius got to his feet and brushed off the knees of his trousers.

"It's been planted here," Josiah said. "Recently. What the hell is going on?"

Victoria pointed to the plant with her stick. "The first plant I found, the one that was dug up, had the same distinctive heart-shaped spot near the center leaf vein and the same ruffles on the leaf edges."

Dr. Cornelius tugged his magnifying glass out of his shirt pocket and examined the leaf. "If I'm not mistaken, this is the variety I would expect to find on the Island. But this is definitely not its normal habitat."

"It's right in the middle of a marked-off area," Victoria said.

"Dead center." Dr. Cornelius got to his feet again, dropped his magnifying glass into his pocket again. "I'd like to look around some more, Josiah. Can you show me other house sites?"

The day had grown warm and Victoria unzipped her heavy sweater. She started to walk with the two men when she heard a rustling in the woods. She stopped.

"Are we going too fast for you, Mrs. Trumbull?"

"No," Victoria said. "You go on ahead. I'm going to rest for a minute or two."

"We'll wait with you," Josiah said. "We're in no hurry."

"No, go ahead. I'll catch up if I feel like it." She heard the faint rustling again.

"If you don't mind, I'll take Dr. Cornelius up to the rock, then, and we'll be back in a few minutes. Are you sure you don't want us to stay with you?"

"Go ahead, please." Victoria seated herself on a rock to one side of the cleared area and waited. She watched until the men were out of sight and listened to the sounds in the woods, twigs snapping and branches swishing. A song sparrow called. A beech leaf fluttered to the ground. Another twig snapped.

"I know you're there," Victoria called out softly. "They've gone up to the rock and won't be back for a while."

Something moved.

"I won't harm you. I'm going to sit here until they come back. I'd like to see you."

Quite suddenly, there he was in front of her, a tall, gaunt man with dark sunken eyes. His short hair was streaked brown and gray and white. Except for a large mustache, he was clean-shaven. He seemed to Victoria to have more lines in his face than she had in hers.

She held out her gnarled hand for him to shake. "I'm Victoria Trumbull."

"I know who you are." He kept his hands by his sides.

Victoria put her hand back in her lap. "You're Phoebe's boy, James, aren't you?"

"I am called Ulysses." His hands were still by his sides.

"The wanderer." Victoria put her hands on the top of the lilac stick. "Where's your dog? He attacked me, you know."

"I'm sorry. He's not a mean dog."

"Where is he?"

Ulysses put two fingers into his mouth and whistled, "Bob white! Bob bob white!" And within a few seconds the black-and-white dog came bounding through the undergrowth toward them, tail and rear end wagging, tongue hanging out. Victoria held out her hand to the dog, who sniffed it and nudged his head under it.

"It makes a difference, I guess, if the boss is here," she said.

"He's defending his territory." Ulysses shifted from one foot to another, as if he were about to take off.

"You've been tracking the boy and me, haven't you?"

"Yes, ma'am." Ulysses stared at her.

"You knew the boy followed your dog into the tunnel?"

"Yes, ma'am." His eyes were set so deep they were almost like holes in his face. "I have his cap."

"And you live in one of the old cellar holes."

He said nothing, but continued to stare at her.

"Does your mother know you live here?"

"I've seen her."

"But she doesn't know you're here?"

"I don't know what she knows." He shifted from one foot to another, still staring.

"How long have you been here?"

He shrugged. "Two years. More or less."

"Do you work?"

He shrugged again. "Carpentry. Odd jobs."

"And nobody recognizes you, not even your mother." Victoria looked into his eyes. "How sad. Don't you think she'd want to see you? To know you're near her?"

"I'm dead, as far as she's concerned."

"Children never are." Victoria looked down at the dry grass at her feet. "If I were to come back with the boy sometime, would you let us see your home?"

Ulysses was silent.

"If we promise not to tell anyone else?"

"Nobody's ever been to my place."

"The boy and I are coming back tomorrow afternoon by ourselves."

"I know, I heard." Ulysses glanced up and Victoria followed his gaze. She heard voices from the direction of Sachem's Rock. When she turned back to Ulysses, he had faded away like a figure cut out of her imagination. She heard the clump of boots and Dr. Cornelius and Josiah appeared.

"Sorry we took so long," Josiah said. "We checked out four of Ness's house sites."

"And you found cranefly orchids?" Victoria asked.

"On three of the four sites."

"Damndest thing I've ever seen," said Dr. Cornelius. "As if somebody else is trying to use the endangered species act without knowing what it involves. You can't simply plant a rare specimen and halt whatever it is you're trying to halt. Whoever is doing this is working against us, actually. We've got to find out who it is and stop him."

~ ~ ~

The next afternoon Josiah went alone to meet with Harry Ness in his house on Edgartown Harbor. An iron gate that hung from white-painted brick posts barred the entrance. To the left of the gate was a speaker set into the gatepost. Josiah announced himself and the gate slid open silently and closed silently behind him. He drove down a long approach paved with Belgian block that bisected a green meadow. Three chestnut horses grazed on the bright new grass. The road dipped slightly and then, ahead of him, filling his view from one side of the windshield to the other, was an Italian villa of white marble. A curving double stairway led up to a second floor. Josiah's impression was of overwhelming expense, of dozens of dazzling windows, of costly gold leaf, of a slate roof, of at least six tall chimneys.

He pulled up next to a Porsche with a yellow finish that seemed to consist of many coats of lacquer, and headed toward the grand stairway. Before he reached it, a wiry man in shorts and T-shirt jogged toward him from a side road. He was about the same height as Josiah. Sweat dripped from beneath a terry cloth headband.

He jogged in place. "You must be Coffin." He extended his hand, which Josiah shook, a hard, big, sweaty fist. "Ness," he said, still jogging in place. "Loch Ness. Doing my daily dozen," he explained, puffing slightly. "Want to see the place?"

"Yes, certainly. Of course."

Ness took the marble steps two at a time. Josiah trailed behind him, thinking that Ness, at least fifteen years older than he, was in better shape.

They went through a massive oak door that opened directly into what seemed to be a huge kitchen. Through an archway in the kitchen he could see a bank of windows at the distant front of the house that looked out over the harbor. Between him and the windows were several groupings of couches and easy chairs in pastel chintz, each grouping arranged on a large Oriental carpet that was placed with meticulous carelessness on the marble floor.

"I didn't mean to be so late," Ness apologized. "Have a seat at the kitchen table while I run upstairs and change. Can I get you a beer first? A diet soda?"

"A glass of water would be fine." Josiah looked around for the kitchen table and decided Ness meant the one beside him, a table three times the size of the conference room table in the Trust office, made of some exotic wood inlaid with arabesques of lighter and darker wood.

"A man after my own heart. Nothing beats good fresh H-two-Oh."

Josiah turned so he could look behind him into the kitchen where he heard water splashing into a sink. Under the windows that faced onto the driveway was a twenty-foot-long counter topped with green marble. Stainless steel refrigerators, freezers, and cupboards lined the wall next to the counter, and in the center of the floor was an island with an eight-burner commercial stove. Pots and pans hung from a low beam above it.

"I'm the cook in the family," Ness explained. "The wife doesn't go in for kitchen duty, but I love it." The water continued to flow. "Have to let it run a few seconds. Well water, you know. A hundred feet deep. Good and cold. Takes a while to get up here." He went around the stove and reached into a cabinet opposite the sink, filled two glasses, and brought them to the table. Josiah noticed that the glasses, frosted by the cold water in them, were crystal.

"Practically everything in the place that can be crystal is crystal," Ness said, almost apologetically. "The wife's name is Crystal. She likes it when I give her that sentimental stuff." He left the vast kitchen area and padded across the inlaid marble floor. "Slippery," he said over his shoulder. "Have to watch your step. I'll be back as soon as I change. Make yourself at home. Look around."

He walked lightly from the marble onto the Oriental carpet that muffled his footsteps and disappeared around a corner.

Josiah didn't move from his seat at the table. He could not imagine making himself at home in this palace. He sipped his water and gazed out the windows at the green lawn on one side, saw one of the horses lift its head high into the air and trot closer to the house. He could see the blue harbor through the front windows, saw a white sail pass below the house into the inner harbor. He was startled when, much sooner than he had expected, he heard Ness return.

"I suppose you want to get down to business." Ness had come around the corner, across the carpet, and his worn boating shoes slapped on the marble floor. He had changed into a yellow knit shirt and rumpled tan cotton trousers that looked as though they had been left too long in the dryer. "We can look around the place later, if you want."

After a few polite remarks, the house, the Trust, the horses, the car, the truck, Ness's background, Josiah's background, Ness sat back in the armchair at the head of the table, rested his elbows on the chair arms, and held his fingertips together in a sort of tent. "What did you want to see me about?"

Josiah, who usually had no trouble dealing with power, started to stutter.

"I suppose it's about the Sachem's Rock property?" Ness said, as though to put him at ease.

Josiah nodded. "It's one of the most beautiful unspoiled large tracts on the Vineyard."

Ness nodded. "Yes, it is."

"You probably know our position at the Trust." Josiah sat forward, hands in his lap. "We don't want to see that land developed."

"Your opinion is certainly valid, I'll give you that," Ness said. "I'm sure you recognize your opinion is only one of many." He tapped his tented fingertips together as he spoke. "Other people have ideas about the best use of that land. I happen to believe mine is the best and wisest use."

"Sixty houses is high density," Josiah said, moving his hands from his lap to the inlaid top of the table. "Sixty houses means roughly two hundred fifty people. I mean, at two cars per household, a hundred and twenty cars. Probably twenty dogs, the same number of cats. The impact of that intensity of development will destroy the habitat of a lot of plants and animals, both rare and not so rare."

"Each house will be surrounded by about three acres," Ness said, tapping his fingertips. "They'll scarcely be in sight of each other."

"Each homeowner will want to landscape his property, plant specimen trees and exotic shrubs, put in a lawn, use fertilizers."

"Quite frankly, Coffin, I don't see anything wrong with that. Human beings are a species too, after all."

Josiah had avoided saying anything about the cranefly orchid. He was not sure how much Ness already knew, and he needed to learn more about who was moving the plants and why. "There may be rare species of plants on that land."

"Fine. I'll have a plant expert go over the property a couple of weeks from now with a fine-tooth comb. See what's growing. If it's rare, I'll build a shrine over it. No problem." Ness tapped his fingertips.

"If there are endangered species on property about to be developed," Josiah pushed a lock of hair off his forehead, "the state's endangered species act kicks in. The state people will need to make their own survey."

Ness's tanned face showed a faint flush. "This is a free country, Coffin. I bought that property. I own it, free and clear. I paid cash for it." He put his hands flat on the table with a decisive slap. "No one, not even the state, can tell me what to do with my property." He pushed his chair back, stood, and paced the length of the table and back again. "I like nature as well as the next guy. Look at my place." He swept his arm toward the manicured lawn. "I hunt. I fish. By the way, I'm going after oysters tomorrow afternoon on the Great Pond. Care to join me?"

Josiah shook his head.

"Almost the end of the season. Months with the letter R in them, you know."

"Yes, I know. But no thanks."

"By the way, I am fully aware that you've engaged Mrs. Trumbull and that kid to trespass on my property and I've said nothing. I respect the old-timers on the Island who think they have a right to walk anywhere they please. But I must tell you, she's trespassing. And sooner or later I'm asking her to keep off my property."

"Mrs. Trumbull has been walking only on the ancient ways," Josiah said. "Ancient ways are public rights-of-way."

"We'll see about that, won't we?" Ness stopped pacing and stared at Josiah. "I'm not sure you want to engage in a battle with me, Coffin. Go along with me and I'll see that your Conservation Trust is rewarded. We'll carve off a nature sanctuary on the property, bring in rare plants, that kind of thing." He turned to the window that overlooked the driveway, then swung around again. "But if you fight me, I'll exercise my rights to do what I want with my own property. I have one hell of a lot larger budget for legal expenses than the Trust does, even though I realize you, its director, are an astute and competent attorney in your own right, and can probably hold your own with any two of my attorneys. But I've got six attorneys. Eight. Ten. Can you fight that?"

Josiah stood up. "The Trust would like to make you an offer, Ness. We're prepared to pay you what you paid for the land, one million dollars cash, plus another million in installments."

Ness laughed. "And what do you plan to do with the property?"

"We had been negotiating with Mrs. Eldredge to put a conservation restriction on it, keep it in an undeveloped state in perpetuity. She would have a right to live on it for the rest of her life. Her children too, if she wants."

Ness laughed again. "She doesn't want anything to do with that cuckoo son or that flaky daughter of hers. Or her tattooed granddaughter, for that matter."

Josiah went on. "She said you had agreed to let her live in her own home for the rest of her life, that you would not be building in her lifetime."

"She misunderstood." Ness put his hands in the pockets of his slacks.

"I don't think so." Josiah stood too, put his hands flat on the table, and leaned on them.

"Think whatever you want to think." Ness jingled change in his pocket. "I paid Mrs. Eldredge one million dollars, a fortune for her. I had my lawyers put the money into annuities and trusts to protect her — we didn't need to do that — we paid all the back taxes and all the fees, we had all the paperwork drawn up at our expense. She's got a fixed income of a hundred thousand dollars a year minimum, living on interest alone. She can travel, buy a place in Florida, keep an apartment here on the Island, if she wants. If she misunderstood us, I don't know what more we could have done. It was all in writing. All she had to do was read it."

"It was my understanding that Montgomery Mausz represented both you and Mrs. Eldredge." Josiah leaned forward over the table.

"That was between Mausz and Mrs. Eldredge," Ness said. "Mausz was on a retainer to me. Mrs. Eldredge had a right to pick any lawyer she wanted. I can't answer for Mausz's ethics, especially not now." He jingled the coins in his pocket.

"Better leave that one alone, Coffin. If you want to save some plant or bird or fish or butterfly, I'll work with you. But I do it on my terms, you understand? You remember that so-called endangered fish that stopped that billion-dollar dam? As I recall, a couple years later the stream biologists found a whole colony of the damned things upstream and in other streams where they hadn't even looked before. So much for endangered species." He turned again to watch the horses. They had stopped grazing and were rollicking over the green lawn. Josiah could see the glint of steel horseshoes in the sunlight as they kicked up their feet.

"Pretty," Ness said and turned back again. "As I was saying, I don't want some sophomore in biology at Boston University holding me up because she thinks she's found some species of rare ragweed or something. I'll work with you, Coffin, but I'm not taking orders from you or any of your minions, you understand?" Ness jabbed his forefinger at Josiah for emphasis. "Understand?"

"I think you've made your point, Ness. I've got to go."

"I haven't shown you the rest of the place." Ness was the cordial host again.

"I'll take a rain check, thanks." Josiah headed through the kitchen to the big oak door.

"Let me get that door for you," Ness said. "It's alarmed."

~ ~ ~

While Josiah was engaged in the one-sided duel with Loch Ness, Page Bachwald of Park and Rec had stepped up onto the porch at Alley's with a pen and an official-looking document in her hand. She addressed Joe, the plumber. "You live in West Tisbury, don't you, Joe?" she asked. Although the afternoon was warm and the four people on the porch were in shirtsleeves or sweaters, Page was wearing a pink parka with its fake rabbit-fur hood thrown back.

She held the document out to Joe, who was leaning against the post watching Taffy. The dog was in the pickup, snapping at flies. "Early for flies," he said to Lincoln, who was standing with his back to the sign lettered, "Canned Peas." Without looking at Page, he reached for the petition, which had about six signatures on it. "I'll sign. What's it for?"

"Don't make the X too big," Donald said.

Sarah flicked an Oreo crumb off her black sweater, embroidered with turquoise and red Navajo-inspired designs. "You're not a West Tisbury resident." She was sitting next to Donald.

"Who cares? It's all one Island."

"What's the petition for?" Donald asked.

"To ask the selectmen to place an article on the town's warrant to buy Sachem's Rock for a park." Page reached a small hand behind her neck and lifted her hair away from the neck of her parka.

"It'll never fly." Joe held out his hand. "Lemme sign it."

"You can't, Joe," Sarah said. "They'll throw out her petition."

"Ness has that land already sewn up," Lincoln said. "He's even got the lots surveyed. He won't sell."

"If we get the whole town behind us, we have a chance. People can make a difference." Page emphasized the word can with a downward thrust of her fist.

"I'll sign," Sarah said. "Doesn't mean I'll vote for it. This town is spending money faster than we earn it."

"Thought those Indians paid you pretty well for that job up to Gay Head," Joe said.

" 'Native Americans,' not 'Indians.' 'Aquinnah,' not 'Gay Head.' And yes, they pay me just fine, thank you." Sarah turned to Page. "How many signatures do you need?"

"Only ten. I have six already." She gave the petition to Sarah, who signed neatly and passed it to Lincoln.

Lincoln read it. "I don't know. How much would we need to ante up?"

"We thought we might sweet-talk him into one and a half million." Page fluttered her dark eyelashes at Joe.

Joe guffawed. "Sweet-talk. Ness? You gotta be shittin'!" He whacked her pink-clad arm with his folded up *Island Enquirer.* "You've seen his logo, haven't you? A sea serpent circling the globe. That's him. He'd strangle his grandmother for her land."

"He's not so bad," Sarah said. "Go on and sign, Lincoln. All that petition means is that the selectmen have to put it on the warrant. You don't have to vote for it."

"You talk to anyone in town hall about this?" Lincoln pointed down at the petition he was holding.

"Park and Rec voted unanimously," Page said.

"A bunch of ninnies." Lincoln passed the petition, unsigned, back to Page.

"I'm the chairperson of Park and Rec." Page turned on him, eyes brimming.

Joe snorted. " 'Ninnies.' Haven't heard that for some time. More refined than 'assholes.' "

Page flushed and snatched the petition.

"Don't let them get your goat, kid," Donald called out as Page trotted to the parking lot, hair bouncing on her pink hood.

"Don't let the animal rights people catch you wearing that fur coat!" Joe shouted to her back.

"You don't need to be so nasty, Joe." Sarah passed him the cellophane bag of Oreos. "Anyway, it's fake fur. Have a cookie."

~ ~ ~

CHAPTER TWELVE

Everybody Wants That Land

THE delegation of five doctors, Erickson and Jeffers from the Island, and Gibbs, Sawicki, and Billings from off-Island, invited Harry Ness to lunch at Goose Neck Golf Club, entirely appropriate and nicely casual. It was the day after Josiah had spoken to Ness.

Doc Jeffers and Dr. Gibbs were already seated. Jeffers had left his helmet with his motorcycle and had unzipped his black leather jacket, exposing a blue scrub shirt. Dr. Gibbs brushed hair away from her forehead.

Doc Jeffers was saying to Dr. Gibbs, "I've put my boat in the water. Next nice day, I'll give you a sailing lesson."

Dr. Gibbs turned her elegant head away from him. Her eyes were as black and glossy as her hair with its white wings. "I know how to sail, thank you." She moved her cashmere cardigan from the chair next to her as Dr. Billings approached the table. Jeffers rose, and the older man shook hands with him, leaning over the table to do so, his liver-spotted hand holding his tie against his blue and white striped shirt.

"You a sailor?" Doc Jeffers sat again with a clank.

"No." Dr. Billings's jowls quivered. "I get seasick."

Dr. Gibbs looked at her watch.

Doc Jeffers turned to her. "When I made my rounds this morning your guy looked pretty good. When are you discharging him?"

Dr. Gibbs stared at him as if he were a not-too-bright patient. "Not for a week at least," she said finally. "He hasn't recovered his short-term memory yet. He doesn't recall what he was doing when the tree came down on him."

"How's his thorax?" Dr. Billings asked.

"Recovering surprisingly well. His right lung had collapsed. We've re-inflated it and it's holding. The ribs seem to be healing as well as can be expected."

"Nice bit of work there." Doc Jeffers bared his teeth.

Dr. Gibbs ignored the look. "He's not a smoker and he's in good physical condition. Both in his favor."

Doc Erickson arrived at the table with Dr. Sawicki. Erickson was wearing his usual rumpled linen jacket over his madras shirt and Sawicki was natty in a sports coat, obviously tailor-made to minimize his girth.

"Before Mr. Ness gets here I should say, once again, that I don't want to be involved in a public golf course." Dr. Gibbs brushed her hair away from her forehead with the back of her hand. "I don't object to elitism."

"I feel the same way." Dr. Billings patted Dr. Gibbs's arm in an avuncular manner.

"First things first," said Doc Erickson. "We don't know whether Ness will sell to us or not. I asked the rep from DufferPro to join us today, but he had another commitment."

"More important than a ten-million-dollar golf course complex on Martha's Vineyard?" Dr. Sawicki pursed his small mouth and puffed out his cheeks.

"We are simply exploring possibilities," said Doc Erickson. "None of us has taken a step yet that we can't back out of."

"Here he is now," said Doc Jeffers, who was facing the door.

Doc Erickson stood and signaled Ness with two raised fingers. Ness was wearing a navy blue blazer, tan trousers, and boating shoes with no socks. They introduced themselves all around and Ness sat between Dr. Billings and Doc Erickson.

"Care for a drink?" Doc Erickson asked Ness as the waiter approached.

"Poland Spring, thanks."

The conversation touched on the weather, on Goose Neck, on Doc Jeffers's Harley-Davidson that Ness had admired. They spoke of the yellow custom paint job on Ness's Porsche, of Doc Jeffers's sailboat. Ness said he had a sixty-five-foot motor sailer tied up at the dock that he could see from his kitchen window. He invited all of them to drop in sometime, and they said they would love to. The two Island doctors spoke of Dr. Sawicki's orthopedic practice and told Ness how much the Island needed Sawicki. Sawicki blushed.

Doc Jeffers nodded at Dr. Gibbs. "Our friend here is quite a surgeon. If she hadn't been on-Island the other day, the patient, Kirschmeyer, would never have made it."

Dr. Gibbs said coldly, "Please, Doctor. Patient confidentiality."

"Really?" Ness looked up. "Kirschmeyer."

"You know him? Doc Jeffers asked.

"How is he doing?" Ness asked Dr. Gibbs, without answering Doc Jeffers.

"We don't discuss patients. Or their cases, Mr. Ness."

Ness nodded.

"You know him?" Doc Jeffers asked Ness again.

"Name's familiar."

Lunch arrived and they chatted civilly about Island politics, off-Island politics, international politics.

And then it was time to get down to business.

Ness brought it up. "I assume you've asked me to lunch to discuss Sachem's Rock. I take it you want to make me an offer."

Four of the five doctors exchanged glances. Dr. Gibbs looked down at her salad plate with its shrimp tails and tufts of parsley.

"I'm not sure we've got that far in our thinking," Doc Erickson said. "We're exploring possibilities."

"I see," said Ness. "Such as?"

"We hoped to build a golf course complex, clubhouse, country inn. We've talked about a system of public trails, but we haven't agreed on that yet." Doc Erickson reached down for his briefcase. "I'll show you some of the sketches, if you'd like."

"I don't believe I need to see them. What sort of offer were you thinking of making?"

They looked at one another, then at Doc Erickson.

"We can go as high as two point five million."

"You know the appraisal on the property?" said Ness.

"I know it's higher than that," Doc Erickson said.

"Ten million." Ness looked around the table with a frown. No one met his gaze. "Ten million dollars."

"We can probably go to three million."

"Gentlemen — and Dr. Gibbs," Ness nodded at her, "thank you for a de-lightful lunch." He pushed his chair away from the table and stood. "I must be going."

"The investors haven't discussed this yet," Doc Erickson said quickly, "but I'm sure we might come to some agreement about making you one of the partners in the project."

"I think a golf course would be more ecologically acceptable to the Island than a housing development," Dr. Billings said.

"Hardly a 'housing development,'" Ness said. "Three-million-dollar homes. Besides, some environmentalists question how desirable a golf course is, in the grand scheme of things." He wadded up the napkin he had been holding and tossed it on the table. "I must be going. I'm hoping to bag a few oysters while they're still in season. Thank you all." He nodded to them. "My invitation stands. Drop in anytime. My door's always open."

The five doctors were silent while Ness left the restaurant.

Doc Jeffers was the first to speak. "Prick," he said. "I'll bet dollars to doughnuts he's the one who hired Kirschmeyer."

"You have to hand it to him," Dr. Billings said. "He's not the biggest developer on the East Coast for nothing."

"I'd like to see his place sometime," Dr. Sawicki said. "Understand it's quite a spread."

Dr. Billings straightened his tie. "Maybe we could include a small hospital in the golf complex, the Ness Memorial Hospital. Might appeal to his vanity."

"We have enough problems with one hospital on this Island," said Doc Jeffers. "Don't get me started on that."

Dr. Gibbs lifted the cuff of her silk shirt and looked at her watch. "I can make the two-forty-five boat if we're all through. How would you like to settle up?"

"I'll take care of it," Doc Erickson said.

"Can I give you a ride to the ferry on my bike?" Doc Jeffers asked.

"No, thank you."

"I'll call you about that sailing lesson."

"Don't bother." Dr. Gibbs put on her cashmere cardigan. Doc Erickson got her coat from the checkroom. She slipped on her gloves, picked up her slim leather attaché case, and left.

"What's with her and sailing?" Doc Jeffers said to the men at the table. "Most women like my lessons."

Dr. Sawicki shook his head and his cheeks wobbled. "Wrong woman, Jeffers."

"You haven't done your homework." Dr. Billings patted his tie with a blue-veined hand. "I gather you didn't know she won the single-handed Newport to Bermuda race two years ago in a thirty-two foot Hinckley."

"Her own boat," said Dr. Sawicki.

"Oh," said Doc Jeffers.

~ ~ ~

Before he changed into his long johns and wool pants and bundled up in his plaid shirt to go oystering on the Great Pond, Harry Ness stood at the windows of his bedroom and looked down at the boats passing below the bluff on which his house stood. Not many yet. It was still early in the season. He could see Crystal jogging on the beach toward the yacht club, her two wolfhounds prancing beside her as if they were on tiptoe. When she moved away from him like this, he liked the way her tight ass was an extension of her long legs. Even now, years after they'd been married, he got a hot feeling of lust when he saw her like this, running with her dogs.

He left to get a sweater, then returned to the window.

He couldn't understand men who went for younger women. What could you talk about? Music? What book they'd last read? The life they'd lived? Part of the fun was talking about things you had in common. How could you talk with a kid who'd never protested the Vietnam War? Kids who knew the Beatles only as classical music?

As he slipped the sweater over his head, he thought about the surgeon, Dr. Gibbs. She was close to his age, and what a woman: bright, cool, as gorgeous as any movie star with that white skin, black eyes, and black hair with its wings of white. The way she surgically handled that oafish Jeffers.

He got knee-length wool socks from his bureau and sat on the window seat to pull them on while he watched Crystal run out of sight beneath a dock, then appear again on the other side.

Minerva Peabody was another woman who made him feel all man. That outdoorsy look really turned him on, that sun-bleached salt-sea-smelling hair, the freckles on her turned-up nose. The preppy clothes, sleekly muscled tan arms and legs. What could she ever have seen in Mausz? Crystal, he was sure, didn't suspect anything was going on between him and Minerva. He and Minerva had gone to extreme lengths to keep their relationship quiet, which was part of the thrill. On this Island, you had to be careful. Rumors spread from Edgartown to Aquinnah faster than the wind traveled. Her husband had been an ass, an inept attorney, but Ness had kept him on retainer because of Minerva. With Mausz gone, certain problems were beginning to crop up. She was getting possessive. Moving in on him. He'd thought about that, and decided he'd better ease himself out of the affair, and soon. This afternoon, maybe. He was going to have to tell her it was all over. Nothing he couldn't handle. It wasn't the first time. She had her own money, so he wouldn't be able to buy her off. He'd have to think about it, the best way out. That was usually the worst part of these things, easing out of them without its turning nasty.

On the beach below, Crystal stopped to talk with someone, a bulky older woman bundled up in a sweater and a kerchief worn like a peasant's. He saw

Crystal throw her head back and laugh at something the woman said. God, she was such a nice person. He loved that about her. He took a deep breath. Women really did make the world a better place.

Crystal moved on, and Ness wondered how he could approach the surgeon. With that thought he felt a glorious new surge in his gut. It would be different from any game he'd played before. He would have to do a juggling act to keep all three women separate, all three balls in the air. He laughed at the thought. It made sense to reevaluate his relationship with Minerva.

Ten minutes later Ness clumped down his marble stairway, waders slung over his shoulder. He stopped abruptly when he saw a short, stocky, bearded man waiting at the foot of the steps.

"Who the hell are you? And how did you get in here?"

The man looked up at Ness with intense, almost luminous eyes. "My name is Tom More," he said. "A woman with two dogs let me in. Your wife, I take it."

Ness said, "I'm just leaving."

"I see." More waited.

Ness paused on the last step and looked down on the man. "Why don't you call for an appointment? Stop by for," he paused, "a cup of tea."

More continued to look up at him with those luminous eyes. "May I ride with you to the gate? I left my truck up there." He nodded toward the entrance.

"I suppose so." Ness went to his four-wheel drive wagon, opened the tailgate, checked for his wire basket and clam fork, and tossed in his waders. He slammed the back shut and stepped up into the driver's seat.

"Hop in," he said to More.

"I'd like to explain why I need to meet with you."

"I can guess." Ness backed into the paved turn-around. "You're offering to buy the Sachem's Rock property for your commune."

"We don't think of it as a commune."

"Whatever," Ness said. "I don't have anything to say to you. Everybody on this Island wants that piece of land to do their thing. Golf course. Playground. Campsite. Country inn. Nature preserve. Casino. Commune. Haven't heard from the people who want to create a zoo, yet." He grinned. The chestnut horses lifted their heads from the velvet grass as they drove past.

"Very funny," More said. "I'm prepared to offer you whatever it takes to buy that property from you."

"You don't have enough money to buy that land from me."

"I have a backer who's interested in my project, enough to put in quite a bit of her money."

"Oh? 'Her?' Who might that be?"

"I'm not at liberty to say," More said.

They were within sight now of the long white picket fence that divided Ness's property from the road. Ahead of them was the iron gate between granite gateposts.

"How much are you talking about?" Ness said.

"Two and a half million," said More.

Ness alighted. "The doctors offered me three and threw in a partnership."

"I might be able to match that."

"Look, buddy, I'm not interested. My project will provide housing for sixty families."

"In three-million-dollar houses."

"That's right. Just because a person can afford to pay three million dollars for a house doesn't mean he shouldn't have a place to live."

"You're exploiting that old woman you bought it from, the Island, the land itself, and the people who'll buy your houses."

"I don't think so," said Ness. "It all depends on your perspective. How much are you charging your homeowners? Three hundred thousand? And you have, how many, fifty of them? If I'm figuring right that comes to fifteen million. Costs you, what, twenty thousand to put up those cracker boxes with their composting toilets and solar panels?"

More stared straight ahead. "Forty thousand," he said.

Ness went on as if he hadn't heard. "So fifty times twenty thousand dollars plus, let's say I sell you the land for three million, comes to what? I don't have my calculator. Roughly fifteen million less, let's say, five million expenses. Leaves you with a tidy ten million net, all for yourself. Not bad."

"Let's multiply out the same thing for you," More said.

"No, no. I'm in the catbird seat. You want to buy into it. Don't give me any of that for-the-betterment-of-mankind shit."

Ness slowed the vehicle before the gate, which slid open automatically, drove through, and stopped next to More's pickup. He thumped his chest with his open hand. "I'm at least honest enough to tell myself my business is for the betterment of Loch Ness." He waited for More to open the door. "Next time you're in the neighborhood, give me a call first. Be glad to show you around. Maybe you can give me some advice on some of the small construction jobs I've got around the place."

"I need to talk with you for ten minutes, fifteen at the most," More said, without moving. "What about later this afternoon?"

"I believe we've about exhausted the subject. I don't intend to sell, you can't come up with the money that would induce me to sell, your housing plan sounds one hell of a lot less acceptable to the town and the Island than mine, and will bring in one hell of a lot fewer taxes than mine. Can you get that door open? It tends to stick."

More gave the door a shove and climbed out.

"Give me a call sometime," Ness said. "I'd love to show you the place."

More slammed the door shut and walked to his pickup.

~ ~ ~

While Tom More was attempting to meet with Loch Ness, Victoria gathered up her cloth bag and her lilac wood stick, and went around to the front of her house. When she heard a vehicle coming from the direction of Edgartown, she stuck out her thumb. The vehicle, one of the Arujo Brothers septic system pumpout trucks, stopped, and took her to the West Tisbury School, which was just letting out.

Robin was racing around the side of the building, his jacket flapping, his shirt untucked. It looked as though he was about to whack one of his classmates with his book bag. Victoria couldn't see who. She called to him.

"How'd you get here?" he asked when he reached her, out of breath, shoes untied, glasses down his nose.

"I got a ride," Victoria said vaguely. "Tie your shoelaces and tuck in your shirt."

Robin put his book bag down and bent over his sneakers.

Victoria looked around to see if there was anyone she knew. Ira Bodman was waiting in his red pickup for his daughter.

"Are you going up North Road?" she asked when he rolled down the window.

"Sure, Miz Trumbull. Can I give you a lift?"

"Do you have room for two of us?"

Ira looked through the dusty back window into the bed of the truck, where his black Lab was beating its tail joyfully against the metal sides. "You and Robin?"

Victoria nodded.

"The kids can ride in back with Douggie."

His daughter Tiffany skipped up to the truck and Robin skulked over.

Tiffany whined. "Not him, Daddy! He's disgusting."

"I'll walk." Robin pushed his glasses back onto his nose.

"Both of you get in, and shut up!" Ira started up the truck with a roar. The kids scrambled into the back and Ira took off. "Not riding with the chief today, Miz Trumbull?"

"She has other business." Victoria changed the subject. "Isn't it a lovely day?"

"Nice day for a walk," Ira agreed. "I see you and Robin been up there to the rock quite a few times lately. Trying to get in a last walk or two before Ness locks it up?"

"Something like that." Victoria smiled. "Is Phoebe still in her house?"

Ira made a wry face. "Ness is giving her six months before she has to leave. Generous bastard."

"She must be sorry she sold out."

"If it was me, I'd for sure rather have the house and land than the money," Ira said.

They passed the split oak on the corner, and farther on, passed the entrance to Seven Gates. A flock of crows flew up from the big meadow, then settled again. The trees on the far side of the meadow shimmered green.

Ira jerked his thumb at the entrance. "Everybody there in the duchy wants their gardens tilled right now, this minute. You'd think I was the only guy on the Island with a tiller."

"They probably think you're best."

"Probably so," said Ira with a tight smile.

When he dropped them off at the trailhead, Tiffany and Robin climbed over the back of the truck and dropped to the ground. She stuck her tongue out at him and he swung his book bag at her. She climbed into the passenger seat and her father drove off.

"Must you do that?" Victoria said to Robin.

"She started it."

Victoria grunted. "Your shoelaces are untied again. I'll show you how to tie them properly, if you don't know."

"I know how." Robin bent over to tie them.

While they were retracing their path to the orchid sites, Victoria told Robin about meeting the underground man.

Robin bounded up the trail and back again. "No kidding! Maybe he'll let us go into his cave. I wonder if it's dark in there? Do you suppose he's got electricity? A generator? Maybe he uses candles. I wonder how he cooks. Do you suppose he has windows somewhere so he can tell what the weather's like outside? How does he go to the bathroom?" Robin blushed suddenly.

"He said no one had ever been in his house. Don't get your hopes up."

When they stopped so Victoria could rest, they heard leaves rustling. Ulysses stepped out of the undergrowth onto the path.

Robin stood still and stared. Ulysses stared back. He wore a tan and green and brown camouflage suit that blended into the spring woods.

Victoria broke the silence. "I hoped we'd see you this afternoon. This is Robin."

Ulysses nodded at the boy, who continued to stare at him.

"You're the underground man, aren't you?" Robin sounded awed.

"Did you tell anyone you were coming here?" Ulysses asked Victoria without answering Robin.

She shook her head. Then she had a sudden horrible thought. For all she knew, Ulysses might be the killer, the person who had murdered Mausz. No one but she knew Ulysses was here, not even his mother. Victoria was the only person who had seen him. No one except Ira Bodman knew she and Robin were coming here today. If they disappeared, no one would know what had happened to them. She recalled her first encounter with the dog, how alarmed she'd been when it attacked her. What did she know about Ulysses? Nothing to make her feel comfortable. He was Phoebe's son. His name was James Eldredge, he lived in a cellar hole, and he was a bit different. She was willing to take risks herself, but she had no right to endanger Robin.

"I think we need to go home again, Robin," she said abruptly. "I just remembered something."

"Do we have to? We just got here." Robin dug the tip of his sneaker into the soft sand of the path.

Ulysses stared from her to the boy and said nothing.

"Your parents don't know we're here. Neither does my granddaughter. We need to go home now."

"But I want to see his cave."

"Come along. Right now." Victoria turned her back on Ulysses and started back down the path.

"You said you'd let me see his cave." Robin didn't move. "You promised."

"I've changed my mind. Besides, he didn't agree to let us see it."

Ulysses snorted, and when Victoria looked back, he was grinning.

"Victoria Trumbull, afraid?"

"Of course not." She turned. "Come along, Robin."

"Why can't we leave after we see his cave?"

"He hasn't invited us. Come along. Right now."

Ulysses whistled, "Bob white! Bob white!" then muttered, "I'm the one who should be afraid, not you." Within seconds his dog bounded out of the brush, Robin's cap in his mouth, tail wagging.

"Hey, Mrs. Trumbull. Look! He's brought my hat." Robin knelt down and put his arms around the dog's neck. "Thanks, dog." The dog dropped the cap. Robin picked it up, brushed it off, and set it on his head.

"Can we see your cave? Can we?"

Ulysses gazed at Victoria with his deep eyes.

Robin had put his arms around the dog's neck again. Ulysses stood with his feet apart blocking the path. He nodded slightly to Victoria.

Victoria gave in. "We can't stay long." She trailed behind Ulysses while Robin and the dog bounded down the slope. Ulysses waited for her where the ground leveled, then waited for her to rest. When she indicated she was ready to go on, he followed a deer path a few feet, then bent and tugged at a small pine stump on the slope. A square of ground, four by four feet, lifted up, and Victoria looked into a black hole with a ladder leading down into darkness.

~ ~ ~

CHAPTER THIRTEEN

Discovery at the Great Pond

TOM More drove from Loch Ness's gate to Minerva Peabody's on North Water Street. Montgomery Mausz's widow ushered him into a solarium that overlooked the harbor and indicated a chair at a glass-topped table. Even though it was still early spring, Minerva glowed with a healthy tan. Her blond hair was streaked with what looked like the effects of sun. Her beige slacks exactly matched her sweater.

"Harry Ness has his weaknesses, Tommy. I know most of them. More tea?" Minerva poised the teapot over the china mug in front of Tom.

"Please." He blotted his mouth with a small linen napkin and nodded. "Nice tea. Good color."

Minerva smiled. "I made it myself with rose hips."

Tom picked up the mug. "How are you holding up since, um, your husband was found?" Tom shook his head.

"You don't need to pretend, Tommy. Whatever Mickey and I had between us at one time was long gone. I'm sorry Victoria Trumbull was the one to find him, and so long after he died."

"Strange, where she found him. Very strange."

"Yes, it is," Minerva agreed.

"At any rate, it's not something you'd wish on an elderly lady."

Minerva poured more tea for herself. "I knew, of course, that Mickey was having an affair. It wasn't his first. Quite frankly I didn't care who the woman was so long as they were discreet. But that's not why I asked you here, Tommy."

"I'm at your service. You know that."

Minerva laughed. The freckles on her turned-up nose crinkled. "Money talks, doesn't it? There's almost nothing you can't buy if you have enough money. Isn't that right, Tommy?"

Tom flushed. "That's hardly the case between us."

"Tommy, I don't care that your discretion can be bought." Minerva picked up her mug. "I've looked at this as an investment, backing your Utopia."

Tom was silent. Finally he said, "I met with Ness briefly this afternoon."

"Oh?" Minerva put her cup down. "What was his reaction?"

"He wouldn't talk to me. He was leaving to go oystering on the Great Pond." Tom avoided Minerva's eyes.

"Did you have a chance to tell him you have a backer ready to buy that land?"

"Yes. I got that much in before he cut me off."

"You didn't tell him who that backer was, did you?"

"Of course not, Minerva."

"He told you he was going oystering," she murmured. "I wonder who else he told?"

Tom glanced at her. "What did you say?"

"Nothing, Tommy." Minerva stared at him over the rim of her mug. "Let's get down to business, shall we? And the reason I asked you here."

Tom moved his chair slightly away from the table so he faced her more directly, settled into the chair again, gazed at her intently, and waited.

Minerva laughed. "Come off it, Tommy. You can manipulate your flock all you want with your soulful eyes, but don't try it with me. And don't look so pained."

Tom took off his glasses and brushed his hand across his eyes. "Jesus, Minerva."

Minerva continued. "I'm willing to pay whatever is necessary, Tommy. Three million, four million, eight million. Ten million. I don't care. I'll pay whatever it takes. However, I want my name on the deed, is that clear? You can build your housing complex on it; we can work out a long-term lease. But I will be the owner. I hope that's acceptable."

Tom thought for a few moments. "Yes. You can be assured of that."

Tom More stood and dropped his napkin on the table. "I believe this arrangement will benefit not only us, but all the investors in Cranberry Fields."

Minerva tapped her manicured fingernail on the glass tabletop. "I hope I can count on your total discretion, Tommy."

Tommy bowed his head to her and left.

~ ~ ~

Casey had already turned out the lights in the police station and was at the door when the phone rang.

It was a woman's voice. "Chief O'Neill?"

"This is Chief O'Neill. Can I help you?"

"My name is Crystal Ness?" The voice went up in a question.

"Yes, Mrs. Ness."

"My husband hasn't come home yet. He was supposed to be here two hours ago. I'm worried about him."

"You're in Edgartown, aren't you? Have you spoken to the police there?"

"He's not in Edgartown. He's in West Tisbury. On the Pond. He went oystering this afternoon. By himself. This isn't like him at all."

Casey sighed and turned the lights back on. "Perhaps he lost track of time. Ran out of gas. A couple of hours isn't long on this Island."

"He always calls me if he's going to be late. On his cell phone. He always calls. Always." Crystal's voice had a trace of hysteria. "He was going out in the boat he keeps at the gunning camp."

"Camp?" asked Casey.

"That's what he calls his cabin."

"It's probably something simple, Mrs. Ness, but I'll drive down there and check. I'll phone you in an hour or so."

"This isn't like him — honestly it isn't . . ."

After Casey hung up she called Bill Burnes, the marine conservation officer, who said he'd launch his boat at the landing in three-quarters of an hour and would motor over to the gunning camp.

"Probably nothing," Bill said. "A guy gets out on the Pond and forgets what time it is."

"Not once it gets dark, he doesn't," Casey mumbled.

She phoned Victoria next. "Where have you been?" she said when Victoria answered. "I've been trying to reach you all afternoon. I even came by the house."

"I have things of my own to attend to."

"Where have you been?"

"Out."

"Okay, okay." From where she stood Casey could see one of the swans on the millpond, picked out by moonlight. "Okay, Victoria. I hope you know where the Ness gunning cabin is."

"We Vineyarders don't call them 'cabins,' we call them 'camps.' The gunning camp was part of Freeman Athearn's farm," Victoria told her. "Freeman sold the land with the buildings to Harry Ness seven or eight years ago. The old-timers used the camp for duck hunting. Why do you ask?"

"Mrs. Ness called. Her husband hasn't come home."

"I'll be ready when you get here." Victoria cut off the phone connection with a decisive click.

"What was that all about?" Elizabeth had come into the cookroom while Victoria and Casey were talking.

"She means well, but I'm tired of people minding my business."

Elizabeth laughed. McCavity had wrapped himself around her leg and she bent down to ruffle his fur. "So where are you off to now, Gram, you and the police chief?"

"Harry Ness is missing."

Elizabeth stood upright. "No kidding!"

Victoria held out her coat and Elizabeth helped her into it as vehicle lights jounced into the driveway.

"Take care," Elizabeth called after her grandmother.

The road to the gunning camp was overhung with oak trees that became more and more stunted as Casey and Victoria neared the Great Pond and the sea beyond. The half moon dodged in and out of scudding clouds, casting enough light so shadows of branches formed a dark network on the light-colored road. As they neared the Pond, trees became stunted brush and the brush ended at the grassy clearing. A low-shingled building stood at the edge of the woods, pale in the moonlight.

Casey parked beside the building. The grass around them was cropped short and littered with small dry turds.

"Sheep?" Casey pointed her flashlight at a pile of droppings.

Victoria looked down. "Freeman Athearn has a deal worked out with Mr. Ness. Freeman's sheep mow the grass and Ness buys a couple of lambs every year. Freeman butchers the lambs and packages the meat for Ness's freezer."

Casey could see a line of surf, phosphorescent white in the shifting moonlight, and could hear its distant mutter on the other side of the bar. The wind had picked up, and small breaking waves covered the surface of the Pond and lapped along the shore.

Casey was thinking about ghosts when Victoria whispered, as if someone might be listening, "He probably keeps his boat in the boathouse on the other side of the point. As I recall, there are webbings or ropes that hang from the rafters. They go under the boat and you turn a crank to lift it out of the water."

Casey strode along the sandy track that Victoria told her led toward the point. Victoria fell in next to her. The wind was southerly, directly in their faces, hissing in Casey's ears, blowing her hair back from her face. The moon disappeared behind a ragged black cloud and shadows raced in front of them. Casey could feel the world spinning through dark space. She glanced at Victoria as the moon sailed out from behind the cloud, casting a shadow of Victoria's great nose across her cheek. Her head was high, her back was straight, she was smiling.

They came quite suddenly to the boathouse, half hidden by a fringe of prickly gooseberry and wild rose. Racing shadows danced across the roof, blinked across the whitecaps on the Great Pond. Everything seemed to be moving, the surface of the Pond, the boathouse, the land itself. For a moment, Casey felt dizzy, whirled around in space on a hurtling planet. She felt as if she needed to hold on to something to keep from flying off.

Victoria broke the silence. "It's been this way forever. It makes you feel insignificant, doesn't it? The moon and the clouds, the Pond and the sea, the wind. The boathouse was built before I was born and will probably outlast both of us."

Casey pushed through the bushes, wiped her hand across a window to clear away the salt spray, and beamed her light inside. "I can't see anything in there. No boat, certainly."

"Perhaps he leaves it on the shore now that winter's over." Victoria stepped carefully down the small bluff onto the beach, bracing her hand against the shingled side of the building.

They looked for the boat or marks of its keel, following the shoreline of the cove. The sheltered cove was eerily silent. When cattails and marsh grass blocked their way they retraced their steps back around the point, where the wind hit them again. Victoria balanced herself as she walked along the stony beach, stick in one hand, the other arm out to one side like a tightrope walker. There was no sign of a boat, no keel mark, not even any footprints in the sand. Only theirs.

"I hope that's Ness now." Casey cupped her hands around her ears to block the wind so she could hear an outboard motor.

"It's Bill," Victoria said as the boat came into sight.

Bill's boat slid onto the beach, scraping on sand and stone. He lifted the motor into the stern. The trailing wake caught up with a slosh that skewed the boat around. "Kind of a wild night." His life jacket, pale and bulky against his dark uniform and dark skin, made him look huge. "No sign of his boat?"

Casey shook her head. "Guess we need to go out there and take a look." She waved a hand at the breaking whitecaps.

Bill looked down at them. "It's chilly on the water. You going to be warm enough?"

"I'll get a couple of windbreakers," Casey said. "We might get wet."

When she returned, Bill had pulled life jackets out from under the stern seat, and Casey and Victoria buckled them over their windbreakers.

Victoria sat on the middle seat. Casey sat in the bow facing her. When they were settled, Bill shoved the boat off the beach, started the motor, and headed out into the wind. The bow slapped the breaking waves, sending a spray of water across Casey's back.

Victoria spoke above the sound of wind and the motor. "Oysters would be in shallow water, right along the shore, no more than three or four feet deep."

"And he probably worked in the lee of the shore to keep out of the wind," Bill called back. "His engine may have quit on him. He may be broken down someplace."

"His wife said he has a cell phone," Casey's voice was broken up by the pounding of the boat on the waves.

"Cell phones don't always work this far away from the transmitting tower," Bill said.

The moon ducked behind a cloud. For a few minutes, until the moon sailed out again, Casey could see Victoria and Bill only as shadowy forms. Victoria's face was wet with spray. She blinked as another wave splashed her. Casey was watching her when Victoria raised her hand and pointed. "There it is."

The boat was drifting off the next point about a hundred yards offshore, sheltered from the wind. Bill steered toward it, and as he did Casey turned suddenly. The boat heeled and shipped water. Victoria leaned to the other side and the boat leveled.

"You don't want to move too fast in a boat, Chief. Not that I want to tell you what to do," Bill said.

"I'm sorry, guys. I'm not cut out for this seagoing stuff."

They came alongside the drifting boat, an aluminum dinghy with its motor lifted into the stern.

"Is it his?" Casey asked.

"Looks like it," Bill said.

"I wonder where he is?" Victoria held a hand on each gunwale. "Could he have fallen overboard?"

Bill looked toward land. "If he did, he could have walked to shore from here. It's not deep, not over his head, certainly."

Casey unsnapped her handheld radio and called Junior, who was in his cabin on the opposite shore of the Pond. "Come on over. We need your help."

They circled the boat, and Casey turned her flashlight on the murky water, its beam a lance of green light.

"Can't see a thing," she said.

Bill pulled an oar out from under Victoria's seat and thrust it down into the water. "Four feet. Too deep to get out and wade. I'll tow it to shallow water."

He looped a line through a ring in the bow, knotted it, and tied the other end around a cleat. He started slowly toward the boathouse. The wind was at their backs now.

They hadn't gone more than a few feet when Bill stopped the motor. "It's not towing right." Ness's boat wallowed sluggishly behind them.

"It acts as though it's full of water," Victoria said. "Or anchored."

He tugged on the line connecting the two boats and they came together again.

"There's a line running off the stern." Victoria pointed. "It's there, under the motor."

"Hold his boat, Chief," Bill said. "The line may be fouled. Maybe he set an anchor. Odd to pay out so much anchor line, though."

Casey and Victoria gripped the side of Ness's boat while Bill hauled in the line. "Heavy," he muttered. "One big anchor," he was saying when a large, bulky shape, entangled in the anchor line, surfaced at the stern of the two boats.

Casey let go of the gunwale. "Guess we found Ness."

Victoria held the flashlight while Bill hauled in the line. As the object surfaced, they could see first a pale face, then a sodden wool jacket. Bill grabbed hold of the back of the jacket.

Casey paused while she decided how best to relay information to the hospital without alerting everybody else on the Island. She turned to Victoria. "Does his gunning camp have a phone, Victoria? I don't want to use the radio."

Victoria shook his head. "I don't think so. Is his cell phone still in his boat?"

"Right," Casey said. "Good thought."

"I'll look." Bill stood carefully. "You sit still, Chief." He stepped from his boat into Ness's, and in a few moments handed a small cell phone to Casey, who called the hospital. Doc Erickson was on duty, and she told him what they'd found. Doc Erickson said he'd alert the state cops and Toby, the undertaker.

"We'll have to get the body to shore," Bill said.

Casey put the cell phone in her windbreaker pocket and slumped down in her seat. "First Mickey Mausz, now Ness," she mumbled.

Bill cleated the line to Ness's boat, and started up again. No one spoke as Bill maneuvered both boats back to the boathouse.

"Don't want to disturb things more than I have to," Bill said finally. "Can't tell what happened to him until someone examines the body."

The two boats rocked in the chop, occasionally bumping together with a thunk. Casey heard dipping oars and flashed her light at the boat approaching them. Junior, whose back was to them, turned his head and nodded. He pulled up alongside Bill's boat, shipped his oars, and held on.

"Any idea what happened?" Junior asked.

"Nope," Bill said.

"Crystal Ness said she had a bad feeling." Casey shook her head. "I don't look forward to telling her she was right."

~ ~ ~

CHAPTER FOURTEEN

Victoria and Phoebe

IT was after midnight when Casey drove Victoria home.

"How about a cup of coffee?" Victoria asked.

"That would hit the spot." Casey locked the Bronco. "I don't think anything will keep me awake after this evening."

"Crystal and he had no children," Victoria said as she measured out the coffee. "They were devoted to each other. Now she has no one."

Casey seated herself at the table in the cookrooom. "She was brave about identifying the body. No hysterics or anything."

"Wonder if this is the end of it," Victoria said. "First Montgomery Mausz and now Harry Ness."

Casey shrugged. "Mr. Ness's drowning could have been accidental. Out alone in a boat with nobody to help if he got in trouble. Not real smart."

Victoria paused while she poured the coffee. "I'm willing to bet Harry Ness's death was no accident."

Casey stirred two spoonfuls of sugar into her coffee.

"Too much is happening around that piece of property," Victoria mused.

"Sachem's Rock?" asked Casey.

Victoria nodded. "I can't help but believe those two deaths are connected in some way."

"It's pretty strange, all right." Casey shrugged. "But that's life, Victoria. Accidents happen a lot more often than murder."

Victoria went on. "I wonder how Spencer Kirschmeyer fits into the picture. Why was he listening to Zack and me?" She smoothed the tablecloth in front of her. "How is he, by the way? Mr. Kirschmeyer, that is."

"He's conscious, eating solid food and bitching like crazy. He still doesn't remember why he was here on the Island or what he was doing bugging your place." Casey sipped her coffee.

Victoria shook her head. "Strange." She glanced at her reflection in the night-dark window and saw herself peering back through the steam.

"I wonder who Mausz's mystery woman was," said Casey. "The one he was supposed to be going to Aruba with."

"It will come out eventually. You can't keep secrets on this Island. In the past that's what made children behave themselves and kept adults from straying."

"Speaking of secrets, Victoria, are you going to tell me where you were all day, or not?" Casey set her mug on the table.

"I think I've got some cookies. Do you like gingersnaps?" Victoria pushed herself away from the table.

"You're not answering me, Victoria."

Victoria shook some cookies onto a plate and put the gingersnap box back on the shelf over the stove.

"Well?" said Casey. And when Victoria still said nothing, "I suppose you went back to Sachem's Rock. Did you go with Robin?"

Victoria nodded.

"And?"

Victoria sat down again and looked into her mug.

"You know, Victoria, cops have to level with each other."

Victoria smiled at that. "Yes. We did go back there. Elizabeth drove us."

"I suppose you were looking for that tunnel where Robin got stuck. And the underground house."

Victoria held her coffee mug in both hands and sipped.

Casey sighed. "Victoria, you're exasperating."

"I promised not to tell anyone," Victoria said. "Don't lean back in that chair."

"Ah! I understand." Casey set the chair back on all four legs. "You found the underground house and you found the underground man or woman who lives there."

"Man." Victoria swirled the coffee in her mug.

"You know how dangerous that was, to go hunting for some lunatic all by yourself . . .?"

Victoria refused to meet Casey's eyes. "Robin was with me."

"Worse still. Putting Robin in danger when there's a killer loose and nobody knew where you were all day."

Victoria looked up. "You don't need to berate me."

"Damn!" Casey slapped her hand on the table. "Okay, what was the place like, Victoria? You can tell me that much."

Victoria settled back into her chair. "The underground man pulled a stump handle that opened a hatch. A ladder went down into a dark hole."

"And you climbed down?"

Victoria nodded. "It was like a boat. You know the way you go down a ladder into the cabin?"

"No. I don't know."

Victoria thought a moment. "You face the wall and go down backwards, holding a railing. There were about twelve steps."

"Was it dark? Are there any windows?"

"He had a glass prism in the roof, like a sailboat. The only visible part outside is flat glass about two inches wide and six inches long. It widens inside like an upside-down funnel and lets in a surprisingly large amount of light." Victoria thought back to this afternoon's excursion. It seemed a long time ago. "The house is on the side of the hill."

"Where we found you and Robin climbing up to the path?"

Victoria nodded. "The house has a window on the hillside where you would never see it if you didn't know where to look."

"So it wasn't a pitch-black cave?"

"It was cozy," Victoria said.

"Was it an old cellar hole, like we were discussing?"

"Yes, roofed over with heavy beams and boards. He must have put tarpaper or plastic on top of the boards to keep them from rotting, then piled the dirt on top of the plastic. You would never know from the outside that the ground was hollow."

"What's it like inside?" Casey asked.

"It's divided into three rooms." Victoria sketched a rough plan on the back of an envelope. "A living-dining room, kitchen, and a bedroom with a portable toilet in one corner. The floors are brick. Probably the original flooring in the cellar. The walls are rough-cut boards. Really very comfortable.

"What about heat? And cooking?" Casey leaned over to examine the drawing.

Victoria continued to sketch. "He said he doesn't need much heat because even in the winter when it's cold outside, the temperature below ground is in the fifties. He has a tiny stove set on top of concrete blocks that he uses for heating and cooking. It's like a boat. Everything is built in and tidy." Victoria wondered if she was giving away too much of Ulysses's secret, and decided it didn't hurt to describe the inside of his house. "He has a kerosene lamp so he can read in bed."

"He likes books?" Casey asked.

"Apparently. He built bookcases into the walls in the living room next to a sofa and easy chair he picked up at the dump. He's hung paintings on the walls."

"That brick floor must be chilly."

"He's got rugs on the floor. He'd picked up everything at the dump, the rugs, the books, the wood. His place is warm and, once he lighted a lamp, quite light."

"What does he do for water?"

"He had a dozen or so plastic jugs. He must fill them at the spring. I guess they were full of water."

"Who is he, Victoria?"

Victoria's mouth set stubbornly. "I think I've told you all you need to know."

Casey got to her feet. "This has been a long day. Get some sleep, Victoria. Who knows what tomorrow will bring."

~ ~ ~

At the hospital the next morning, Spencer Kirschmeyer called for the nurse, who immediately paged Doc Erickson.

"Our boy says it's all coming back, Doc," she told him outside Kirschmeyer's door. "Want me to stick around?"

"Please," Doc Erickson said. "Won't hurt to have you hear what he has to say."

Kirschmeyer was sitting up. His head was no longer bandaged and his hair, which had been shorn, was a gray fuzz with lines of railroad-track stitching running across it.

"How are we doing today?" Doc Erickson asked briskly as he examined the chart at the foot of Kirschmeyer's bed.

The nurse was folding the blood pressure sleeve. "Blood pressure and temperature are normal."

"Been up and about?" the doctor asked.

Kirschmeyer grunted. "What about that steak you promised?"

Doc Erickson smiled slightly. "How do you want it?"

"This side of purple."

"Lucy tells me your memory's coming back."

"Spotty." Kirschmeyer winced. "I remember standing under the old lady's tree in the rain."

"Anything before that?"

"Yeah. Rented a car at the airport, drove around some, got a hotel room somewhere."

"The Harbor View," Doc Erickson said.

"Yeah. I remember sticking a transmitter on the old lady's window. I was holding a tape recorder. It was a fierce thunderstorm. Pouring rain."

"Do you recall what you were listening for?"

Kirschmeyer grimaced. "That's confidential."

"I understand," Doc Erickson said. "I suppose the name of the person who hired you is, too. Without giving me names, do you recall the details of who it was and what you were doing?"

"Yeah." Kirschmeyer nodded and winced.

"Take it easy," Doc Erickson said. "You're still tender. I want you up and walking around. Not too much, now." He turned to his nurse. "Let him have steak for supper. Rare. Salad."

"Right," the nurse said, writing on her clipboard.

"You're doing better than anyone expected, Kirschmeyer. You'll be almost as good as new in a few weeks." Doc Erickson headed for the door.

"Hey, Doc."

Doc Erickson turned. "Yes?"

"Will my memory recovery completely?"

"Your memory will come back. Probably be back to normal in a week or so." The doctor paused at the door. "I don't know whether this means anything to you, but Harry Ness, the developer, drowned last night." He watched his patient's expression.

Kirschmeyer's face paled. "What do you mean?"

Doc Erickson shook his head. "The West Tisbury police chief and Mrs. Trumbull, your old lady friend, found him. Drowned — with an anchor line wrapped around him."

"Shit," Kirschmeyer said, and lay back on the pillows.

Doc Erickson nodded. "I thought so." He closed the door softly between himself and his patient and padded down the corridor.

~ ~ ~

By noon that day, well before the weekly *Island Enquirer* had a chance to cover Ness's drowning, the news was all over the Island.

Minerva Peabody was at the Net Result buying lobster meat when she overhead Dolly Browne tell another customer that a man had drowned on the Great Pond the previous night. He'd been fishing for oysters, Dolly said. When Minerva opened her wallet to pay for the lobster, her hands shook so badly she dropped a twenty on the floor. She bent down and picked it up. Dolly was saying to the other customer that the man had got himself tangled in his anchor line. Dolly's brother-in-law had told her about the drowning, she said, and he'd heard about it in the Thrift Shop, where he volunteered. Mr. Norton, behind the counter, said, "You'd think a man would know better than to go out alone in his boat. Asking for trouble."

When Minerva got home, she put the lobster meat in the refrigerator and called Tom More, who was there within fifteen minutes.

By the time Tom had seated himself across from her at the glass-topped table in the solarium, she could speak almost normally.

"Harry's dead, Tommy. They found his body."

Tom had been watching the small ferry make its run across the harbor to Chappaquiddick. "That's what I heard," he said, not looking at her.

Minerva tapped her fingernails on the glass top of the table. "I don't suppose you know anything about it, do you, Tommy?"

Tom swiveled abruptly. "I hope to hell you're not implying what I think you are."

"Whatever I'm implying," Minerva kept her voice under control, "the situation has changed now, Tommy. I'm sure you understand."

"What are you talking about?"

"The property. Sachem's Rock."

"Minerva . . ." he started to say.

She interrupted. "Listen to me, Tommy. Harry's dead. That means I no longer need to buy that property. That should have been obvious to you the minute you heard."

Tom folded his arms over his chest and crossed his legs.

"I no longer want to buy it, Tommy," Minerva repeated. "What happens to that property now is no longer a concern of mine."

Tom sat motionless. "Who gets it?"

"Crystal, probably."

Tom paused several moments before he said, "Or possibly you, Minerva?"

She laughed. "No, I don't think so, Tommy. You can forget that."

"You and Ness had a thing going, right?"

"You know we did."

Tom shrugged. "Well, isn't it possible that he wanted to thank you for the good times?"

Minerva laughed again. "You've got it all wrong." She looked past him out the tall windows to the harbor. "I wonder how much Crystal knows."

Tom said nothing.

"I don't suppose it matters now," Minerva said. She watched as an osprey swooped out of the sky, dived at the water, and rose with a struggling fish in its talons. "You do understand what I'm saying, don't you?"

Tom said nothing.

Minerva continued. "I assume you plan to go ahead with the Cranberry Fields development?"

"I have to," he said in a low voice.

Minerva laughed softly. "Yes, indeed. You've collected all that deposit money from your communal-living people and now you've spent it."

Tom stood suddenly. "What makes you think that?"

"Come off it, Tommy. I don't just think that, I *know* it."

Tom sat down again.

"It would be embarrassing, to put it mildly, if they started asking for their deposits back, wouldn't it? How much time do you have, Tommy, before that happens?"

Tom rested his elbows on the chair arms. "Six months, roughly."

"I won't ask what you spent it for."

"I invested it."

Minerva laughed again. "High tech computer stock? A sure thing? I suppose you bought on margin when it was going through the roof?"

Tom said nothing.

"You couldn't wait, could you?" Minerva went on before Tom could respond. "For your own sake you'd do well to find out — and soon — who owns that property. When the new owner's name becomes public, which it will soon, the whole world will be lusting after that land."

"What about our agreement?"

"What about it?" Minerva tapped her fingernails again. "Surely you recall the agreement was that you would keep quiet about Harry and me." She gazed out at the harbor and then turned again to him. "Harry's dead. You do understand, don't you? — Harry's dead. Since you 'invested' your people's money, you have nothing with which to buy the land even if it becomes available, isn't that right?"

Tom said quietly. "I'd need your help, Minerva."

She snorted. "Why should I help you? That pathetic 'poor me' act doesn't work. Haven't you learned that by now?" Minerva continued to tap her fingernails on the tabletop. Tom turned away.

"If I don't finance your scheme, bail you out, where will that leave you — back in hiding for another five years?"

Tom swiveled back to her. "What are you talking about?"

"The statute of limitations hasn't run out on the embezzlement from the architectural firm in New Hampshire, has it?"

Tom stared at her.

"Don't be cute, Tommy. As you well know, there are ways to find out things people don't want uncovered. We could turn this blackmail scheme of yours right around, couldn't we? Except I no longer have anything to hide, and you've got nothing I want. Right?"

Tom stood up suddenly and headed for the door. "I don't want to listen to any more of this, Minerva. Where are you getting this baloney?"

"You knew it was Harry who hired Kirschmeyer, didn't you?"

Tom stopped, his hand on the doorknob. "The investigator. I suspected as much. Is that where you got that piece of information?"

Minerva smiled. "Harry prided himself on his thoroughness. He checked up on everybody with an interest in Sachem's Rock."

"Who else did he tell?" Tom spoke so softly Minerva almost missed it.

She didn't answer his question. "Kirschmeyer is likely to be discharged from the hospital within the next couple of days," she said. "It might not hurt you to talk to him. He undoubtedly collected information on your competitors, too."

Tom held out his hands, palms up.

"That broke?" Minerva laughed. "I feel sorry for you. Have him send the bill to my post office box. I'll do that much for you. No name, please. Leave me alone now, Tommy. I have things I need to do."

~ ~ ~

Tom More had counted on Minerva for financial backing. He had been so confident that he had taken a flyer in the stock market with his investors' money. It had been a sure thing. Tom bought on margin. And that was when the slump came. It would be a temporary slump, he was sure, but it brought on the margin call and he was wiped out. That was it.

At first, he was not worried. He felt sure he could count on Minerva's support. After he'd found out about her and Ness last fall, he had invited her to invest in his Cranberry Fields project. He told himself it wasn't blackmail. He was simply offering her an opportunity with a return on her investment.

When he found out about Minerva and Loch Ness, Tom had been out in his boat oystering on the Great Pond. It was only a fluke that he had seen them the first time. They were in view for only a few seconds when he spotted them slipping into Ness's gunning camp. Ness had looked around as he opened the door, presumably to make sure they hadn't been seen. At that moment, Tom had glanced up from raking up a cluster of oysters. Tom's boat had been drifting, motor off, partly hidden from view by a plum bush on the point.

He had let the boat drift around the point before he started the motor again. While he drifted he thought about Minerva and Loch Ness. If they wanted to keep a secret so badly, perhaps she would be willing to help him buy that property. It was a thought. He'd seen them twice since then, once right after Victoria Trumbull had found Mausz's body.

It never occurred to Tom that Minerva might change her mind about backing Cranberry Fields once Ness was dead.

~ ~ ~

"It's that tart's doing," Phoebe said to Victoria that afternoon as they sipped tea in Phoebe's parlor. Phoebe was in her rocking chair, Victoria was on the couch. Elizabeth had driven her grandmother to the homestead at Sachem's Rock and had left her there, promising to come back after she'd done errands.

Phoebe rocked vigorously. "I'd rather have a hundred houses here than let her have this property. Her and her druggie friends. Tattoos. Nose rings. Crinkly hair. You should have seen her. Like a Fiji Islander."

Victoria balanced her teacup and saucer in her lap. "Did you know that Mr. Ness planned to force you out of your house?"

Phoebe paused for a long time, then shook her head. "I suppose I should have read the fine print. That'll teach me." She laughed shortly, a forced laugh. "Some lesson. I listened to that snake-in-the-grass lawyer, Montgomery Mausz. Well, he got what he deserved, I'd say." She touched her napkin to the corner of her eye.

"And then some."

Phoebe leaned forward in her rocker and held out a plate of vanilla cookies to Victoria. "Want another?"

"No, thank you. You heard what happened to Harry Ness last night?"

"I don't listen to the radio."

"He drowned in Tisbury Great Pond."

"Last night? You don't say!" Phoebe's pale eyes widened.

"The police chief and I found him."

"How'd it happen, do you know?"

"He was fishing for oysters and evidently got caught in the anchor line."

"Can't say as I'm grief-stricken. I suppose that changes things. About my land, that is."

"I'm not sure how, though." Victoria moistened a finger and picked up a cookie crumb from her saucer. "I suppose it depends on whether the land is in his company's name or his own."

"His own," Phoebe said. "That much I do know. He bought it outright in his own name."

"Then I suppose his wife will inherit it."

Phoebe leered. "Never can tell."

Victoria looked up at Phoebe's tone. "What do you mean by that?"

"I understand he had an interest, shall we say, on the side."

"Another woman?" Victoria was surprised. "I thought he was devoted to Crystal."

"Maybe he was devoted to his wife, but he was a man, wasn't he?"

"Where on earth did you hear that?"

"I may not have a radio or TV, but I'm not completely cut off from the world." Phoebe closed her mouth with a self-satisfied smirk.

"He certainly wouldn't leave something that valuable to a mistress," Victoria said.

Phoebe continued to rock. "Never can tell," she said. "You find what you and that boy were looking for?"

Victoria flushed. "I should have asked your permission."

"Pooh!" said Phoebe. "You've never needed to ask my permission to walk my place. Besides, it's not my place anymore. Who's the boy?"

"Robin White."

"Is that Audrey's son?"

"Her grandson. Jessie's son."

"Got my generations mixed up. Didn't think Audrey was old enough to have a grandson."

"She's in her sixties."

Phoebe rocked. "So. Did you find what you were looking for?"

Victoria settled back on the hard sofa, balancing her cup as she did. "Josiah Coffin . . ."

"I know the boy," Phoebe interrupted. "Works for that conservation group. Go on."

"Josiah was hoping we could find something that would halt Mr. Ness's development plans."

"I take it you found something?" Phoebe's eyes glistened. "I don't know as it's going to make a difference, now. I've got my money and my marching orders." She wiped the back of her hand across her eyes. "What a stupid old woman I was to trust those people."

'Where do you plan to go, Phoebe?" Victoria said gently.

"I've no idea. I've never lived anyplace else. Never wanted to. Never been anyplace else, either. Never wanted to go to Florida with the old folks. I figured on dying right here, in my own bed. Even after that man bought me out, I figured I'd live out my days here. After I'm gone, I don't suppose it matters." Phoebe rocked. "I've washed my hands of my son and daughter. And that granddaughter, too." She rocked faster. "Wasn't she mad, though, when she heard how the lawyer told me everything!"

"Montgomery Mausz, you mean?"

"No other. She called him up from California hoping he'd spy on me. On me! I guess he turned the tables on her. She flew here as soon as she heard I might sell the land. All lovey dovey. Butter wouldn't melt in her mouth. I knew what she wanted. Her father's daughter, all right."

Victoria thought about Phoebe's son, who lived in a hole in the ground at the foot of Phoebe's hill.

Phoebe went on, rocking vigorously, her face flushed. "That girl was so mad, it wouldn't surprise me if she hadn't killed him out of sheer meanness."

Victoria set her cup and saucer on the floor. "Surely you don't mean that, Phoebe."

"He was killed right around the time she was here. That cold snap back in February."

"Don't even think like that, Phoebe. She's your own flesh and blood even if you don't approve of her lifestyle."

"Humpf." Phoebe got out of her rocking chair and went to the window. She looked down at the ice pond in the distance. "I've always liked that view. Summer, fall, winter. Always changing. Better than watching TV." She turned back to Victoria. "Change your mind about more tea?"

"I guess I will," Victoria said, holding out her cup for Phoebe to pour. "Maybe Ness's death will buy you some time."

Phoebe brushed her hand across her eyes again.

Victoria thought for a few moments. Should she say anything about Ulysses? Phoebe's son James?

"What say?" Phoebe glanced at her, and Victoria realized she must have said something out loud.

"I was thinking about your son. When did you see him last?"

Phoebe paused before answering. "It was before the war. Vietnam, you know." She turned back to the window, set both hands on the sill, and spoke as if to herself. "He enlisted against my wishes. Lied about his age. Never did get along, James and me. Too much like me, I suppose."

"Was there an actual break between you and James?"

Phoebe came back to her rocker and sat again. "After the war he went crazy. Dope, it was. He nearly killed that wife of his, not that she's much of anything. It was dope, all right."

"Vietnam damaged a lot of people who fought in it, men and women both. We called it shellshock after the First World War." Victoria added, "Have you tried to get in touch with your son?"

"How?" said Phoebe, rocking again. "Supposing I wanted to — and I don't much — where would I start? He knows where I am. If he wants to come to me, I'm here. At least for a few more months."

Victoria watched Phoebe over the rim of her teacup. "It might be nice to have a man around."

"No, thank you. I'm too used to doing for myself. I don't want some crackpot underfoot, me waiting on him, cleaning up messes after him. No, thank you."

"Wouldn't it be nice to have him on the Island, at least? He wouldn't have to live under the same roof," Victoria said.

"I suppose the Island is big enough for the both of us." Phoebe crumbled the cookie she was holding without seeming aware of it. Crumbs dropped into her lap. "I don't know where I'll end up, though. On the Island or in some old age place in Florida. Consorting with a bunch of old people who think they've found the Fountain of Youth. They're not there to die, oh no. Face lifts and tummy tucks and dyed hair . . ."

Victoria interrupted Phoebe, who was getting quite animated, two pink dots on her cheekbones. "With Ness gone, Phoebe, perhaps things will be different." She saw a movement outside and stood up. "Here's Elizabeth now."

"Never did tell me what you found," Phoebe said.

"It was nothing." Victoria avoided Phoebe's bright eyes. "Showing Robin the ancient ways."

"You expect me to believe that, I suppose. Well, come again. Don't see many people these days."

Elizabeth knocked on the door and entered. "Am I too early?"

"We were just finishing up," Victoria said, shrugging into her coat.

Phoebe waited at the front door until Victoria had seated herself in the car. "You're so interested in that good-for-nothing son of mine," she called out. "You happen to see him, tell him the least he can do is give me a call." Victoria lifted her hand in acknowledgment.

"What was that all about, Gram?" Elizabeth asked once they were on their way home.

"Phoebe knows more than she's letting on," Victoria replied.

~ ~ ~

When Doc Erickson made his rounds that same afternoon, he stopped in at Kirschmeyer's room. He peered over his half glasses at Kirschmeyer, who was sitting on the edge of the bed in a backless hospital gown.

"I see you've gotten your way," Doc Erickson said brusquely. "They're discharging you tomorrow afternoon." He frowned as he wrote something on his clipboard. "If I had my way, we'd keep you here another couple of days at least. Here, sign this." He passed the clipboard to Kirschmeyer, who scrawled his name on the form and handed the clipboard back. "You were pretty badly beat up, and it's only been a week."

"Yeah, Doc, I know. Thanks for all you guys did." He slid off the bed and flinched as his feet touched the floor. He was broad and muscular and several inches taller than Doc Erickson.

Doc Erickson stepped back. "You've got to take it easy for a couple of months," he warned, looking up at Kirschmeyer. "I'm serious. Go lie in the sun on some tropical beach and ogle the scenery."

Kirschmeyer limped over to the washroom, opened the door, splashed water on his face, and rubbed it vigorously with a towel. "I've got some unfinished business," he mumbled.

"Came close to never finishing it. That was a damned near thing. If it weren't for Dr. Gibbs . . ."

"The lady surgeon," said Kirschmeyer.

"The *surgeon*," Doc Erickson corrected. "If it weren't for Dr. Gibbs, they'd be shipping your remains off-Island to your next-of-kin."

Kirschmeyer limped back to the bed and eased himself onto it again. "Tell her thanks for me, Doc."

Doc Erickson tucked his clipboard under his arm to free his right hand and shook Kirschmeyer's much larger one. "Good luck," he said. "Take care of yourself. Don't get into any more trouble."

~ ~ ~

CHAPTER FIFTEEN

Kirschmeyer Gets an Offer

THE next morning Casey parked the police Bronco in Victoria's drive and went into the kitchen. Victoria was in the dining room, searching through a stack of papers on a chair next to the table.

Casey looked at her watch. "Are you almost ready?"

"I'm looking for a book I wanted to read from."

"Are you reading your own poems?"

"I thought I'd read a story for a change. I hope I can hold their attention that long."

"I suppose they fall asleep."

"That or they wheel their chairs out of the room when they've had enough." Victoria continued to sort through the pile, stacking papers and magazines on the table in some kind of order.

"I think you're a hero to read at the nursing home every week the way you do. I know they love having you come."

"They like any kind of distraction." Victoria held up a small battered book. "Here's what I was looking for."

"*Winnie-the-Pooh?*" Casey asked, surprised. "Christopher Robin?"

Victoria nodded, and moved the sorted papers back onto the chair. "That's no kind of life. The nurses take good care of them, the food is good, the setting is pleasant. But . . ."

"But it's not like home with kids and grandkids and people dropping in and all the confusion of normal life."

"I'll read the story about Pooh floating into the sky holding onto a balloon and pretending he's a small black rain cloud."

Casey laughed.

They drove to the hospital the back way, past the airport and the blinker and down Barnes Road. Casey parked near the Emergency Room entrance and waited until Victoria slid out.

"Got everything? Your books? Will you be warm enough?"

"Heavens, yes. They keep it like a hothouse."

As Victoria walked away from the Bronco, Casey rolled down her window and leaned out. "I'll see you in about an hour. I have some business with the Oak Bluffs chief. I may be late."

"I'll wait inside." Victoria looked through her cloth bag. "I've got my crossword puzzle. I may drop in to see that man who was under my tree."

"Spencer Kirschmeyer. That would be a nice thing to do."

"I have his glasses." Victoria held them up, wrapped in a paper napkin. "I hope he didn't need them."

"His glasses were probably the least of his worries. Okay, then. I'll be seeing you." Casey rolled her window back up and drove away.

Victoria tugged open the Emergency Room door and went into the admitting area. Doc Jeffers was on duty. Victoria could see his motorcycle helmet on the floor behind him. "Morning, Mrs. Trumbull. Found any more bodies?"

Victoria smiled, waved airily, and kept going without reply. She turned right at the entrance to the operating room just as the door opened. A tall woman in a blue hospital scrub suit almost bumped into her. "I'm so sorry," the woman said, then stopped. "You're Mrs. Trumbull, aren't you?"

Victoria nodded and examined the woman. "And you must be Dr. Gibbs. The surgeon who saved the man under my tree. Everyone says you performed a miracle."

"The patient had a lot of luck, including the fact that I was on-Island that day."

Victoria's face was sober. "If only I'd . . ."

Dr. Gibbs wagged a slim finger at her. "Don't think like that, Mrs. Trumbull. He's going to be fine. In fact, we're discharging him this afternoon."

Victoria set her bag on the floor. "Would it be all right if I stopped by to see him when I finish reading to the elderly?"

"Certainly. I would think he'd like to meet you in person." Dr. Gibbs pulled off her protective cap and shook out her hair.

Victoria looked at her watch, picked up her bag, and moved on. She went up the ramp that connected the hospital to the nursing home, turned down a corridor that smelled of new carpeting, and walked into a sunny room where a half-dozen people waited for her, all of them younger than Victoria, most of them in wheelchairs.

She shook hands with each one. She did that every week. Limp hands, strong hands, gnarled hands. Hands that once had held on to important lives and now were plucking at the cloth of gift robes or hospital gowns. It was immeasurably depressing to Victoria, who was not easily depressed.

Once she'd asked about their grandchildren, about the afghan one of the women was crocheting, and listened sympathetically to complaints about it being too cold (or too hot), she sat in the armchair next to a wooden table where she would have enough light to read.

Her listeners were restless. Victoria hadn't even reached the part where Pooh fell into the gorse bush when she heard snores and saw that one of them was fast asleep. A second swiveled his chair around and left.

"Perhaps this isn't what they want to hear," Victoria said to the nurse's aide who was sitting to one side of the room.

"They enjoy it, Mrs. Trumbull. But you know the way it is. It's not you."

Victoria finished early and retraced her steps through the maze of corridors. She never felt old until she came here to read. Then every one of her ninety-two years seemed to weigh her down. The long corridor seemed endless. She was sorry she hadn't brought her walking stick. Silly that she was so vain about using it. Elizabeth understood, and had given her the stick. She had sawed off a branch of the old lilac tree for her to use when she was hiking. People of all ages used hiking sticks, Elizabeth had told her.

Victoria rested on a bench under one of the windows.

"Hi, Aunt Vic. Bet you've come to see Mr. Kirschmeyer."

Victoria, who had been staring at the water marks on the carpet where the windows had leaked, looked up to see her great-grandniece Hope, a nurse at the hospital.

When Victoria nodded, Hope held out her arm. "I'm going that way. I'll walk with you."

Victoria took Hope's arm, raised herself from the bench, and together they went to Kirschmeyer's room. Hope peered around the curtain that hung from a track on the ceiling between two beds.

"Visitor, Mr. K. Are you decent?" she said brightly.

Victoria heard a mumble that sounded like, "Who in hell would visit me?" before Hope pushed the curtain aside.

Victoria's impression was of a huge man who took up most of the narrow hospital bed. Not fat, large. His hair was gray fuzz, obviously just growing back in. He had thick eyebrows that met over the top of his nose like a bottle-brush, thick lips, and heavy wobbling jowls. He was lying on top of the covers in his hospital gown. He quickly pulled a blanket over him, but not before Victoria saw his muscular hairy legs.

"Who are you . . ." he started to say. Victoria saw his expression change from puzzlement to embarrassment to concern. Then, "You're Mrs. Trumbull. Victoria Trumbull."

Hope grinned at her great-grandaunt. "I'll leave you two," she said, wiggling her fingers. "Bye!"

Victoria held out the napkin-wrapped glasses. "I brought these to you. At least, I think they're yours."

Kirschmeyer unfolded the napkin. "Yeah. They're mine. Where did you find them?"

"Where the tree fell. I thought you might need them."

"Yeah. I do. Thanks," he said gruffly. "You want a seat?" He indicated a chair by the window.

Victoria sat, out of breath from the walk down the corridor. "I hear you're being discharged today."

"That's what they tell me."

"Are you all right? Are you fully recovered?"

"Enough to get by, I guess. I gotta get out of this place." He gestured around the room with a large hand.

"I know what you mean," said Victoria. "It's a lovely hospital, but it's a hospital. Will you go home from here?"

He looked out of the window onto a small garden between two wings of the building before he replied. "I got business I have to take care of."

"You were working for Harry Ness, weren't you?"

Kirschmeyer grunted. "No secrets around this place, are there?" he mumbled. "What I was doing was confidential. Between him and me."

"It's common knowledge," Victoria said. "If it's not being too nosy, did he pay you before he drowned?"

Kirschmeyer paused for such a long time, Victoria thought she might have offended him. Finally he said, "Ness gave me an advance plus expenses. The advance ran out. He owed me."

"I'm sure his estate will cover it."

Kirschmeyer shook his head, and winced as he did. "I doubt it. I got nothing in writing. He didn't want people to know I was doing work for him."

"I guess you figured he wasn't likely to die before he paid his bill."

"That's for sure."

Victoria had a fleeting idea. "Where will you stay? I assume the Harbor View is out of your budget range?"

"Right." He indicated a newspaper that was on the table next to his bed and held up a pair of drugstore glasses. "The hospital loaned me these. I've been looking at want ads. Not a lot available in my price range."

Victoria took a deep breath. "I occasionally rent rooms."

"Yeah?" He stared at her.

Victoria spoke with what she felt was the right degree of assurance. "Would you like to strike a deal?"

~ ~ ~

CHAPTER SIXTEEN

Kirschmeyer on the Case

"LADY, I don't know a thing about plants." Kirschmeyer sounded appalled when he heard Victoria's proposal. "You want a scientist, not a PI." He straightened the pillows behind his back and sat up.

" 'PI'?"

"Private Investigator. Detective. That's what I do for a living." Kirschmeyer opened the top drawer of the bedside table and lifted out his wallet. He flipped it open to his license, which Victoria examined.

"Divorces," he said. "Background checks. Get the goods on people doing stuff they shouldn't."

Victoria handed the wallet back to him. "That's exactly what I have in mind."

"You want me to go hiking around in the bushes looking at some goddamn plant? Same place that lawyer was killed? No, thanks." He shook his head.

Victoria settled back in the chair. "You won't need to do that," she said. "I already have."

Kirschmeyer groaned.

Victoria continued. "In exchange for doing some investigation for me, you may stay in my downstairs room until you finish your own business. I don't know what your rates are, but we can work something out between us."

"Let me get this straight, lady. You found some rare plant." Kirschmeyer leaned back on his pillows.

"A cranefly orchid. Several, in fact." Victoria looked at him with concern. "You're not really recovered yet, are you? Perhaps you should stay an extra few days."

"I been here long enough. Too long." Kirschmeyer closed his eyes briefly, then opened them again. "So you found this rare orchid. You go back the next day and it's gone. Dug up."

"That's right," Victoria agreed.

"Then you go there the next day and the plant's back in the ground where it was in the first place."

"Only it's a different plant."

"Yeah? I don't get it. So what?" Kirschmeyer flinched as he breathed out.

Victoria averted her gaze. "It's a different subspecies or variety. I'm not sure which."

"But it's a cranebill orchid, right?"

"Cranefly," she said.

"And then you find that somebody planted the first orchids where someone else wants to build a house?"

"Exactly right."

"And you want me to find out who's digging them up and who's planting them again?" He raised his eyebrows.

"Yes."

Kirschmeyer ran his hand over his bristly hair. "This is the craziest thing I've ever heard of."

"Whoever's been moving the orchids around is causing a great deal of trouble," Victoria said.

"So what?"

Victoria was losing patience. "It's one hundred eighty million dollars' worth of trouble, that's what. Someone cares enough to go around murdering people." She glared at him. "Are you interested in my proposal or not?"

"I heard Loch Ness's death was an accident, not murder."

"You heard wrong. Somebody killed him. I thought detectives didn't take murders for granted." Victoria sat forward in the chair.

"Look, lady, I'm not Sherlock Holmes. I'm a garden variety catch-your-husband-sleeping-with-another-woman kind of detective."

"I see I'm wasting my time." She got up to leave.

"Wait a minute, I'm still thinking."

"Take your time." Victoria sat down again and looked at her watch. "I'm supposed to meet someone in five minutes."

Kirschmeyer sighed. "Okay, lady. I'm not agreeing to the deal, but I'll look at the room." He added, "I know where your house is at."

"I guess you do. I've got to go now."

~ ~ ~

As they were driving back to West Tisbury Victoria told Casey about the deal with Kirschmeyer. Casey sounded aghast. "You don't know anything about the guy, Victoria. A private eye from Bridgeport creeping around your house spying on you? Are you nuts?"

Casey waited for a car to pass before she turned onto the Edgartown Road.

"I often rent rooms to people I haven't done a background check on," Victoria said stiffly. "He's coming to see me directly from the hospital."

"I'll stick around. Ask him a few questions."

Victoria looked straight ahead. "I'm capable of taking care of my own affairs, thank you."

They dipped into the small valley that marked the beginning of Victoria's property. Casey turned left into the drive.

Victoria held onto the door handle to steady herself. "I've got to have something done about this driveway."

"Better than speed bumps, that's for sure," Casey said. "Okay, Victoria. Give me a call if you need me. And take care, will you?"

Victoria waved and disappeared into the house.

An hour later, Kirschmeyer showed up at the west door. When Victoria answered his knock, he was facing out, examining the uprooted stump of the great silver poplar.

"It's a wonder it didn't kill you," Victoria said as he swiveled around to face her. "You know, don't you, that you're not supposed to stand under tall trees in a thunderstorm?"

Kirschmeyer muttered, "Thanks a lot."

"Where's your car?"

"I left it on the mainland."

"You came from the hospital by cab?"

Kirschmeyer nodded.

"Cabs are an extravagance. How are you planning to get around? Surely not by cab? I ride with the police chief."

Kirschmeyer snorted. "Cops and I aren't on the same wavelength. I'll find a used car. Something cheap."

Victoria showed him the downstairs room and how to find the bathroom. They sat at the table in the cookroom with cups of tea and negotiated.

"The room's not too bad," Kirschmeyer said, and when Victoria scowled he added quickly, "It's pretty nice, actually." He leaned back, tipping his chair.

"Don't do that," Victoria said sharply, and he set the chair down. She went on. "We don't know what the person who dug up those plants was trying to accomplish. If he's hoping to stop development by planting an endangered orchid in the middle of a house lot, that's not the way it works. All he's doing is damaging the rare plants that he's dug up. On the other hand, he might have been working for Mr. Ness."

"Yeah?" said Kirschmeyer.

Victoria sipped her tea. "Someone working for Mr. Ness might have been trying to get the plant *off* the property."

"So it wouldn't be the same person who's planting them again," said Kirschmeyer.

"Probably not."

"You say the new plants didn't come from the Island?"

Victoria shook her head. "The state botanist says they probably came from someplace south of New Jersey."

"That helps me a lot."

"Probably North or South Carolina or Georgia."

Kirschmeyer shifted in his chair and winced. "So that's my assignment."

Victoria regarded him. "You really are not fully recovered, are you?"

"I'm getting there," he said.

"You're going to bed. Right now," she ordered. "I'll heat up some chicken soup and you can have that with a mug of hot lemonade and whiskey."

Kirschmeyer got carefully to his feet. "Okay, lady."

"My name is Victoria Trumbull."

"Okay, Mrs. T. I'll start tomorrow. No guarantees."

"About a car," Victoria said when he was at the door.

He turned. "What about it?"

"You'll need some wheels to get around tomorrow."

"Yeah." He started toward his room again.

Victoria called after him. "You may borrow mine."

He asked, "You got a car?"

"Why are you acting so surprised?" Victoria turned back to the table, her nose lifted.

"No reason. No reason at all." He waited.

Victoria nodded toward the Norway maple at the end of the drive. "It's that green Chevrolet."

"The Citation? That's an antique."

She turned and stared at him. "Of course it's not. It's only a few years old."

"More like twenty. Does it run?" Kirschmeyer leaned against the kitchen counter.

"It did until recently."

"How recent?" he said suspiciously.

Victoria paused a moment before she answered.

"Until I had to give up my license."

"Yeah? What for?"

Victoria paused again. "I'd rather not discuss it."

"Okay, okay." Kirschmeyer shrugged. "Is it registered? Tags and all?"

"You may have to do something about that. I believe the registration is a bit out of date."

"Well thanks, I guess. I'll see if it runs, and if it does, I'll take care of the paperwork tomorrow."

After Victoria settled Kirschmeyer into his room with his soup and spiked lemonade, she gathered up her hat and coat, her lilac-wood stick, and a paper bag of stale bread and walked to the police station. Casey was on the phone.

"That was the state forensics people," Casey said when she hung up. She looked puzzled.

Victoria unbuttoned her coat. "Oh?"

"Montgomery Mausz was not killed where you found him, Victoria."

Victoria fanned herself with her coat. "How on earth do they know that?"

"They went over every inch of the ground. Took samples. Measured stuff. Found old footprints, I guess. Drag marks. The forensics people can do magic tricks with stuff you and I can't even see." She indicated Victoria's brown paper bag. "What do you have there, lunch?"

"Bread."

"As if those geese and swans don't get enough to eat," Casey grumbled. "Anyhow, the forensics people think he was killed somewhere near where Robin disappeared."

Victoria stopped fanning herself. "Oh?"

"I guess they measured the direction of the drag marks or footprints or whatever. Who knows?"

"The weather hadn't destroyed the evidence?"

Casey shook her head. "It's amazing what they can figure out." She studied Victoria, who was staring at her. "What's the matter?"

"Nothing."

"You thinking about the underground man?"

"I've got to go." Victoria started to lift herself out of the chair.

"You just arrived. You're thinking it might have been the underground man, aren't you?"

Victoria said nothing. She buttoned her coat again and started for the door.

"Who is he, Victoria? Are you going to tell me, or not?"

"I gave him my word."

"We might be dealing with a killer, Victoria. You've been taking crazy risks. Did it occur to you that the guy probably *is* the killer?"

"He's not a killer," Victoria said stubbornly.

"Yeah, sure. They said that about Son of Sam." Casey got up and stood between Victoria and the door. "Come on back, Victoria, and sit down. We've got to talk."

~ ~ ~

Kirschmeyer was up early the next morning, working on Victoria's green Citation. After a couple of hours, Victoria heard the engine start up with a ragged roar, and when she looked out she could see the car wobbling down the drive, a cloud of black smoke belching out of its tailpipe.

Kirschmeyer returned around noon. "I see you got it running," Victoria said.

"Yeah. New battery, new plugs, new license plates, new registration, new insurance." Kirschmeyer stamped his boots on the grass mat outside the kitchen door, dislodging a small pile of sand.

"Would you like some lunch?" Victoria offered. "Toasted cheese sandwiches. And you may have half of my beer."

Kirschmeyer's eyes brightened. "I could go for that." He sat in the captain's chair by the door with a sigh.

Victoria buttered the outsides of the cheese sandwiches and slapped them into the black cast iron pan with a sizzle. "Did you find what you were looking for?" she asked.

"I don't know," Kirschmeyer said. "I went to the airport. I figured if anybody was shipping orchids, they'd air freight them to the Island. That girl at the counter said a shipment got flown in a week or so ago. Marked 'Live Plants. Perishable.'" He sighed again. "She noticed it because there's not much activity this time of year."

Victoria glanced at him. "You'd better lie down after lunch." She flipped both sandwiches and set a lid on top of the pan. "Where was it shipped from?"

"Some place in North Carolina." He closed his eyes.

"Go on," said Victoria.

"That was about it."

Victoria set the sandwiches on plates, and Kirschmeyer got up unsteadily and took them from her.

Victoria asked, "Who was it addressed to?"

"It wasn't. Just said, 'To be picked up.' "

Victoria took a bottle of Rolling Rock out of the refrigerator and handed it to Kirschmeyer, who set the plates on the cookroom table and opened the beer.

"I'd like a small glass. You take the rest," Victoria said. "Who picked the package up?"

Kirschmeyer shrugged.

"Was it a man or a woman? Did anyone remember what the person looked like?" After Victoria poured a small amount of beer for herself she slid the bottle toward him.

"Thanks. The girl who was on duty that day is on maternity leave," he said.

Victoria sipped her beer and blotted her lips. "When is the baby due?"

Kirschmeyer had wrapped both of his hands around the sandwich and had just taken a large bite. "It's here already," he said, his mouth full.

"She was working right up until . . .?" Victoria had cut her sandwich into small squares and was holding one square up to her mouth.

"Yeah. That's the way things are done these days." Kirschmeyer eyed the green bottle appreciatively, tilted his head back, and drank. "Ahh!" he said when he put the bottle down.

"Didn't the person who picked up the plants have to sign anything?" Victoria said.

"Evidently not."

"Well."

Kirschmeyer finished his sandwich. Victoria had scarcely touched hers. "Here, you can have the rest of mine."

"You sure?" He reached over and slid her sandwich onto his plate. "So I went to the hospital. That niece of yours . . ."

"Hope. My great-grandniece."

"Yeah. Well, she's in the baby department. Acted like I was her good ole buddy. Took me to see the new mother."

"That was nice of you," Victoria said. "Was the baby a boy or a girl?"

"To tell the truth, I didn't ask. They all look alike to me. I didn't want to stick around."

"Afraid you'd run into Doc Erickson?"

"Yeah." Kirschmeyer finished off his beer and wiped his hands on the napkin, which he wadded up beside his plate. "He wanted me to stay a few more days."

"This is yours," Victoria said, pushing a wooden napkin ring toward him.

Kirschmeyer looked at her from under his eyebrows, flattened out his napkin, rolled it up, and slipped it into the ring.

"Did she recall anything about the person who picked up the orchids?" Victoria asked.

"Yeah. But I don't know how much help it is." He pried something from between his teeth with a fingernail. "She remembered him because he was strange."

"Strange?"

"His eyes, she said. Like in a skull. A tall skinny guy. Weather-beaten."

"Mustache?" Victoria asked.

"Yeah. Mustache. She said he was, like, spaced-out." He belched and immediately looked sheepish. "Pardon me."

Victoria ignored it. "Ulysses," she said softly. "I wondered . . ."

"What did you say?"

"Nothing," Victoria said.

~ ~ ~

CHAPTER SEVENTEEN

Sooner or Later

"IF you're heading into Vineyard Haven around three," Victoria said as they were putting away the lunch dishes, "I need a ride to the school."

"Sure, Mrs. T. Anytime," Kirschmeyer replied. "I thought you rode with the lady cop?"

"This doesn't involve her," Victoria said.

"Yeah?" said Kirschmeyer, but Victoria had walked away.

When they arrived at the school later that afternoon, Robin was racing around the side of the school, shirt untucked.

"Who's the kid?" asked Kirschmeyer.

"Robin White," Victoria answered.

Robin looked up with a grin, wrinkled his nose to work his glasses back in place, and darted toward the green car.

"A grandkid or something? Great-grandkid?"

"A friend," Victoria said. "Would you mind dropping us off at the Sachem's Rock trailhead on your way?"

Robin climbed in behind Victoria. "Cool car," he said. "I didn't know it ran."

"Barely," Kirschmeyer muttered. He set both hands on the top of the steering wheel and glanced at Victoria. "What are you gonna do there?"

She stared straight ahead. "I have to see someone."

"Yeah?" Kirschmeyer waited for her to say more, but she continued to avoid his gaze.

"What in hell's going on, Mrs. T?"

"Will you or won't you take us?" Victoria held the door handle, about to get out of the car.

"Sure Mrs. T, sure. But . . .?"

Robin settled himself into the back seat.

Victoria said, "I have to attend to something."

Kirschmeyer snorted. "And I thought I kept *my* mouth buttoned."

He drove them to the trailhead and waited while they got out. "How are you gonna get back?"

"She hitchhikes," said Robin, jerking a thumb at Victoria.

Kirschmeyer looked away from the road briefly. "You shouldn't hitchhike. It's not safe."

"Mrs. Trumbull knows everybody," said Robin.

"You're gonna get yourself killed."

Victoria collected her cloth bag and lilac-wood stick from the front seat of the Citation. "Come, Robin."

Robin had run on ahead when Kirschmeyer called after them. "How long you gonna be?"

Victoria turned. "A couple of hours."

"I'll come back for you at five, then."

She looked at her watch. "About two hours. Thank you. That would be nice."

"Mrs. T, are you sure you know what you're doing? This is the place they found that body."

Robin circled back to the car. "Mrs. Trumbull found him," he said with pride.

"Yeah. And they haven't caught the killer yet. I don't think this is real intelligent, Mrs. T."

"Five o'clock," said Victoria, adjusting her tan hat.

She and Robin followed the familiar route past the now-green marsh. Robin stopped suddenly, bent over and tied his shoelaces. "Do you think he'll be home?" he asked.

He usually is at this time of day."

"Doesn't he work?"

Victoria stopped to catch her breath and leaned on her stick. "Sometimes, I guess. Mornings, probably."

"Are we going to his cave?"

"He likes his privacy. We'll sit by the path and wait for him."

Robin leaned over and picked up a fallen pine cone. "He probably needs to let his dog go out."

"He probably does."

Robin tossed the pine cone into the air, let it drop on the ground, and kicked it with the side of his foot. "Does that detective think the underground man is the killer?"

"I don't know what Mr. Kirschmeyer thinks. He seems to have something else on his mind."

"Maybe he's the killer," Robin said.

Victoria shook her head. "I doubt it."

They walked again until they reached the spot where Robin had disappeared only a few days ago.

Victoria eased herself onto the log where she'd sat before, using her stick for support. She straightened her coat under her, pursed her lips, and whistled, "Bob white! Bob white!"

Robin put his hands over his ears. "Cool!" he said with admiration. "How'd you do it so loud?"

Victoria smiled. "I'll wait here for the underground man. Don't go too far away."

"I hear something," said Robin. He peered through the trees down the slope. "Here comes the dog now. Look at that! You called him and he came."

The black and white dog bounded up the hillside, wagging his tail, tongue hanging out. Behind the dog was Ulysses. His eyes were deep set and sunken, the way the woman at the airport had described them to Kirschmeyer.

"Can we talk here?" Victoria asked.

He nodded.

"Hey, dog!" Robin called, running up the path away from Victoria and Ulysses, looking over his shoulder at the dog. "Come get me!"

The dog barked and started after the boy.

"Is that all right?" Victoria asked.

He nodded. "You wanted to talk."

"The police chief got a call from the forensics lab."

Ulysses was quiet.

"They determined that Mr. Mausz was not killed where I found him. He was carried or dragged there." Victoria gestured down the hill. "From somewhere around here."

Ulysses's hands were still. "Do they know about me?"

"I told them how Robin and I were being followed, and I told them about Robin getting stuck in the dog's tunnel." Victoria stopped. "Casey — the police chief . . ."

"I know who she is."

"Casey concluded that I'd visited someone around here, so I had to tell her about your underground house."

Ulysses turned slightly toward the slope that led to his house. He suddenly made a fist of his right hand and smacked it into his left palm, startling Victoria.

"It was too good to last," he muttered.

"There's more bad news, I'm afraid," Victoria continued.

He looked down at her.

"After the forensics lab called, Casey decided the killer is – you."

Ulysses shook his head.

"You didn't kill him. Did you?"

"No."

"But you know something about it, don't you?"

Ulysses nodded.

Victoria waited. A beech leaf drifted down. A squirrel chattered. A blackbird caroled from the marsh.

Ulysses hunkered down next to Victoria's log, picked up a handful of leaf litter from the path, and sifted it through his long fingers, from one hand to the other.

"You must feel uncomfortable about trusting me after I gave you away."

"No," Ulysses said. "That's not it." He continued to sift the dirt and pine needles and dried leaves and sand, moving it from one hand to another as he squatted next to Victoria. She waited. She heard a car go by on North Road. Finally he spoke. "I knew they'd find me sooner or later."

Victoria heard Robin playing with the dog in the distance. He must have tossed a stick, because she heard something hit a tree trunk and drop. The dog barked and swished through the underbrush.

Ulysses stood up and dusted off his hands. "It was in February."

Victoria waited.

"There's an old cart track below my house."

"I know where it is."

"No one uses that track. But I heard a car." Ulysses put his hands in his pockets and looked in the direction of the ice pond, which was not visible from the path. "It was a new four-wheel-drive vehicle."

"Do you think they knew anybody lived right there?"

He shook his head. "It didn't seem so." He went on, "There were three people, two men and a woman."

Victoria realized she'd been holding her breath, and let it out softly.

"What did they look like?"

"I couldn't see the woman. She was bundled up in a down parka with the hood up."

Victoria shifted on her log seat. "Was she tall? Short? Slim?"

Ulysses shook his head. "Couldn't tell."

"And the men? What did they look like?" She looked up at him.

"One was shorter than the other. He was bundled up like the woman."

"So you couldn't identify him either, I suppose. The third person — the other man? Was it the one who was killed?"

"Yes," Ulysses said. "Fuzzy gray beard and side hair, bald on top. Glasses. Not dressed for the weather. He was wearing a heavy wool shirt."

"Then what happened?"

"I couldn't see so good. The bearded guy didn't get out of the car right away. The others seemed like they were dressed for a walk."

"It was during that cold spell, wasn't it?"

"It was snowing. They started to squabble. Finally the bearded guy got out of the car, yelling at the woman."

"Were all three arguing?"

Ulysses shook his head. "Him and the woman were having a real set-to. The short man turned his back on them. He stayed by the car. They walked away."

"Could you tell what they were arguing about?"

"No. I only heard voices, hers and his. I had to get back to what I was doing."

"I don't blame you." She looked past him into the woods, which were showing delicate tints of green.

"After a while I heard the car leave."

"Could you see who was in it?"

Ulysses shook his head. "I was gluing a chair. Couldn't leave it. At first I thought it was just a family fight."

"The woman and man seemed to know each other?"

Ulysses shrugged. "I guess. Then I wondered what they were doing here, and figured maybe it had to do with the land. The old lady . . ."

"Phoebe. Your mother."

"Yeah. My old lady. She was planning on selling out. You know about her?"

"We're friends." Victoria poked at something on the path with her stick. "That may have been it. The land. What happened next? That wasn't the end, was it?"

Ulysses stood uncertainly. Victoria heard a feeble whistle, "Bob white!" She heard the dog bark. Ulysses didn't seem to notice. He was gazing into space beyond the bare trees.

He focused on her again. "When I went out the next morning, I found the guy." He corrected himself. "The dog found him. Behind my place. Up by the stone wall."

"Dead, I suppose."

"Dead."

"Could you tell what had happened?"

"Looked like he fell against the stone wall. Hit his head."

"Then what? I suppose you carried or dragged him away from your house so people wouldn't come snooping around?"

Ulysses nodded.

"You know you're not supposed to move bodies, don't you?"

Ulysses nodded.

"You're supposed to report that kind of thing to the police."

Ulysses nodded.

"You've got to tell Casey what you saw and did."

"They'll say I killed him."

Victoria thought. "Probably so."

Both of them were silent. Victoria could hear Robin laugh and the dog bark in the distance. Another beech leaf fluttered to the ground.

Finally Victoria said, "They'll come after you if you don't. That would be worse. They know you're here somewhere, and they'll search until they find you."

Ulysses looked around. "I've got to get out of here."

Victoria flicked a small stone with her stick. "You don't want to run again." She looked up at him. "We've got to find the killer, and we've got to find him quickly."

Ulysses took a deep breath and let it out for a long sigh. "All I wanted was to be left alone."

"I know," Victoria said softly. "I know."

She didn't have the heart to ask him about the cranefly orchids.

~ ~ ~

"I have to go to the lumberyard," Kirschmeyer said to Victoria the next morning. "Talk to someone there."

Victoria glanced up from her bowl of Shredded Wheat. "You look much better. I hope you slept well."

"Slept like a log. Want to go with me for the ride? Nice day."

Her face lighted up. "I'll get my coat while you're having breakfast."

Manter's Lumberyard was off the Lambert's Cove road, not far from the Conservation Trust office. Kirschmeyer drove past Up Island Cronigs and the new fire station and turned left onto the narrow winding road. The shrubbery around Uncle Seth's Pond would have new spring leaves in another week. They turned into the lumberyard beyond the pond.

"The man I've got to see rents the shop next to the main building," Kirschmeyer explained as he parked between stacks of vanilla-scented new lumber.

"Who are you going to see?" Victoria asked.

Kirschmeyer looked at her with a smile. "*You* don't tell *me* everything."

"I don't care whether you do or not." Victoria settled back into her seat.

"I don't suppose it hurts to tell. I'm seeing that guy who wants to build a commune at Sachem's Rock."

"Tom More," said Victoria. "I know who he is. What are you seeing him about?"

"Now that *is* my business," Kirschmeyer said, getting out of the car. "I shouldn't be more than fifteen minutes. Are you gonna be okay?"

Victoria held up her crossword puzzle book.

But she found it difficult to concentrate on her puzzle. The image of the desolate look on Ulysses's face haunted her. Who were the people who had stopped in front of his cellar hole and argued? Mausz, of course. But the woman. Was she a client? The mysterious woman friend? His wife? Ulysses had intimated that they seemed well acquainted. And who was the other man? She sat up straight. Tom More. That's who the other man was. Tom was short, shorter than Mausz, who had been only average height. That made sense. Tom More wanted the land for his commune. Mausz was the lawyer for Phoebe. And he was also the lawyer for Ness. He was undoubtedly double- or triple-dealing, playing one buyer against another. The killer must be Tom More. He must have killed both Montgomery Mausz and Harry Ness. Victoria remembered how she had seen someone dropping bags of oyster shell cultch overboard the day after she had found Mausz's body. She would call the shellfish warden when they got home to see if More had a boat on the Great Pond. It made perfect sense, she thought. The people at Alley's said Tom More was like a cult leader. She recalled his hypnotic eyes and shivered.

Why was Kirschmeyer meeting with Tom More now? That didn't make sense. What was taking him so long? She realized with a shock — Kirschmeyer was in danger.

While she waited, Victoria's muscles had stiffened. She opened the car door and carefully set first one foot then the other on the ground, held on to the door-frame, and stepped out. She mustn't move too quickly until she limbered up. She reached into the car for her cloth bag, replaced her fuzzy tan hat with her police deputy cap and set the bag on the floor. She retrieved her stick and walked slowly toward the shed. As she approached the building she could hear the sound of a motor and, over the noise of the motor, raised voices. Before she opened the shed door she paused to think. Was it possible, just barely possible, that Spencer Kirschmeyer was the culprit? The timing was wrong. Besides, when Loch Ness died — was killed, she corrected herself — Kirschmeyer was in the hospital, definitely not able to get about. Nobody could fake that injury.

She tugged the shed door open and the sound of the motor was louder. It took her only an instant to realize what was happening. Kirschmeyer was facing her, hands high in the air. She noted, in that instant, that his face was pasty white. His eyes were huge behind his spectacles. His jowls quivered.

The motor cut off suddenly, an air compressor, she realized. The shed was deathly quiet.

Tom More was pointing some kind of weapon at Kirschmeyer's stomach, something that looked like an orange death-ray gun. On the side nearest Victoria it had a foot-and-a-half-long plastic hose that snaked across the floor in front of her. Kirschmeyer babbled something, over and over, that sounded like, "Don't shoot me. Don't shoot!"

"Put that down, Tom!" Victoria demanded in her best schoolteacher voice.

Tom turned toward her and lowered his weapon. The air compressor kicked on again. He glared at her, his eyes dark, and lifted the weapon in her direction.

Victoria looked around quickly, saw the plastic hose in front of her, leaned down, and tugged it. Tom's weapon jerked toward the ground. There was a loud SNAP!

Tom More screamed.

Kirschmeyer kept his hands in the air. Sweat poured down his pale face. His glasses had steamed up.

"Do something." Victoria said to him. "Take the nail gun away from him before he does any more damage."

Tom stood still, mumbling incoherently.

"You shot yourself in the foot," Victoria said after she had examined him. "It doesn't look terribly serious. They'll probably have to give you a tetanus shot."

The Cranefly Orchid Murders

Kirschmeyer started to say something, but before he could, Victoria went on, "We'd better leave him nailed to the floor until the police get here." She located the phone. As she picked it up and started to dial she told Kirschmeyer, "Find a chair for him to sit on. He can't be comfortable."

Kirschmeyer took a grayish handkerchief out of his pocket and wiped his glasses and his forehead before he found a stool in the back of the shed and placed it behind Tom.

Victoria was speaking into the phone. "We've nailed the killer, Chief," she said to Casey. "You'd better come with the ambulance."

~ ~ ~

A Gift of Crystal

TOM rode to the hospital in the Tri-Town Ambulance. Victoria and Casey followed in the police Bronco, and Kirschmeyer brought up the rear in Victoria's battered green Citation.

The EMTs had pried the nail out of the floor, but had left it in Tom's toe.

Victoria and Kirschmeyer waited outside the Emergency Room. Casey followed the EMTs, who wheeled Tom into one of the examining rooms laid out on a stretcher. "I didn't kill anybody," Victoria heard Tom say. Then "Ouch!" as Hope gave him a tetanus shot.

"When they get you fixed up we'll take you to the station and you can make a statement," Casey told him. "I have to give you the warning, you know. You can have your lawyer there if you want."

"I don't need a lawyer. You don't need to warn me. I didn't do anything. Christ, can't you be more gentle?" The last to Hope, who was pouring antiseptic on his toe.

"We'll have it X-rayed and then Doc Jeffers will want to take a look," Hope said brightly. "He'll probably remove the nail. Doesn't seem all that bad, if you ask me."

"I'm not asking you," Tom grunted. "Jesus! Ouch!"

"Lie down," Hope said. She wheeled the stretcher from the Emergency Room toward Radiology.

"I didn't kill them!" Tom said over his shoulder to Casey, who was following the stretcher.

Casey turned to Victoria, who had stood up as the stretcher passed her. "*Them?*" she said.

~ ~ ~

The five golfing doctors met at the Harbor View Hotel over drinks later that afternoon. Golden light was settling over the harbor. The days were noticeably longer.

Doc Jeffers held up his glass of tonic. "Here's to Crystal Ness and her two hundred acres of prime real estate."

Dr. Sawicki passed a plump hand over his scalp. "Does anybody know what she's decided to do with that land?"

"She's decided against her husband's development, and she's also decided against our golf course," Doc Jeffers replied.

Dr. Sawicki shook his head. "Weird that Ness kept that land in his own name rather than setting up a trust."

Doc Erickson took his pen out of the pocket of his madras shirt and signed the tab the waiter had left on the table. "Ness expected to live forever. Didn't think he needed to hide behind a trust. In addition, he didn't trust lawyers."

Doc Jeffers held up his glass in a kind of salute.

Doc Erickson continued. "He didn't give a damn about taxes or inheritances. He had money to burn. You had to respect him."

Dr. Gibbs flexed her long fingers. "What *does* Mrs. Ness plan to do with it?" she asked. "Do we know?"

"Well," said Doc Jeffers, "besides her husband's trophy houses and our golf course, there's still that community housing project and the conservation group. Were those all?"

"A Native American gambling casino," Dr. Billings said.

"The campground," Dr. Sawicki said, and blushed suddenly.

Dr. Gibbs gazed at him over her pinkish drink. "What do you know about that group?"

"I, er, I had occasion to meet Page Bachwald. The chairperson of Park and Rec."

The other three doctors looked at Sawicki.

Dr. Sawicki swallowed and loosened his tie slightly.

" 'Occasion'?" Dr. Gibbs said.

"One of her boys broke his arm. I set it."

Dr. Gibbs nodded. "I see."

Doc Jeffers guffawed. "Orthopedic practice on the Island looks better all the time, right, Sawicki?"

"The golf course was a good idea," Doc Erickson said. "But you can't win 'em all. At least we saved ourselves some money."

Dr. Billings lifted his chin and stretched his neck. "I'm afraid I lost interest when I found the club would be open to the public," he said. "I've applied for membership in Goose Neck."

Dr. Gibbs sipped her drink. "Goose Neck coined the word *exclusive.* You certainly won't have to worry about the unwashed public there."

Dr. Sawicki's face had returned to its usual pallor. He laughed. "I'm surprised they even allowed you to fill out the application forms."

"Not funny, Doctor," Dr. Billings said stiffly. "Besides my professional credentials, which, as you know, are considerable, my family has substantial financial assets. Furthermore, my ancestry traces back to, not one, but two passengers on the *Mayflower*."

"That should do it," Doc Erickson said heartily.

Doc Jeffers moved his booted feet with a clank and grinned. "Doesn't all that inbreeding worry you?"

"Goose Neck's got an eight-year waiting list. You planning to live that long?" said Dr. Sawicki.

Dr. Billings rubbed his thumb against his index and middle fingers with a dry sound. "You have to talk to the right people."

"Yes, indeed," Dr. Gibbs said. "Money does talk, doesn't it?"

"It doesn't hurt." Dr. Billings changed the subject and turned to Dr. Gibbs. "I understand you discharged your patient, the crushed thorax case."

Dr. Gibbs stirred her drink with the slice of orange impaled on a plastic straw. "He discharged himself, actually," she said. "Dr. Erickson and I both felt he should have stayed in the hospital longer. A week more, at least."

Dr. Sawicki patted the shiny top of his head before he asked, "Have you done any follow-up on him?"

Dr. Gibbs smiled. "In a way. You knew it was Victoria Trumbull's tree that fell on him?"

The others nodded.

Dr. Sawicki added, "I understand he's staying with her. I suppose she feels responsible for him."

Doc Jeffers laughed, showing his great white teeth. "I doubt it. Victoria's probably enlisted him to help her solve the murders."

Dr. Sawicki looked up quickly. "Murders? Plural?"

"She claims Loch Ness was murdered," Doc Erickson put in.

Dr. Billings straightened his tie again. "Surely not. Who examined the body?"

"I did," said Doc Jeffers. "He drowned. Bump on his head consistent with his stumbling against something on board his boat, then falling overboard. Happens all the time."

Dr. Gibbs looked thoughtful. "I suppose someone could have hit him over the head?"

Doc Jeffers leered at her. "Start with the simple explanation. Fisherman goes out alone — what do you expect?"

"Maybe Mrs. Trumbull is right. Perhaps he wasn't alone," Dr. Gibbs said.

~ ~ ~

"I'll be goddamned," said Josiah. He had slit open a large, brown, registered, return-receipt-requested envelope that Zack had picked up from the Vineyard Haven Post Office, and was staring at the contents. "I can't believe it." He stood up and went over to the window. "It can't be happening." He peered out at the cranberry bog, bright red in the afternoon sunlight.

Zack unfolded himself from his chair and reached over to the sheaf of papers on Josiah's desk.

He read. He pushed his glasses back into place. He combed his hair out of his eyes with his fingers. "Holy cow!"

Josiah turned to him. "What do you make of it?"

"Is someone playing a joke?"

"Pretty expensive joke. All that legal stuff looks real enough."

Zack laid the papers back on the desk. "What are you going to do?"

"I guess I have to assume it's real," Josiah said slowly.

"And then . . .?"

"Then, I guess I'd better call on Crystal Ness and thank her." Josiah gazed at Zack for several moments. Then, quite suddenly, he whooped and made an exuberant leap, high enough so he hit his head on the low ceiling. Rubbing the top of his head, he bounded over to Zack, pulled him out of the chair, and threw his arms around him. "The cranefly orchid did it," he shouted. "Get Victoria Trumbull over here right away. Get Robin out of school." He raced to his desk. "Dr. Cornelius. Where's Dr. Cornelius's phone number?"

"Holy cow," said Zack, shaking his head. "Holy cow!"

~ ~ ~

The Cranberry Fields group met in emergency session in the basement of the senior center.

"He was trying to help us, is all," Marguerite said, knitting vigorously. "He wanted to double our money."

"If I wanted to gamble, I'd bet on the horses, not the stock market," said the balding middle-aged man who was sitting in his usual seat at the rear of the group. "What happened to that anonymous donor who was going to put in so much money?"

Cynthia Riggs

"After Mr. Ness died, she lost interest, I hear," someone said.

"Where do we go from here?" Sanders said. "I shelled out ten thousand bucks I couldn't afford, with a promise for another twenty."

"Thank the good Lord it was only ten thousand. Could have been worse."

"That represented all our savings," the gaunt fortyish woman seated in front of Deborah said. "It took us years to accumulate that much."

Deborah disentangled her two-year-old from her lap and set him on the floor. "You know, it was, like, kind of stupid for all of us to think about setting up our community on a piece of real estate like that. We could go someplace out West where we could afford to buy land. Where there aren't so many people. Where we can, like, farm and work and raise our kids and have dogs and free-range chickens. And if Marguerite wants, she can get away from other people's kids and paint pictures of mountains and cactus like what's-her-name."

"Georgia O'Keeffe." Marguerite's face flushed a becoming pink. "Thank you, Deborah."

"I don't care whether I live right here on this particular spot or not," the bald man said. "Out West sounds good to me. Anybody want to look into it?"

Sanders scratched his head. "I'd be glad to, but where do we get the money to start over?"

The long silence was broken by a knock on the wall at the foot of the stairs.

"I hope I'm not interrupting anything." It was Carole, the center's director. "But the Papa Bear delivery man brought this big envelope and said I was to give it to you right away." She looked around at the somber group. "Is everything okay? No more bad news? I was sorry to hear about Tom More getting arrested . . ."

Sanders took the envelope. "We're okay. Nothing we won't get over."

"I'll leave you then." Carole went back up the stairs.

Marguerite twitched a length of yarn out of her tapestry bag. "What is it?"

"Who's it from?" asked the gaunt woman.

Deborah picked up her two-year-old. "Open it!"

The bald man shook his head. "Probably more bad news."

"Hold on, don't rush me." Sanders fished a knife out of his pocket, opened a blade, and examined the envelope carefully before he slit it open. "Some Boston lawyers' office. No one I ever heard of."

"What does it say?" several people chorused.

The bald man laughed. "Maybe it's a summons to testify against More."

393

Marguerite knitted furiously. "I wouldn't want to do that."

Sanders took a great sheaf of papers out of the envelope and stared at the one on top.

"What is it?" several people asked at once.

Deborah called out, "Is everything okay?"

Marguerite looked anxiously at Sanders's face, which seemed to have lost most of its color. "Are you all right?"

Sanders dropped the envelope and the papers on the floor and sat down with a thump. Marguerite set her knitting down next to her and got to her feet.

She picked up the papers Sanders had dropped. "Oh my!" She put a hand up to her mouth.

The bald-headed man strode to the front of the room and snatched the papers out of Marguerite's hands. "For God's sake. What a bunch of incompetents." He looked at the papers. "What the hell!"

"What? What?" said the group.

"It's from Mrs. Ness. Loch Ness's widow."

"Yes, yes! Go on!"

Deborah said sourly, "Probably offering us the land, now that we can't afford it."

The bald man slapped his hand on the legal papers. "Listen to this. She says, and it's all here, she says her heart is still in Nevada, and if we're interested, and if we're willing to change the name from Cranberry Fields to The Loch Ness Memorial Ranch, she'll deed us a thousand acres of land near Tonopah."

Sanders scratched his head. "Where in hell's Tonopah?"

The bald man looked over the frame of his glasses. "Out West."

"Desert. Cattle. Mining," someone said.

Deborah got to her feet again. "I'll see if Carole has an atlas."

Sanders picked up a gavel from the podium at the front of the room and banged it for attention. "I don't know about the rest of you, but I'd be willing to look into this, see what it's all about."

"I hear her father was a big wheel in the Mormon Church," the bald man said.

Deborah turned on her way to the stairs. "She was a showgirl in Las Vegas. Her father didn't care much for that, I bet."

The bald-headed man said, "Mormons are pretty *broad*-minded — get it? 'Broad-minded'?"

Marguerite turned to him. "Not amusing. Tasteless, in fact."

Someone in the back of the room said, "A thousand acres is a lot more land than two hundred acres."

Comments flew around the group.

"Taxes are lower, too, I bet."

"Good place for the kids."

"Not exactly waterfront."

"Neither was Sachem's Rock."

Sanders said, "Maybe the first thing we should do is send a delegation to Mrs. Ness to thank her."

"Why not? Well, why not?"

~ ~ ~

In the West Tisbury police station, Tom More was a small frightened man, no longer the charismatic leader of a band of zealots. He was still protesting. "I didn't do it! For God's sake, I didn't kill anybody!"

"Sit down," said Casey.

Victoria found a cardboard box and set it in front of him so he could put his foot up. He limped over to the chair, his high-tech cast thumping with every other step, and sat with a plop.

Casey had called the State Police, who said they would come to her office, and they told her to hold Tom there.

"You don't have to talk, you know," Casey said again, replacing the phone in its cradle.

"I waive my Miranda rights, or whatever it is. I didn't do it, I tell you." Tom lifted his foot onto the box with both hands and grunted.

"Let's start with what you allegedly did do, namely threaten Mr. Kirschmeyer with the nail gun."

"It wouldn't have hurt him," Tom said.

Casey looked over her desk at his foot.

"It wouldn't have killed him even if I'd aimed it at him."

Casey picked up a pen and tapped her desk with it. "Whether it would have killed him or not, it comes out to assault. Would you care to explain?"

Tom pounded on her desk. "He's a goddamned blackmailer. An extortionist. A bloodsucker."

"Yeah?" said Casey.

"It has nothing to do with Mausz."

Victoria moved one of the extra chairs next to Casey's desk and sat. "An eye-witness saw you get out of the same car Montgomery Mausz was in just before he was killed."

Tom started to sweat. He took off his glasses and wiped them on a tissue he plucked out of a box on Casey's desk.

Casey continued to tap her pen. "Is that true? What Mrs. Trumbull just said?"

Tom looked around the small station house before he replied. "No. It can't be."

Casey stopped tapping. "Oh?"

He wiped his forehead and continued to hold the wadded-up tissue.

"An eyewitness identified you," Victoria insisted.

"Nobody was around." Tom suddenly seemed to realize what he had just admitted. He shifted uncomfortably in his chair. "Okay. Yeah, I was there. But I didn't kill him."

"Who was the woman?" Casey asked.

"His wife. Minerva Peabody."

Casey asked him, "Mind if I tape this?"

"Yes, I mean no. Go ahead and tape it."

Casey set the tape recorder on her desk and turned it on. "Go ahead, Victoria. You were in on this part of it."

Victoria faced Tom. "Mr. and Mrs. Mausz argued, isn't that so?"

"It had nothing to do with me. They got into a squabble about his girl-friend."

Victoria's hooded eyes were fixed on Tom. "Was that all they argued about?"

"I didn't want to get involved in a family spat."

"Was that all they argued about?" Victoria repeated.

"I walked away from them. It wasn't my fight."

Victoria asked for a third time, "Was that all they argued about?"

Tom sighed. "They went from fighting about his girlfriend to fighting about the land."

"Go on."

"She told him it was illegal or unethical for him to represent both buyers and sellers, and said she was reporting him to the Bar of Board Overseers."

"You mean the Board of Bar Overseers."

"Whatever. He said they wouldn't listen to her, and she said she'd filed for divorce and he'd be getting the papers when he got back to his office. She told him to move out of her house." Tom paused. Outside, a car door slammed. "It had nothing to do with me."

The station house door opened, and two state troopers entered. Casey stood. "We're taking his statement. One of you can have a seat at Junior's desk."

One of the troopers was heavy-set and white; the other was short, wiry, and black. The black cop sat on the edge of Junior's desk. The other pulled out the chair behind Junior's desk and sat. "Don't let us interrupt," the black trooper said.

Victoria looked over at them briefly, then went back to her questioning. "Go on."

Tom shifted his injured foot with his hands. "Mausz said he had tickets to Aruba and he didn't plan to stay in that mausoleum for the rest of his life anyway. It went on and on like that."

Victoria stared fixedly at him. "The land. What did they say about the land?"

Tom looked down at his hands, which were clenched in his lap. "Minerva told him she wanted that land. She told him if he knew what was good for him, he'd make sure Ness didn't get it."

"Did she say why she wanted it so badly?" Casey asked.

Tom shifted uncomfortably. "The argument was going round in circles. You know the way it goes. His girlfriend, the land, divorce. They walked away from the car up that hillside beside the stone wall."

Both of the state cops had folded their arms. The one sitting on the edge of the desk crossed one foot over the other. The one sitting behind Junior's desk looked out the window at the pond.

Victoria continued with her questioning. "Then what happened?"

"Minerva came back alone. 'So who won?' I said. 'I did, naturally,' she said. 'What a fool he is,' she said." More, who had been avoiding Victoria's eyes, looked directly at her. "Actually, she called him an asshole. Her quote, not mine."

Victoria's expression didn't change. "Go on."

"Then she said, 'Let's go.' I said, 'Hadn't we better wait for him?' She said, 'He can find his own way to Aruba from here.' I said, 'He's not exactly dressed for a long hike.' She said, 'It won't kill him.' " Tom looked from Victoria to Casey to the two state troopers. "Those were her exact words: 'It won't kill him.' "

"So you left him there? Did Minerva tell you what had happened on the hillside?"

"She said he swung at her, but she's taken courses in defend-yourself-against-rapists, so she deflected his arm and knocked him down and left him."

Casey stood up. "Get yourself a lawyer. You need one, whether you want one or not."

~ ~ ~

CHAPTER NINETEEN

What the Old Lady's Up To

WHEN Casey drove Victoria home, Kirschmeyer was waiting for her at the kitchen door with three stalks of chrysanthemums done up in clear plastic. "I gotta thank you, Mrs. T. That was some quick thinking."

Victoria took the flowers with a smile, cut the stalks to fit the green glass vase, and filled the vase with water. "I need to ask you something, Mr. Kirschmeyer."

"Call me Studs," he said, placing both hands on his chest. "Ask me anything you want."

McCavity appeared in the kitchen from some hiding place and wrapped himself around Victoria's legs.

Victoria set the vase in the center of the kitchen table. "Tom More mentioned something when we were at the police station." She bent down to pat McCavity, avoiding Kirschmeyer's eyes. "Blackmail and extortion. Was that why you went to see him?"

Kirschmeyer coughed and looked behind him nervously.

Victoria went on. "I know Harry Ness didn't get around to paying you for the investigation you did for him. Was there something you found out about Tom More that you thought he might pay you to hush up?"

"Look, Mrs. T, I owe you. But . . ."

"No one else needs to know." Victoria took the chrysanthemums out of the vase, broke off an inch more of stem, and put them back in the water. She tilted her head critically. "I'll feed the cat and make tea."

Kirschmeyer was silent while the water heated. He stood by the west door, staring at the stump of the fallen tree, hands clasped behind his back. McCavity made soft noises while Victoria opened a can of cat food, dished some into his bowl, and put it on the floor.

When the tea was brewed, Kirschmeyer carried it into the cookroom. Victoria shook gingersnaps onto a plate. Neither had said a word during the tea-making ceremony.

Finally Kirschmeyer spoke. "I wouldn't have called it blackmail or extortion. But I guess maybe he could have seen it that way."

"You asked him to pay you for the information you'd found for Harry Ness, was that how you put it?"

Kirschmeyer stirred sugar into his tea. "Yeah. That was about what it amounted to."

Victoria held her mug in both hands and looked at him through the steam. "Can you tell me what it was?"

He let out a great sigh and set his mug on the table. "I guess I can trust you."

Victoria said with some asperity. "I should think so."

McCavity sprang into Victoria's lap and turned, eyes half-closed, to face Kirschmeyer.

"I traced him back to when he first came to the Island, about ten years ago. No one seemed to know where he'd come from before that. He just appeared one day, started working as a carpenter, and the first thing anybody knew, he had his own business and was building eco-homes."

Victoria stroked McCavity.

" 'Eco-homes?" she asked.

"You know, solar energy, floors made out of recycled tires, composting toilets, the whole nine yards."

"Of course. I recall now. There've been articles about his houses in the *Island Enquirer.*"

"I couldn't find out anything about him before then. It was like he got born ten years ago. Just showed up on the Island full-grown."

"That seems odd."

"Damn right it was odd. I said to myself, 'What's he hiding?' I figured it must've been something serious."

"What did you do then?"

"Well, you know, if I'd been able to check back, found he'd served time, no big deal. He would've paid his debt to society, as they say. So the guy deserves a break. But when I found nothing — not one damn clue — it made me think he was hiding something big. A lot worse than serving time." Kirschmeyer popped a gingersnap into his mouth and chomped down on it with a crunch.

"And you found something."

"Yeah. I figured he comes from New England — you know, the way he talks, and all."

"Yes." Victoria nodded. "I know what you mean."

"Then I figured he had to have been in the business for a while. He knows a lot about building houses."

McCavity kneaded Victoria's thighs. She disengaged his sharp claws. "That was clever."

"So I called around."

"What a huge undertaking."

"You said it, Mrs. T. Here on the Island, this little tiny place, there's about a dozen home building companies, plus a bunch of architects and engineers. You just multiply that out."

"How did you ever do it?"

"As I say, I got buddies. I figured the guy probably changed his name and his appearance. He's got that big beard. But he could hardly change those eyes of his or how tall he is. You've seen how he wears those high-heeled boots?"

"I noticed," Victoria agreed.

McCavity, still in Victoria's lap, licked his paw and started to scrub his ears.

"I asked about a short guy with bright eyes. Couple of my contacts said a guy of that description had worked for them twenty or more years ago. Stayed a year, two years, then moved on. He'd changed his name, all right."

"What was his name before?" Victoria asked.

"Ted Moskovitz." Kirschmeyer passed the plate of gingersnaps to Victoria, who shook her head. He helped himself to another.

"Same initials," Victoria mused.

"That's what people usually do. A new name with the same initials. In case they've got something with initials on it, they won't have to change it."

Victoria thought for a moment. "It was Sir Thomas More who wrote about Utopia."

"Yeah? He live around here?"

Victoria laughed. McCavity, startled, jumped off her lap and walked away. "He lived in England around the time of Shakespeare, in the 1500s. He wrote about an imaginary island called Utopia where everything was perfect."

"Yeah?"

"That's what our Tom More had in mind with his Cranberry Fields, I suppose. A new Utopia. His idea must have gotten out of hand. I can't imagine why he felt he had to kill anybody." Victoria shook her head. "What did you find out about Ted Moskovitz?"

"One of the companies he'd worked for told me where he'd gone to, an architectural company in New Hampshire that specializes in environmental homes. Where he got his ideas, I guess. I called them, and — Bingo!"

"Oh?"

"He worked for this company, Green Architects Limited, for five or six years. They promoted him to supervisor, then a couple years later to handling contracts and money. Then, bam!" Kirschmeyer slammed his fist on the table, and one of the gingersnaps bounced off the plate onto the table. "One day he disappeared. And so did a pile of money, like around two hundred thousand."

Victoria brushed cat hairs off her lap. "Dollars?"

Kirschmeyer nodded. "Green Architects tried to track him, but he'd vanished clean off the face of the earth."

Victoria smoothed the tablecloth in front of her. "Strange," she said. "It's not that easy to vanish."

"That's for sure. I figured, if I was going to disappear, where would I go? And I figured I'd leave the country, go someplace in Central America, like Costa Rica. They love Americans down there, and I hear it's a nice place to stay."

McCavity scratched at the kitchen door. Victoria got up stiffly and let him out. "Is that what happened? He left the country?" she said when she returned.

"Right. I know this girl works for an airline, so I had her check for More or Moskovitz around the time he disappeared. It wasn't all that easy because the records were in some back storage. That's why I'm so bullshit about Ness getting himself killed without paying me."

"That *was* unfortunate. His death."

"This girl found the records. He'd used his own name, Moskovitz, his own passport, and sure enough, he'd gone down to Costa Rica. Lived there for about five years, then came back here on a new passport with the name Tom More."

"Interesting," Victoria murmured.

She sipped her tea. "What happened at the lumberyard when you confronted him today?"

"I was upfront. I told him about Ness hiring me, about me not getting the money, about how I'd shelled out a lot from my own pocket, and asked how's about him reimbursing me."

"I suppose you told him what you'd learned?"

"Yeah, of course." Kirschmeyer pushed his chair back from the table and crossed his legs.

"Then what?"

"He says, 'That's ridiculous,' or something like that. I says, 'I've got proof.' He says he doesn't have any money. I laughed in his face. 'You mean,' I says, 'You're developing two hundred acres of prime real estate on Martha's Vineyard and you've got all these investors and you don't have any money?' He got red in the face. 'Come on, come on,' I says." Kirschmeyer gestured with both hands. "That's when he picked up that death-ray gun."

"It was a nail gun," Victoria said.

"I never seen one before. How am I supposed to know what it was?"

"It looks pretty lethal," Victoria admitted. "I suppose it could kill you if it was aimed exactly right." She sniffed. "It's not the weapon *I'd* choose, though."

Kirschmeyer shrugged. "So that's where we're at."

Victoria thought. She glanced up at the baskets hanging from the whitewashed rafters. Finally she said, "Why don't you write out your report and give it to Crystal Ness with your bill? I'm sure she'll honor it."

Kirschmeyer wiped crumbs from his mouth with a paper napkin, wadded up the napkin and dropped it on the table. "Ness didn't want anybody to know I was working for him."

"The situation has changed. Decidedly. I'd go to her, if I were you, Mr. Kirschmeyer . . ."

"Studs."

Victoria coughed delicately. "Yes. Well. I'd also give a copy of the report to Chief O'Neill. She'll know how to handle this."

Kirschmeyer shook his head. "I don't like the idea of cops getting involved. Especially a lady cop."

Victoria fixed him with her deep-set eyes. "You realize you're in danger, don't you? I don't know how long they can hold Tom More, but the minute they release him, he'll obviously try to silence you. The safest thing for you to do is to notify the police. Right now."

Kirschmeyer lifted his shoulders.

"I mean it." Victoria slapped her hand on the table. "Tom More has nothing to lose. You do. Go to Chief O'Neill right away."

~ ~ ~

Joe stepped up onto the porch at Alley's. "You heard about Tom More shooting himself in the foot?"

Lincoln laughed. "What you call 'toe nailing,' right?"

"It's not funny," said Sarah, who was sitting on the bench next to Donald. She stirred her coffee. "You know how much it hurts when you stub your toe. Imagine getting a nail in it." She shuddered.

Joe laughed.

Donald leaned forward, his elbows on his resin-splotched jeans. "I hear Miz Trumbull rescued the detective."

"She knew more about nail guns than he did." Joe chortled. "He thought it was a death ray."

"How long are they keeping More in jail, anybody know?" Lincoln asked from his spot next to the door.

They looked at each other questioningly.

Donald said finally, "I hear Miz Trumbull thinks he killed Mickey Mausz."

"No way to prove it," Lincoln said. "Some guy who's camping out there moved the body."

"Yeah?" Joe rocked from his heels onto his toes. He put his hands in his pockets. "Where'd you hear that?"

"It was probably on the scanner," Sarah put in.

Joe continued to rock. "Tom More's got a pretty good deal, being locked up in that country club."

Donald leaned back against the wall behind the bench. "You heard about the quee-zine at the jail?"

"It was in the paper," Sarah said.

"What about it?" Joe stopped rocking.

Lincoln rubbed his back against the doorframe. "They got a French chef serving time for doing drugs."

"Yeah? That's what they eat, French quee-zine?"

Sarah finished her coffee and folded the paper cup. "Makes you think, doesn't it?"

"So all they can hold Tom More for is the threatened assault on the private eye?" Lincoln looked around at the others.

"I guess." Sarah shrugged. "I don't think they can keep him there forever, eating French cuisine at taxpayers' expense."

"Somebody told me the private eye isn't pressing charges," Donald said.

Joe looked up with interest. "Yeah? How come?"

Just then, a white VW convertible pulled up in front of the store and Elizabeth went around the car from the driver's side and onto the porch. She greeted the four, and went inside. Victoria rolled down her window and waved. "Nice day," she said.

Joe straightened up. "Yes, ma'am."

"Where are you off to, Mrs. Trumbull?" Sarah called.

"An outing," Victoria replied. "What my grandfather called 'a cruise.'"

Elizabeth came out of the store with a stack of mail. "What a waste of paper." She held up a half-dozen catalogs. "Stuff we'd never buy."

"Someone does," Sarah said.

Elizabeth flipped open one of the catalogs to an ad for a Potty Putter. "Want to play golf while you sit on the john?"

Sarah laughed. "So where *are* you and your grandmother going?" she asked. "Back up to Sachem's Rock, now she's nabbed the killer?"

"I'm taking her there, but I have to get back to work. I wish Robin was with her."

"I suppose she'll hitch a ride home again?"

Elizabeth said quietly, "I worry about my grandmother sometimes, but honestly, she's impossible. There's nothing I can do to stop her."

From the porch they could see Victoria's owl-like profile, her beaky nose and hooded eyes. She seemed to be writing something. She looked up from whatever she was writing. Her chin jutted out stubbornly.

"I see what you mean," said Sarah with admiration.

Elizabeth handed the mail through the window to Victoria, got back in the car, made a U-turn in the middle of the road, and drove off down Brandy Brow.

After a few minutes' silence, Joe said, "What do you suppose the old lady's up to now?"

~ ~ ~

Victoria stopped by the log where she'd summoned Ulysses before and sat. She was tired and felt, for the first time, that perhaps she'd bitten off more than she could chew. Robin was in school, and she missed him. But she needed to talk to Ulysses alone. When she caught her breath, she pursed her lips and whistled, "Bob white! Bob bob white!" remembering how Robin had been awed by her loud whistle. She smiled.

Soon the dog bounded up the hillside followed by Ulysses.

"We caught the killer," Victoria called out as soon as she saw him.

Ulysses smiled grimly. "Yes, ma'am. I heard."

"You don't need to worry about being accused of murdering Mr. Mausz now. But you have to talk to the police chief about moving the body. You're not supposed to do that, you know."

Ulysses squatted beside Victoria, picked up a handful of leaf litter from the ground.

Victoria watched him for a few moments. "I don't know for a certainty, but I don't think they'll do any more than give you a lecture."

The black and white dog lay down on the path in front of Victoria. He put his head on his paws and looked up at Ulysses through sad eyes.

"He misses the boy," Ulysses said abruptly.

"He's in school. I wanted to talk to you alone."

"About giving myself up."

"That, but something else, too." Victoria poked the ground between her and the dog with her stick, inscribing small circles. The dog lifted his head and dropped it back on his paws.

Ulysses waited.

Finally Victoria said, "Why did you dig up the cranefly orchids?"

Ulysses stood suddenly, dropped his handful of dirt, and dusted off his hands. He said angrily, "I didn't dig them up."

"Someone air-shipped live plants to you."

"Maybe they did. But I didn't dig up anything."

"I suppose those were cranefly orchids in the shipment?" Victoria continued to draw circles in the dirt.

Ulysses nodded.

"Will you tell me what that was all about?"

Ulysses hunkered down again beside Victoria.

"I followed you and the boy, from the first time you came here together."

"I knew someone was."

"I wasn't the only one following you," Ulysses said.

Victoria raised her eyebrows. "Oh?"

"Somebody else was. You heard them. Not me."

"Who was it?"

"I could never get close enough to see."

"Could you tell if it was the caretaker?"

"It wasn't him. He makes the rounds of the main trails twice a day with his dog, regular as clockwork. Then he leaves."

Victoria thought over this new information. "Then who dug up the plants?"

"Whoever was stalking you."

"But you definitely didn't?" Victoria looked at him.

Ulysses stood up and paced back and forth for several minutes. Then he said, "Someone finds some rare plant or animal on this land, developers would back off. Why should I dig up something that might save my family's land? Used to be my family land."

"That's true," Victoria conceded. "Who could the other person be, I wonder. Someone working for Harry Ness?"

Ulysses said nothing.

Victoria asked, "How do you happen to know so much about cranefly orchids?"

"I looked them up on the library computer after I heard you and the boy talking about them," Ulysses said.

Victoria stopped drawing circles with her stick. "The new orchids — why have them flown in? And where on earth did you get them?"

Ulysses didn't answer directly. "I heard when you and the boy found them. He made enough fuss."

Victoria put her stick aside. She shifted so she could reach a napkin in her trousers pocket and wiped her nose with it. "I was afraid Robin would trample them."

"That other person must have heard the boy, too. I went back later to see what you'd found and the plants were already gone."

Victoria whistled softly. "Someone worked fast."

"I read all about those orchids. They aren't rare in the South. There's plenty of them in North Carolina and Georgia." Ulysses walked a short distance up the path and back again. He continued, "I have an Army buddy who works in the Smoky Mountains, North Carolina. I asked him to find me some plants and send them to me."

"You don't have a phone, do you?"

Ulysses grinned. "I faxed him from the drug store."

"I see," Victoria said. "You know the orchids your friend sent are different from the ones that were dug up? The ones that grow here naturally?"

Ulysses shrugged. "It was the best I could think of."

"I suppose you re-planted the original orchid plants on the house sites?"

Ulysses shuffled his feet in the dry litter. "Yes, ma'am."

"Why?" Victoria asked.

"I didn't find the original plants until after I got the new ones from the Smokies. I thought that whoever dug them up would have gotten rid of them fast. They probably wouldn't dump them on the ground or bury them. For fear they'd grow back, you know?"

Victoria nodded.

"I decided somebody must have come by car, but didn't park near where you and the boy always start walking."

Victoria put the napkin back in her pocket. "I'd have seen them, if so. I wonder how they knew when Robin and I would be here."

"You weren't exactly sneaky," Ulysses said, and smiled.

"Hmmm," Victoria murmured.

"A couple of other roads lead in here. One is the old road that goes by my place. The other is off Tea Lane."

"The way I go to Phoebe's — your mother's."

"Yes, ma'am. The Tea Lane road seemed like where they'd most likely park. There's an old trash barrel there. Nobody ever empties it, but whoever wanted to get rid of the orchids probably wouldn't know that."

"It must be full of rubbish if it's never emptied."

Ulysses shook his head. "It's not public property. Nobody goes there. The barrel had a couple bottles, a lot of leaves, some soggy paper. I thought I'd find the orchids there, and that's where I did. In the rubbish."

"So you planted them where Ness was planning to build the houses."

"Yes, ma'am. Didn't see any point in putting them back where they were, what with the new plants growing okay."

Victoria sighed. "That explains a lot."

"I heard the fellow from the state . . ."

"Dr. Cornelius?"

"Yes, ma'am. I heard him say it was the wrong habitat, the house sites."

"They probably won't survive there," Victoria agreed.

"I'll move them back to where you found them."

Victoria laughed. "That will confound Josiah and Zack." She paused for a few moments. "Ulysses?"

"Ma'am?"

"Your mother would like to see you."

He turned his back on her. "I haven't seen her for twenty years."

The dog sat up and laid his muzzle on Victoria's knee. She patted his head. "It's time you went to see her, Ulysses."

"I got nothing to say to her." Ulysses turned back to Victoria.

"I don't think she has anything to say to you, either," Victoria said. "But you should go see her anyway."

"She sold the land. It's not hers anymore. She'll be moving off one of these days."

"Things have changed," Victoria said. "You know Crystal Ness gave Sachem's Rock to the Conservation Trust?"

"I'd heard so. They'll be moving me off, too, I imagine."

"I don't think so," Victoria said. "Josiah Coffin told me he needs a caretaker for the property. I recommended you. I think he plans to work out something so your mother can stay in her house."

"Does she know?"

Victoria shook her head. "That might be a good excuse to talk to her."

"I don't know," Ulysses said, turning away again.

"She doesn't want you living with her and taking care of her. She'd hate that." Victoria patted the dog, who moved closer to her. "She wants her place to herself. Just like you. But it would be nice for her to know her son's around somewhere."

Ulysses wiped his hands on his trousers. "I guess I better talk to the police chief."

~ ~ ~

CHAPTER TWENTY

The Road to Edgartown

CASEY hung up the phone and sighed. "Let's go, Victoria. Mr. Ferro's lost his car again. He's sure it's been stolen."

Victoria was sitting in the wooden armchair in front of Casey's desk, her blue coat flung over its back. "This must be the third or fourth time."

Casey stood and buckled on her belt. "More like the fifth. Last time he forgot he left it at Up Island Cronigs, and came home by shuttle bus." She led the way down the station house steps to the parking area. Victoria took her usual seat in the Bronco.

As she started up the vehicle and backed out onto the Edgartown Road, Casey muttered, "Things were never like this in Brockton. We had proper crime there."

"Don't murders count as crime?"

"Victoria, honestly! There's no proof — no indication, even — that either Mausz or Ness was murdered. The only crime that was committed was your underground friend moving the body. Nothing else."

Victoria pulled down the visor to check the angle of her cap in the small mirror before she responded. "You can't deny that Tom More attempted to kill Mr. Kirschmeyer."

"For a murder attempt, that was pretty feeble. Kirschmeyer didn't even press charges."

"Which leaves Tom More free to kill again."

"Be careful who you say that to, Victoria. That could be libelous." Casey looked in the rear view mirror and turned onto Old County Road. "Ness's death appears to be an accident, pure and simple, even though I know you'd like it to be murder. And Mausz's death — well, it could have happened the way Tom More said. Mausz and his wife argued, she left him to go off to Aruba with his girlfriend, and he fell and hit his head on the stone wall. There's no way we can prove otherwise."

"That's what Tom More wants us to believe," Victoria said stubbornly, and changed the subject. "I suppose we have to respond to Mr. Ferro's stolen car complaint as if the car really has been stolen, don't we?"

"If I were to ignore the complaint and tell him his car will show up where he left it, that'll be the one time somebody does steal it. He really shouldn't be driving still."

"Humpf," said Victoria.

"You wouldn't be riding with me if you hadn't given up your license, Victoria."

Victoria rolled down her window and looked out.

"You know, don't you, they're releasing Tom More today?"

Victoria turned. "How can they possibly?"

"I told you — Kirschmeyer won't press charges," Casey said. "You can't lock up somebody just because you think he's a killer."

"He *is* a killer."

"Victoria, I swear, one of these days I'm going to ask the selectmen to send you to police school."

"When?" asked Victoria.

Casey turned onto the dirt road where Mr. Ferro lived. "I'd tell you to go find the proof, but you probably would."

"It's outrageous," Victoria said. "With Tom More out of jail, Kirschmeyer is now in danger. Kirschmeyer can't defend himself. He should be in bed still." Victoria studied Casey. "He did go to you with what he found out about Tom More, didn't he?"

Casey shook his head.

"I told him to."

"Well, he didn't."

"I suppose I should let him tell you." Victoria thought for a moment. "Tom More's real name is Ted Moskovitz. Kirschmeyer traced him back more than twenty years and found he'd absconded with two hundred thousand dollars he took from an architectural firm in New Hampshire."

"Yeah?"

Victoria told Casey what she'd learned from Kirschmeyer. When she finished she said, "I wonder why Kirschmeyer's not pressing charges against him?"

"Who knows?" Casey responded. "You were the only witness to the nail gun incident. Do you have any idea who made the first move? Did Kirschmeyer threaten More with something? What he'd found out about him maybe?"

"Ahhh!" said Victoria.

Casey slowed to go around some deep ruts in the road. "Sounds as if he did. Blackmail, maybe?"

"Something like that," Victoria said.

They bounced along for another quarter-mile before they came to Mr. Ferro's house, a shingled one-story Cape with plastic deer in front of the door.

"I wouldn't think he'd need the statues," Victoria said. "There are plenty of real deer about."

"If it were anybody but Mr. Ferro, I'd think he was using these as decoys. He wouldn't be the only one planning on a venison stew," Casey said.

Mr. Ferro, a slight, dark man with wispy white hair, was waiting for them at the end of his driveway. He was wearing a sagging yellow cardigan and worn leather bedroom slippers.

"They must have come while I was taking a nap," Mr. Ferro said when Casey got out of the Bronco with her clipboard.

"When did you last use the car, Mr. Ferro?" Casey asked.

"This morning. I went to Alley's to pick up the paper."

"Did you drive it home, sir?"

"I'm sure I did."

"Did you meet anyone at the store you knew, sir?" Casey asked.

"Yes, that woman who works at tribal headquarters in Gay Head."

"You mean Aquinnah," Casey said.

"Sarah something."

"Right," said Casey. "Did you leave the keys in the car, sir?"

"Of course," he said indignantly. "I was only in the store a few minutes."

Casey sighed. "Why don't you come with me, sir? We'll take a look around before I report it stolen."

Mr. Ferro shoved his hands deep into the pockets of his sweater. "Time is of the essence."

"Yes, sir," said Casey.

"You haven't left something on the stove, have you?" Victoria called out from the front seat.

"Yes. Thanks for reminding me." He held up a finger. "I'm heating a cup of coffee. I'll be right out."

"You'd better change your shoes, while you're at it."

While Mr. Ferro was shuffling back to his house, Casey said, "What do you bet Sarah brought him home, and his car's in Alley's parking lot? With the key in the ignition."

"No bet," said Victoria.

~ ~ ~

Kirschmeyer was getting ready to leave when Victoria came home later that afternoon. He was wearing his leather jacket and was jingling the keys to the Citation.

"They're letting Tom More out of jail today," Victoria said. "You've got to watch out for him."

"Thanks to you, he can't get around too good, himself, Mrs. T," Kirschmeyer responded.

Victoria took off her coat and laid it over the back of a kitchen chair. "He's probably planning to make you victim number three."

"I'm not worried," Kirschmeyer said, moving toward the door. "I'm off to see Mickey Mausz's widow now. You need anything at the Edgartown A&P while I'm in town?"

"No thank you," said Victoria. "What are you seeing Minerva about?"

"Tying up some loose ends," Kirschmeyer said vaguely.

Victoria sat down heavily. "Surely you're not trying to sell information to her, are you?"

"Who, me?" Kirschmeyer slapped his hand on his chest, and coughed.

"You're still not back to normal," Victoria said. "You've got to take it easy."

"I'm only visiting that nice refined widow. I don't expect any gymnastics, Mrs. T." He leered. "I'm sure she'll behave herself."

"That's not what I meant," Victoria said.

After Kirschmeyer left, Victoria puttered about the kitchen. She emptied the dishwasher and put the cups away. She kept thinking about Kirschmeyer. He was not as strong as he pretended to be. If only she were still driving she could follow him to Minerva's, or wherever he was going, make sure he was all right.

She thought, too, about Tom More being released from jail this afternoon. The jail was in Edgartown, only two streets from Minerva's. It was quite likely that Tom More and Kirschmeyer would run into each other. Victoria thought some more. She had seen Minerva's car near the senior center during one of Tom's Cranberry Fields meetings. Suppose Tom should decide to visit her when he was released from jail. Suppose he should run into Kirschmeyer.

Victoria dropped the dishtowel she had been holding on the countertop and called Casey. "Do you remember telling me — when you took my license away — that you'd drive me wherever I wanted to go if I asked?"

Casey said "Yeah?" with more than a touch of suspicion.

"I need to go to Edgartown," Victoria said. "To see Minerva Peabody. Will you take me?"

Casey hesitated.

"If not, I can always hitchhike," Victoria said.

"Okay, Victoria. Give me about ten minutes to finish up here, and I'll be by."

Victoria paced the kitchen. Should she take a weapon of some kind to defend

Kirschmeyer against Tom More? Her lilac-wood walking stick would do. It was tough. And not likely to look suspicious.

When Casey came to the door, Victoria was ready.

"How long do you expect to be?" Casey asked.

"I don't know," Victoria replied. "Do you have your handcuffs and gun with you?"

"For crying out loud, Victoria. I suppose you're planning on having me arrest Tom More, aren't you?"

"Yes," said Victoria.

The road to Edgartown had been an Indian trail originally. It ran in a straight east-west line from Edgartown to West Tisbury, across the glacial outwash plain, dipping into sudden valleys that hid oncoming cars. When Victoria was a girl, she had gone with her grandparents and aunt in the horse and wagon to pick blueberries on the great plains. The road ended at Main Street. The white clapboard building that faced them was the jail. Between the jail's front door and the brick sidewalk was a white picket fence, festooned with neatly pruned climbing roses, almost in leaf in the mild spring weather.

Casey slowed before she turned onto Main Street. "There's your car, Victoria. In front of the courthouse."

Victoria stared at it. "Anyone leaving jail will see it."

"It's distinctive, that's for sure." Casey glanced at Victoria. "All those dings and dents."

"Mr. Kirschmeyer must be at Minerva's already. What time was Tom More going to be released?"

Casey looked at her watch. "About three-quarters of an hour ago."

Victoria straightened her cap. "We've got to hurry."

"I agreed to drive you here, Victoria, but not in an official capacity. If you need help from the police, I'll call the Edgartown cops for you. This isn't my jurisdiction."

Victoria ignored her. "We'll need to be surreptitious. I'll go in the front door, you go around to the back."

"No way. Absolutely not. As a police officer, I can't simply walk into somebody's house without an invitation. Or probable cause."

"There's plenty of probable cause," Victoria said. "If you won't do it, I will. You wait in the car."

Casey sighed. "I'm calling the Edgartown chief to let him know what you're doing. And take off your cap. This is *not* official police business."

Victoria twitched off her baseball cap and flung it onto the seat. Her hair stood up in white feathery tufts where the cap had been. She slammed the door of the Bronco, and marched down the driveway to the right of the house, swinging her lilac stick in front of her.

"Hey, Victoria," Casey called softly. "Where are you going?"

Victoria called back, "This is no longer your business." In a few moments she heard Casey's voice on the radio, and smiled to herself.

Victoria knew Minerva's house well. One of Victoria's sisters had owned it years ago, long before Minerva had bought it. Minerva had modernized the house and had added a solarium that overlooked the harbor. Victoria marched up the back steps and opened the door that led into what used to be her sister's kitchen. The kitchen no longer had her sister's comfortable clutter. It was as immaculate as an operating room, and looked like something out of a fashion magazine, dazzling white with stainless steel appliances on spotless counters. She shook her head and went slowly toward the dining room that opened off the kitchen.

After the bright kitchen, the dining room was dark. Victoria heard raised voices coming from the front of the house, but the door between the dining room and the parlor was closed and she couldn't distinguish words. She could tell only that a man's voice was shouting angrily and a woman's was responding softly. Victoria tiptoed uncomfortably, her arched-up toe rubbing painfully against her shoe, until she realized the two people were so intent on their argument that they would never notice her footsteps. She needed to size up the situation, and she needed to conserve energy for whatever was going to happen next. She grasped her walking stick firmly and edged around the dining room table, sliding one foot after the other. Her eyes had not adjusted to the gloom. To give herself support, she trailed her hand along the backs of the chairs drawn up to the table. As she got closer to the parlor she could make out distinct words. Not enough to understand what was being said, but enough to give the impression of fear and anger. Victoria could smell fear around her, a rusty metallic scent that permeated the dining room. The woman sounded like Minerva, the man like Kirschmeyer. If so, where was Tom More? Perhaps she was mistaken. Perhaps he had not come here after all. Casey was calling in the Edgartown police, and this might be a false alarm. However, the voices sounded nasty enough.

Victoria paused, her hand on the last side chair. She had to make a decision, and make it quickly. She could see a crack of light showing around the edges of the closed parlor door. The scent of fear was strong, as if it were here, in the dining room.

She slid one foot forward, then another. Suddenly, her foot rammed into something soft and bulky on the floor, and, startled, she cried out. She put her hand up to her mouth, too late to muffle the sound. The voices in the other room stopped. Victoria stood still, her heart pounding.

"What was that?" the woman said.

Victoria couldn't hear the response.

Then Kirschmeyer shouted, clearly, "What in hell are you doing, lady? Put that down!"

Victoria skirted the mound on the floor, barely registering the fact that it was the size and shape of a person. She hustled to the parlor door and wrenched it open. The sudden light was so brilliant it made the parlor seem like a stage. Kirschmeyer had both arms over his head.

"Hey, cut it out! Put it down!" he shouted.

Minerva turned when Victoria burst through the door and faced her. She was holding a large polished brass candlestick by its stem. Minerva's face was white, despite her tan. Victoria noticed in that brief second how her freckles contrasted with her pallor.

"Leave her alone, Mr. Kirschmeyer!" Victoria ordered.

Minerva laughed.

"She's trying to kill me," Kirschmeyer blurted out.

Victoria turned to Minerva. "Put the candlestick down. You're safe now."

"Safe!" shouted Kirschmeyer. *"She's* safe?"

Minerva laughed again.

Victoria, leaning heavily on her stick, walked quickly between the two into the front hall and flung open the front door. "Police!" she called out loudly. "Police!"

"I hear you, Victoria." Casey was standing on the brick sidewalk in front of the house. "The Edgartown cops are here." A police car had stopped in the middle of South Water Street, its blue lights rotating.

Victoria reached into her pocket for a napkin and wiped her forehead. "I believe we may be too late," she told Casey.

Casey turned to the two patrolmen, one a tall, lanky blond, the other a much shorter black woman. "It's your turf, fellows." She hitched up her belt and followed the two into the house.

Minerva had collapsed into a chair. She was still holding the candlestick, which dangled from one hand. Her left elbow was on the chair arm, her forehead rested on the back of her wrist.

Kirschmeyer stood where Victoria had first seen him. He was sweating profusely, and his breath came out in a wheeze.

The Cranefly Orchid Murders

Casey looked from Kirschmeyer to Minerva to Victoria. "Okay, Victoria. What's up?"

Victoria leaned on her stick. "I believe you'll find Tom More in the dining room," she said.

~ ~ ~

CHAPTER TWENTY-ONE

The Song Sparrow Sings

"THERE'S a body in there," Victoria said, pointing to the closed door. The three police officers fanned out, Casey circled behind Kirschmeyer, the female Edgartown officer behind Minerva, and the blond officer stood to one side of the dining room door and flung it open. He came out immediately.

"Barbara," he said to the woman officer. "I want you here in the parlor. Chief O'Neill, come in here."

Casey glanced around at the four in the parlor before she followed. Minerva still held the candlestick. Kirschmeyer stood in the center of the room, sweating profusely, and Victoria stood between them, her back to Kirschmeyer. Barbara stood to one side, watching all three, her right hand touching the gun at her belt.

Victoria glanced behind her at Kirschmeyer, who was having a coughing fit. He pointed to the candlestick Minerva was holding. "She clobbered him with that. She must have. She was about to clobber me, too."

Victoria looked back at Minerva. "Was he threatening you?" she asked.

Minerva laughed.

"Jesus! She was threatening me," Kirschmeyer said, and coughed again. "You got here in the nick of time again, Mrs. T." He coughed.

Victoria stared at him for a moment, then said, "You'd better sit down, er, Studs."

Minerva laughed again. "Really, this whole thing is just too ridiculous. I can imagine what the neighbors are thinking."

"I suppose Tom More pushed you too far, didn't he, Minerva?" Victoria said. "How sad."

Minerva began to talk. "I must say, Mrs. Trumbull, you're the only person on this entire Island who seems to have any concept of reality." Minerva leaned her back against the chair and closed her eyes. "None of them would be dead today if it weren't for their own behavior. In every case it was their own fault." She looked up at Victoria, who was leaning on her lilac-wood stick. "I certainly didn't plan to kill any of them."

At that, Victoria glanced around at Kirschmeyer, who had collapsed onto a footstool, his head down, holding his hands between his knees.

The dining room door opened, and Casey looked in.

"I think we need Officer Barbara to take Minerva's statement," Victoria said.

"I don't believe I'm qualified." She smoothed her hair, tousled where she usually wore her blue cap.

"No, no, I insist on talking to you, Mrs. Trumbull," Minerva said. "I refuse to talk to a policeman. You are more my sort of person."

The Edgartown police officer, who was standing behind Casey, stepped forward. "You have a right to have your attorney present, Mrs. Mausz," he said formally.

Minerva turned to Victoria. "Tell him it's Peabody. Minerva Peabody. I don't go by Mausz."

The police officer said, "Yes, ma'am."

Minerva waved dismissively. "I'm fully aware of my rights, Mrs. Trumbull. My husband was a lawyer, after all. The officer has my permission to take notes, if she must, but I don't intend to speak to anyone but you."

Minerva was still holding the candlestick. The square base was blotched with a gummy substance. Tom More's blood, Victoria thought.

The blond officer spoke to his partner. "Put the candlestick in an evidence bag, Barbara, and label it."

"Of course, certainly," said Minerva, holding the candlestick out to Victoria, who backed away with her hands behind her. "Evidence. Sorry about that."

The officer, Barbara, tugged a plastic bag out of an inside pocket of her uniform jacket and slipped on surgical gloves.

Barbara's boss moved back into the dining room and shut the door quietly.

Minerva started to say something but interrupted herself. "I'm forgetting my manners, Mrs. Trumbull. Won't you sit down?" She half rose, then sat again with a sigh.

Victoria turned to see what Barbara was doing. The officer was standing between the two front windows, writing in a small notebook. Victoria moved a parlor chair closer to Minerva and sat down, holding her stick in front of her.

Minerva sighed again and leaned back. "Actually, they made me kill them. All three of them." She paused for several moments. Victoria waited. "Mickey was playing one person against another. He was utterly amoral. On the land transaction alone, he was acting for Mrs. Eldredge the seller, for Harry Ness the purchaser, and for Tom More, who hoped to obtain it somehow from Harry. I believe he was working for the doctors on their golf course plan as well."

She stopped to take a breath. In the distance a song sparrow sang, the first Victoria had heard this spring. A car passed in front of the house.

Victoria swallowed. Her eyes felt raw and scratchy. She asked Minerva, "Why did you kill your husband?"

"It was entirely fortuitous, Mrs. Trumbull. I didn't intend to kill him on the

Sachem's Rock property. I'd been asking him repeatedly for a divorce and he refused."

Victoria was not sure how to respond. She nodded, and looked down at her toe, which protruded from the cutout in her shoe. Her toe throbbed.

Minerva paused. "I suppose that's not entirely right. He didn't refuse. He demanded that I settle a rather large amount of money on him before he would agree to a divorce." She gazed at Victoria, who had looked up. "I suppose you know Mickey had no money. The money's mine. I was damned" — for the first time Minerva was animated — "I was damned," she repeated, "if I was going to settle my money on him. A womanizer, that's all he was. And not terribly successful at womanizing, either." Minerva's face flushed.

Victoria looked away again.

Minerva went on. "So for some time I had been thinking how to get rid of him. I didn't really intend to kill him at first. And it never occurred to me that Sachem's Rock might be the ideal place. Ironic, isn't it?" Minerva smiled. "Mickey, Tom, and I drove to the property. Once we got there, one thing led to another. I told Mickey what I thought about his ethics. Rather, his lack of ethics. With respect to legal matters, that is. I said I intended to inform the Board of Bar Overseers — not that I expected it to do any good." Minerva gave a slight shrug. Victoria listened without interrupting. She could hear Barbara writing. "That got to him. Not the threat of divorce but his exposure to his legal colleagues. He got quite belligerent."

Victoria tried to shift to a more comfortable position in the lumpy parlor chair. "I can imagine how upsetting that must have been. Did he threaten you?"

"He was verbally abusive," Minerva replied. "He called me some ungentlemanly names. He was quite beside himself about the ethics question." She looked toward the front windows. The sunlight had lighted up the tree in front of her house. "He denied he was acting unethically. At that point I told him not to bother to come home." She indicted the wide, painted floorboards. "Here, that is. I own the house. I bought it, but it was his home as well."

Victoria heard the scratch of the police officer's pen on her notebook. She could hear movement behind the door to the dining room. "What did your husband say to that?"

"He laughed. He said he wasn't planning on coming home anyway — he said 'home' with a kind of sneer. That was when he told me he was going to Aruba. With the woman he'd been seeing."

"I don't blame you for feeling humiliated. Had you known about this other woman?" Victoria asked.

The sunlight had moved to Minerva's face, and she shifted slightly. "Mickey was never what you'd call faithful. I accepted that, as long as he was discreet about his affairs. I had my own life, after all, and my life involved less and less of Montgomery Mausz."

Victoria tried again to get comfortable in her chair. "This must be difficult for you to talk about."

"Not any longer, Mrs. Trumbull."

Victoria waited. Behind her Kirschmeyer blew his nose.

Minerva continued. "Then, I'm sorry to say, I raised my voice and we got into a shoving match. I knocked him down, stunned him." She seemed to think Victoria needed an explanation. "I've studied defensive maneuvers at the women's support group."

Victoria nodded. "Is that when you left him?"

"No, I'm afraid not. He'd fallen near a stone wall, and I picked up a large rock and smashed him on the side of his head. I was angry. As I'm sure you can see, I was justifiably angry."

Victoria felt her stomach rumble. She held her stick tightly. "Did you go back to the car then?"

"Yes." Minerva moistened her finger and rubbed at a spot on her tan slacks. "Originally I had planned to drive there with Tom, who wanted to look over the property for his Cranberry Fields development. It was he who invited Mickey to come with us, thinking, apparently, that Mickey had agreed to represent him. When Mickey and I started to argue, we walked up the hill to have some privacy, and Tom stayed with the car."

Victoria's mouth was dry. She wanted to be back in the police Bronco pointing out new spring growth to Casey. When Minerva didn't say anything more, Victoria asked, "As I recall, that was during that spell of awfully cold weather, wasn't it?"

"That's right. In fact, it was snowing. I was dressed for the cold, but Mickey wasn't. He was wearing only a heavy wool shirt. He was so intent on arguing, he never noticed the cold or the snow."

"After you hit him with the rock and returned to the car, did you tell Tom what had happened?"

"Well, I wasn't entirely candid with Tom, Mrs. Trumbull. I told him that Mickey had hit his head, which was technically true. I let Tom believe that I was upset at Mickey's womanizing and that I'd decided to let him find his way home alone."

Victoria shifted again in the uncomfortable chair. "Apparently Tom was convinced," she said. She heard voices in the dining room and wondered what Casey and the Edgartown officer were doing with Tom's body. The song sparrow called again. "Was it necessary to kill Harry Ness? Had he done something to you?"

"You knew I killed him, didn't you, Mrs. Trumbull?" Minerva laughed again. "Everyone else was calling that an accident, but you knew. Good old Harry. He told me over and over again, 'If it weren't for Mickey, I'd leave Crystal for you, just like that.' " She snapped her manicured fingers together. "That sweet Mormon showgirl of his. Harry and I had been seeing one another for well over a year."

Victoria looked back at Kirschmeyer, who hadn't moved. He was leaning forward on the footstool, his hands still between his knees.

"Crystal had no idea," Minerva continued. "Harry told me his wife didn't understand him. Crystal hadn't grown with him, he said. He told me over and over how much he appreciated my sensitivity." Minerva's face twisted in a pained expression. "He was so sincere. I believed him. We had our trysts at the gunning camp on the Pond, a place that Harry and I loved."

Victoria nodded. She, too, knew the Pond.

"Crystal didn't care for roughing it, Harry had told me. We would go out in his boat, eat oysters that we fished from the Pond, and spend idyllic hours together. Sometimes I'd have a glass of sherry. Harry didn't drink." Minerva looked down at the floor.

Victoria waited for Minerva to continue, and when she didn't, asked softly, "What happened that day?"

"It never occurred to me that Harry intended to stay with his wife. Never. We had such a wonderful relationship, both physically and intellectually. If it weren't for Mickey . . ." she rubbed at the speck on her lap. "Both Harry and I had discussed what our life would be like if I were free of Mickey."

Victoria ran a gnarled finger across her forehead, lifting her hair away from her scratchy eyes. She had to keep Minerva talking, she told herself. Behind her, the police officer rustled a page in her notebook and then was silent. Victoria swallowed. "Did Harry ever suggest killing Mickey?"

"No, of course not, Mrs. Trumbull." Minerva sounded appalled. "Harry assumed Mickey would eventually go along with the divorce. As did I." Minerva reached for a tissue from a box on the small table next to her, and blotted her eyes, which had begun to tear. "But then, once I got rid of Mickey, what do you suppose happened?" She gestured toward herself. "Harry dumped me. That's what he was telling me that last day. We were out on the Pond. It was quite warm for this time of year. There was no wind, and the sky was that brilliant spring blue that artists love. The water was only about three feet deep where we were, so we could reach the oysters from the boat with a rake. I had no idea what he had in mind. Dumping me, that's what it was."

Victoria steadied herself on the chair and waited.

Minerva blotted her eyes again. "After dull years of being married to Mickey, it was exciting to be with Harry Ness. He was so brilliant. So sure of himself."

Victoria nodded.

"We were out in the boat when he told me that it was over. Just like that. He said, and I remember his exact words. 'Minerva, my owl.' " She looked at Victoria. "That's what he called me, his wise owl. You know the owl was Minerva's bird, don't you?"

"Yes."

"He said, 'Minerva, my owl, our fling has been wonderful.' Right away I assumed he was telling me he was leaving Crystal for me. I put my arms around him and said, 'It will be marvelous to make it permanent, won't it, darling?' He said, and I will never forget how he looked, 'I'm afraid that's not what I meant. It's over, Minerva.' I felt the blood drain out of my face. 'You'd better sit down, Owl,' he said, looking concerned. 'I didn't mean to shock you. I assumed we both knew this wasn't permanent.' I sat down on the thwart suddenly, and the boat rocked. 'That's not so,' I said. 'You said . . .' At that point he got quite cross. 'Forget what I said.' He practically snarled at me. 'Things have changed. It's over.' I protested. 'But . . . ' I said. 'It's over,' he said again. 'Get that into your head.' He'd never spoken so harshly to me before. I couldn't believe it was my Harry talking. I simply could not believe it." Minerva lifted her hands from the arms of the chair and dropped them again.

Victoria heard the officer behind her scribble. Another car went by the house. A horn honked somewhere. The Chappaquiddick ferry whistled. Dust motes danced in the sunlight.

Victoria didn't know what to say. Behind her Kirschmeyer coughed and shifted his feet.

Minerva went on. "Then Harry said, 'Let's celebrate the good times we've had together, okay? A fond farewell. I have a bottle of champagne cooling back at the camp. Just for you, Owl.' That seemed like the ultimate insult. I was supposed to drink champagne by myself to celebrate his dumping me? It was all planned, I realized. He turned his back to me to haul up the anchor, and I snapped. I grabbed a wrench from the toolbox he kept next to the console, and with all my strength I hit him on the left side of his head. Without a sound he slumped over the gunwale. I lifted up his feet and he slid overboard easily. He had been hauling up the anchor, and when he went over, he got tangled in the line as the anchor went down again."

"How did you get home?" Victoria asked softly.

"The boat was on the anchor, but it was a fairly long line. With one of the oars I paddled as close to shore as I could get, the length of the line. Then I waded ashore on Plum Bush Point. The water was only a couple of feet deep. I walked to where I'd left my car, drove home, and changed my clothes."

Victoria felt dizzy and nauseated. "And Tom More? What happened with Tom?" she asked in a thick voice.

"You knew the sort of person he was, didn't you, Mrs. Trumbull?" She glanced at Victoria, who was watching her through half-closed eyes. "He tried to extort money from me before Harry died. Once Harry was dead, he tried again."

Victoria was puzzled. "What was he blackmailing you for?"

"He knew about Harry and me, and was threatening to make a scene about our relationship. With Harry dead, it didn't matter. That's why it was so foolish of him."

Victoria thought a moment. "Was that why you wanted the land so badly? To give to Tom?"

Minerva nodded. "It was worth it to me at the time in order to keep Harry's and my secret. I could afford the money and I was amused by Tom's project. Tom planned to set me up as an investor, so it wasn't as if I was simply paying blackmail money. I expected a return on my investment."

"So you agreed to help Tom acquire the property from Mr. Ness . . .?"

"Yes. Harry didn't know I was behind Tom's bid to buy the property from him — and I certainly didn't want him to know."

"When I came in just now, I stumbled over the body in the dining room. It is Tom's, isn't it?"

Minerva nodded.

"Do you want to tell me how that happened?" Victoria asked.

"Tom came here, right from jail, and told me he had proof — I don't think he did — but he said he had proof that I had killed both my husband and Harry. He needed money, he said, to pay off his Cranberry Fields investors, and he wanted enough to leave the area and get a new start somewhere else."

"And then?"

"I laughed at him. I said Harry's wife had given the property to the Conservation Trust, so there was nothing I could do about that even if I wanted to. I asked him why he expected me to bail him out when it was he who stupidly gambled his investors' money away on those Internet stocks."

Victoria watched the dust motes dance in the sunlight. "What did he say to that?"

"He said again that he had proof I'd killed both men. I told him that was impossible since, as I'd said, I didn't kill them. He couldn't have had proof. I knew I was safe. The police were calling Harry's death accidental, and they had decided to believe Tom's story about my leaving Mickey to find his own way home. I told Tom he'd made his own bed and . . . you know the rest of the saying."

"Yes," said Victoria. "Then what happened?"

"Tom got quite upset. He was stalking around the room, like the little banty rooster he is, pontificating about how he had enough information to send me to jail for years, if not for life, and it finally got to me."

"Oh?" said Victoria.

"He was pacing and forth in the dining room like a little Napoleon in those high-heeled boots of his, and I simply lost control. I picked up one of the candlesticks from the table, and whacked him with it on the side of his head."

"You knew by then just where to hit, I suppose," Victoria said dryly.

"Just as he fell on the floor, someone knocked on the front door. I closed the door between the parlor and the dining room and answered."

"And it was Mr. Kirschmeyer."

Victoria looked around. At the sound of his name, Kirschmeyer had looked up.

"Yes. I couldn't believe it. That lowbrow," Minerva gestured toward Kirschmeyer, "had the audacity to ask me for money to cover up his findings about Tom's background and his suspicions about me." Minerva pointed to herself. "Me!" she said.

At this, Kirschmeyer spoke. "It wasn't to cover up nothing," he said. "I knew you and Loch Ness was close. He hadn't paid me. I figured you'd honor his commitments."

Victoria said, "I suppose that's when I appeared after stumbling over the body."

Minerva nodded. Everyone was quiet. Barbara, the police officer, had stopped writing.

The dining room door opened and Casey looked in. "Are you finished, Victoria?" She and the other Edgartown officer came into the parlor, both wearing surgical gloves.

"The ambulance should be here momentarily," Casey said. "Officer Murray here called for it. The emergency room is standing by. Both Doc Erickson and Doc Jeffers were there."

"Is Tom still alive?" Victoria asked.

Minerva let out a shriek and stood abruptly.

Casey shrugged. "Barely. I'm staying with him until they get here." She started back to the dining room, then turned. "Here's your cap, Victoria." She took the crumpled baseball cap out of her pocket and handed it to Victoria. Victoria smoothed out the wrinkles, and put it on. Sunlight glinted on the gold stitching: "West Tisbury Police, Deputy."

~ ~ ~

THE END

ABOUT THE PUBLISHER

Vineyard Stories is in the business of book development and publishing on the Island of Martha's Vineyard, Massachusetts.

The focus of this independent company is on books that tell stories of and by Islanders.

The co-owners and editors are Jan Pogue, a journalist with newspaper experience in Baltimore and Philadelphia, and John Walter, a former editor at Washington and Atlanta papers, *USA Today,* and the *Vineyard Gazette.* Ms. Pogue has written commissioned nonfiction for Bookhouse Group, Inc., of Atlanta, and is coauthor of a forthcoming book on the American Cancer Society.

Current Vineyard Stories books include *Behind the Times on Purpose: The Charlotte Inn of Martha's Vineyard,* and *Delish: A Martha's Vineyard Cookbook* by Philip and Shirley Craig. The company has also published a retrospective of an Island landscape artist, *Allen Whiting: A Painter at Sixty.*

CONTACT

E-mail: info@vineyardstories.com

www.vineyardstories.com